MY DECEMBER DADDY

DADDY

A Boy for All Seasons novel

by

LETA BLAKE

An Original Publication from Leta Blake Books

My December Daddy
Written and published by Leta Blake
Cover by Morningstar Ashley
Formatted by BB eBooks

Print Edition

First Print Edition, 2022
ISBN: 979-8-88841-001-1

Other Books by Leta Blake

Contemporary

Will & Patrick Wake Up Married
Will & Patrick's Endless Honeymoon
Cowboy Seeks Husband
The Difference Between
Bring on Forever
Stay Lucky

Sports

The River Leith

The Training Season Series
Training Season
Training Complex

Musicians

Smoky Mountain Dreams
Vespertine

New Adult

Punching the V-Card

'90s Coming of Age Series
Pictures of You
You Are Not Me

Winter Holidays

North's Pole

The Mr. Christmas Series
Mr. Frosty Pants
Mr. Naughty List
Mr. Jingle Bells

A Boy for All Seasons
My December Daddy

Fantasy

Any Given Lifetime

Re-imagined Fairy Tales

Flight
Levity

Paranormal & Shifters

Angel Undone
Omega Mine

Horror

Raise Up Heart

Omegaverse

Heat of Love Series
Slow Heat
Alpha Heat
Slow Birth
Bitter Heat

For Sale Series
Heat for Sale
Bully for Sale

Audiobooks

Leta Blake at Audible

Discover more about the author online

Leta Blake
letablake.com

Gay Romance Newsletter

Leta's newsletter will keep you up to date on her latest releases, sales and deals, future writing plans, and more from the world of M/M romance. Join Leta's mailing list today.

Leta Blake on Patreon

Become part of Leta Blake's Patreon community to support her indie publishing expenses and to access exclusive content, deleted scenes, extras, and interviews.

Acknowledgments

Thank you to the following:

Family: Mom & Dad, Brian & Cecily

The Behind-the-Scenes Gang: Keira Andrews (developmental edits), Amy Schaeffer (beta that turned into developmental edits), Sue Laybourn (developmental, copyedits, and proof), Devon Vesper (proof), Willow Board (copyedits and proof), and Emily Hernandez (beta).

Without the Behind-the-Scenes Gang this book would be a mess. Thank you to everyone's dedication and commitment to bringing this book to the readers.

Friends: Kim, Punny, Danielle, Keira, Cara, Cynthia, Geralynn, and Wendy for endless love and support.

Most of all, thank you to my readers for making all the hard work worthwhile. You bring me so much joy and make this career possible.

Special Acknowledgments to the Community

Thank you to Sherry, Melinda, Gary, Mark, Griff, Chris, and Rob for talking with me over the years about their respective Daddy/girl and Daddy/boy play. I'm especially grateful for our more recent, heartfelt conversations about what that play means to you and what it satisfies within you. Obviously, no two people are the same—and none of you are either—but it is so helpful, especially when writing outside of my area of expertise, to talk with individuals who are willing to be candid and honest, not to mention self-aware.

Thank you to certain LiveJournal communities of old for introducing me to the above folks and for teaching me so much about nontraditional bedroom play. It felt safe to meet and discuss everything in those protected, dedicated online communities. The fact that our friendships continued outside the community is a bonus.

Thank you to Melanie for helping me find the right research materials on the history of Daddy/boy culture in the queer community. And, of course, thank you to the men throughout the years who have written and spoken openly about these modes of play, especially the responsibility Daddies feel toward all aspects of their boys, as well as the long-standing traditions behind the roles.

Speaking with practitioners and studying the background of Daddy/boy has made it beautifully clear how this play is so much more than a kink. It's a wonderful, sexy, intense, and emotional way for two men to connect. I hope I've honored this history and your experiences with the portrayal of Matthew and Erik in this book.

I admit, I hadn't anticipated writing a Daddy/boy book. It had never been one of my personal kinks, and in the past, I'd even dismissed it fictionally for myself. But when characters showed up in my imagination insisting that I tell their story, I dedicated myself to learning about Daddy/boy dynamics, studying the history of it in the queer community, and talking with practitioners. In the process, my eyes have been opened to new horizons, and I hope readers' eyes are opened as well (if they aren't already) to the beautiful intimacy of this play.

For the muses, who insisted

&

For Willow, who went above and beyond

Content Warnings: Daddy/boy dynamics, internalized homophobia, shame play, on page enema, NO age play

PART ONE

The Daddy Experience

CHAPTER ONE

Matthew

FATE IS AN odd thing, isn't it?

If I hadn't had too much to drink last night, sitting not only alone but *lonely* at the hotel bar after the dull-as-dishwater conference I'd attended on behalf of my accounting firm, I might not have accidentally set my alarm for seven p.m. instead of seven a.m. And if I'd set my alarm for the right time, I most certainly wouldn't have missed my flight out of Asheville.

If I hadn't missed my plane, I wouldn't have returned to the hotel to book myself in for another night while I attempted to wrangle a new flight or a rental car for a non-exorbitant price the next day.

And if I hadn't returned to the hotel, I never would have known it was hosting a very different crowd over the weekend for a fascinating special event.

And if…

Well, you get the point.

If it hadn't been for all that, I wouldn't be here now, in the middle of the Blue Ridge Kink Club's Christmas Auction, having paid thirty dollars at the door for the privilege of sipping a watered-down drink and watching people in all kinds of bondage and kink gear getting their wild on. Nor would I be walking through the various kinky offerings for the auction.

For one thing, I'm not from around here, so a lot of this stuff—like the whipping, for example—would be hard to collect on, and for another thing, I'm not sure I'm even kinky.

I've only been out as a gay man for a few years, having waited until my parents died to be true to myself. During those long, dark years in the closet, I gave (more like endured) my share of quick and raunchy blowjobs, but those kinds of experiences aren't what I want or need anymore.

That's something I'm still trying to figure out. What do I want? What *do* I need?

Hookup apps have been informative. Actual *hookups* themselves would have been even more so—but so far the apps have mostly been helpful in terms of highlighting what I don't want. Not that I can explain what *that* is in any detail either.

I just know of everything I've done to explore my sexuality—whether it's the nasty furtive stuff of my youth or contemplating possible hookups—none of it has been fulfilling or right.

All I've ever wanted is to feel *right*.

During my stay for my business meeting, I'd already explored the hotel's various amenities. All typical and not worth checking out again. I'd already walked around Asheville and enjoyed its offerings, though it's always lonely being in a new place with no one to share it with.

So, after a solitary dinner at a local restaurant, when I returned to the hotel to see signs for the Blue Ridge Kink Club Christmas Charity Auction stating 18+ members of the general public were welcome to pay for entrance and even more welcome to bid, I decided to see what it was about. Because I still haven't found what I'm looking for, and, who knows? Maybe it's here.

Right about now, as I pause in front of one particular offering, I'm not sure how I feel about my choice to come to the auction tonight. It might have opened a Pandora's Box for me.

Because I'm captivated.

The offering is presented on a black, trifold poster, like I used in school to show the findings of my science projects on the toxicity of soil or the effect of ultraviolet light on bacteria growth. Except sexy. Across the middle-top portion intriguing words are written in silver-glitter marker to stand out on the dark poster: *I'll Be Your December Daddy.*

The left-hand side of the trifold presents a handful of photos framed with tinfoil, shining in the low light of the hotel's ballroom. In the photos, a tall, handsome man wears nothing but a pair of jeans tight enough to display his powerful thighs and thickly-muscled ass.

In one picture, he stands with his legs spread while a young man, perhaps twenty-three or so, kneels at his feet. The boy is also shirtless; his shoulders are scrawny, and the musculature of his back shows his youth. But what grabs my attention is the combination of the older man's hand resting in the boy's hair and the boy's wide-eyed adoration.

I swallow hard.

The next photo is similar—the boy is kneeling again, but this time both are fully dressed and wearing Christmas sweaters. The man keeps his hand on the boy's shoulder, and the boy leans against his strong leg with an expression of contented bliss. My chest aches, and I rub it anxiously. I've never felt that kind of satisfaction in my life. Not even once.

But I crave it. And it might seem silly, but the thought of having someone to wear a hokey holiday sweater with makes my throat tighten with longing. I've never had that, either. My parents always declared Jesus-is-the-reason-for-the-season, and due to their rigid brand of religious devotion, the holidays were never silly or particularly joyful in my home.

The next photo is the boy alone. He's opening a Christmas stocking with a smile of delight. Next up is a picture of the two of them cuddling on a brown leather sofa, a Christmas tree lit up next to it, and the boy tucked in by the older man's side. There he rests, safe and sound, cradled in his Daddy's arms. Eyes closed. Asleep.

I imagine there are carols playing softly, and it's late on Christmas Eve. *All is calm, all is bright.* I lick my lips, wondering what it would be like to be held like that, to be cherished, to trust and adore a man like this boy does. If only for a few days, a night, or hell, even an hour or two.

And at *Christmas?* Even sweeter.

Of course, if I lost my mind and bid on this "December Daddy" and somehow won him, he wouldn't really be my Daddy on the twenty-fifth—this man surely has his own plans. But it would be close enough. I've never celebrated Christmas the way I've always dreamed of. Even when my parents were alive, aside from the night we decorated the tree, we'd always kept a sober and serious holiday.

I've never been treated by anyone, not even my own father, with the strong, tender kindness radiating from the Daddy in these photos, nor have I felt the open-hearted joy I see written all over the boy's face.

Feeling lightheaded, I pull my gaze from the display to read what's actually being put up for auction, because it can't be a relationship like these two share. No one can auction something as intense as that.

*Daddy Erik is offering one Not-So-Silent Night—a Christmas-themed Daddy/boy Experience. He'll deliver Daddy/boy dynamics, and a very merry faux-Christmas morning complete with a stuffed stocking, gifts from Santa Daddy, and other agreed upon "presents" for being a good boy. No prior experience is required. Kinks and all other physical interactions negotiated in advance. Either party may cancel this arrangement **at any time for any reason**. Proof of STI testing* ***required. No*** *more than one night.* ***No*** *repeats from prior years. And* ***absolutely no*** *drinking or drugs allowed during our time together.* ***References available.***

I take a quick gulp of my whiskey, already feeling like Daddy Erik's eyes are on me, and I'm breaking one of his rules. Breathlessly, I turn my attention to the paper beneath the trifold where people can make their anonymous bids, curious how much money has already been put on this man and the offered experience.

On the left side of the paper there's a column for the private PIN number we were given at the door, and next to it, a line for the bid being placed.

Both those columns are empty.

Not a single person has bid on Daddy Erik's offer. I can't imagine why. Many of the other kinks at the auction have multiple lines of bids already. Is there something about this man that makes him undesirable? A reputation that the Asheville kink community is aware of but I, a stranger to town, am not?

As I ponder that possibility, my gaze strays to the photos again. I don't see any red flags in the pictures. Everything appears soft and lovely between these men. This Daddy obviously knows how to make his boy happy and give him the perfect Christmas.

I imagine myself kneeling at his feet with his hand in my hair, and my blood rushes south. It's arousing to contemplate being on my knees for a man like Daddy Erik, but more than that, I know deep down I'd feel so *relieved* to be there. At his feet. Under his hand.

I take in the pictures again, scrutinizing Daddy Erik's face for any hint of malevolence or cruelty, trying to understand why no one here wants to take him up on his offer. I see nothing but the open-hearted adoration of his boy and an easiness between them I envy.

As if I can tell a bad person from his looks alone. So foolish.

And yet...

Self-conscious, I dart glances around the room to see if anyone is observing me—someone who might warn me away from this man and his tempting December Daddy Experience. But no one is paying the nerdy quiet guy and his watered-down whiskey any attention at all. Per the usual.

I pick up the pen and before I know what I'm doing, I've bent over the auction paper to write my PIN number at the top of the first column. Pausing midway through, I'm halted by something stamped at the top of the auction paper.

The minimum opening bid.

My brows hit my hairline. No wonder the columns are empty. The opening bid is eye-wateringly high. Enough to make me stop and reconsider.

Clearing my throat, I think of my bank account and rake my gaze over the pictures again. The clench of yearning in my heart, so strong and primal, makes it hard to catch my breath.

Until tonight, until the last few minutes, even, I never knew I wanted this, and yet now I want it so much I'm more than willing to part with an absurdly high sum just to experience an approximation of whatever that boy is feeling at his Daddy's feet.

Still, that much money for one night is beyond indulgent and bordering on rash. I hem and haw again, wondering when was the last time I treated myself? When my folks were sick, I'd dedicated my time between work and caring for them. When my parents passed on, I'd spent two years sorting out their estate.

When I decided to come out as a gay man, I admitted it to three friends and have never done anything else about it. I haven't dated. I haven't partied. I haven't played or indulged or fucked around.

I've been boring. A cardboard person. I've been afraid and cautious. I've been alone.

So if I want to spend a shit-ton of money to have a handsome man hold me, buy me presents, and give me the kind of Christmas I've dreamed of? Teach me what it means to be gay and loved? That's my prerogative. And if it's only for one night? That's all the better, isn't it? I can test it out. Have my physical needs met for the first time and see if this Daddy/boy dynamic is truly something I want. No strings attached.

And if this *is* what I want? If I like it as much as I think I will?

I'll need to consider reworking and reactivating my dating app profiles, at the very least. Maybe more.

I add the rest of my PIN number to the sheet, set my maximum bid significantly higher than the already high minimum, and swallow the rest of my drink in a single gulp.

Then I leave the auction.

Rushing on anxiety and excitement, I swing by the hotel bar. I need a strong drink this time and request two shots of whiskey to take the edge off. As I swallow them, liquor burning my throat, it's as if I might levitate off the bar stool and fly to the ceiling. I can't believe what I've done.

They'd told me when I entered the auction that if I bid on anything tonight, they'd use the contact information associated with the PIN number to let me know if I've won. I keep checking my phone as if the notification will come through at any moment.

Absurd.

It's not until I'm back up in my hotel room, brushing my teeth before bed, that jumbled worries begin to rise up from beneath my excitement. What if this isn't safe? What if he's dangerous? What if he's unkind? What if I'm not good enough to be a boy to a handsome man like Daddy Erik? He looks younger than me, and the boy pictured with him was younger than me *by far*. Maybe it's not done for someone in their forties to want to be a boy? Maybe it's weird or something? What if I'm making a fool of myself? What if he doesn't want me?

I laugh bitterly at my reflection. Why is the thought Daddy Erik might not want me more frightening than the thought he might hurt me? I've told myself I'm going to find a way to love myself better from now on, and yet if Daddy Erik hurts me, I feel, deep down, I might deserve it.

But *oh*, how I want him to want me.

What if he can't? What if he won't?

But what if he *does*?

I climb into the wide hotel bed, strung out with desire and anxiety. I'm half-hard thinking of a night with Daddy Erik—snuggled against him, safe and adored—so I work to get myself off, but I can't seem to get there. My fears keep pushing in. I let go of my reluctant cock, curl up on my side, and stare out the window instead, watching the Christmas decorations sparkle and blink all around the mountain town.

My thoughts fall into the same rhythm as the blinking lights. I'm exhausted, but I can't fall asleep.

What if…what if…what if…

CHAPTER TWO

Erik

"ESPRESSO DOUBLE SHOT over ice—oh, with oat milk, please." I put my request in at the counter before turning to scan the festively decorated nooks and crannies of Caffeine Dream, looking for a young man who seems like he's looking for someone, too.

Matthew Angel, the boy whose enormous bid had won my offer for a December Daddy Experience at last week's Kink Club charity auction, has been cagey about sending me a photo. Maybe he's afraid I'm the judgy sort of man who cares too much about clear skin or weight or overbites or what-have-you.

I'm not. I like a boy who's fallible and human, someone to care for and correct, but I've never been worried much about whether a boy's appearance meets gay culture's overly rigid beauty standards.

My first boy was a chubby little angel, and my second had acne and a sleepy eye, and I loved them just as much as my third boy, who was, by any measure, a knockout of a twink. Not that I'm going to *love* Matthew Angel. Feelings aren't something that can be auctioned.

But I'll respect him and treat him well for the time he's won, like any Daddy should. And if somehow we click? If he wants more? Forget it. My heart's not up for being broken again. Because that's how these things always end, and the fact of the matter is I'm *not* ready for that. It hurt too much last time.

I brush the miserable thought away and scan the room again.

Whatever Matthew's fears might be, I have no idea what he looks like. I've tried googling his name, but I just got a ton of returns for a director in Hollywood and another set of returns for a figure skater training under my old favorite, Matty Marcus.

Between the two of them, there were way too many hits to comb through trying to find a picture of a random twink who's won my services. So, I'm left running my eyes over every young, potentially gay guy in the room. Since Caffeine Dream is right next to Asheville's newest gay club, that description fits more than half of the clientele this early on a Saturday morning after a fun Friday night.

None of the young men meet my eye. I'm having no luck trying to suss out which of them might be Matthew Angel, a.k.a. the only boy to bid on me.

There is a hot, older little number, though. He's standing near the window, coat draped over his forearm, cradling a coffee mug in his hands, and staring at me with wide eyes. He's got salt-and-pepper hair and a nice tight body wrapped up in a pair of well-fitting slacks and a green button-up with the edge of a white undershirt peeking out from the collar. A satchel hangs across his chest. He's a little breathless, and his cheeks are red from being caught staring at me.

I like the look of him.

Hell, I wouldn't mind getting my hands on him later in the coffee shop bathroom, if he's still around after my meeting with Matthew. I suppose I do need to get my dick wet with someone new. Rip the Band-Aid off. Brandon's been gone for over six months, and I need to get past this stupid post-breakup, grief-powered-celibacy thing.

Especially if I'm going to be a good Daddy for Matthew Angel next weekend. It won't do to go into that kind of situation with six months of pent-up need in me. I run my eyes over the blushing salt-

and-pepper hottie again. Yeah, this guy will be a tasty bite…

But for now, I need to stay focused on finding my temporary, only-for-Christmas boy.

I turn my attention back to the barista as he finishes up my drink, wincing as he fumbles it, spilling coffee everywhere.

"I'm so sorry," he says, grabbing a rag to wipe it up. "I'll have to make another."

"No problem," I assure him. Accidents happen. No one's perfect. All sorts of easy clichés are poised to roll off my tongue, but I keep them in. There's something about the barista's nose and chin that reminds me of Brandon. My stomach twists. I sigh. When will it stop hurting?

Memories flow over me as the barista starts my drink over.

First up, as always, is Brandon the day we met at my training center. He'd been so adorable, shifting from foot to foot, hands stuffed into his parka pockets, not sure what was ahead of him. Not sure if he had what it took to succeed. That was before we'd recognized we wanted each other or that I could help him with more than strength training and kettlebells.

God, he'd been so young and in need of so much guidance. He'd been perfect…

More memories wash through my mind. Brandon naked in my bed, laughing as I danced for him. Brandon kneeling for me, his eyes wide and adoring. Brandon taking his first sip of Hungarian coffee. Brandon walking hand-in-hand with Ferko, the Hungarian fields rolling away in front of them, beckoning them into a new future. Brandon telling me goodbye.

After Brandon left, I haven't held it together as well as I promised him I would. It's hard to go from being Brandon's lover, trainer, advisor, and Daddy for three years to being none of those things to him anymore. Not unexpected, but hard.

I've been taking my time processing that sadness. Do I even

know who I am when I'm not someone's Daddy? When I'm not *Brandon's* Daddy? All the questions. All the doubts. Christ, I've felt it *all* since he left me. Grief, sadness, loneliness, regret.

All of it.

Truth be told, I can't believe I've gotten myself into a situation where I'm going to play Daddy again for the first time after losing him, and it's going to be with a total stranger. Talk about a numbnuts move to make.

"Sorry again, sir."

"It's all right." I tip the barista before taking the proffered glass of iced espresso. Sipping it, I walk to a table by the window, choosing it because it has two seats: one facing the door and one facing the inside of the café. I take off my coat and scarf, draping them over the back of the chair, and sit facing the door.

Glancing at my watch, I see I'm three minutes early, so Matthew isn't late yet. Though I prefer my boys to arrive a little early rather than just on time. It's respectful, and it's flattering to a Daddy when his boy is eager. If Matthew Angel and I agree to a night together, I'll have to coach him on that.

We've texted a few times since Nick sent me the contact information for the boy who's won me, and I suggested a FaceTime call, but clearly skittish about turning me off in some way, Matthew has insisted on meeting in person first. Even though it means he's had to drive all the way from Nashville, which is quite a haul just to meet someone face-to-face.

But I get it, and I respect it, too. There's nothing like an in-person meeting to feel out someone's vibe, and since the Daddy/boy experience Matthew's bid on is an intimate, private one, I think he has every right to inspect the goods—me—in person.

Everything matters in an exchange like this: scent, the sound of a person's voice, how they handle the unexpected. Everything. He's smart to ask for a personal meetup. That's also why I'd set my opening bid so high. I don't play with just anyone, and ever since Brandon left me, I don't play with *anyone* this way at all. I only agreed to the auction because…

I sigh.

Well, there were a few reasons, but I'd mainly agreed because my best friend, Nick, thought it would be a good way to get back on the horse, so to speak. He'd been relentless about it, urging me to participate in the auction until I caved. I thought I'd set my price high enough to discourage bidders. Matthew Angel must be some rich trust-fund kid to have the kind of money I've demanded. Spoiled. Used to getting his way.

Could be fun to teach him a lesson or two for a night.

My stomach flip-flops, and I can't discern if it's excitement or anxiety.

Okay, so maybe I *am* a judgy asshole after all, because the longer I wait for Matthew to show up—I glance at my watch; he's still not late—the more worried I'm getting about it all. What if I can't do this? What if I don't like this guy? What if I hate how he looks, sounds, or smells? Aside from two other charity auctions years ago, I've never played Daddy to someone I don't know. All my boys have been special to me, hand-chosen, but Brandon had been *really* special.

I'm able to admit it now: I'd been head-over-ass in love with him. Even though that hadn't been our agreement, and even though I'd known from the start how it would end. But love doesn't care about agreements or plans or endings. It jumps in and grabs a person at its own whim. Kink with love, though, is divine play. It's changed my idea of what I want from a partner forever.

So a stranger—a potentially unattractive stranger at that—is not how I've imagined wading back into the kink pool. Doing this right before Christmas had been part of my plan to avoid this very scenario. I'd chosen a difficult fulfillment date, as well as set a high opening bid, because I'd wanted Nick to leave me alone, but I'd also wanted to make damn sure no boy bid on me.

But a boy had, and now, despite myself, I'm intrigued.

Matthew has been vague by text, not only about his appearance but also about his desires and experience in kink, saying he'd rather "discuss it all in person." Which has me curious as hell about why he bid on me at all if he's so shy.

It doesn't matter. No matter what his experience level is in kink, I'll still define with him, well in advance of our night together, what his expectations and preferences are, what our lines and limits will be, and discuss whether we both can agree to them. If he wants to do all that in person rather than by text, I get it. Maybe he wants to size up my facial reactions, observe my body language during the discussion… Or maybe he's worried about some of the same things as me.

I've got a lot of questions for him. What was he doing at a BDSM auction in Asheville when he lives in Nashville? Does he have prior negative experiences with the kink clubs over there, so he's branching out? Why is he willing to engage me for a Christmas kink night just one day before Christmas Eve? The longer I wait, the more questions pile up. My leg begins to jiggle, rattling the table. Unbecoming, really, so I push my hand against my knee, putting a stop to it.

At that moment, a young man walks in wearing tight leggings, furry boots up to his knees, and an oversized gray sweatshirt reading *YES, DADDY* in big red letters. He's also wearing a set of felt reindeer antlers on his head, and his strong thighs look like they'd grip my hips just right if we fucked face-to-face.

I tilt my head as he begins to search the room. As he twists and turns, his sweatshirt rides up in the back, exposing his ass, round and firm like an apple. I'm pleased. If this is Matthew Angel, he has nothing to worry about. Physically, he's just my type of boy.

I sit a little straighter, prepared to wave him over as he continues to search the room.

"Hi." A voice intrudes on my attempt to get Matthew's attention.

I glance up. It's the hot salt-and-pepper guy who's been watching me since I came in. He's even cuter up close, with big, wide hazel eyes and soft lips that would be so pretty around my cock. His pants fit well, showing off his juicy ass, and his shirt skims over his chest, demonstrating he's slim and fit. Sexy. Manly in that older guy kind of way, yet feminine in his softness and bashful smile.

I like him all over again, and I'm game for a suck-and-fuck in the bathroom once Matthew Angel and I have set our terms for the December Daddy Experience and called it a day—*if* we call it a day, because I might be willing to give Reindeer-Yes-Daddy-boy a sample of Daddy Erik *tonight* if he wants. With an ass like that, I'm beyond tempted.

"Hey," I say, trying to peer around the guy, ready to wave Matthew over from where he's still hunting for me on the wrong side of the shop.

The man shuffles awkwardly. "Should I sit here?"

"Sorry, no, I'm waiting on someone."

"Yeah," he says. "You're waiting on me."

I chuckle, thinking for a moment he's just given me a cheesy pickup line, and I'm rather admiring him for it, when I realize, no, he's serious and embarrassed. And oh.

Oh.

Well, that's interesting. And not what I've been expecting. I guess what they say about assumptions is true. I've made an ass out of myself and made *him* feel like an ass with just a simple laugh. Not cool. No, not cool at all.

"You're Matthew," I say without a hint of question in my voice now that I know. Truly, I should have guessed as soon as I saw him.

There's no mistaking the very submissive way he's been staring at me—eager and yet a little intimidated by the presence of a dominant man—but I'd ignored it. Stereotypes and all that. Not good.

But, c'mon, I should know better.

Matthew swallows hard and grips his coffee mug a little tighter. He nods at the empty seat. "So, may I?"

"Of course. Please do." I chide myself that I hadn't stood after he walked up, that I haven't pulled out the seat for him, and generally haven't behaved like a good Daddy at all. I glance toward the young guy I'd assumed to be Matthew and see him sling an arm around an older man, a few years older than me even. The man kisses his forehead. So that's his Daddy. All right then.

Reverse, rewind.

I turn my attention to the real Matthew across from me. He's trembling and flushed as he lays his coat out across the back of his chair, slinging his satchel over it as well. Little beads of sweat rise along his hairline, and he gulps again as I study him.

Aside from my surprise at his age, I can't find a reason to complain about what I'm seeing.

Matthew is a sexy-as-fuck, almost-silver fox. Spotting the snatch of dark hair sticking up from beneath his undershirt, I revise that mental description to almost-silver otter. Everything about the auction makes a lot more sense now.

The man who's bid on me isn't a twenty-something twink with trust-fund wealth to burn. No, this guy has got his own money—as evidenced by the quality of his clothes, the price of his watch, and his bearing, which is professional, if rather shy.

To be honest, Matthew is my type for a hookup, but he isn't my fantasy for Daddy/boy play at all. But I didn't put *my* fantasy up for auction, did I? I put someone else's fantasy up for auction, and now it's my duty to fulfill it.

Besides, fantasy is never reality. Brandon ended up being so much more than I'd imagined when I first met him, and found myself attracted to his perfect, youthful representation of my ideal boy. He'd been so much more, for better and for worse.

So, yeah, fuck fantasy.

Reality is I've got a guy across from me who I find attractive, so I should be happy for small miracles. This could have been so much worse.

But meeting Matthew has left me off-balance. I'd expected a boy—a young man—and while *Boy* as a role isn't defined by age, all of *my* boys have been younger than me.

I sip my coffee to cover my puzzlement, and Matthew twists his hands in his lap, gazing at the table with pink cheeks over his freshly shaven beard-line. Hell, he's so insecure in this moment, I can almost taste it. I need to do something. Say something. The *right* thing.

But what is that?

"I've never done this before," Matthew whispers before I figure out how to stop myself from fumbling the situation further.

Oh, well, that's…wow. A Daddy/boy virgin, huh? This information changes the whole game. I've got *to get myself together. Now.*

"That's fine," I say, pleased my voice doesn't squeak or give away more of my disquiet. "Lucky for you, I have." He chuckles, low and sweet, and I relax some.

"As with any kink, the important thing is to be completely honest with each other. I want to know exactly what you're looking for during our night together, and I'll be upfront about what I can deliver. Are you game?"

He chews his lower lip before replying, "You require complete honesty?"

"Yes."

Matthew's lips quirk up. "A kinky friend of mine told me a commitment to total honesty is the only way to have a truly good

Daddy/boy experience."

"He's right." I tilt my head, something about Matthew making me wonder just how much of a kink virgin he really is. "Don't worry. We can go slow."

"Slow is good," he says, glancing up with another shy smile. "I like slow. Soft. Gentle."

The dimple in his right cheek does funny, fluttery things to my stomach. "Is that what you're going to want?" I ask. "Gentle?"

He swallows and glances around, checking to see if anyone's listening to us—they aren't. No one gives a shit about what people talk about in here. Asheville's known as the Seattle of the South, so it's full of artists, rednecks, craft beer aficionados, random freaks and weirdos, and everyone's used to everything nowadays. There's nothing left to shock anyone around here.

"I think so? I don't know for sure what I want." Matthew breathes shallowly as he meets my gaze. "I want what I saw in the pictures. Cuddles on the sofa. Kissing by the fire. Presents. Sleeping in your arms." He grows even brighter red.

I'm worried for his health. It can't be safe for a grown man to be this embarrassed this easily. Also, if Matthew is new to Daddy/boy play and perhaps even new to kink itself, we're going to need to take our time. We've already rushed ahead too quickly due to the awkwardness of our initial meeting. I should fix that.

"Let's back up," I say, putting out a hand and touching his fingers where they're still twisting together on the tabletop. "Let's go all the way back to the beginning."

"All right."

I stand, and pull him up, too, before putting out my hand. "I'm Erik Garner. It's nice to meet you."

"Matthew Angel," he says, and his hand in mine feels strong and right. I'm tempted to bring his fingers to my lips and kiss them, but now's not the time for gestures like that. He's definitely submissive, and I'm drawn to that a lot more than I'd ever thought I would be in an older man. At the very least, it'll be helpful for easy Daddy/boy play.

"Have a seat," I say, gesturing back to the table.

Matthew sits again. I notice he's less tense.

And I smile, taking my chair across from him. I lean forward, elbows on the table, bracketing my drink. "So, how was your drive from Nashville?"

"It was great. The weather was nice. Blue skies and white clouds are even prettier against the winter-gray mountains, you know? Lots of pretty views."

"And it wasn't too much of a trip for you?"

"No." He cleared his throat. "You're from here? Asheville?"

"Not always, but it's my home now."

"Asheville's changed a lot over the years."

"You've visited here often?"

"Sure. Ever since I was a kid, I've come over from time to time. My folks liked to make a weekend of it. You know, see Biltmore House, and afterward spend the night in a hotel with a pool and room service before heading back home."

"Ah, the Biltmore Estate."

"You're probably accustomed to the grandeur of it by now, huh? Maybe it's not as special to you?"

"Nah, I'm still a fan of the Biltmore," I say with a grin. "It's too beautiful and too over-the-top not to love it."

"I've always wanted to spend more time discovering the hiking trails there, but I never have."

"They've got some good ones." I move on, trying to get more of a bead on his personality. "So, based on what you just said, am I right to assume you're from Nashville?"

"I'm from the Murfreesboro suburb, actually. I moved to Nashville proper for college. Belmont."

"Oh? You're a musician?" I sit a little straighter, curious. He doesn't look like a musician. He looks like an accountant.

"Not really. Don't get me wrong, I love music, and a part of me always wanted to be gifted enough to make a life of it, but it turns out I'm not cut out for making a career out of it. I quickly realized I was swimming in far too big of a talent pool."

"But you play or sing?"

"I play some guitar, some piano, but to be honest, my voice is bad," Matthew says with a pretty smile, showing he has cute dimples. "After a semester, a kind and honest professor sat me down to spell it out for me." He shrugs, and it still obviously shames him, though he's trying to hide it. "Music was a pipe dream for me. I don't have anything special."

I scoff. "What does a professor know about that?"

"Enough." He waves his hand a little swishily, and I like that too. I'm always fond of a man who moves with some grace instead of thunking around like a macho hunk of meat. Matthew goes on, "Anyway, I switched to MTSU and got a degree in accounting instead."

Ding, ding, ding, give me a prize.

"Ah."

"And you?" Matthew asks with a sudden slyness, despite his still bashful smile. "What does a guy have to major in to become a Daddy?"

I laugh. He's got a sense of humor. Excellent. Between that, his hot body, his nice face, and his quite evident natural submission, I feel confident we can have a good time together. My shoulders loosen, and the anxiety that's been balled in my stomach ever since Nick notified me I'd been won in the auction dissolves away.

I lean back and smile at him. Matthew's eyelashes flutter, and my pulse rushes faster. Something about him makes me feel protective and strong, older than him, even though I'm not. Which works well for me. It fits his winnings.

"So, let me guess." Matthew flirts prettily. "You had to get a degree in discipline?"

"You're gonna be fun," I say.

Matthew meets my gaze with flushed cheeks and a shy smile.

Damn, he's adorable. And he doesn't even seem to know it. Just the way I prefer my usual boys—sweet, eager, and in need of a confidence boost. What that says about me, I don't care to know, but when my boys leave—and they always do—they're stronger, better, more confident men. And that's my doing. I help them grow up. Like a Daddy should.

So what if Matthew's older than me? He still fits the type.

"Am I allowed to tease you? Was that rude? Should I apologize?" Matthew asks, uncertainty flooding his expression again.

I take up my glass. "Hell no. I like a boy with a little sass."

"I don't know what I like," he confesses. "Can you help me learn?" Matthew bites his lower lip and glances up at me through his lashes in a way that makes my balls tighten.

Submissive and eager to learn? Sexy as hell? Someone who is *nothing at all* like Brandon in looks, or demeanor, or style? Yeah. Okay. I don't know what it is about this guy, but he's got me ready to flip this table and drag him out of here all caveman-like. When he licks his lips and takes a little gasping breath, my nipples go hard, and my cheeks flush too.

"I'd be honored to help you learn. It'd be my pleasure."

"Thanks," he says, flashing that dimple.

The night I've promised in exchange for him giving a hell of a lot of money to a call center for LGBT adolescents already seems worth it.

"You're welcome," I say. And I mean it.

I don't know if it's because I haven't had sex with anyone since Brandon left, but Matthew's natural eroticism is hitting me hard, like he's my own surprise personal catnip. Our night together might not be for another week, but I'm horny for him now. Maybe he'll let me fuck him in the bathroom before we continue our talk? If I can get this weird buzzing attraction out of my system, I'll be able to think more clearly for our negotiation.

But no. That's not how I should be thinking at all. I'm the Daddy here. I'm in charge. I need to act like it. From start to finish.

Cracking my knuckles and trying to ignore my simmering arousal, I start. "Let's go ahead and begin a deep dive into our histories and experiences. The best way to have a good kink experience is wide-open communication. It's imperative we be completely honest with each other."

"I understand."

"Great. You can ask questions at any time, of course. When we're playing, I'll have some rules about etiquette and manners, but for now feel free to interrupt me whenever questions come to mind."

"All right."

I lean back, stretching my legs out to the side of the table, enjoying his easy acquiescence. Fuck, I'm actually excited about this. I'm deep-down *excited* for the first time in a long time.

Matthew is patient as I sip my iced espresso, and his eyes meet mine when I begin to talk again. "So, as to your first question about what it takes to become a Daddy, you deserve an answer to that. Obviously, you saw my poster at the auction."

"I did. I also know I'm the only person who bid on you, which, I admit, makes me feel wary."

"It would. I understand. Let me assure you I'm well known within the local kink community, and I'm happy to provide references if you'd like."

"I got them from Nick, the guy who let me know I'd won. I even called a few already."

This boy might be uncertain in many ways, but he's old enough to know he needs to do due diligence.

"And?"

"I wouldn't be here if they weren't glowing."

I chuckle. "Indeed. You're still right to ask what my qualifications are for any sort of scene, much less a scene that's expected to run a full night. I'm impressed."

"Thank you." He pushes a hand through his hair, fluffing it. "I wanted to make sure we're a good fit, and we want the same things. That's why I wanted to meet face-to-face. To get a read on you and on this."

"Of course. It's always better to have conversations about kink face-to-face." I smile and lean close, scenting his cologne which reminds me of fresh rain in the forest. Crushed, damp pine needles and leaves. "And let me guess, you wanted to check on the little things, too? Right? Like how I sound, how I smell?"

Matthew blushes again. "If I say yes, does it make me shallow?"

"Of course not. Sensory things are important in this experience." I grin. "You, for the record, smell amazing."

"Thank you." He smiles. "I admit I hadn't thought much about how you might smell or sound. I'd been more focused on how you might *feel* in person. Like in an energy sort of way, for lack of a better description. I needed to know if we would feel nice together when interacting."

"Of course. That matters most of all," I admit. "But, for me, smell is important too. It's hard for me to be intimate, even in a nonsexual way, with someone who doesn't smell *right* to me. I need to resonate with a man's scent."

"Makes sense." Matthew leans across the table and sniffs the air. When he sits back, he smiles wryly. "You smell like nothing much."

I laugh. "Ivory Soap and water for me. Plain and simple. But, don't worry, I like a well-groomed boy, and that includes a boy who wears a nice scent like yours."

Matthew goes red again, and I wonder how much darker he can flush before he has an aneurysm. I also wonder if he blushes all over. I can envision pinkness all the way down to his dark bush. If this interview goes well, I'll get to find out.

"But back to your initial question. You asked what's in my education that qualifies me as a Daddy." I resist the impulse to reach across and wipe my thumb over his still damp lower lip. I'm not sure what it is about Matthew, but he has an energy, a vibe, and a look that, in combination, seem to hit my id right where it aches the most—my balls.

I'd still like to take him back to the men's room, guide him to his knees, and tell him to suck Daddy's dick like a good boy *right fucking now*. I wonder how much he'd blush then.

Focus. Christ, Erik, calm the fuck down.

Under the heady spell Matthew has cast on me, I would have forgotten about the young man I'd originally set my sights on, except he and his Daddy pass our table. As my gaze follows his path to the exit, his bubble butt and eager youth seem a lot less appealing in comparison to Matthew's elegant, submissive shyness. I believe I got the better deal today. Sometimes reality is far more intriguing than fantasy.

"Your 'education.'" Matthew snorts, grabbing my attention back from the departing twink. "Is there a university official who bestows Daddyhood on only the Daddiest of undergrads upon graduation?" Matthew asks, taking a sip of his coffee and giving me another sly smile.

"If only," I say, chuckling again. "But if there was, would there be a correlating designation of 'boy' assigned as well?"

"The universities could pair them up. Make it a dating service."

Shy, sly, *and* silly.

Nice. That bodes well for him being naughty too.

"Alas, I had to settle for graduating with a degree in Sports Medicine. No Daddy designation at all on my diploma."

"A shame." It takes him a beat to process what I've said, but then his gaze skims over my body. "Ah. I see. You're a jock."

"Of sorts. I've never been into team sports, but growing up on a horse farm outside of Charlotte, I'm a big fan of everything involving riding. I'm also drawn to sports which maximize a body's full potential."

"Like bodybuilding?"

"No, more like martial arts, or acrobatics, or dance."

"Ohhh."

"In school, I studied Sports Medicine because I wanted to work with martial artists, dancers, gymnasts, and aerialists. After I left college, I got a job offer I couldn't resist. It required a move to Florida, but it was worth it. I learned how to help train actors and stuntpeople in the best ways to fall—mainly from horses, but really from anything." I shake my head as I remember starting out in the industry. "It's wild to think that was over ten years ago now."

"But you're only what? Twenty-six? Twenty-nine tops?"

I smile again. *This guy. He knows I'm older than that. Cute.* "Thirty-five."

"You look great."

"Thank you. And you're?"

Matthew swallows, his fingers drumming against the side of his half-full mug. "Forty-one."

"Nice. You look younger." He doesn't, but the lie is an easy way to assure him I find him attractive, since that's clearly part of where his insecurity is coming from. If I thought assurances that I also like to play Daddy to older men would benefit him, I would have gone that route. But that lie feels harder to pull off, since it's closer to revealing the more damning truth: I've never had a boy this old before.

"I've always been a late bloomer." Matthew bites his lip again, and I swear to God if he does it one more time, I'm going to stand, frog-march him to the bathroom, and…

For fuck's sake, hold it together, Erik!

I should have gotten myself laid before this meeting with Matthew. Or, say, *anytime* since Brandon left me six months ago. I should have *at least* rubbed one out this morning. Poor planning on my part. "Slowly blooming has served you well."

Does that even make sense? I hope so.

"Thanks, but I know I'm very much middle-aged."

Now I'm confused. "What's that mean to you?"

He shrugs. "Just I get it's weird wanting to be someone's boy at my age."

I frown, the waver of insecurity in his voice touching my heart. "Nothing weird about it at all."

"No?"

"Lots of boys are older."

"Really?" He sounds hopeful.

His wide-eyed need is so at odds with his professional appearance that the Daddy in me roars to the surface, wanting to take him under my wing, take him apart, figure him out. But all I say is, "Sure."

It's true in theory, even if I've never had an older boy in practice.

"Sorry," he says, leaning back and fluffing his hair again. I get a whiff of his cologne, as well as a hint of his sweat.

Matthew dabs at his forehead with a paper napkin he grabs from the dispenser. He smiles with a touch of embarrassment before crumpling it and tossing it onto the table. He meets my gaze again. "I'm sorry. I've derailed the recounting of your list of, uh, 'Daddy qualifications.'"

I chuckle again. "Right. So that's my education and work history. I began in the coaching and training business in Florida, but I've since started my own firm, again specializing in working with actors, stuntpeople, dancers, and aerialists. I've been hired by circuses, ballet companies, and individual actors. But I get most of my business from television series and film work these days."

I glance out the window at the brightness of this midwinter day and add, "The cool thing is I can work from anywhere. Florida's hot and flat, and I missed North Carolina, so I came home. These days most of the actors and stuntpeople I work with come to me to learn how to ride, to fall, to get up. In fact, I joke that my main job is teaching people how to get up. Over and over."

Matthew's eyebrows lift in curiosity.

"Get hit." I mime it with my hands. "Fall. Get up. Get hit again." I grin. "It's harder than you'd think to get up from the ground properly, especially in a way that looks good on camera. I'm willing to bet you've never had to give much thought to how smoothly you get up from the floor. For actors and stuntpeople, they need to make it appear effortless and easy. In things like battle scenes where the actors are on horses in a historical show or movie, there's a ton of training to be done there. So those folks come to *me* most of the time, though I do go to them when necessary. I spent four months on a shoot in Hungary a year ago training actors and stuntpeople for a variety of things: martial arts, sword work, riding horses—"

"Falling from horses," Matthew teases.

"Yes. And falling from rooftops, from moving carriages, from punches, and falling, falling, falling, and getting up."

"Wow."

"It's a cool job," I admit.

That time in Hungary was the beginning of the end with Brandon, though. He'd come along as he always did on my extended shoots, and he'd found a few things I hadn't anticipated: a love for the language, a love for teaching, and a new *lover*. All in Hungary. Across the world from here. As much as he'd loved being my boy, he'd found things he loved more. It still hurts to remember the sense of betrayal I'd fought and failed to conceal when I found out about Ferko.

"So all this training of people, I suppose it helps with the Daddy stuff because…" Matthew trails off, wanting me to fill it in for him. I'm happy to.

"Because I'm skilled in directing, guiding, teaching…all good things when it comes to being a Daddy."

"Yes," he whispers, and his eyes gleam.

"I have a small farm up Patton Mountain," I motion toward the southeast, and the various mountains ranging out in that direction. "It's where I spend the holidays and where I plan to host our Experience."

"Oh?" His eyes light up. "That sounds perfect. Very Christmassy."

"Yeah, it's gorgeous. My favorite place on earth. It's so peaceful there. I have a main house, a couple of rocky mountain pastures, and a barn with four horses, many goats, and four dogs."

"You live there?"

"Only on weekends. I have a small house in town I stay in the rest of the week. I leave the care of the farm to my mom," I tell him.

"You're close to your mom?"

"She's my best friend."

"Ah." Matthew presses his lips together. "Does she…uh, know?"

"That I'm queer? Yes."

"About the Daddy kink?"

"Most parents don't want to know that level of detail about their children's sex lives," I say. "My mom's no different. She knows enough, though. Brandon called me Daddy full-time, and she figured out what it meant pretty quickly." I snort. "It took some getting used to, being okay with her knowing about my Daddy/boy kink, but she's supportive. That's what matters."

"Brandon?"

"My last boy." Matthew's eyes hold questions about him, and I don't want to answer. "Anyway, that covers my personal and educational background. But my kink credentials are just as, if not more, important."

"Oh. Right."

"My training in kink began while I was still in college. I had a relationship with an older Dominatrix back then. She taught me a lot about being a sub and supported me when I started seeking out play partners as a Dom. I learned how to spank, how to use a paddle and a flogger," I count these off on my fingers, "and how to safely engage in some of the more, let's say, *traditional* BDSM activities. But truth be told, my interest in that aspect of the kink scene waned fast. Pain isn't my cuppa—giving it or receiving it. I'm much more psychological in how I typically like to play."

Matthew clears his throat and surprises me with his next question. "So you're bisexual?"

"Pansexual." I'd expected him to ask more about intense pain play and my aversion to giving or receiving it, but he doesn't seem disappointed by my position. I guess I'm just accustomed to a lot of subs being less than understanding of how I can be a Dominant without wanting to hurt them. Which is one reason why I call myself a Daddy and not a Dom. There are different expectations associated with the term.

"Okay." Matthew nods for me to go on. "How did you start to identify as a Daddy?"

"When I met my first boy, Duncan. I was twenty-eight. He was nineteen."

Ah, my Duncan. A sweet cinnamon roll of a kid who could

deepthroat my cock like a pro and make me come so hard my knees shook. I'd loved being his Daddy and bringing his confidence level up. After years of being bullied in high school for his weight, he'd needed some intense bolstering. I'd thrived on encouraging him, championing him, teaching him how to get up after every fall—literal or metaphorical—and helping him grow.

I've never felt prouder than seeing how my guidance aided him in making a better life for himself. I've always felt like I gained something too—from all my boys. "We had a good relationship, and I learned a lot from him."

"I see."

"We lasted until he graduated from college." I pick up my glass and take a deep swallow to cover the pang that sentence provokes.

That's the pattern, isn't it?

First Duncan, then Garrett—both gone within weeks of graduating. Of my three former boys, only Brandon ended up staying longer. A year and a half longer, to be exact. Then he'd taken off with Ferko, disappearing into the heart of Hungary and taking *my* heart with him.

Melodramatic maybe. But true.

"I've had three long-term boys." I interrupt my own thoughts before I grow gloomy with memories. "Several more for short-term play."

"The boy in those photos? The one from the auction? He was short-term?"

Why does Matthew have to zero in on my sore spot? "No, that was Brandon. He was my most recent boy. He was with me for five years. From the ages of nineteen to twenty-four."

"So you *do* prefer your boys on the younger side."

I frown again. I don't know why I don't want to admit it to him. It sounds tawdry when it's said that way, but I can tell by Matthew's guileless wide eyes he doesn't mean anything by it. The question is more about his own insecurities than any accusation about my preferences.

Still, the truth is I've always had a taste for "chicken meat," as the old-timers call it, at least when it comes to my Daddy/boy fantasies and play. Matthew is going to be a big exception to my general rule. But I don't want him knowing that. And I definitely don't want him to *feel* it, so I hedge.

"Not really. My preferences run to a boy who's submissive, eager, and wants to be enjoyed."

"That's pretty broad."

I shrug. "There are thousands of ways to be attractive in this world. I prefer to focus on a boy's personality."

Which is true, but I *do* have a type of boy I prefer, and a type of man I like to casually fuck, and, in the past, "never the twain shall meet" and all that jazz. Matthew seems to be crossing my wires. Unexpected, but not unwelcome.

But whatever. It doesn't merit close examination. Despite how much ground we need to cover during this conversation for the sake of consent and safety, the December Daddy Experience he's won is just for one night. I don't need to disclose my heart to him. This is business, and I need to keep that in mind.

Besides, Matthew lives in Nashville. He bid on me for a charity auction for a night of fantasy. My very real attraction to him is a bonus, nothing more than that.

I clear my throat and push on. "What kind of Daddy experience were you looking for when you bid on me? Because as I said earlier, I'm not into the harder kinks, and that's non-negotiable."

"Of course. I understood that from the disclaimers on the poster at the auction, not to mention you reinforced it just now with the story of your kink history. You've been very clear. I'm okay with all of it."

"Good. Don't get me wrong. I have no problem with the fact

that other people get off on intense pain play, but it isn't what I enjoy, and I won't do it."

"Boundaries are important," Matthew agrees before chewing on his bottom lip again.

My groin tingles with a hot rush of blood. Fuck me. It's all I can do not to lean forward, pull it free from his teeth, and press a soothing kiss to its plump redness before urging him down to his knees, right here in front of everyone…

Weird. Not my usual kink.

But for some reason, Matthew's elegant masculinity makes me want everyone to see him with me, to know I'm going to own a piece of him they'll never get to have.

Wow. I'm out-of-my-mind horny today. I should get up and go jerk off in the bathroom before continuing this conversation, just so I can clear my head. I clear my throat instead and continue.

"So let's get to the meat of it, all right? We should lay out our experiences and expectations today, so we have the best chance of an enjoyable night together. Obviously, a plan can always be tweaked later, and we'll both always have a safe word, but the important thing is open communication."

"That sounds good," Matthew says, turning his mug around in his hands. "But I have to confess I'm not experienced with *that* either."

"Lots of people aren't." I smile again. "Why don't you start with what you want? Then I can spell out what I'm looking for in return, and we can see if this is a good fit for both of us. If we find either of us isn't up for playing, after all, I'll pay you back for what you donated to the charity, all right? No pressure there."

"No!" Matthew's outraged at my offer. "I wanted to give to the charity no matter what. Besides, your offer explicitly stated 'no refunds.' I knew what I was signing on for," he insists.

"All right." No need to go easy on Matthew. If he's going to be my boy for even a night, it's good he's already eager to honor his commitments. Another thing I find I can admire in him and something I can praise him for later.

"All right." Matthew smiles in relief that I've agreed to let him pay even if we don't engage in the December Daddy Experience after all. He fluffs his hair again, and I make note of it, as well as the lip-biting, as big tells about his state of mind. Anxious. Excited. "Well, like I said, I'm not sure what I'm looking for, but I think whatever it is, I'd like it to feel loving, and…" Matthew pauses to think. "Firm."

"'Firm?' What does that mean to you?"

"Strong. I might want a *little* discipline. Nothing hardcore. I want a Daddy who can be soft but also scolds me when I need it." He meets my gaze with a sharp, challenging expression: *Is that you? Can you do that for me?*

"I'm not averse to a little spanking," I offer.

His pupils dilate, and my cock swells. "Okay," he agrees. "Right. Discipline."

"You're looking for strength and discipline. Got it." I nod.

Matthew takes a sip of his coffee and nods, too. He puts on a very businesslike expression and sits straight. "In that case, let's move on to the next question."

Ho, ho, hot damn. Let's do this, boy.

He's adorable, all serious like this. Butterflies tumble in my gut.

The waitress stops by our table to check if we need anything, and to top off Matthew's mug. He takes a long swallow, moaning gently. "This is fantastic coffee."

My dick surges with blood again. This boy's going to make some delightful noises when I crack him open. When is our night together? Next weekend?

It can't come soon enough.

CHAPTER THREE
Matthew

WHEN ERIK WALKS into Caffeine Dream, the first thing I notice is he's even more handsome in person than he was in the pictures on the charity poster board. Wearing jeans, a T-shirt, a gorgeous black leather jacket, and a red scarf, he looks the epitome of cool.

As I watch him scan the room for me, trying to sort out which of the many gay men in the room I might be, I take him in from head to toe, and I am captivated by what I see.

He's broad, strong, and built like all my boyhood fantasies of firemen, cowboys, and police officers. He moves like he's in command, and that's what stays my feet, keeps me glued in place even as he meets my eyes, and then moves on, not suspecting I'm the boy he's been auctioned off to.

I feel like I need his permission to approach, that I shouldn't bother a sexy hunk like him with my timid, uncertain Daddy/boy fantasies. He no doubt deserves someone better than me. Someone younger, prettier, and without so much baggage. That's what keeps me from stepping up to him and announcing myself.

Until I see his eyes catch on a young, blond man who's entered wearing an oversized sweatshirt and a smug expression. When Erik's eyes catch on the boy's bubble butt and smooth down over his thighs with a satisfied smile, it's like my feet develop a mind of their own, and next thing I know, I'm standing by him at his table, asking if I should sit.

It's ridiculous, but a thrum of possessiveness sings through me even as he still tries to make eye contact with the young blond.

I'm your boy. I bought you.

Which is silly because you can't buy a person. That's part of why I'm here, after all. To ascertain mutual consent in this situation that's otherwise so borderline lacking in it. I even have some forms for him to sign, procured from my friend Doug. He's not only a great attorney but also kinky, and thus willing to write up some quick, marginally binding contracts regarding Erik's and my agreement here today. Because you shouldn't just *trust* someone you bought at a kink charity auction.

But when Erik replies to my request to sit with, "Sorry, no, I'm waiting on someone," I find the snark coming out quicker than I can stop it. "Yeah, you're waiting on me."

I love his laugh immediately. It's gravelly and leaves me feeling like he's just slid a firm, strong hand up the inside of my thigh and taken hold of my cock. Like he owns it already now. I even chub up a little, as embarrassing as that is. All that from just the way he laughs.

When I sit across from him, the conversation goes off my planned script right from the start. It's clear he isn't expecting me, which is embarrassing and stressful. But I get it, too, because I thought I *was* expecting him. I'd at least seen pictures—but he's so much more than I thought.

He's got a strong, stubbled jaw, and his lips are on the thin side, but despite his initial discombobulation, they give him a rock-steady appearance.

And speaking of rock-solid. His body.

Erik's snug T-shirt fits like a glove over his thick shoulders and sculpted pecs; the arms are tight around his biceps, leaving me with a strong urge to reach out and feel the size of them. His muscled thighs strain against his jeans, and I can see a nice hint of the size of his package from the way his legs are splayed. Not that I'm a size queen. Or, rather, I wouldn't even know if I was. But it's just another way Erik is a lot more than I'd known to expect.

His light brown hair is cut military-style short, but it flatters his strong face. He looks capable and sure of himself. I ache over the way he's sprawled in his chair so easily, and how he leans forward to gaze at me like he might order me to my knees right here and now, stroke my hair, and call me his boy.

If he wants that? I'll do it.

My cheeks heat. It'd be so humiliating to kneel like that in public, and yet I know I'll feel proud to be under his hand. Which is a dangerous thought. I still know so little about him.

I try to direct us back on track, asking questions about his credentials, and listening to his answers. Training actors to ride horses? And fall off them? What a fascinating job. It's easy to want to know more about that, but again we go off the rails, falling into teasing and silly commentary, poking at the thick attraction between us. I'm not alone in it, right? I can't be this hot and bothered by him while he's sitting there unmoved. Surely?

As we chat, I study his cinnamon-brown eyes. They're alternately merry, measuring, and alluring. Before long, I can tell he's found something he likes about me, even if I'm not young like his other boys have been. That's exciting but also intimidating. The urge to hide which dogs me in my professional life, keeping me from putting myself up for the promotions and advancements I deserve, nearly leads me to hide my red face in my hands.

But I don't. The easy power of Erik's command holds me in place even though we haven't formalized anything yet. For some unknowable reason, I already need to show him respect, look him in the eye when I speak to him, even when it's hard, answer his questions, and ask some, too. I'm compelled to be myself for him—sassy or shy—whatever, whichever. I sense he likes it either way.

Both ways.

I believe he already likes *me*.

Which is thrilling but also scary.

Because I've never done anything like this before, and I've never been taken seriously by a guy as sexy as Erik. In person, he's so alluring to me, so charismatic in a way I can't define. Every few seconds I'm tempted to tell him to forget it all, to get up and run back to my car.

It's only parked a few streets away. He won't chase me down. Even if it *is* a hot fantasy I'd like to explore one day. Being chased by a big, sexy man, panting hard as I try to get away from him, getting grabbed from behind and…

Lord, where is my brain?

Erik has me feeling way more things than I expected when I bid on him in that auction, and that's saying something, because he'd stirred my interest like nothing else ever had in those photos he'd taken with his…his…*ex*-boy.

My stomach sours a little when I remember the boy in the pictures. It's not fair, but I'm not thrilled Erik has a string of boys behind him. Of course he does. Why wouldn't he? Most men our age—straight or gay—have a lot of exes of one stripe or another, and there's no reason to think Daddy Erik should be any different. I shouldn't want him to be! It means he's got experience and "know how."

That's what I'd wanted when I bid on him: someone who's done this Daddy/boy thing before, someone with experience as a queer man who can show me the ropes—someone I can be vulnerable with, because I want to trust a Daddy just wants to take care of me, raise me up. But I realize, as he discusses his past boys, I'd wanted to have all those things without thinking too closely about the very real young men he's had before me.

Before this moment of hearing their names, and of seeing the tender expression in his eyes as he mentions them, it's been easy enough to replace the boy in the photos with myself in my mind. To imagine only how *I* will feel in his arms, curled on the sofa, in front of a fire, opening a gift he's bought for *me*, held in his strong arms and fucked firmly, taken even harder as I beg for his strength…

Fuck, that's so hot. And frightening.

Can I even *let myself* be that vulnerable with a man? I don't know. It's a beautiful thing to fantasize about, but I've never been able to do it before.

What if, in the moment, when we're "playing" as he puts it, he looks at me and sees my wrinkles, sees my gray hair, and finds me lacking?

Faced with Erik's very real person and his easy discussion of his past, I realize how *not real* everything about this fantasy has been up until now. I'm out of my depth in more ways than one. In secret and humiliating ways. My inexperience with Daddy/boy activities, with living out even basic, common fantasies, with *everything* sexual is mortifying in a man of my age.

I remember what Doug told me as he'd pushed the blank contract into my hands: *To avoid a bad kink experience, you must be brutally honest with yourself and with your Dom or Daddy. Even if it's uncomfortable or frightening. There's no place for withholding information out of embarrassment or shame. Otherwise, you risk getting seriously hurt, physically or emotionally.*

"Tell me what you're thinking," Erik says. It's a command, and I realize I've been quiet for some time, turning my mug around and around in my hands, and letting our conversation lapse into silence.

"I think I need to be honest with you," I say, meeting his gaze and hoping what I say next isn't a deal-killer, because I already know I *do* want to work out a contract with Erik for this December Daddy Experience. I'm aching for the opportunity to call him

Daddy, and have him pretend to love me, even if he can never love me for real, even if I never find anyone who can.

"That would be best, yes," he says.

"I've never done this before."

"So you've said."

"Any of it." My voice squeaks on the words.

He blinks at me. "Define that more clearly, please."

"I…" Mortification stops me from saying more.

Erik reaches out to take hold of my hands and turns them so he can grip my fingers. "Look at me as you say it," he says. "Show me your face."

I let out the breath I've sucked in; even so, my voice cracks. "I'm a virgin."

He blinks a moment. "In what way?"

My gaze swerves to the table, but he squeezes my fingers until I look up again. "I've sucked a bunch of men off. Jerked off a handful more—no pun intended, heh." I giggle but sober quickly, shame like an ache in my breastbone. I whisper the rest. "But I've never had a man get *me* off, and I've never had my dick sucked, and I've never been fucked. I've never even been kissed."

Now it's his turn to suck in a breath, but after the moment of shock passes, he asks, "Not even with a woman? Or a non-binary person?"

I shake my head.

"No one at all?"

"Just my hand. I guess I did some shameful humping once with a high school friend. He got off, but he wouldn't kiss me, and he pushed me away before I could come."

"Selfish prick."

"Ruined our friendship, too," I say with a grimace. Erik squeezes my fingers again. I catch my breath and go on. "I've sucked off fifteen men in my life. Yes, I've kept count." *Because I'm that pathetic.*

"Why has there never been any quid pro quo?"

I lick my lips and glance away, but he rubs his thumbs over the back of my fingertips, coaxing my gaze back to his. "I liked being used."

"All right."

"But I'm past that now." I bite into my lower lip, trying to ignore the pain in my chest, threatening to turn into tears in my eyes. "I want to be adored."

He nods, stays silent.

"I don't know how…" I clear my throat. "I don't know how to find that. When I saw the photos on your poster at the auction…" It's probably annoying I keep trailing off, but I can't help it. I keep losing my words.

Erik doesn't rush me, though. It's as if he knows this is already so intense for me: holding his hands, gazing into his face, being honest and exposed. I'm scared and feel like I might lift out of my body in a strange ecstasy born of too much vulnerability.

"I'd never even considered wanting a Daddy/boy interaction for myself before I saw your poster." I remember how transfixed I'd been as soon as I saw those photos. "But once I did? I just knew. In my bones. I need this. I mean, I've seen that kind of thing in porn, of course. Who hasn't? But it's not the same as doing it, is it?"

He nods again.

"Like, I didn't think *I* needed or wanted anything like that. Not what I saw in the videos online. Definitely not. But your poster was different."

"Maybe because, in porn, Daddy/boy play is often paired with other kinds of dominance, like rough sex, dark humiliation, and sometimes pain."

"Maybe. I'm not sure that's it. Like I said, I understand the urge. The urge to be hurt or treated badly. Before, up until recently,

I wanted to be used, but now…" I shake my head. "Am I making sense?"

"Of course. Fantasies change, desires change—we *all* change over time. But tell me, Matthew, what do you think caused this change in your fantasies and needs? What prompted this switch from enjoying being used and discarded, to…" He pauses as if he's making sure he's phrasing it the right way. "To wanting to be adored?"

"That's not—I didn't—"

I glance around, trying to see if anyone's listening to us. I can't believe I'm saying these things to anyone at all, much less to a man I want to play out Daddy/boy fantasies with. A man I've been stroking myself off thinking about every night for the last week, ever since I got back from Asheville and received the official notification I'd won him in the auction. And I can't believe I'm saying it all *here*, sitting in a busy coffee shop where anyone could listen in on us. And yet…

No one is.

It's like there's a magic privacy wall around us. No one's paying any attention, and between the jangle of "Santa Claus is Coming to Town," the chattering of so many caffeinated people, the clatter of knives and forks on plates, and the rattle of tea and coffee cups finding their place in their saucers, it's way too loud for anything I say to travel much distance anyway.

I take a slow breath, and Erik's eyes soften as he smiles at me. "C'mon, you're doing great," he says. "Tell me about it. I won't judge you."

"My parents died," I said, and my throat almost closes on the words. Now I'm blinking, and those are definitely tears in my eyes. Shit. He's going to think I'm such a wreck. "I'm sorry. You didn't sign on for this when you put your offer up for auction. I bet you just wanted a simple, fun, *young* boy to spend a Christmas-themed night with, right? And that's…that's not me. I'm sorry. We don't have to do this."

"Hey, stop. Don't make assumptions about what I want," he says.

"Then what did you want?" I ask.

Erik smiles, brings one of my hands up to his mouth, and brushes a kiss over the back of my knuckles. My stomach flutters. So gentlemanly. So sweet.

"Nope," he scolds. "Don't turn away from my question. We'll get to what *I* want later. We're talking about you right now."

His reprimand hits me like a zip of lust, and my dick, which has gone through the stages of chub, fully hard, and back to chub once already during this conversation, grows hard again. I shift in my seat as it swells against the seam of my pants. I tingle with heat when he kisses my knuckles again, and my cock throbs. "Fuck," I whisper.

Erik laughs. "Yeah. We can talk about that, too, if you want—we'll address the ever-important question: to do anal or not to do anal—but first things first. We need to get comfortable with each other. I'm not going into a scene like this with you until I know you better. It's too important. *You're* too important."

"Me?"

"Yes. You." He rubs my fingers again. I feel like soaring out of the chair and up to the ceiling, where I'll plaster myself on my back, and spin around in ecstatic, possessed glee. I'm important? To someone like Erik? If I'd known I could buy this feeling, I'd have gone to a kink charity auction years ago.

"Go on," he urges me. "Your parents died. I'm sorry to hear that. But I'm not sure how it answers my question about what's changed about sex for you."

"It changed *everything* for me," I confess. I worry for a moment he doesn't hear me in the clang and bluster of the room, but his eyebrows lift, and it's clear he heard me just fine. "My folks were your typical Southern Baptists in a lot of ways. Non-drinkers, homophobic, puritanical. But they were my parents, and I loved them."

"Of course."

"Plus, I'm adopted."

Erik's fingers start a steady, reassuring stroking on the backs of my hands, and the roiling anxiety in me calms as I continue to talk. He listens with a calm, measured acceptance which goes beyond understanding. It's impossible and delusional, I know, but it's very much what I think it might be like to be held with unconditional love. That thought makes me want to cry or run away. I keep talking instead. "I always felt like I owed them, you know? For saving me?"

"Saving you from what?"

"From a fate worse than being adopted by them. Who knows where I came from? Who knows who might have adopted me if they hadn't?"

"That's a negative outlook."

"Maybe, but most parents don't choose their kids. They just have one themselves. My parents chose me, you know? They didn't have to. They could have chosen someone else."

Erik makes a low noise, like he's considering my words. "You were a baby?"

"Yes, but I always felt the weight of it. I was determined to be the son they'd wanted and tried to conceive for so many years before turning to adoption. I wanted to be the man my folks wanted me to be, even if that meant denying who I truly am, who I want, *what* I want..."

Erik's eyes shine with understanding. "You were closeted until their deaths."

"Yes."

"They never knew?"

"My mom, maybe? I think she suspected, but she stopped asking me about my lack of a love life a few years before she got sick. My dad never asked me anything after high school came and went without me dating at all." I pause, gather myself. "It was cancer for both of them. Lung for him, ovarian for her. The strangest timing. Six months apart."

"That sucks."

I chuckle despite the lump in my throat. "It does. And when it was all over, after their estate was settled, and it was all done, I found myself alone. *Really* alone. Let me tell you, I did a lot of soul-searching." I sigh. "And I found a lot of regrets."

"I'm sorry." His fingers are still moving on mine.

"In the end, I decided I needed to accept who I am and live my life as an out gay man." I put up a hand to stop the congratulations I can already see forming on his lips. "But it isn't as easy as all that, now is it?"

"I imagine not. But tell me why."

"I don't know, to be honest. After all these years of hiding, I'm not sure how to open up?" I take a shuddering breath and charge on, feeling like I'm laying my insides out on a table for display. "It's like I only know how to get on my knees and let a man fuck my mouth. I'm…I'm actually very good at that?" I say it like a question because my throat's gone so tight now I can hardly squeak air through it.

"You're doing a great job opening up to me right now."

I squeeze his fingers. "I've told you more in the last few minutes than I've told my therapist in two years."

"Why?" he asks again. His eyebrows crinkle, concern radiating from him.

"Because she's so damn nice," I bite out. "How can I look at her and say these things? Say I've let men pull my hair, let them come on my face and spit on me, and then watched them walk away?

How can I tell her, in all her apple-cheeked sweetness, that I've never asked for *anything* for myself in return?"

"Did you like it? Being humiliated and left hard with no orgasm as a reward?" he asks, ignoring what I said about my therapist, digging right into the heart of it.

"No."

"Ah."

"And I *didn't* like that I didn't like it, either, if you know what I mean. Nothing about it pleased me."

He nods, and his eyes grow soft. "I'm sorry."

"It's fucked up, but back then, I just wanted them to treat me the same way I felt about myself. All that self-loathing and fear— that I was letting my parents down, letting God down. And because I was a believer in those days, that I was letting myself down by being queer."

I hear the way my voice has gone rough with old pain. "I needed someone to do it to me, physically, so I could express the disgust I felt. It was the only way I could find to admit it, you know? At home, with my folks—even once I was an adult, I still lived with them—I had to be so neutral all the time, so tidy and tight. I couldn't be a mess."

"Mm."

"But when a man—"

A straight couple stops near our table, and I clam up. Erik doesn't move, doesn't say anything at all. He just keeps on stroking the backs of my hands with his thumbs, and he waits. The couple talk about what they're going to have for dinner, what time the man should pick up their dog from the doggie daycare, and the woman says she'll meet him at home after she goes to the drugstore. They leave.

"Go on," Erik says.

"When a man used me, treated me like shit, I felt relief. I didn't *like* it, but it was as if someone saw the truth of me."

"I'm so sorry."

"Anyway," I say, lifting my chin to declare it. "I don't want that anymore."

Erik's lips rise at the corners in an encouraging smile.

"I'm learning to love myself. It's slow and hard, and it's about more than just accepting who I am as a gay man. I've joined some DNA sites to maybe find my birth parents, and I've decided I'm going to pick up playing music again—just for myself, but still—"

"But still," he agrees.

"So, yeah. That's where I am. I'm learning. How to be a gay man. How to love myself. And I need help. When I saw your poster, how you held your boy—" my throat goes tight again and tears well. One slips down my face, and when I tug my hand so I can wipe it away, he releases me, but reaches out to wipe away the tear. His fingers are gentle on my cheek.

"I understand," he says.

"Do you?"

"Yes. And I can help you."

"You can?"

"Of course."

"When?"

"During our night together."

I'm so relieved I take slow breaths just to keep from breaking into an embarrassing sob. How did he do it? How did he pull all this out of me? I barely know him, and yet I've unburdened myself to him, told him things I've never admitted out loud to anyone.

I should ask my therapist for my money back. Erik's done more for me in half an hour than she's done for me in two years, just by being the kind of man I can say all this to. I really do have to quit seeing her, if nothing else.

After a few tense moments, Erik glances around the coffee shop and says, "I can't tell you how important and precious it is that you shared all this with me. It's going to make what we do together better in every way. This kind of vulnerability is necessary to have the best kink experience possible, so I want to thank you for this."

I can't say anything, so I just nod.

"At the same time, I can tell you're feeling overwrought now, and I get it. This has gotten intense. Let's take a break. Go on a walk. Work out some of your tension before we go ahead with our planning." He glances at his watch. "Do you have time?"

I'm so tempted to agree to his suggestion without asking any further questions. Erik's been so kind to me, so laid-back and open, and I've bared my soul to him, it can't hurt to bare more. But I'm not sure we should go somewhere to fuck quite yet—especially since I haven't ever done that before.

But if I leave here with him, if we go somewhere private? If he touches me, lifts my chin, and kisses me? I'm going to let him do *whatever* he wants. And that's not how this is supposed to go.

Get a grip.

I need to keep a clear head and get him to sign the contracts Doug drew up for us. I should call the rest of his references and check them, and I should go on back to my car and drive to the hotel I've reserved at the halfway point in Knoxville after all that. But I'm swept away in lust and the strange high from having exposed my rawest truths, and though I should reel it back in, I don't want to.

Erik has let go of my hand and risen already, putting on his jacket and wrapping his red scarf around his neck.

"I don't know," I say, stopping him mid-wrap. "Where did you have in mind?"

If he says his place, I need to say no, but I'll say yes. I want him. I want his hands back on me anywhere I can get them. I want to see how he handles me once I'm naked and trembling and—

"Let's start with a walk," he says. "The city is decked out for the holidays. Some cute shops we can go into, too."

"'Cute shops?'" I'm confused. *We're not going to go cut this tension between us? We're not going to fuck? We're going to* shop?

Erik smiles. "I like cute things."

I recognize he's telling me I'm cute. My heart double-beats. Oh wow. I spilled all that emotional crap to him, and he's not running. He's calling me cute. What's *his* damage? I should know that before I go anywhere at all with him or sign a contract to spend the night as his boy. Before I let myself get carried away.

"Okay," I hear myself say. "Lead the way."

"I will."

CHAPTER FOUR

Erik

ASHEVILLE IS FULL of artisans, and the shops, art galleries, and restaurants downtown are all festooned with creative, unique, and beautiful holiday decorations. Green and red ribbons wrap around lampposts, twinkle lights in windows, and the full cast of *The Grinch* has been knitted by artisans and propped up in cotton batting within the windows of the wool store. Each window is done up with lights and shiny things for the season.

I hadn't intended to spend the whole day with Matthew. I'd expected to meet up with a somewhat experienced kinkster or boy, not a man like Matthew: virginal in every way. Unless I want to call the entire thing off, I'll need to be much more careful with him than I'd realized. That takes time. Today, luckily, I have all the time in the world to devote to getting to know Matthew, so our time together next week can be safe for both of us.

For now, we don't talk further about Daddy/boy fantasies, our sexual or personal histories, or what we plan to do together during the night he's won from me.

Instead, we chat amiably about our jobs, TV shows we like, and other mundane matters as we duck in and out of a few little shops and galleries.

Accounting is as dull as it sounds, he tells me, though he gets a hit of dopamine when the numbers add up just right, and he's satisfied when he knows he's done a good job for the client.

"But it's nowhere near as exciting as what you do. Have you

worked with any famous actors?"

"Depends on what you mean by famous. I haven't worked with Chris Evans, or *any* of the Chrises, for that matter, but there's a certain female movie star from a famous superhero franchise who I trained in combat moves, sword fighting, and fitness. I sign NDAs for most of the big names, so…" I mime zipping my lips. "I can't say more than that. But she's a pretty big star, one of the biggest names I've worked with."

"Was she nice?" Matthew asks as I hold the door open to the next art gallery that has presented itself. I've already determined Matthew is an art buff, based on the three other galleries he asked if we could go into. He has a keen eye and opinions about what he likes—and snide comments about what he doesn't. It's amusing.

"She was professional. Focused. I'm not sure 'nice' is beneficial when you're at her level. She wasn't an asshole, though. I'm not saying that."

"I get it," Matthew says, stopping in front of an intriguing painting depicting a loaf of Wonder Bread strapped to the back of a red fox wandering in a winter wood. He tilts his head, taking it in. "She had a job to do, and you were there to help her do it. It's the same with my clients. Our business relationships aren't about being nice." He steps closer to the painting, squints at the paint strokes before stepping back to my side. "Oil on wood. I've always liked how smooth it is. If the artist had put a gloss on this, I'd be tempted to buy it."

I watch him studying the painting, admiring how his eyes have wrinkles fanning out lightly from the edges, noting that while the salt is heaviest next to his temples, it's also scattered throughout his dark hair, and smiling at the dimple in his cheek which begs a finger to be pressed into it. "Have you been to the art museum here? It's small but has some nice pieces," I say.

"I have, actually. When I was here the weekend of the auction. I came to most of these galleries then, but they've already changed out a lot of their pieces." He walks to the next work—a sculpture of a brown mushroom with an open door in the stem. Inside is a warm, cozy kitchen with built-in, glowing, homey windows in the cap.

He glances over his shoulder at the tall, blonde gallery representative. She's standing back from us, giving us space to examine the art in our own time and way, but monitoring us in case we have questions.

Pitching his voice lower so the woman can't hear him, he says, "While we were in the last gallery, I realized we sort of rushed it earlier, didn't we? Like we just skipped right to the part where we try to make this—" he motions between us "—work for our night together."

"Skipped right to it," I say with a laugh. "Yeah. Men tend to do that."

It's true men don't beat around the bush when it comes to what they want. It's one of the things I've historically loved about being a single man who also digs guys: the possibility of uncomplicated, animalistic, hot hookups.

And I'd have happily skipped right to fucking Matthew in the bathroom. At least I would have before I'd unearthed just how vulnerable he is. Now I don't want to skip right to anything. Or rather, I still *want* to, but I shouldn't. Even if he's tempting, what with the way his clothes cling in the right places, and how he walks around with that odd innocence in his eyes, so out of place in a man his age.

"Yeah, I guess men typically do," he agrees. "But I don't. Not ever."

"I understand."

We move on next to a painting; this one is by a different artist. It's a fiery work of orange, red, and pink. Matthew stares at it, crossing his arms over his chest, his jaw tightening.

"You don't like it?" I ask.

"It's good," he answers, but he's tense again. If it's not the painting eliciting this in him, it must be me. This won't do.

"Something got you worried?"

Glancing back again to make sure the gallery employee is still out of earshot, he nods. It's adorable how shy he is. I want to protect that part of him. It's endearing.

"Out with it," I tell him, using my firm Daddy voice. It does the trick.

He capitulates, sending me a worried glance before lifting his chin and saying, "You should know I didn't go into that charity auction looking for this, or for you, or, well, looking for anything at all."

We step over to the next painting. It's similar to the last, but in purple, gray, and pink.

"I see. Why *were* you at the charity auction? I admit I've been curious."

I recognize it might be easier for him to continue to open up without being literally face-to-face; the act of studying the art is a good buffer. The intensity of our conversation in the coffee shop isn't something he seems eager to rekindle quite yet, and that's fair. We both need some breathing room after how raw that became, and this more businesslike discussion is worthwhile, too.

When Matthew doesn't answer right away, I say, "Asheville is a long way from Nashville, and while the Blue Ridge chapter has a good reputation, I know if you wanted to explore kink, you didn't have to come this far. Nashville has several stellar kink clubs."

Moving on to a concrete sculpture of a boot with black painted roses blooming from the sole, Matthew's arms tighten across his chest as he whispers, "I wasn't in Asheville for the kink club at all. I was there for a business conference. I missed my flight, and given the current economy, renting a car to drive back was going to be almost as expensive as another night in the hotel and taking a discount airline's flight home the next day. Not to mention a lot more strenuous."

I can see it all: Matthew, frustrated and tired, returning from the airport after missing his flight.

"I see. You were staying at the hotel, got a little bored, and noticed an interesting BDSM convention going on in the conference area, complete with an open-to-the-public kink auction, and you thought, 'Hell yeah, looks like fun.'"

"Yes. Well, maybe not *fun*. More like interesting. Because until that night I'd never thought of myself as kinky." He blushes, and I'm amused.

There's nothing as delicious to me as when a new boy shows his true colors for the first time, and Matthew's flying them for me now, as uncomfortable as it might be for him, and as frightened as he is. Deep down, he's excited. I sense it in him and echo it in myself.

He continues, "I'm sure that sounds weird given how badly I've let myself be treated by men. But even that never felt kinky because I didn't *like* it. What I'm saying is I never *wanted* to be kinky. I would like you to understand that."

"Does the idea of kink upset you?"

"No."

I place my hand on his lower back, supporting him. "And if it turns out you *are* kinky—like *really* kinky—will it scare you?"

"I don't know. Maybe. I'm still just trying to be gay. Like out and gay."

"Right."

We both realize we've been standing in front of the shoe sculpture for a very long time when the woman begins to make her way toward us. She must have interpreted our quiet, serious discussion as real interest in the work.

I wave her off, and she falls back.

Matthew and I move on, passing by the next work with just a glance. It's a shattered mirror taped back together in a gilt frame with glitter-backed duct tape. I get the impression Matthew thinks it's gauche by the way he very literally turns his nose up at it.

Next to a passé watercolor landscape of the Blue Ridge mountains, Matthew pauses, but he's not seeing the art. All his attention is on me, even if he's gazing at the blue mountains against the orange sunset; I feel it like the heat from a fire.

After a few beats, he says, "So that's how I came to be at the auction. I didn't make a dedicated trip over here from Nashville just for it. I knew nothing about it or you before that night. I'm not a stalker or a fan of yours or anything."

"I didn't think you were." I'm not sure how he thinks I'd even have any fans in the kink world; I've been monogamous with Brandon for most of the last five years and haven't played since. Though I do have a YouTube channel unrelated to kink where I post various training routines and workouts, and it's starting to get quite a following. I suppose I might have some fans from that.

Matthew turns to me, glances over my shoulder, and ascertains the position of the ever-hopeful sales lady before he meets my gaze. Lifts his chin. Squares his shoulders. A smile starts on my lips. I'm impressed by his boldness and by how the hazel of his eyes shifts in the light from the wide windows at the front of the store.

"So now I've explained myself, I guess I'm curious…"

"Go on."

"What were you hoping for when you put yourself up at the auction?"

The truth—that I'd hoped to set my opening bid so high no one would bid on me—isn't something I'm prepared to share. I think it'll hurt his feelings, and, worse, he'll think I don't want to be here with him. He'll call the whole thing off. I don't want him doing that. Because no matter how reluctant I'd been before, I'm into this now.

At that very moment, Matthew's stomach growls, and mine takes it as a cue to do the same.

I clasp his arm and steer him toward the front of the gallery. "C'mon. I'm happy to tell you about my reasons for putting myself up for the auction, but how about we do that over lunch?"

Somehow the morning has flown by, and we're staring one o'clock in the face. Neither of us have eaten since breakfast, and our drinks at Caffeine Dream weren't filling.

"All right. Lead the way," he says again, and I love the way he lets me take control. It's flawless, like he's been trained to submit, and yet it's just natural. Easy.

As I take him out onto the sidewalk, he follows without any resistance, and when I point at a restaurant—my favorite down-home Southern food joint—he nods and asks no questions, trusting me. Such a good boy. Christ, I'd like to pull him close, squeeze his ass, and tell him how very good he's being, but we aren't there yet. We still need to finalize things.

After we've ordered, and the waitress has left us alone in the back of the restaurant near the big window, I come back to his question in the gallery. Matthew doesn't seem surprised I remembered or worried I wasn't going to keep my word that I'd explain myself to him. He fluffs his hair, sits back in his chair, and takes me in as I talk, his eyes soaking me up like he's thirsty and I'm fresh rain.

"Though you and I are just planning for one night together, any Daddy/boy scene can be an intensely intimate thing." I reach out and take hold of his hand again, loving the ease with which he gives it. For a newly out gay man, it's remarkable. "In fact, it *should* be very intimate, or what's the point of it?"

Matthew nods.

"So when my last boy, Brandon, left to pursue a new life—" *and love*, my hateful brain helpfully reminds me "—I needed some space away from kink and Daddy/boy play in order to move on from that relationship."

"Did he hurt you?" Matthew asks. "When he left?"

"I can't say I didn't know it was coming."

But I hadn't known. Not like I should have. I'd loved Brandon so hard and so blindly by that point, I'd imagined he might be the one who didn't leave.

But boys always leave. They should. It's a Daddy's job to raise them up.

I'm not going to tell Matthew that, though. He doesn't need to see my vulnerabilities. I'm the Daddy here. It's my duty to hold *his* vulnerabilities and rawness, my job to scold and coax him to independence. So that's what I tell him. "Boys are meant to leave their Daddies. They grow up and go off."

"Right. But I'm already grown," he says.

"Not in this way. Not when it comes to being a gay man."

He nods.

"After Brandon left, once I was ready to get back in the saddle—"

"With Daddy/boy play," he interjects. "Not relationships, right?"

"Right. I'm not looking for anything serious. I decided the charity auction would be a good way to dip my toe back into the kink community."

"Just your toe?" he says a little cheekily, and I should tease back, but I don't.

"I need to see if I still want to be someone's Daddy, or if moving on from Brandon means moving on from that, too."

My last words surprise me. I hadn't even known I felt this way, but as soon as they're out, I see the truth of them, and I can tell by the downward, caring quirk of Matthew's strong eyebrows that he knows now just how much Brandon hurt me by leaving.

"So, you've been doubting whether you want to be a Daddy to anyone else?" he asks.

I pause as the waitress approaches with our orders of biscuits, gravy, sausage links, and sweet potato fries. As soon as she's gone, I take up where I left off, the words having come to me as she arranged our plates and asked if we needed straws.

"I haven't doubted whether I still get off on the dynamic; I do. But after three serious and intense Daddy/boy relationships, I'm not sure I want to dive back into that again. I've wondered if, instead of the full-time intensity I've engaged in with boys in the past, maybe I can enjoy doing it more casually." I poke my fork into the sausage and dip it into the gravy before I add, "Truth be told, I don't think I want to go through another boy leaving me again. It's too hard, even though it's what I prepare them to do."

So much for not showing my vulnerabilities, so much for me being the strong, impermeable Daddy for this new-to-kink man.

But Matthew doesn't even flinch. He picks up his fork, takes a bite of biscuit slathered in gravy, and after swallowing, says, "You think casual kink with a boy like me can let you have your cake and eat it too. All the joy of the dynamic, but none of the pain of a real relationship."

"It seems too good to be true. But it would be nice if it works out that way."

It won't.

I'll want to find another long-term boy and raise him up strong, and then one day, he'll want to go. They always do. They *should!*

And I'll suffer again.

That's the cycle, because I'm good at my role, and despite how tawdry it sounds, my preference does run young. And young men don't want to settle down with their first Daddy. They want to go out and explore the world, be free, make mistakes, and, hell, maybe even *be* the Daddy one day themselves.

That's what I know, but despite my runaway mouth, I'm *not* going to tell Matthew this.

Even if we hit it off—and we have—and even if our one night together from the auction is fantastic, and even if we end up arranging another few nights just for the hell of it, there's no way we'll fall into the kind of Daddy/boy relationship I crave.

He lives in Nashville.

He's middle-aged.

He has a life of his own, and there's no reason to think he'd want to leave it.

I need a boy to live with me—for me to care for, feed and clothe and scold and fuck.

No, Matthew is one night. For a charity auction. Maybe we'll add a few hookups afterward if it's hot enough for us both. But then it will be over. He'll move on and hopefully come out of this experience with some good memories, enhanced self-respect, and a readiness to start looking for healthy relationships with men local to him.

"I hope it works out for you," Matthew says, but he sounds as doubtful as I feel. Which isn't great. I need him to believe I can handle him, and I need him to forget all about my scabbed-over inner wounds. I never should have shown them to him.

"Let's not focus on that."

"Right. We should talk about the details of our night, shouldn't we?"

The light from the windows glistens on the white strands in his hair, and gleams against the dark. His eyes glow a greener hazel, and I find I'm happy he requires extra time and care. I don't want to rush the day away. I'm enjoying drawing out this time with

Matthew. If we nail down the details, and wrap things up, I'll have nothing to do but head back to my shared, rented house to be confronted by the loneliness I've felt ever since Brandon left. Matthew is so much more interesting than that.

Glancing at my phone to check the time, I say, "The afternoon is still young. I'd enjoy spending more time with you, if you feel the same."

Matthew's eyes light with pleasure. He lowers his lashes, but his lips lift at the edges, almost as if he's trying not to show how happy he is that I'm not ready to send him packing quite yet. "I have some time." He glances at his phone's lock screen and seems to ponder a moment before meeting my gaze. "In fact, I can stay for dinner if you'd like. My treat."

"No," I say sternly.

He winces, and I realize I haven't been clear enough.

Note to self: Matthew needs absolute clarity.

"I'll pay. You're the boy in this December Daddy Experience. Don't forget that."

"Oh. I suppose I did win you, and you didn't come cheap."

I laugh. "No, I didn't. But when you're with Daddy, he always pays. Understand?"

"Yes." I can see in his eyes he wants to say 'yes, Daddy' but holds it back.

Gratified, I add, "Dinner sounds wonderful. Until then, let's just enjoy each other's company. There's so much more to having a fun experience together than hashing out whose cock goes where and when and how often."

Matthew blushes again, and it seems to get prettier and more appealing each time he does it. "I'm rather invested in the answer to those questions, I have to admit."

I clear my throat. My dick is interested, too, but if we close out those details, our excuse to linger in each other's presence will disappear. "And I'm invested in finding out what flavor of chocolate truffles you like best."

Matthew laughs, bafflement crossing his face. "Why?"

"The better to stuff your stocking with," I say with as much innuendo as possible.

He laughs again and chews another forkful of biscuits and gravy as he fights an irrepressible smile.

"Seriously, though, there are two wonderful candy stores very nearby. I'll be curious to see what you like. For stocking purposes."

Matthew agrees chocolate truffles will make a nice dessert.

Satisfied, I sit back in my chair, and once we're finished with our meals, I pay and we exit onto Wall Street, making our way toward Chocolate Fetish, with Matthew stopping curiously outside many of the holiday-bedecked stores. As the scent of peppermint drifts out onto the sidewalk, mixing with the jangle of bells from a charity Santa Claus, I urge him inside of each one.

"Window-shopping is for the weak-willed," I tease. "The real test is going in and leaving without buying something."

As we go in shop after shop, I keep a close eye on what Matthew is drawn to. I notice which clothing items he ponders for a long time, and what scents he lingers over in the candles, handmade soaps, and incense sticks. This information will come in handy when I buy him presents for under the tree later.

In Chocolate Fetish, I make a mental note of which truffles he struggles to choose between as he points out his favorites. I buy a half-dozen for him as dessert. Leaving the store, we find a nearby bench and open the small box. So much for willpower. I'm charmed as he takes a bite of one chocolate truffle and moans at the flavor, before holding it out to me.

"Want to taste?"

Licking my lips, I lean forward to take a careful bite of the chocolatey, gooey, orange-flavored treat. "Mm."

"Yeah?"

I nod.

Matthew takes another bite and holds the last of it before my lips, popping it inside when I open. The chocolate and orange flavor fills my mouth, and fondness fills my heart as I watch him studying my reaction. His nose is red from the cold, and his lips are pink from the way he chews his bottom lip all the time. And when I smile at him, all chocolate-y and messy, he grins back. That dimple. It does me in.

I nearly lean forward to rub my nose against his cheek. But I don't.

Packing up the rest of the candies into his satchel, he stands and opens the top buttons of his long woolen coat. Then he reaches out to me, simply standing there as I hold his cold fingers.

"Let's go," I say, rising, too.

Matthew doesn't let go of my hand as I lead him across the street toward Page Turner, a local bookstore I've always loved. The atmosphere is warm and welcoming, and the owner, Charlie Page, is familiar with me from my frequent visits.

At Christmas, the store decorates with faux greenery and red and gold ribbons, and the scent of peppermint and pine fills the air. I'm certain it's from an air freshener or scent diffuser, but it takes me instantly back to my childhood and the good memories Mom and I made together back then. The only negative is I adore the scent of paperbacks, and the Christmas-y odor edges it out.

Page Turner is a unique store, owned by a unique man. Charlie is a local fixture with a mop of wild curls and an earnest belief he's psychic. During the Christmas season, he does solstice tarot readings, and hosts Ghosts Of Christmas Past, Present, and Future séances. The store itself has a genre fiction focus—all romance, horror, sci-fi, and fantasy. As a sci-fi fan, it's my favorite bookstore in town. There's also a surprise poetry section in the back.

"Ah, I missed coming into this place last time I was here. I think I was too eager to get to the galleries up the street." It's warm in Page Turner, and Matthew tugs off his coat, revealing his green button-up and that interesting tuft of hair at his collar again. "It's nice." Sniffing, Matthew drapes his coat over his arm and holds it in front of his body. His eyes light up. "Smells great too."

I peel off my leather jacket as well, holding it similarly, and motion him deeper into the store. "C'mon."

Matthew and I wander together back into the stacks of books. There are a good number of folks in the store, bustling around, looking for Christmas gifts, and I'm disappointed Charlie is distracted helping them. He's always good for a fun conversation, and I think Matthew would find him to be a hoot. Instead, I lead him back toward the secret poetry section. It's not so crowded.

In every other store, I've let Matthew take the lead once we were inside in order to catalog his preferences, but here I want to show him some of mine.

"Poetry," Matthew says, running his fingers over the spines in front of him. "You're a fan?"

"I am. How about you?"

"I'm not an anti-fan, but I wouldn't call it my go-to reading choice."

I begin searching through the offerings. Charlie is good about adding new voices to the section. "Ah."

"But I'm familiar with a lot of poetry. I went to a private liberal arts high school."

"Any particular favorites?"

"Not really. I have one volume at my house—a collection of love poems my father gave to my mother on their third date. He knew he was crazy about her pretty much immediately."

"That's sweet."

"They were truly in love." Matthew says, a fond smile shadowed with grief passing over his face. But he shakes it off. "How about you? Who are your favorite poets?"

"Michael Donaghy," I say, pointing out a volume of his work. "Imtiaz Dharker is a unique voice as well." I scroll my finger across the volumes, searching for my favorite. "Ah, this is a good one." I tug free *Crush* by Richard Siken. "Possibly my favorite."

Matthew takes the book and flips through a few pages.

"There are poems in there that'll make you feel like someone peeled you open, examined your guts and wrote them down. Some will make you feel like they forgot to stitch you back up again."

Matthew chuckles.

I still need and want to know so much more about Matthew before we can move forward with his winnings—just little things like what does he fantasize about when he jerks off, what does he want our night together to look like, and can I be the one to show him what his dick and hole are meant for?

Because, fuck, do I ever want to teach Matthew to surrender to pleasure and to joyously experience orgasm with a man. It might be "caveman" of me, but the idea he's never done that before, and he'd be trusting me to be the one to teach him? It's a serious ego trip, and I need to keep an eye on that, too. There's nothing like ego to get in the way of a good kink experience.

But still, as he'd said earlier.

But *still*.

"What's your favorite poem in this collection?" Matthew asks, flipping through *Crush* with an easy, open attitude I appreciate. If he's willing to learn about poetry from me and willing to learn about sex, too, I can teach him about so much more: fitness, health, horses, goats, NASCAR, and, most of all, how to fall and get up again.

"Mm, so many are good. I can't choose," I say. "Here, let me buy it for you."

"Oh, you don't have to—"

"Shh," I stop him from pursuing the formality of refusal. We both know he wants the book, if only because it's a present from me. But, more important than that: "I want to. You take what Daddy gives you, and you appreciate it," I murmur, instructing him because he doesn't know yet.

Matthew falls silent and then nods, handing the poetry book over to me. "Thank you." He glances up at me, holds my gaze for a second, and adds, "Thank you, Daddy."

A shudder rocks him as his eyes go glassy. I *know* he's hard now, and I am too. I've never seen or felt anything like it in my life. My boys don't get off on calling me Daddy in that casual, quiet, almost heart-stoppingly sweet way. My boys are usually brattier, drawing the word Daddy out into a whine or overexaggerating it with a bat of their eyes, or a sugary-sweet smile. Matthew's use of the title is so fucking earnest. It's incredible. I want to kiss him, but…

No. Not now. Not here.

We have serious things to discuss first.

I lead him to the register where a teenage part-timer is working and buy the book for him. I keep hold of the bag, carrying it for him as we step out onto the sidewalk. The sound of church bells ringing and the rise and fall of violins, banjos, and the music of other street performances adds a fierce cheer to the air.

As we put our coats back on, I feel like someone's carved a new space for me today: a space that's all Christmas and Matthew and being a grown man's Daddy. It's hot and exciting, and I acknowledge I'll need to thank Nick for bullying me into participating in the auction. My gut says this is going to work out well for me. Everything about this day—the air, the ringing of bells, the moment—is permeated with so much promise.

"Let's talk," I say, as I steer Matthew toward a bench on Wall Street. I adore the way he follows me without any resistance, trusting my guidance. It makes me wonder if he's like this with everyone. Is he a pushover at work? Is he in need of learning how to say no and how to set boundaries?

I make a mental note to investigate this, if I can, between now and our night together. I want to tailor our experience for his maximum growth potential. But right now, I love that he lets me take charge. I just worry—would he let just anyone take charge of him? Because that can be dangerous.

The very thought of him being "guided" by some of the sadists I've met in the kink scene makes me sweat and feel irrationally protective.

Chatting on the bench about poetry Matthew read years ago in school, I notice our words are growing obscured by the amplified piano and guitar performance taking place on the corner. Busking has begun. The sun is setting. There's a soft orange glow behind the buildings, and the Christmas lights blink on all along the streets. It must be after five o'clock now. The Winter Solstice is in two days, and until then, night keeps coming earlier and earlier.

We sit and listen to the buskers, Matthew bobbing his head to the beat, and after a few minutes he begins "playing" piano chords on his knees. His smile is easy, and his lips are glossy from where he's licked them. I worry they'll get chapped in this cold. I reach into my coat pocket, pull out a Chapstick, and present it to him.

He hesitates only a moment before accepting, rubbing the slick stuff on his full lips.

He hands it back.

I can't stop staring at him, taking in his profile, his eyelashes—so dark, and his eyebrows—so strong and yet delicate, too.

"Is everything okay?" he says, turning to me with color on his cheeks which isn't from the cold. He's felt my eyes on him, and it's making him feel *something*. I don't know if it's arousal or worry or embarrassment. I choose to remove all mystery.

"I want to fuck you," I say to start, which is blunt and rougher than it should be. I'm the Daddy. I should be finessing this. But with each passing minute I want more and more to get inside his hot body, take his virgin ass, and watch his face as I bottom out inside him, tagging his prostate with each thrust. I'll do it again and again until he paints his stomach with his own load.

Which is a filthy and crass thought to share, but I share it anyway before asking, "How much hair do you have?" I ask. "All over? Or just on your chest?"

Blushing redder than can possibly be healthy again, he indicates with a sweep of his hand that hair grows on his chest, belly, and down to his groin. "My back, though—luckily, there's almost none there." His breath comes in quick pants as he gets the answer out despite his embarrassment. "My ass cheeks have some but not a lot, and it's a little hairy around my hole, but I can shave or—"

"No. That's perfect."

"It is?"

"I told you. I like an eager boy. There are thousands of ways to be sexy and physically attractive. Hair, no hair. I like it all. But on you? I like hair."

He turns his gaze from me to the buskers, busily working Christmas music into the air, stirring hearts with a rousing rendition of "God Rest Ye Merry Gentlemen." After a few awkward seconds, he asks, "Um, what about you? How much hair and where?"

"I've got light chest hair, but otherwise, I'm pretty bare except for my pubes."

Matthew swallows hard. It's adorable how unaccustomed he is to discussing these things. Negotiating sex and hookups and talking about preferences in body and build is second nature to most gay men his age. But not Matthew. No, he's still innocent. I find that more enticing than I'd ever anticipated.

"So, with my curiosity settled on that front, let's talk business."

Matthew seems a little dizzy as he processes what I've just said. "Oh, uh, I have contracts," he offers, opens the satchel he's been carrying and brings out a handful of pages secured to a clipboard. "We can fill this in as we talk, and then we can see about the rest."

"The rest of what?"

He bites his lower lip, glancing up at me with a mix of coyness and hope in his eyes. "See about having sex today?"

"Today," I repeat, and my cock is so ready for it. My nipples go hard, my balls lurch, and I want to press against him here on the bench and kiss his mouth. "Not today," I grit out. "We can't today."

We can, my dick cries.

We can, every cell of me choruses.

But we *shouldn't*.

"No? Did I misread you?" He sounds so disappointed and embarrassed. Fuck.

I turn to him, putting my fingers under his chin and forcing his gaze up to mine. His hazel eyes are soft and shining with insecurity. That contradiction between his age and his experience makes me want to protect him. "It's only 'no' because, after what you've told me today, about your history, experience, and why you bid on me, I'm not going to take you home and screw you like you're not important, or like you're an easy hookup."

"Oh." He tries to pull away, but I hold his chin steady.

"You're very important, Matthew."

"To who?"

"To yourself first and foremost." I refrain from saying "to me" because I barely know him, and it would ring false. But he's going to be important to some man, someday soon. I just know it. "You deserve to feel cherished, and with your first time, there should be no rush. It should be as if you've got all the time in the world to feel everything, every last inch, understand? Next week, during our night together, I want you to let me show you how to open up and accept it all." The innuendo is heavy, but I mean it that way, too, so I let it fall between us, crude and needful. It's everything we both want right now, but I'm going to resist until it's right. "Got it?"

He ducks his head, jerking his chin free of my fingers. I consider scolding him, demanding he look at me again, but I give him a minute to compose himself. He's vulnerable, and I need to give him space to step into this role with me. The moment in the bookstore when he'd called me Daddy showed how it affects him, but he's still not sure. He's like a newborn lamb on wobbly legs. Too hard a nudge and he'll get knocked down when I mean to be lifting him up.

"All right," Matthew agrees. "So, even though we want each other—we do want each other, right?" He sounds mortified to ask, but also desperate to know. So insecure. I stamp that out.

"I want you." I take hold of his hand, pull it over my crotch and let him feel my thickness. He lets out a shuddery sigh before I move his hand away.

"And we really have to wait until the night I won from you?"

"Yes. That's best."

"Why?"

I have a ton of excuses—my client appointment tomorrow morning (yes, I work on Sunday; there's no rest for the wicked.) My rented house in town is plagued with roommates since we each only need it a few days a week, and yet often at the same time. My main place is a long drive up the side of a snowy mountain in the dark, and Matthew shouldn't make the drive for the first time at night. Plus, my mom will be there since she isn't leaving to spend Christmas through New Year's Day with her sister and my cousins until Tuesday. I haven't changed the sheets…

But none of those things would have stopped me if Matthew

had been the young man I'd expected him to be at the coffee shop this morning. That young man with the apple ass, I'd have taken back to my room at the rented house, fucked him into the mattress, and done little more than slap his ass as a thank you before he was dressed again and out the door.

Matthew's first time deserves so much more than that.

A tension hangs in the air, thick with want and a knowledge that resolving this could be as easy as me saying, *"Let's just go to my place now."* I bite my tongue.

His expression shifts as a clear understanding takes hold. I'm not going to offer to fuck him tonight, no matter how much he wants me to. No matter how much *I* want to.

"Yes," he agrees. "Daddy knows best." He darts a heated glance up at me from under his lashes again, and this time his voice holds a little teasing; he's not being quite as earnest and respectful as he'd been in the bookstore.

"I *do* know best."

Matthew's clever smile turns soft. "Thank you, Daddy."

Goddamn, the way he says that is like a bolt of lightning in my gut, shooting into my balls and making me so fucking hard I struggle to stick to my decision not to take him home right now. But I'm determined to make his first time special for him. To make it last. To make it something he'll never regret or look back on and feel cheap.

Even though he's paid for it.

I never want him to feel like it's something he *had* to pay for. I want him to understand the night we'll share is something he deserves. Because it's a Daddy's duty to teach his boy to love himself. Going home with a man he's just met to let that man take his precious virginity—a social construct, certainly, but so the fuck what?—without any buildup or ceremony or time for treasuring is not the best way to love himself. Matthew deserves better. Any boy of any age does.

Not that Matthew can't love himself with casual sex once he's learned how to have it in a way that isn't degrading for him. Of course he can. And yet I don't want him to. I want him to learn to be adored, just like he's asked, and that means letting only men who can see him—*really* see him—touch him, enter him, pleasure him.

That's a ridiculous way to be thinking, and unlike anything I've ever thought about anyone other than Brandon. Even with my other two boys, I never minded the idea of Duncan and Garrett sleeping with other men, so long as they didn't break our rules of condom use and discretion. But there's something about Matthew's eyes, his urgent need to be mentored, that has me feeling more protective than I've felt over anyone, even Brandon.

I want Matthew safe. I want him to always be as casually submissive as he is now, clueless in his trust. I want for his naïveté to stay intact. I hope I can help show him how to be with a man in such a beautiful, natural way that he doesn't settle for less out of desperation.

"C'mon, put that away for now, and let's go," I say, standing and reaching for his hand.

Matthew tucks his clipboard back into his satchel and takes my hand with that same willingness to be guided he's demonstrated all day. I don't deserve this from him yet, but it gladdens me. It makes me even more determined to prove to him that his trust in me isn't unfounded, even if it is unearned. But it makes me uneasy, too. Not every man will want to take care of him like I do. Some men will want to use him. Make him feel old or worthless. Degrade him for fun.

The thought curdles my stomach.

I've known men like that. I need to teach Matthew how to avoid them. But I just have tonight to teach him—well, and the one night he's won. That's barely enough time to help him learn how to take my cock and accept a blowjob, or how to kneel at his Daddy's feet and wait to be rewarded as a good boy.

How can it be enough time to teach him that his eager submission is beautiful but shouldn't be bestowed so indiscriminately?

My mind whirls. The responsibility of taking on Matthew like this is enormous. I've accepted it, and yet... Is it bigger than the container it's meant to fit in? I think it might be. One night can't hold everything I know he needs to learn.

Matthew follows me through town, and if I led him to my car right now and drove him up the mountain to my home, he wouldn't protest or say a word. I just know it. Hell, I'm not sure he'd even insist on being returned to his car before Monday, when he would, by all rights, need to be at work. I sense his need to surrender is that strong, and my urge to let him is just as potent.

It's all so heady and tempting, but it's also powerful to do the right thing by him, and to know *I'm* going to handle choosing how he experiences physical pleasure for the first time. *Me.*

It's mind-blowing, knowing he's going to let me help define this critical moment for him, and that his surrender is the exact opposite of the surrender he's offered to those men who've fucked his mouth and given him nothing in return. It'll be the submission of a boy to his Daddy. It'll be the *trust* that Daddy is going to make things right for him.

What a fucking delight. Holy shit. I'm going to have to buy Nick two drinks.

Make that ten drinks.

CHAPTER FIVE

Matthew

THE CHRISTMAS LIGHTS glisten and blink on the buildings all around us like a jolly theme park. Asheville spreads out beneath us from our perch at a tall table by wide windows in this hotel's rooftop bar. I sip the drink Erik ordered for me without my input.

It's a mocktail—no drinking during any of the Experience is a rule of Erik's after all, and he doesn't bother to explain it, just proceeds as if my enjoyment of the drink is assumed. And he's not wrong. I love the nutmeg, cinnamon, and ginger flavors—like Christmas in a glass.

I sit patiently as he sips his own mocktail and watches me like I'm a rare bird he wants to catch but is also certain will take flight if he moves too fast. I want to assure him I'm not going anywhere, but part of me thinks he's interested in the chase. He wants to net me. Claim and tag me. Then release me back into the wild.

I'm fine with that. I'll be the rare bird for him. I'll let him think I'm special.

It feels so nice to have someone look at me like he does. It's enough to make me wonder if the drink is alcohol-free after all. I feel like I'm spinning, dizzy, and floating away all at once.

"Like it?" he asks after a few quiet minutes of observing me.

I pretend I'm appreciating the Christmas lights when I'm truly soaking in his attention, hoarding the sensation of his interest for later, when I can be alone with my thoughts and fantasies. I pick up the drink and we clink glasses. "I do," I say after I swallow another sip. "It's delicious."

He nods as if he already knew that, and I guess he did. I wonder how many other boys or men he's brought to this bar. Did he bring the last one? Brandon? The one who broke his heart? Or is this a place he typically comes with hookups? I know he's familiar with the bar's menu. He didn't even glance at it.

"I'm sorry if you thought it was a cruel tease to bring you here," he offers with a sly smile that makes my stomach do a backflip. He gestures around the place. "They have a great bartender here. Makes the best mocktails in town."

I glance around at the glistening tables, the polished wooden bar, and the shimmering Christmas décor, all gold and silver, very high-class and expensive. The hotel rooms on the floors below can only echo this theme of wealth and pleasure. Too bad I'm not going to be seeing one of them tonight.

I laugh at his comment, because it's true. My eyes must have lit up like Christmas trees, given the hope that'd gripped me when he first led me into the hotel's lobby.

Erik had taken one look at me, squeezed my fingers, and said, chuckling, "Sorry, kiddo. I'm taking you to the bar, not to bed."

Honestly, I'm not sure what I love more, that he called me "kiddo" like I'm younger than him—like I'm really his boy—or the sound of his laughter, which is gritty, like sandpaper and honey, and makes my stomach do funny things.

"I'm all right with cruel teasing if Daddy makes it worthwhile later," I say, and shiver again at calling him that aloud.

Erik's own response to the word isn't negligible either. He swallows and blinks rapidly as if trying to bring his focus back from wherever that word sent his mind.

"Put the contract you brought on the table. We'll review it now and see if I find it suitable," Erik says. His tone sounds gruff, but the light in his eyes is hot, and I know he wants me. What a shocking, strange feeling. How electrifying. I almost can't believe it.

"Yes, Daddy," I murmur, and I'm rewarded yet again with another immediate reaction from him: blown pupils, a stutter in his breath.

I hadn't known how powerful this Daddy/boy dynamic would make *me* feel, nor what effect I might provoke in a man whose kink aligned with the one I aim to explore. But every time I call him Daddy, I'm half convinced Erik is going to grab me, drag me to the bathroom or another private spot, and fuck me right away.

The hotel is incredibly posh. I don't think the management would appreciate him screwing me in the bar bathroom or in the alcove by the vending machines in one of the hallways. Or in the stairwell between floors.

I would appreciate it, though.

I think?

…Maybe not.

To be honest, Erik's right. If I let him do that to me, it's not that much different than letting those other men fuck my face. It's not how my first orgasm with another man should go. More importantly, it's not how my Daddy wants his boy to feel.

That, more than anything else, makes me want to let Erik dictate everything about how I surrender to him. Yes, I'm going to take advantage of the night I've won from Erik. I'm going to try the full Daddy/boy Christmas Experience and let him show me how a man can adore another man. Decorating a tree with him, opening presents, a cozy night by the fire? That's just a heartwarming, memorable bonus.

Today with Erik—even though we've just met—for the first time in my life, I've felt something like romantically cherished. Maybe even loved. It might be a bought and paid for "love," and Erik might have sold his "affection" for a charitable cause, but it's the closest thing I've ever felt to that kind of tenderness.

I know it's not real, not like the kind of love that leads people to get married, but it's man-to-man love; it's human, and it's caring. It's enough for me.

Or maybe, more honestly, it's a start.

"Would you like another?" Erik asks, nodding toward my almost empty glass resting beside the small stack of papers I've put between us.

"No thank you, Daddy."

"Are you sure? Anything you want, sweet boy," Erik says.

I shiver again, like I did in Page Turner, and he smiles at me. "Why does it feel so good when you call me boy?" I ask, self-conscious but needing to know.

Erik's smile is gentle, and his eyes are so warm and kind. I want to melt into them and be held in his strong arms. It's a primal urge I can't explain, but he understands. "Because you're a boy in the presence of a Daddy. It feels good because it's right. When you're with me like this, as a boy, you seem to easily fall into a headspace that feels like relief, like home."

"Yes," I agree. If "home" is arousal, and "relief" the promise of orgasm and being held lovingly after, then okay. But that's not a home I've ever known before. I suppose it's the home Daddy Erik is going to teach me about so I can find it with someone else someday. Fuck, I can't wait. I want him to show me tonight.

Now.

Earlier, in the back of the bustling bookstore, as he'd run his fingers over the spines of the poetry books, I'd imagined him pressing me back against the shelves, his hard, big body rocking against mine as he unzipped my pants and pulled my cock out because he wanted to pleasure me, too. At his command, I'd have come all over—

"Matthew?" Erik asks in a tone that makes me think I didn't

answer a question.

"Sorry, what?"

"Are you going to have trouble getting home tonight?" He glances at his watch. "Nashville is a long way. Four or five hours, right? I should have asked earlier, but I got lost in the moment with you."

I smile, duck my head, and try not to give in to the urge to plead for him to take me back to his house tonight and dispose of my pitiful lack of experience. *Daddy knows best*, I repeat to myself. "I'll be fine."

"I'll be happy to pay for you to stay here tonight if you'd like, in this hotel. It's my fault we haven't concluded our business yet. I was enjoying being with you."

"Would you stay here with me, Daddy?"

He runs his fingers over my jaw before drawing his sweet touch away. "No."

"Ah." I'm disappointed again, even though I'd known that would be his answer. "It's too far for me to go all the way to Nashville, but I've arranged for a hotel in Knoxville tonight. I'll stop there and drive the rest of the way in the morning. I'll be home by noon."

"Then I'll pay for that hotel."

"It's okay, I can afford—"

"That's not the point. Daddy's taking care of his boy until he's safely home. I'll pay for the hotel. What do you say, boy?"

"Yes, Daddy. Thank you," I whisper, and that reactive shudder grips me again, leaving my nipples taut. Seeing him in control of this situation, certain and secure, I nearly melt from how attractive he is: everything from the muscles in his forearms flexing in the low light of the bar to the way he runs a hand over his military-short hair is an aphrodisiac to me right now.

"Good. Let's get on with the negotiation and contract," he says, motioning at the papers I've put on the table. "I don't want you driving over the mountains too late into the night. It's supposed to get icy in the early hours."

I nod, and that new, exciting feeling of being cared for washes over me. "Thank you."

"Thank you what?" he prompts.

"Thank you, Daddy."

I don't know what I did that was different, but this time he throws back what's left of his mocktail like it's got alcohol in it to steady himself and meets my gaze with hot, demanding eyes. "Fuck, yes," he says. "You're so goddamn pliant."

"Is that good?"

"Good? It's a fucking dream come true."

"Is it, *Daddy?*" I'm being a tease now, but the sexy, sliding smile that takes over the bottom half of his face tells me he likes it. "Am I really a dream come true?"

He growls lightly, and the sound makes my dick rock-hard. I shift on my seat.

"You are so…" He pauses to lick his lips and rake his gaze over my body. "Unexpected. The best surprise I've had in years, and we're just getting started. Our night together is going to be amazing."

"I hope so, Daddy."

"Did you know your body is fucking delicious?"

"No?"

He ducks his head to the side, checking me out again from head to toe. "That ass."

I sigh. "Not a bubble butt." Despite all my efforts at the gym, my ass always holds a little weight instead of rising high and firm.

"No," he agrees. "But it jiggles just right. It's been all I can do not to grab it when I'm walking next to you." Leaning forward, voice low, he teases, "Bet it'll be good to sink my teeth into when we're alone."

I squeeze my eyes shut, a surge of need almost blinding me.

He leans back and clears his throat. "My apologies. It's not fair to say all this when we're supposed to be putting down boundaries and getting clear on what we do and don't want."

"It's okay." But he's right. We're supposed to be setting things into neat, steady lines for clarity's sake, for consent, and to ensure that next weekend is a transaction between us and nothing more.

But what if I wish for something more? If we're this reactive to each other, if I'm such a welcome surprise, maybe...

I shove that thought away. I can't let those sorts of dreams enter into this equation at all. Hopes for more will ruin the experience and taint it in my memory when it doesn't go beyond the one night.

Besides, if it's just for one night, that's freeing, isn't it? I have no hope of seeing Erik again after it's over, so I can surrender to him. Open myself up completely. Be his boy, let him be my Daddy, and never have to face it afterward if it's too much, if I feel too raw.

Something tells me he's going to demand full exposure of my body and soul—that the insistence I meet his eyes as I confessed my situation is just the beginning. I know I need that to grow, to come into my identity as a gay man and maybe as a "boy." But I also don't think I'll be able to tolerate that kind of intimacy in the moment if I think I'm ever, *ever* going to see him again.

So no.

No thinking of a future.

This experience is going to be my gift to myself, an evisceration of my deepest needs, an airing of my raw wounds, trusting that Erik is strong enough to hold all of it, and I'm going to try so hard to love myself in those moments.

I'm aware I'm going to get so much more out of this than Erik will, more than he can ever understand. There's no way whatever small satisfaction he gets from being the man to expose my inner soul will ever truly be equitable. We'll be unbalanced, and I can't live like that.

So my gift to him will be that after our one night is over, I'll never contact him again.

"Did I offend you?" Erik asks, and I realize I've been turning my glass around and around in my hands, studying the last sip of Christmassy goodness as I sort out the thoughts and feelings rampaging through me. I meet his inquisitive gaze and cock my head. *What have I missed?*

"Is biting your ass—or any of your body—off limits? If so, that's okay."

I smile and shake my head. "No. That's not it. Anything is on the table, Daddy."

Erik's eyes light up with heat, but he banks it. "You can't say things like that to a man you've just met," he scolds before pulling the contracts closer and looking them over. "These are good. Very clear. Who drew them up for you?"

"My friend Doug. He's a lawyer."

"Ah. And he's into kink himself?"

"Yes. He's got a husband and a submissive—they call him a slave, and he lives at their beck and call, from what I can tell."

"Mm." He continues to read over the contract. "I don't typically sign these with my boys. Our relationships have been organic for the most part. But I've signed a few agreements when I've played short-term, so this makes sense. I was going to send you something like it after we'd hashed out the details, but I appreciate how your friend Doug has left blanks for us to fill in. He must use these contracts on the fly at times."

"He might. He's very into risk reduction, and that includes liability."

"I see."

"He likes to keep things tidy that way."

"Mm-hmm." Erik puts the contracts down on the table and turns his attention back to me. I feel it like a physical touch. It's both warming and a little intimidating, given how serious he is right now. "And how did you meet Doug?"

Is that possessiveness I hear in his voice? That's flattering. But I stay focused on being as open and honest with him as I can. If I want to experience this with Erik, I'm going to be as raw and real as I've ever been before. It'll be hard, but it's easier than it might be if he weren't a stranger and if I weren't committed to keeping this to just one night.

"I met Doug back in college at MTSU. He was my roommate. I let him rough-fuck my mouth a few times a month."

Erik blinks. "And this man is now a friend? Someone who treated you like disposable trash?"

"It wasn't like that. I begged him to use me." Erik seems poised to argue, but I persist in my explanation. "He resisted for a long time, said I deserved more…"

"You did."

"But when he went through a dry spell, he got horny enough to give in."

"You begged him to do it, but you didn't like it?"

"No. I didn't like it. I mean, I didn't get hard or get off. I just felt relieved that someone used me as hatefully as I felt I should be used."

"Matthew…"

"But Doug's not like that. I mean, he's a Dom and a sadist, but he'd have reciprocated if I'd wanted. But I didn't let him." I glance at the table. A familiar shame settles on me. It's how I used to feel when I was hanging out with my dad, and he'd give me that quiet, disappointed sigh that let me know I wasn't the son he'd hoped I'd be. Or when my mom would cast her eyes down over something I'd said or done, like she thought or knew I'm a queer.

Overwhelmed, I choke out, "I'm sorry, Daddy. Please forgive me."

Even more shamefully, my chin wobbles and hot tears prick my eyes. Erik takes hold of my chin and forces me to meet his gaze. With his other hand, he wipes the tear that squeezes out despite my best attempt to squelch it.

Quietly, he asks, "Matthew, tell me again why you want to do this with me."

My voice shakes, and I press a hand over my breastbone, rubbing as I answer. "To learn to love myself, to learn to enjoy sex with men, to take pleasure in it—to let someone give me pleasure."

He strokes his thumb over where my dimple lives on my cheek, caressing the spot. "Right. How do you feel about what happened with your friend Doug?"

He says "friend" like it's a curse word, and I dare to meet his gaze with a hint of defiance. "He *is* my friend." But that's all I have in me. I close my eyes against his too-knowledgeable face. How does he see me so clearly when we've only just met? "But the truth is I'm ashamed. Doug's always treated me like I'm a charity case since. Even when he helped me with this contract, I felt his pity."

Erik strokes my cheek again. I can't help but wonder how we look to others in the bar: very intimate. They'll assume we're lovers. Next week, I suppose we will be. For one night. "How many times?"

"What?" I ask, confused.

"How many times did Doug use you? You said you'd kept count of the men, but did you also keep count of the number of *times* each man degraded you?"

My shoulders hunch with shame, and I feel how his hand is keeping my chin from ducking lower. "Thirteen. Doug fucked my mouth thirteen times while we roomed together."

"Then *he* should be ashamed."

"But I wanted him to do it."

"He should be *ashamed*," Erik repeats. "It's one thing when it's consensual humiliation kink between men who know what they're doing—and it's another when it's taking advantage of a vulnerable, self-loathing young man just to ease some horniness and—"

My mouth trembles. I've never been defended in this way. Never imagined I would be, and yet part of me wants to leap to defend Doug. I'd begged him to treat me badly. It'd just been a matter of time before Doug had given in.

Erik must see something in my eyes that stills him. He releases my face and quirks an apologetic smile. "I'm sorry. I'm out of line."

I think he probably is, but his protectiveness has me feeling like I might crawl on the floor at his feet if he'll just stroke my hair, call me a good boy, and take care of me tonight and again next week. I've never felt so valued—and he barely knows me! This defense of my person, of my worth, makes me hungry for more. I feel all *kinds* of things I shouldn't—because I like it too much, and if I'm not careful, it'll make me want things I can't have.

I'm getting a glimpse of what a cruel man Erik can be, cruel and beautiful and loving too. How does he do that? Show love and respect without knowing a person? How does he give all that just because it's the right thing to do? Is that what being a Daddy means? That's not what my father was.

"You're angry with me for saying all that."

"No."

"You should be. I went too far. We haven't even made an agreement about our night together yet, and here I am lecturing you on the past, which you can't change."

"You're lecturing me on my *attitude* about the past, which I can change. Doug *is* my friend, and he's apologized many times for giving in to me. But back then I needed that kind of treatment. It felt necessary, like popping a blister. Being treated like crap helped me release a feeling which, if I'd held it in, would have hurt me so much more."

"I'm sorry."

"I am too." I take a big breath. "I'm ready to feel good when I have sex. Heck, I'm ready to *have* sex, to know how to ask for it, and…" I deflate a little, brushing my hair away from my forehead. "Look, I know I'm not healed enough yet to start a relationship with anyone. That's why I bid on your offering at the auction. But I *am* ready to feel pleasure, to get fucked, to maybe fuck someone too, if that turns out to be something a man wants of me. I'm ready to learn how to let someone give and receive all that instead of just asking them to use me like I'm trash." I point at the contracts and keep on talking. "Listen, I want the following things—"

Erik picks up the pen and flips to the page of the contract where Doug has added blank lines for us to write in what we agree to do together and what our limits are.

"I want you to be in charge of *everything* when I'm with you— what we eat, what we drink, where we go, what we do." I hadn't even known I'd wanted that until he'd ordered my mocktail without asking for my input, and now I want him to do it again. The entire time we're together. For everything.

He writes this down.

"I want to be told how to please you with how I look, smell, and present myself and in what I do for you."

He nods and adds all of that, along with: *Matthew will either be naked or wear only underwear—gifted by Erik—and nothing else unless instructed by Erik for the entirety of their night together. Matthew will NOT shave his hole, balls, or any part of his body, aside from his face. Matthew may douche or otherwise prepare for anal sex, but he will also submit to an enema administered by Erik when they are together.*

I flush hot and cold, and a weird excitement flutters in me, a strange mixture of dread, repulsion, and wild, lustful desire. "An enema?" I ask.

He lifts his eyes from the documents to me. "Ever done one?"

I shake my head.

"Don't worry. I'll take care of you."

"Yes," I say breathlessly. "I know, Daddy."

Erik reaches out and touches my bottom lip. "You chew here a lot."

"Sorry, Daddy."

"Mm. I should tell you to stop. It's not good for your skin. But the truth is it's a hot tell."

"It is?"

"Yeah. It lets me know when you're nervous or excited." He smooths his thumb against my lip again and swallows when I dare to poke my tongue out and taste his skin. "Very good," he praises. "I like that."

So I do it again. Erik leans close, his eyes bright with desire, and my every cell pricks to attention. My eyelids fall almost closed, and I move toward him, eager to taste his mouth.

Erik pulls back, a wicked smile on his lips.

"No," I whisper. "Daddy, please."

"Please, what, boy?" His voice is like a hand around my balls, and just like that, I'm even more eager to obey him.

Fuuuuuck. I shiver like a tree in the wind, and my still-hard cock pulses, releasing pre-cum. My pants feel too tight, and I wonder if a wet spot is showing.

"Please don't tease me. I'm not sure I can wait if you do."

Erik growls, like *actually growls*, and the sound vibrates over me in a visceral way. I grab hold of my dick, afraid I'll come if I don't, and I moan. Erik reaches out and touches my wrist but doesn't move my hand away from my crotch. "We're in public," he reminds me.

Taking a slow breath, eyes on his, trying to steady myself through his solid, serious, presence, I release myself and grip his offered fingers instead.

"That's right," he encourages. "Hold Daddy's hand. Daddy will help you calm down."

"Fucking hell," I whimper, as if those words could possibly make me calmer. "Why is this so hot?"

A pleased smile slips over his lips. "Boy, stop questioning it. It just is."

I nod, and my breathing takes a few minutes to settle. As I return to myself, my cock no longer threatening to unload in my pants if Erik calls me "boy" again, I add, "During our night together, I want to be fucked, and I want to get sucked, and I want to be cuddled most of all. I want to be held and kissed. Made to feel special."

"That'll be easy as breathing," he says, and I believe him, what with the way he's looking at me.

"What do you want?" I want to please him so badly, and I hope he'll give me instructions on how I can. But his answer surprises me.

"To be the best Daddy I can be for you," he says. "No intense pain play." He writes this down. "Safe words—yellow and red—can be used at all times, even if we're just hanging out, or cuddling. You can use them if you want to stop anything for any reason at all."

"What about spanking?" I'm taken by the size of his hands, the span of his palms, and the surety of his grip on both the pen and on my fingers. My heart skips a beat, and some of my fantasies surge to the surface—being chased, being "handled," being scolded. "What if I'm a bad boy?"

Erik smiles. "There's no way you can be a bad boy for me, Matthew. *But* if you want a spanking, we can see in the moment." He writes, "Spankings are negotiable—either party can request and either can reject."

"Thank you, Daddy."

His voice drops to a silky whisper. "I see. Not all of that internalized shame is gone, right? Daddy might need to spank some of it away to make room for the love?"

I shudder as my eyes fill. I don't know how I'm supposed to drive home after what I've found here today. I've somehow met a man—or bought time with a man—who can see me for who I am, who I've been, and how I want to be.

How can I possibly get back in my car and drive home to Nashville, back to a place where the only person who *knows me*-knows me is Doug? And our relationship is...complicated. Especially so ever since the Christmas a few years back when I'd drunkenly asked his husband, Forest, to please fuck my mouth.

It had been the first Christmas without my parents, and I'd been in a bad place. I'd figured since they had their slave, the boundaries were more permeable in their relationship. I'd figured wrong.

Forest didn't do it. He'd told me to get some self-respect and stop punishing myself for being queer, which had hurt to hear but was the truth after all. And that harsh assessment from Forest had started my quest to love myself. It'd prompted me to start seeing a therapist and to think about what I want and deserve from men, and from myself.

But even though Forest had told me no and set me on a better path in life, Doug wasn't happy that I'd propositioned his husband. Two years later, we're still walking on eggshells with each other. Sure, he'd printed out the contract for me, cautioned me about being impulsive, and made it clear he still cared about my well-being. Even so, it isn't the same. I want our friendship back the way it used to be. But we just aren't there yet.

My co-workers are.... Not much more to say about them than

that. My next-door neighbor is a friend, I guess, but she's almost eighty now; she's watched me grow up, and always wants to talk about the old days of the neighborhood, back when the houses and families were new. Sometimes I think she forgets my parents are dead because she'll ask after them. Maureen is sweet, but not anyone I can depend on, or anyone who sees the real me.

Now. Here. In this moment with Erik, I'm a new, raw person, freshly birthed and seen. Whole. Real. Flaws and all. Erik sees them, and he doesn't hate me for them. In fact, he's looking at me with so much openness and acceptance, I feel its warmth in my bones.

"Is that why you think you might need a spanking, boy? To chase away that shame?"

"Yes, Daddy," I say, letting him see the tears in my eyes. "I need to make room for the love. Help me."

"Don't worry. Daddy will handle it," he assures me, and I almost slide off the high stool at the bar table with relief.

"Thank you."

"A big question we should cover is condoms. I typically use them for sex with someone I don't know well, but this is a different situation. We have some time to plan ahead. There are two options: we both provide recent tests showing that we are STI free, or we just use the condoms."

"Which do you prefer, Daddy?"

"This is up to you, Matthew. If you want to swallow my cum, or have me leave my load up inside you, then we'll need the tests. If you don't think those things are important—"

"I want that, Daddy," I grit out. "I want to taste your cum and hold your load. Daddy, please."

"All right," Erik says. "Do you have a doctor who can do the tests for you? Or will that be a problem?"

"I can get the tests, Daddy."

"Good boy." He smiles. "You love calling me Daddy, don't

you? You can't seem to stop."

"It makes me hard," I admit. "Is that okay, Daddy?"

"Fuck, boy," he mutters, scrubbing a hand over his military cut. "Everything you do is okay, and if it isn't, I'll correct you." He releases my fingers and touches my cheek again. It's like he can't get enough of the dimple there, and for the first time in my life, I'm pleased with my dimple, too. "Don't worry. I'm not going to let you keep on hurting yourself. Daddy's got you now."

He signs the contract and slides it toward me. I review it and think of one more thing to add to the list. I write, "Matthew will address Erik as Daddy whenever possible." I look to him for approval. He nods.

I sign my name, and the contract is done. "I'll send you copies."

"You'll send *who* copies?" he asks with a lifted brow.

"You, Daddy. I'll send you copies."

He grins. "Nice, boy. Very nice. Now, let's get out of here. You have a long drive over the mountains."

Erik walks me back across the city center to where I've parked my car. I stand next to it, aching for him to touch me. Ever since we left the hotel, the entire time we were walking along the street and up the parking garage stairs, he hasn't held my hand or said much at all. Now's the moment I need something more from him, or else my mind will run riot with doubts once I'm alone.

"Text me when you get to that hotel in Knoxville," Erik says. "I'll want to know you're safe."

"Yes, Daddy," I whisper.

"And text me daily between now and next Thursday. Keep me in the loop about how you're feeling, what you're thinking, and what things you're fantasizing about for our night. Feel free to ask me questions or make requests."

"Yes, Daddy."

"And Matthew?"

I lift my head to meet his gaze. "Yes?"

"I'm going to kiss you."

I'm lightheaded as I nod. He touches my chin, lifts it a little, and positions his mouth near mine. "Your first kiss should be sweet," he says. "Gentle." His lips brush mine, dry and tender. "And your second kiss should be passionate."

He grips the back of my neck, and his mouth presses to mine, his lips open as his tongue seeks entrance. I moan and let him in. He does something that sends tingles down my spine, a full-body shudder wracking me, and I lean in for more just as he pulls back, breathing heavily.

"Your third kiss will be from me and no one else," he orders.

As if I'd want to kiss anyone else! "Yes, Daddy."

"Good boy. Now go on. Drive safely."

I climb into my car, and he stands there next to the parking spot until I pull away, a silent observer watching over me.

I feel loved. I know it's all an illusion, something I bought and paid for, and yet...

My heart beats like a drum.

As I pull onto the interstate, my taillights blessing Asheville with their glow, I shake my head at my melodramatic feelings. It isn't real, but it *feels* real. There's no good explanation for that.

Perhaps it's Christmas magic.

CHAPTER SIX

Erik

NOEL'S TURNED ON the Christmas lights, I note as I approach the small, three-bedroom, two-bath rented house I share with three other men. It's not an ideal situation, but with Asheville real estate prices these days, it's the best option for all three of us. If I wanted to buy a place closer to the city, I'd have to sell the mountain house, and there's no way I'm doing that.

Even if I'd rather have had the place to myself after Brandon left, there's no reason to put down that kind of money every month. Noel is a travel nurse who's living here in Asheville for the next three and a half months. He's funny, irreverent, and dedicated to making the holidays bright, as we'd all discovered when he put up a tree, hung stockings, and did up the roofline of our small house in candy-cane striped lights.

Charles is a bit of a mystery to me. He's trying to get a male lingerie business off the ground but isn't too worried about the success of it. He comes from money; I can tell that much. I can see it in the clothes he wears, the car he drives, and even the way he walks. Though the biggest tell is that his uncle, whom Charles is very close to and sometimes stays with, lives in one of the mansions in Historic Montford. That's old money—like old-old.

Still, Charles pays the rent and uses his room in the rented house regularly, and aside from the noise his sewing machine makes late into the night, I have no complaints about him. He's pretty much an absentee roommate.

Then there's Trevor. He's young. Just nineteen and fresh out of his mama's house. But the good news is he's not a jerk, and his parents pay for his part of the rent. Trevor's straight but queer-friendly, and he's in a couple of bands, including a fairly well-known one called Pinky and the One-Eyes.

Trevor works during the day at Early Girl Eatery, saving money for a trip across the country to join the band's lead singer out in Los Angeles. They're hoping they can make it big out there.

At least, that's what I've picked up from the few conversations I've had with the guy. Trevor's busy between his band practices and his serving job, so given my schedule and his, we rarely clap eyes on each other. He and Noel have twin beds and share the primary bedroom. But with Noel's hospital hours and Trevor's all-the-time hours, they don't see much of each other either. Both of them seem to have enough privacy to be satisfied with the arrangement, at least.

The way I see it, I don't *have* to like any of them all that much. The lease for the small house is in my name, and they pay me rent. My only requirements for roommates are that they're queer or queer-friendly, they treat the place well, and they occupy it while I travel for my job.

Roommates can come and go as far as I'm concerned, and when the time comes for one of them—or more, as the case may be—to move out, I'll just put up a new ad. With the economy and Asheville real estate market, I'll have those bedrooms filled again in a heartbeat. It's wild out there.

Keying my way into the small house, I'm greeted by the scent of instant ramen. I'm sure that means Trevor's home, and probably Noel, too. They share ramen a lot when they're in the same space at the same time. Sure enough, after ditching my shoes at the rack by the door and depositing my jacket in the closet, I enter the living room-slash-kitchen to see it's a rare full house.

Noel is by the kitchen counter, stuffing his face with corn chips, while Trevor stirs the ramen on the stove. Charles is sitting on the sofa, hand-embroidering small red roses onto a lacy something. He glances up with surprise as I come in.

"Looks like we're all here tonight," he says. "Guess we can draw straws for who gets to shower first."

"Go back to your uncle's and save us the water," Trevor calls out. "Why do you slum it here with us anyway?"

"Change of pace," Charles says primly, tying off his thread. "You wouldn't understand."

"Well, you're right about that. I sure as hell don't," Noel says. "Your uncle's place…" he whistles. "I jog by it on my practice route for the half-marathon, and it's something else. Don't know why you bother keeping a single room here with us."

"Charles pays the rent just like you two do; he can stay or go as he pleases," I say, leaning against the wall and taking in my three tenants. "So you're all in for the night?"

Three heads nod.

"You?" Noel asks.

"Yup."

It's a good thing I hadn't given in to temptation and brought Matthew home tonight. He'd have been subjected to…

Well, I don't know what any of these guys might have said or done. Charles is my longest-running roommate, having moved his sewing machine and supplies in a few months before I'd even met Brandon. Back then, it'd been just me, Brandon, and Charles in the house, and since Brandon and I quickly became monogamous, he's never seen me with a hookup.

To give Charles credit where it's due, he hadn't even flinched at the Daddy thing. I assume he's more open-minded than the other two are likely to be.

I haven't had a hookup for as long as Trevor and Noel have lived here. I don't know how they would have reacted to me bringing Matthew back home for a fuck, but I can imagine how embarrassed Matthew would have been to face the scrutiny of three strangers when he's so inexperienced with the queer scene. Or any scene.

"I can toss another ramen packet in the pot for you," Trevor offers.

"I've eaten, but thanks." I step farther into the room, trying to decide if I want to sit next to Charles on the sofa, pull up a stool at the bar that separates the kitchen from the living area, or go back to my room to think about Matthew's shy smile, the dark thatch of hair at his throat, and that strange innocence shining out of his eyes.

I've decided on the latter when Noel suggests, "We should have a roomie movie night since we're all here." He accepts a bowl of ramen from Trevor and comes to plop down next to Charles, who moves his white lacy material away from Noel's slurping face and the dangerous bowl of spiced noodles.

"Let's!" Charles surprises me by agreeing. "I call dibs on picking the movie, though."

"We'll vote," Trevor says. "That's what we do in my bands whenever we need to make a choice about something important."

"A movie is hardly important," Charles sniffs. "But fine. Let's vote."

I waver, not sure what to do. I feel obligated to stay with them and watch a movie, almost as if I'm their host and not just a guy looking to make a few bucks from sharing his house with strangers.

I nod, taking the lounger next to the window. It's comfortable but has a side-angle view of the TV.

"*Dune*," Noel suggests.

Charles groans. "It's Christmas. Let's watch something seasonal, at least."

"Like what? *The Grinch*?" Trevor says around a mouthful of ramen.

"I was thinking like, I don't know, something gay *and* bright, like *Dashing in December* or *Single All the Way*," Charles says.

I guess I do listen to everything my mom tells me because I'm aware these are the titles of some queer Christmas movies a couple of streaming services have on offer. Mom's always asking me when I'm going to bring a boy home for Christmas like characters from these saccharine (but adorable, I'm sure) films.

Surprise, Mom, I'm bringing a boy home for Christmas this year, but you won't be around to meet him.

"Aren't those gay movies?" Noel asks.

"You have a problem with it?" Charles says, both of his perfectly-shaped brows rising in challenge.

Noel blows a raspberry and rolls his eyes. "Hell no, but I don't see why we need to watch gay shows to prove it. Right, Trevor?"

Trevor shrugs. "I'm down for *The Grinch*. Don't really care about the romance movies."

Charles huffs. "I'm surprised you aren't insisting on some Marvel smash-'em-up film instead."

"You said Christmas," Trevor says. "I'm giving you Christmas."

"Know when you've lost, Charles," Noel ribs him but then offers a steaming hot spoonful of slopping ramen noodles as consolation.

Charles shrinks farther away. "No, thank you."

My phone dings.

Hey, I'm at the hotel.

It's been about two and a half hours since I watched Matthew pull out of the parking garage. I'd walked around downtown for a little while, trying to shake the sense that I shouldn't have let him go without screwing him after all. Eventually, I'd realized I'd wandered on the Christmassy streets long enough that my car was on the other side of downtown.

It'd been another hike across in the cold to get back to it and make my way to the house. Once here, I'd sat in my warm car listening to a playlist I especially enjoy, texting with a few clients about changes to their training calendars in January, and then more texts with my mom about an issue with our mare's hoof. After that, I'd made notes about the various potential gifts I'd witnessed Matthew's interest in during the day and budgeted what I intend to spend on him.

Spoiler: quite a bit.

Heart trip-skipping, I thumb in my response. *Great. I'm glad to hear it. Thanks for letting me know.*

Reply bubbles appear on the screen. They disappear. They return, and after what feels like an interminable amount of time, a message comes through: *While I was driving, I couldn't stop thinking of you and how much I want this.*

I can just imagine the nerve he's gathered to confess that. He'd probably turned pink as he'd typed it out. I don't keep him hanging. *I've been thinking of you too.*

You have?

Of course.

What were you thinking about me? Specifically.

I'm impressed he's got the balls to ask, and I smile, typing in a reply: *I was planning for our night together. No specifics. It's Daddy's secret.*

I can imagine his reaction to that, too, and my heart speeds up.

"What's that smile about?" Noel asks, slurping up ramen.

"Got a hookup coming over?" Charles asks, his blue eyes shimmering with mischief and interest. "Is that why you looked so disappointed to see us all when you came in?"

"Nah," I say, pocketing my phone as I stand. "But I do need to deal with this. You three enjoy whatever movie you choose. Try not to come to blows over it."

They don't try to get me to stay, though Charles watches me go with the puppy-dog eyes of the betrayed, as if he would have preferred, I hang back and, what? Add in my vote for the romantic movie? Sorry, buddy, but this Daddy is voting for *Die Hard* if the single condition is Christmas.

I walk away as they continue to discuss their options, and my phone pings again before I've made it down the hallway and into the second-largest bedroom in the house. I lock the door behind me, like I had when I was a kid and I'd wanted to keep my mom out of my business.

I flop back on my bed after flicking on the soft light on the night table and unbuttoning my pants. Turning onto my side, my back to the door, I check out Matthew's latest message.

I'm nervous but excited about next week.

Understandable. What are you most nervous about?

I guess that I don't know what I'm doing? That I'll be bad at it or let you down.

You shouldn't be giving any thought to letting me down, Matthew. This is about you. What you like and what you enjoy.

I have no idea what that is, though? It's a little scary to think I'll be the focus. Can we just make you the focus, and I'll be there too?

That's a little like saying I can use you.

There's a long pause, and I wonder what he looks like as he's processing that comment. Is he frowning, tearing up, blushing? I don't know him well enough to be sure. I don't think it will make him angry, though. I think he'll sit with it, feel it, and see that it's true. I'm right, because he replies with:

I suppose so. But you did agree to take control, to handle me, to tell me what to do, eat, drink, and how to be. How to please you. I'm reading it over right now. It's on the contract you signed. I'll send you a picture of it if you want.

I chuckle at his full accounting of our contractual agreement. *I did sign to that effect, and I'll fulfill my obligation. But guess what pleases me the most when it comes to sex, boy? What I'll be demanding of you again and again?*

What?

My favorite thing is making my boy so horny he begs, so turned on he leaks pre-cum, and so aroused that when he climaxes, he loses all sense of place and reason.

Please, Daddy, you're making me hard again.

Daddy knows.

You're not going to make me tell you what I want, though, are you?

No, but I'm going to get your consent every step of the way.

Can't I just give you blanket consent now? Upfront?

I'm afraid not, boy. That's not safe—for you, for me, for anyone. You should never give blanket consent for anyone to take control of any aspect of your life.

Obviously, I don't know how to do this. I need someone to tell me. I trust you.

I know you do. I think that's the appeal of Daddy/boy play for you.

What do you mean?

If you're my boy, you don't need to know it all, do you?

No, I don't.

*If you're my boy, you aren't a middle-aged gay man who doesn't know how to get what he wants. You're mine, and you can just be **handled**. Shown. Taught. You can have everything you've yearned for but never trusted anyone to give you. Until me.*

The wait for a reply is long, and I wonder if I've exposed too much of him too fast. He's a raw wire, an open wound in some ways, and I just jammed a big iron stick of truth into him. That might fry some circuits or make him bleed. I should have been more careful.

He finally sends through: *I need to be handled, Daddy. Teach me.*

I will.

For one night, I just want someone to show me how to exist in my skin. How to truly live in my body as myself.

When we're done with our one night, you'll be ready to live as your true self.

It's a big statement, and I might not be able to pull it off, but in this moment, I believe that no matter what we accomplish or don't accomplish during our night together, he'll have a lot more of an idea of who he is, what he likes, wants, and needs than he did before. He won't feel cheated. I'm quite certain of that.

I might be getting the short end of the stick because I'm going to teach this boy, open him like a box of delicious chocolates—and then send him out for some other Daddy or man or idiot to enjoy. Kind of silly, isn't it? And yet there's too much in the way for us to make something more of this heady attraction.

After a few ponderous moments, I text him again. *It's late. You should get some sleep.*

Yes, Daddy.

Good boy.

We end our conversation, and I sprawl back in my bed, a strange turmoil of emotions twisting around in me. Not festive, not bright. Just a mishmash of excitement, arousal, frustration, sadness, disappointment, and anxiety. The last time I felt this kind of thrill was when I'd first met Brandon. And look how that ended.

Where was Brandon tonight? With Ferko? Was Ferko his Daddy now? He never said or gave any hint as to the nature of their relationship, though Ferko, if I recall correctly, is somewhat older.

Does Brandon even play that way anymore? He'd been such a beautiful, submissive, sexy boy. I'd loved fucking and holding him. I'd adored waking up to his softly sleeping face, and I'd been so happy every time I heard his laughter in another room. Hell, I'd treasured so much about him.

When he left, we'd agreed going "no contact" was best, but sometimes I just want to know if he's all right. I still care about him, even if he's gone for good.

My phone chimes. My heart leaps, hoping it's Matthew again with another question, or, Christ, maybe even Brandon somewhere in Hungary, sensing my sudden missing of him…

No such luck.

How'd it go? Nick asks, checking in, I'm sure, as part of his duties as chair of the charity auction, but also as the friend who'd convinced me to participate.

He's forty-one. That sums up so little about Matthew, but I can't help wanting to needle Nick a little, make him wonder if he'd fucked up by coercing me to put myself up on the auction block.

That a problem?

I take my time responding, getting up to adjust the blinds and take off my pants, shirt, and socks. I settle back on my bed, this time beneath the soft covers. *No. He's hot.*

He sends a "devil horns" emoji. *So you're looking forward to fucking him?*

That isn't the issue. Of course, I want to fuck him. It's just that as excited as I am, as much as I want Matthew, I still think Nick should consider how close a call this could have been. But what-the-hell-ever. What's done is done, and I made my own choices too.

I hadn't been forced to participate in the auction. Some part of me must have hoped that Nick was right, and there was some way I could get back into playing with boys on a more casual basis. Then the universe coughed up Matthew, about whom I have no real complaints, so I reply with, *His ass jiggles like a sweet pudding, and I look forward to eating it.*

Told you this would help get you back out there.

Smug motherfucker. I roll my eyes. *Yeah.*

*Maybe this boy could be **the** boy. The boy to end all boys.*

I type in a single word and shoot it off with a big helping of irritation: *No.*

Why not?

Lots of reasons.

Name one.

I sigh. This is how he got me to do the auction. He's like a damn bulldog when he gets something in his head. He'll be trying to marry me to Matthew before this conversation is done. *He lives in Nashville.*

So? Long distance not your thing?

You know it's not.

That's part of what had ended things with my first two boys, Duncan and Garrett. They'd both been ready to carry on by Skype or what-have-you, especially while they got set up in their new situations. But I'd told them no. Not only were they ready to fly on their own, but I need more than virtual contact. I need flesh and cum and cries of ecstasy in my ear. My phone pings again.

Get over yourself.

Will do.

Nick sends a "middle finger" emoji, and I smile to myself. After several minutes of no further harassment, the conversation appears to be over.

The thing is, whether it's long or short-term, I want the boys I play with to be happy. There's little I want more in life than that. But *I* deserve to be happy too. And for me to be happy, I need my boy close. Or I need to stop having boys at all.

Maybe my mom's right, and it's time for me to investigate whether I can sustain a relationship with a man who wants to be treated more as an equal and resign myself to short-term Daddy/boy interactions outside of that main relationship. Consensual, casual kink.

I roll onto my stomach. Memories play in my mind, beginning with the first day Brandon came into my life and culminating with images of him on his knees for me. He'd always been a hungry little cocksucker, so eager and dedicated to pulling my brains out my dick.

I grow hard remembering the way he trilled his tongue over the head of my cock, and how his lips would become so red as he worked. Erect, I press my dick against the mattress. My mind shifts, and the man on his knees isn't Brandon, but Matthew, and he's staring up at me with those wide eyes, his lips so pink and rosy—like when he bites them—and his salt-and-pepper hair glistening beneath the Christmas lights from the tree beside him.

I close my eyes and let myself drift thinking of Matthew, going back to the moment I saw him in Caffeine Dream and how I'd immediately wanted to fuck him. The way his eyes had been stuck on me, and how innocent and lustful he'd seemed. I'd known he wanted me even then. I go back to the image of him on his knees, his inexpert hand taking hold of me, his tongue poking out to taste my pre-cum…

Fuck, that's hot. I flip onto my back to grab my dick and start wanking as I play the fantasy out further.

What will he look like when he's in nothing but the underwear I buy for him, when I've peeled them off his fine form, and I've got my fingers in his ass? What will he sound like when I'm coaxing all kinds of pleasure from his throat? Will he be the breathy, high-pitched kind of fuck? Or the low, groaning kind? I love making a boy squeal as much as I love making a man grunt.

Since Matthew is both a boy and a very-much-grown man, I'm hoping he'll make both kinds of sounds.

What will he do when I rim him? Will he try to hide himself or show me his blush? He's so expressive. I'll do everything in my power to watch his face—hard when my mouth is attached to his ass, but I'll find a way.

Staring at my ceiling, studying the swirling stars of the plaster, I imagine how Matthew might squirm and buck if I put a vibrating plug in his ass, turning it on every time he was an especially good boy. A little reward for pleasing me.

My phone pings again. I almost don't check it because I'm busy jerking myself off now, but I go ahead and take a glance.

I just came so hard thinking of you, Daddy. Do you want to see a pic?

I groan. I already know Matthew well enough to recognize how much of a risk he must feel he's taking by putting himself out there like this. I have to grip my balls, so I don't blow my load. I manage to use voice-to-text to growl out: *yes*.

The photo that comes through is fucking glorious.

Matthew laid out on white sheets, salt-and-pepper hair damp with sweat, pupils blown wide, and his cheeks, neck, and chest stained red—guess I know the answer to that question now—and ropes of white cum all over his dark chest hair and dotting his small, rosy nipples.

My gut tightens, my orgasm yanked out of me by the sight. I grunt and huff as I shoot, legs trembling and jerking. Cum pools on my stomach, slips down my hips, and wets my sheets.

My brain babbles. *Fucking* fuck. *He made me come with just a picture. And it was a* good *orgasm, too. Holy fucking fuck.*

My phone pings.

Is that okay, Daddy?

I grunt through another aftershock before texting Matthew with trembling fingers, making so many typos that, for once in my life, I'm glad for autocorrect: *Do you want to see how happy you made Daddy? You made me come so hard, boy.*

Please show me.

I take a photo of my own cum-drenched cock and pubic hair and send it through, shivering through a few more aftershocks before he replies.

I want to lick that up, Daddy. May I?

Fuuuck. This boy isn't feeling so shy now, is he? I can just imagine how eager he'll be, kneeling next to me on the bed, lapping at my pooled cum, and those innocent eyes of his watching for my reaction. I text: *I'll make sure you eat all of it when we're together, boy. Every last drop.*

He sends a "loved" emoji, and I groan, wishing I could see his face. We shouldn't have done this. It's not part of the plan. We're supposed to have one night together. I'm not supposed to be sexting him in advance or wondering if I can drive to Nashville tomorrow to suck his cock while he strokes my hair and croons, "Daddy, yes, please, Daddy. Please make your boy come, Daddy."

My phone dings me from my reverie.

Thank you, Daddy. Goodnight.

Goodnight, boy. Sleep tight.

That's more than enough. I hope he doesn't text me again until tomorrow.

That's a lie.

I don't know what it is about Matthew Angel, but I want—no, *need*—more, and I think it's going to be a mighty big problem. A big thorny mess. A sticky situation.

A Christmas conundrum, if you will.

I giggle, high from lust and orgasm, cover my face, and kick at my sheets like a giddy idiot.

Holy shit, what have I gotten myself into?

I can't wait to find out.

PART TWO

The Sexual Experience

CHAPTER SEVEN

Matthew

IT'S LATE MORNING as I pull up the steep incline toward the so-called log cabin at the top of the mountainside—it's more like a lodge, what with its three stories and impressive decks. I'm so nervous I can't stop the quaking of my muscles. I've been grateful for cruise control for most of the nearly five-hour drive from Nashville, since I'm trembling like I've been locked out in the freezing cold.

Excitement, nerves, and a giddiness I've never experienced before run rampant in me. If I appear half as wild as I feel, I must look like a strung-out mess.

I barely slept last night for fantasizing, but refusing to jerk off. At my age, the refractory period of orgasm can be annoyingly long, and I want to come as many times as possible with Daddy.

Thinking of Erik that way is heady, dirty, and fraught, and it gets me so hard and wound up that sometimes I almost see stars from my sheer need. Orgasm isn't even necessary for me to feel like I'm having an out-of-body experience, not with this kink. And all that intoxicating goodness has been without even being in Daddy's actual presence—just teasing texts, and sexy photos, and my own internal longing to bring me to this peak of arousal.

It's been like a week of edging.

I haven't let myself come since I drove away from Daddy, apart from that first night at the hotel. I'd thought I'd come spontaneously if I didn't take myself in hand. So I'd fingered my ass thinking of him, and when I hadn't been able to endure any more, I'd stroked my cock twice before blowing all over my stomach, chest, and the hotel sheets. It'd been explosive. Intense. One of the best orgasms of my life.

Up until whatever happens now.

Whatever Daddy has in mind for me, I'm sure I'm going to come my brains out, and more than once. I shiver as I put the car in park, ducking my head a little to take in the full scope of the lodge through the windshield.

There's a haze over the entire scene—fog's rolled in—and I notice the clouds above are heavy and dark. It's gloomy, almost as if evening has fallen sooner than it should.

But the lodge looks warm and safe, with smoke coming from the chimney, and multicolored Christmas lights strewn along the various deck railings, lining the roof and outlining the windows. The log structure has a rustic feel, but the construction is new and fashioned for comfort; I can see that even from the outside.

I get out of the car, and the sound of my door shutting echoes around the mountainside. I stuff my hands in the pockets of my dark jeans and feel grateful for the soft scarf around my neck and the thickness of my MTSU sweatshirt. It's cold, and it smells like snow is on the way. I tilt my head back, examining the lodge floor-by-floor.

The top floor seems likely to be all one big space, based on the way the windows are situated. From that room, there are sliding glass doors out onto the long upper deck. So it's probably the primary bedroom, which will have, no doubt, the best views.

The middle floor seems to be the main living area, based on the gorgeous Christmas tree with twinkling white lights visible through the big windows facing to the east. If I had to guess, I'd assume it also hosts the kitchen and den and perhaps a bedroom? Maybe not. It depends on whether a formal dining area is important to Erik.

The deck for the middle floor is covered and wider than the one for the master bedroom. There's a wide, cushioned porch swing, an outdoor sofa and table, as well as overhead fans for use in the summer. But, in the spirit of the season, someone has hung multicolored Christmas bulbs from the fan blades, and they shimmer in the gloom like tiny, festive constellations. It's beautiful and just what I need.

My parents' Christmas tree decorations have stayed packed away in the attic, collecting dust. It seems wrong somehow—or at least unnecessary and a waste of electricity—to put up a tree just for me.

Tomorrow, I'll be making the long drive back to Nashville to a dark house for Christmas Eve. It might as well be any other day since I have no one to celebrate with. Doug and Forest clearly aren't ready to invite me to their holiday dinner after what I did the last time I went. I can't blame them.

Erik's home is a festive scene straight from a Christmas card or one of the hundreds of sappy holiday romances I always end up watching for hours on end, even though the tales of Christmas miracles and finding love with small-town handymen leave me feeling more alone than ever.

Again, I sweep my gaze over the merry lights and the warm glow of the tree in the window. At least I'm allowed to enjoy this Christmas wonderland for one magical night. I wonder if the decorations are Erik's or his mother's idea. Do they put them up after Thanksgiving? Six weeks of this would be bliss.

Speaking of Erik's mom, the bottom floor has a separate entrance, and I think it must be hers. The patio outside has another outdoor sofa and a table, and there's a heap of firewood, too. A grill stands off to the right of the patio, out from under the deck above, and it appears well-used. The bottom floor doesn't have any lights glowing within, so I assume she's not home.

I have mixed feelings about that. I don't want her here for our night together, but I'm also curious about the woman who's still this close with her grown son, and who's accepted his kink and his former boy with no backlash. I can't even imagine. My own parents would...

I try to cut the thought off, but it hits me all the same.

They'd be so ashamed. If they knew where I am right now, if they knew what I'm going to do and with whom? They'd fall on their knees and pray for my soul. Mom would wail and cry, and Dad...I don't even want to think of what Dad might do. Tell me to leave his home and never come back? Disown me?

I shake myself.

It doesn't matter now. They're gone. I miss them like a permanent toothache that fades and returns full force when I least expect it. But I don't miss how their religious beliefs and their conservative attitudes kept me so small. Kept me from knowing what I wanted or figuring out a safe, sane way to get it.

Speaking of safe and sane. That's something Doug insisted on talking with me about at length, before letting me come here. Not that he has any real say over what I do in my life, but it'd been nice to see that he cares about me after all.

The concern in his eyes as he'd sat me down over a glass of whiskey at Hummingbird Bar had felt like a warm blanket I hadn't even known I'd needed. For the first time, since the horrible mistake I'd made in propositioning Forest, I'd felt Doug's affection for me.

After reviewing the contract I'd signed with Erik, he'd deemed it superficially safe and sane, so long as *Erik* isn't a risk. At that point, Doug had insisted on taking the names of the references Nick and Erik had given me and calling them himself, saying since he was in the kink world, he'd know better than I what to ask, and what red flags to look out for. After doing that due diligence, he'd texted me: *I think he's safe. Have a good time.*

Safe.

Am I?

Is this truly safe or sane? Tonight? Coming here to this remote house after buying a Daddy at a charity auction? Jazzed up on the idea of being handled and cuddled and fucked by him? That's madness, isn't it? I suppose it is, but I'm doing it. I'm going to live for myself for just one evening, and if it feels right? If it turns out that this is what I want? Then I'll have learned one true thing about myself.

I walk around to the back of my car and pop the trunk. Lifting my suitcase—a small hard-shell that I use for all my business travel—I let it clatter to the gravel drive. It's empty except for one change of clothes, toothbrush, toothpaste, hairbrush, and the contract Daddy and I signed at the bar last week.

A strange noise comes from the right, and I turn my head, seeing through the trees to a clearing downslope from here, on another flat piece of land where, if this were a neighborhood, a neighboring house would have been built.

A red barn, like something out of a children's book, is covered by a ring of fog and glows enchantingly with lights from inside. I hear the odd sound again and recognize it as a horse's whinny. Another sound answers it…the bleat of goats.

My phone buzzes in my back pocket, and I pull it out.

You made it.

I turn around but don't see Erik anywhere. *Yes. Where are you?*

I'm in the barn. Molly gave birth last night, and I wanted to check on the baby.

As I'm wondering who Molly is—an animal of some sort, I suppose—and if I'm supposed to walk to the barn now, or wait for him here, another text comes through.

Molly is a goat.

I laugh and reply: *I figured.*

Hold on a few, and I'll be right there. Wait on the deck. There's a nice view.

Yes, Daddy.

Good boy.

My nipples go hard, my cock thickens, and I'm ready to strip naked right here and let him have my ass over the still-hot hood of my car. But I do as he says, hauling my thankfully light bag up the somewhat steep flight of stairs. Halfway up, I pass a hidden deck set off to the right, with a hot tub behind a tall obscuring hedge. I continue to the middle deck, just a little winded.

Sure enough, now that I can see inside the windows, there's a living area, kitchen, and dining room separated by a long, curved counter built around a thick wooden column that comes straight down from the ceiling—no doubt a support beam. The Christmas tree, also visible through the window, is tall, covered in white lights and multicolored bulbs of all sizes, and there are presents beneath it dressed up in green, red, and white striped paper.

And, if I gaze over the deck railing, Daddy's right. There's a lovely view, a bit obscured now, but this is Appalachia's Blue Ridge mountains, and the blue fog is common and adds to the gentle mystery of the world's oldest mountains. My gaze follows the curves and shadows, the hollows and dips, and the wispy fog dancing through them, until I drop my attention to the red barn to see Daddy exiting it. He saunters over a well-trodden path that leads to the main house.

He's wearing jeans and boots, a T-shirt and a heavy flannel, as well as a thick beanie on his head. The air is cold but not freezing, so he hasn't bothered with a jacket. The way he walks is captivating—strong, assured. There's no hesitation as he takes each step, hands in his pockets, chin raised.

I don't know if I'm supposed to sit and wait, but I can't. I'm too excited. My palms go all sweaty, and my stomach flutters. My legs feel as if they might go out from under me as Daddy reaches the bottom of the stairs and starts up.

Clomp, clomp, clomp.

His boots land heavily on the wooden risers. Ominous. A little threatening. My mind goes wild, offering up all kinds of filthy fantasies—he's going to grab me, bend me over this rail, and—

No, no, he's going stalk up to me, take me by the throat and—

No, he's going to force me to my knees and plug my mouth with his—

No, he's—

He's going to reach the top of the stairs, stroll up to me, his eyes warm and his smile cool and relaxed. He's going to touch my cheek, the way he did when we met the first time, hold my head steady and lean in for a kiss. A sweet, sexy kiss.

I groan, gripping his arms, loving the thickness of his biceps. I lean into his body, opening for his tongue. The kiss isn't aggressive. It's passionate, but he doesn't kiss me like he can't wait to rip my clothes off. I'm thrilled, but also disappointed by that. It's only my third kiss, and I'm not skilled, but I can't be bothered to care when he's teaching me what to do with each gentle caress of his lips and tongue.

Hungry, eager, I chase his mouth when he pulls away. Daddy indulges me with one more peck before putting his fingers on my lips, stopping my next attempt to prolong the kiss.

"It's good to see you, boy."

I nod, silenced by the roar of desire in me.

"Is that how you greet Daddy?"

I start to sweat. I don't want to mess things up already. But Daddy's eyes are patient, and I manage to get out, "It's good to see you too, Daddy." My voice is rough, like I've gargled pine needles. I'm still shaking, and he notices, running his hands up and down my arms. His gaze is earnest, and it makes me ache inside.

"This sweatshirt is too thin for the coming weather, boy. Come on inside. Let's keep you warm."

I let him take my hand and lead me into the beautiful house. The heat from the wood-burning stove is soft—not overpowering, or drying—and I soak it in, letting it still the shivers from the chill, and giving in to the shudders that are nerves alone. I stand beside him as he removes his boots, and I kick off my sneakers. He puts them in a shoe-holder by the door, and I stand there in my socked feet, heart pounding, waiting to see what sexy thing happens next.

It turns out, it's not very sexy at all.

He tells me to leave my bag by the door before leading me past the Christmas tree, the sofa, and over to the counter separating the kitchen from the rest of the living space. Over my shoulder, I see the dining area, but I don't examine it too closely.

"Have a seat." He gestures to the tall bar chairs, shooting me a grin as he goes around and washes his hands in the deep sink opposite me. "How was your drive?"

"Great." I get settled on the chair, blinking around the place, my throat dry and my hands still shaky with nerves. "Weather was good. There was a wreck I passed about an hour outside of Knoxville, but no one seemed injured, and the cops were there. The traffic slowed to a near stop because of lookie-loos."

I'm babbling a little, but I don't know what else to do. I don't know how this *works*.

"Must have been an early morning for you," Erik—*Daddy*—says, getting two glasses from the cupboard, and putting them on the counter between us. "Water okay? I've got some canned sodas if you prefer, but, truth be told, I'd prefer you drank water. Hydration will be important soon enough."

My breath falters. "Whatever you'd like, Daddy."

He grins, and that nervous, excited fluttering in my stomach creeps into my throat. If I were fanciful in nature, I might imagine butterflies were about to fly out. But I'm an accountant, and we're supposed to be boring, staid, and serious.

Maybe I don't want to be anymore. If I ever have been. I remember how, in my youth, I'd yearned to give myself over to music. Even as bad as I was at making it. In private moments, I'd let it steer me, command me, take me over. Numbers and tax returns could never do that. Not for me.

"What time did you leave Nashville?" Daddy asks as he pulls a pitcher of water out of the fridge. He pours it into both glasses.

"Around seven. It wasn't that bad. I didn't get up any earlier than if I'd gone to work."

The pitcher is the kind with a built-in filter, and he refills it from the sink before returning it to the fridge. "Did you stop for food on the road?"

"No, Daddy."

He leans on the counter, elbows down, forearms on display where he's pushed his flannel sleeves up. He gazes at me warmly, even as he clucks his tongue scoldingly. "Did you have breakfast?"

"Too nervous to eat."

"Mm." He smiles at me again, and then turns around to the cabinets, pulling out bread, peanut butter, and a bag of chips. He moves to the fridge and gets out grape jelly. As I watch with my legs jittering on the bottom rung of the bar chair, he puts together a peanut butter and jelly sandwich, plates it with chips, and hands it over. The whole time he's working, silence hangs between us, but it's not uncomfortable, just charged.

"This is great," I say around a mouthful. "I didn't realize I was so hungry."

"Eat up. Then we're going to the barn."

"We are?" I don't know why, but I'd spent the drive imagining that I'd arrive at his cabin—which had been much more rustic in my mind—and we'd get right to it. After all, I just have twenty hours or so, and I have a lot I want to experience with him before my time is up. Many naked things.

"Yes."

As I make my way through the sandwich and chips, I must be exuding my confusion and disappointment, because he reaches out and tousles my hair. "Don't worry, boy. Daddy's got you. Everything's going to be just fine. I promise you'll get what you want."

I nod, sipping the water he's provided, and pushing the clog of peanut butter, jelly, and bread down. I have to trust Erik knows best. That's part of this entire thing, isn't it? Letting him be in charge. Letting him take control of the situation.

"There," he says as I finish up. "Good work."

I flush, a little embarrassed to be praised for eating, like I'm a kid or something—and when was the last time I'd had a PB&J?— but when he turns back from putting the plate in the dishwasher, he sees my expression and says it again.

"Good work, boy. Following Daddy's instructions is key to enjoying yourself tonight. You're starting off on the right foot." He comes around the counter and heads back toward the door where we left our shoes. "This way."

Obeying, I'm soon wrapped up in a too-big blue puffer coat with lined pockets. As he puts a scarf around my neck and pulls a beanie over my head, I'm reminded again of childhood—of my mom and dad bundling me up for the long wait for the school bus on those icy cold winter mornings. Erik's bigger than I am, and I feel small. His hands are gentle as he smooths over the lines of the coat on my shoulders and tucks my ears more firmly beneath the beanie.

"There. You'll be plenty warm now."

He tugs on a barn coat and a lined beanie for his head and opens the door. "After you."

Once outside, he takes hold of my hand and leads me back down the stairs and toward the path to the barn. He swings our hands. "You like horses?"

"I guess?" My chin, cheeks and ears start to ache at the bite of the cold air, and I adjust my scarf to cover my chin. For his part, Erik seems at ease in the winter mountain chill.

"Never been around them much?"

"Not really."

"Goats?"

"Just in a petting zoo."

"Well, you're in for a treat. This is no petting zoo." As we walk, he tells me about Dora, Tyron, Zebra Cake, and Ryder, the four horses living in the stable. "They're all trained stunt horses. They help me do my job, and, in return, I baby the hell out of them."

"Did you name them yourself?" I ask, zeroing in on perhaps the least important thing he's just said, and yet I'm very curious.

"Only Ryder. The others came to me with their names."

"Zebra Cake…" I grin. "Does he have a striped butt?"

Chuckling, Erik squeezes my fingers. "His former person's five-year-old daughter named him after her favorite Little Debbie snack cake."

"Mm, gotta love some Zebra Cakes."

"And he's just as sweet, too."

I smile. "You seem to enjoy your work a lot."

"You don't?"

"Not really." I shrug, blinking as a fleck of what feels like ice pings against my face. "I'm good at it, but that's all. I wouldn't say it makes me happy. It pays the bills."

"Hm." He doesn't ask more, going back to talking about the animals I'm about to meet. As the fog swirls around our feet, the ominous clouds above begin to spit small ice pellets. The weather is calling for snow, but Erik hasn't mentioned it as a potential problem, so I don't worry about it. Daddy will take care of me.

"Then there's Molly, the new mother. This is her first kid."

"Oh? Is that why you wanted to take me out to the barn first thing?"

"Yes, I'd like to check on her again. She's a little out of her depth. That, and I like to see how my play partners are with animals. It gives me a lot more information than they might realize."

Feeling self-conscious, I clear my throat before asking, "What does it tell you?"

"It tells me about their confidence and empathy for a start." A dog barks, and another yips. Two dash around the corner of the red barn, both white and black, and looking almost ghostly in the wafting fog. "That's Kramer and Scott." Erik chuckles again. "And here comes Sally and her son Brodie."

Two more dogs, these brown and white with spots, rush behind the first two, bowl them over, and start tussling in the grass and dirt. Caught up in their antics, I forget to worry about what my reaction to it might mean, and I laugh as the dogs play. Erik does too. The sound of his throaty happiness pops the tension that's been growing inside me since my arrival, and when Erik squeezes my hand again, I'm awash with giddy relief and anticipation.

"Four dogs!"

"There are plenty of barn cats, too."

"You must really love animals."

"You don't?"

"I do." I bite into my lower lip and then admit, "I have a cat. Terrificus Persimmon Mottsanders. Or Simmony Sunshine for short."

"For short," Erik repeats with another delightful laugh.

"Or sometimes it's Terry Ficus. Or Mott the Pissy Pants."

"Which does she—"

"He."

"Ah, which does he answer to?"

"All of them. He's affectionate."

"And where is he this weekend?"

"My next-door neighbor, Maureen, looks after him whenever I travel. Won't even let me pay for it."

"That's kind of her."

The dogs zoom past us, chasing each other and panting hard in the cold air, puffs rising from their smiling mouths. Two of them brush against Erik's left thigh, and he runs his fingers over their backs as they pass. It warms my heart to know Erik likes animals.

If I'd been harboring any fears for the weekend or concerns that the references hadn't been honest about Erik as a person, seeing how he lights up talking about his horses and dogs would have alleviated them.

"We don't usually keep the animals inside. They have several trails on the property where they're free to wander year-round, both the goats and the horses. But with snow on the way, we keep them indoors where it's warm and safe for them." He swings open the big door.

Inside the barn, it's toasty, and the scent of manure and straw clings in my nostrils. Light sifts through several high windows. Dust motes shimmer in the air. It's certainly not silent. There are the bleats of goats, and the huffing sounds of horses, along with some stomping of their feet. An orange-and-white cat slinks forward to wrap itself around Erik's leg when he pauses just inside the entryway. He squeezes my hand again before releasing it and pointing up at the hayloft. "There's Daisy. This one at our feet is Dipsy."

A motley-colored cat regards me from above. I wave at it and smile.

"Come meet Zebra Cake," Erik says, leading me toward the half of the barn that's divided into horse stalls.

As I approach, a brown horse with a white mane sticks his head out and peers at Erik before huffing. Erik laughs and says, "I didn't bring another carrot. You just had one, silly."

The horse rolls his eyes at that.

"Does he know what you said?"

"They're very intelligent," Erik hedges, reaching into a bucket near the stall and pulling out a handful of hay, passing it to me. The scent of it brings back a sharp memory of a Halloween hayride on a neighbor's lawn tractor when I was five or six.

"If you want, you can feed that to him, and he'll let you pat his nose."

I move forward to offer the hay, palm up. Zebra Cake's lips are ticklish on my palm, and I struggle to keep from jerking my hand back as I giggle.

"Ticklish?"

"Yes," I say, stroking over Zebra Cake's velvet snout. He chews as I pat him and admire his shiny coat. "He's beautiful."

"Sweet, stubborn, and good at his job. He's the one I train beginners on. I'm confident he won't get carried away and step on some stunt-hungry actor while they're practicing falling off."

I laugh. "Actors. What a job. Getting paid to fall off horses."

"And to eat nothing but chicken breast and spinach for eight months to achieve that ripped look."

"True. Those actors suffer, I'm sure."

"But I hear the big bucks make it worth it," Erik says with a smirk. "C'mon. Let's see what Dora thinks of you."

I'm not sure what Erik is measuring as I interact with each of the horses, but he seems pleased, and my nerves—which had been sky-high when I'd first arrived—are now showing themselves as buzzy excitement instead of coming-out-of-my-skin anxiety.

When Dora, Tyrone, and Ryder are all done with me, Erik leads me toward the other half of the barn and the goat pens. I'm amazed by the amount of cheerful noise they make, and I gasp as one hops onto the back of another, and then steps over the backs of two of his pen-mates before hopping back down again to butt horns with a gray scrapper of a goat.

"They play like that," Erik assures me. "This is Molly over here."

We step past the main pen, where the majority of goats play, bleat, and chew their feed, to another area cordoned off and protected. It's very warm as well, and I see why. Heat lamps, warming pads, and many blankets cradle the mother and her teetering-on-his-tiny-legs baby kid.

"Awww." The high-pitched squeak that issues from me is a little embarrassing, but I can't help it. "It's so cute."

"Mm-hm." Erik leans against the entry to the small room. "She's a cutie, all right. They always are."

"What's her future hold?" I ask, tilting my head, wondering if the goats are intended for a dinner plate somewhere.

"Not sure. What do you think should happen with her?"

"What are her options?"

He smiles at me and shrugs. "She can stay here and become one of my milk goats, or I can sell her to someone else, and she can be one of *their* milk goats."

"So, she's not going to be eaten?"

"No, sir. Well, not unless a bear gets her when she's out wandering this spring, but the dogs are good at protecting the goats from that."

"I guess if you need another milk goat, you should probably keep her. She was born near Christmas. That seems like a good omen, right?"

"What do you think I should name her?"

Instantly I have an answer, but I blush, pressing my teeth together, too embarrassed to say it aloud.

"Tell Daddy what you're thinking," Erik says, and that tone of voice is back, enough to make me feel scolded but also cared for; it's so odd how something as small as that can create so many complex emotions.

"Miss Merry Joy-Joy."

Erik's lips tremble before he laughs to himself, eyeing the baby. "Miss Merry Joy-Joy it is."

"No! It's absurd!"

"I love it. I'm sure we'll just call her Joy, but her full name will be a joy—ha!—every time we use it." He turns to me, cups the back of my neck, and draws me toward him. Once our foreheads are touching, I smell peppermint on his breath. "Are you ready to be my boy now, Matthew?"

"Yes, Daddy."

"Are you ready for me to take you back to the house, warm you up, and show you what your body's made for?"

I shiver, my cock thickening. "Yes," I gasp. "Please."

"Do you want to know the first lesson?"

I quiver, wishing he'd pull our mouths together, wishing he'd kiss me, and I'm oh-so-tempted to take his mouth without waiting for him to give it to me again. I almost say yes, but then I swallow, take a shaky breath, and say, "What—whatever Daddy wants."

"Oh, Christ, boy," Erik mutters, his hand flexing on the back of my neck, pressing our foreheads even tighter. "Are you sure you've never done this before?"

"I'm sure, Daddy."

"I know you are. It was just another way to praise you, to say that you're so good at being my boy already. That was such a good answer; it's hard to believe you're not a practiced boy."

"I'm not."

"I believe you." He pulls away from me, kisses my forehead, and studies my face for a long moment. I wish I knew what he sees there.

"Daddy?"

"Yes, boy?"

"Can we start? Please?"

He grins. "Let's go. Tonight's going to be beautiful for you. Powerful. Pleasurable. Maybe even scary. But you won't leave me feeling like you've been used. I promise."

CHAPTER EIGHT

Matthew

I N THE DINING area, there's a long wooden table with comforta-ble chairs, and Erik pulls one out, motioning for me to sit. He takes his place at the head of the table where a small stack of papers awaits.

Copies of our STI tests and our contract.

"Thank you for sending me these," Daddy says, picking the pages up and shuffling through them for a moment. "Now, let's both review these test results before we start, noting the date and the findings." He passes them to me, and I look over them and nod before he takes them back and reviews them himself one last time. "You're still good with cum play?"

"Yes, Daddy." I feel lightheaded and high imagining his cum in me—swallowing it, taking it in my ass. I want it so bad I start to salivate.

"Excellent. Before we begin, we agree to everything again. This is our contract. This is what we've agreed to."

I listen as he reads every line aloud. Every single sentence. I want him to be done with it so we can start, but I want to hear him say the words, too. It makes this all real again, contained, and safe.

"What are your safe words?" he asks me when he's done reading over the contract.

"Red and yellow, Daddy."

"And red means?"

"Stop."

"And yellow means?"

"Slow down."

"Those are my safe words, too," Daddy says. "I can use them whenever I want as well. You understand?"

"Yes, Daddy."

"Good. I want you to know, kink can be a fast track to intimacy. It can crack you open emotionally. Are you ready for that?"

I nod.

"Words, please."

"I'm ready, Daddy."

"Whatever you feel, however strong, I'm here to hold you through it."

"Yes, Daddy."

I'm still quaking, and my dick aches from being hard and trapped in my jeans. He stands, puts out his hand, and says, "Good boy. Let's go upstairs and start your enema then."

I swallow. I'd cleaned myself out with a douche before I left this morning, but this is part of what we've agreed to. There's something powerful in thinking of what this will entail. That Daddy will administer it. Most of all? That I'll let him.

He holds my hand as we climb the stairs to the top floor of the cabin, and again I was right. The master suite. A big bed, a wall of glass doors with a gorgeous view of mountains and more mountains, an overly wide and long sofa that is the size of a bed, and a giant high-definition television above it.

But Daddy doesn't linger; he takes me right into the tiled bathroom. There's a big open shower with four heads. There's a massive bath with clawed feet, a modern take on the bathtub of yore, and the water valves are rigged with an enema apparatus. My heart double-beats, and my breath stutters.

The sinks are against a wall that has a door in it, no doubt leading to a closet.

"You won't come until I tell you to," Daddy says calmly. "Understand, boy?"

"Yes, Daddy."

"Have you had an enema before?" he asks, letting go of my hand to go to the bath and start the water, working the cold and hot until the temperature pleases him. He pushes a fancy valve that keeps the water's temperature constant.

"No, just douches, Daddy."

"And you douched this morning?"

"Yes."

"Then this will be easy," Daddy says, coming to me with a warm smile. "You don't need to be afraid, baby. Daddy's got you."

I bite my lower lip, my cock throbbing, and my throat feeling tight. "Can you…"

"What, boy? Talk to Daddy."

"Can you hug me?"

Daddy's smile almost melts my heart as he takes me into his arms, cuddles me close, and tucks my head beneath his chin. I'm grateful he's taller than me. Wider. I feel like a child in his arms. Like I can be his boy. He cradles the back of my head, massaging my scalp and the back of my neck. He whispers little nothings in my ear, soothing words and sounds, and rocks me back and forth on our feet.

When I go limp in his arms, he kisses the side of my throat, and then my cheek before whispering, "Ready, boy?"

I nod.

"Let's get these clothes off." He pauses for a moment, giving me the space to say no or use my safe words before he slips his hands beneath my sweatshirt, and caresses the hair on my stomach and over my chest. "Christ, boy, this is soft stuff."

My cheeks heat. I haven't touched other men enough to know one way or another, but I remember that most of the men I've sucked off had wiry pubic hair, and stiff fur beneath their belly buttons.

"Amazing," he murmurs. "Now, off this comes." He tugs my sweatshirt over my head, and my cock throbs as his eyes go from soft and cool to liquid hot. "Look at my boy," he says, trailing his fingers from my shoulders, over my chest, missing my nipples, and down to the top of my jeans.

He hooks his fingers into the loops of them, but doesn't start to take them off. Instead, he runs his eyes over me hungrily. "Do you know how hot you are?" he asks, and he sounds sincere, though I can't imagine he means it as more than a way to make his boy feel good.

I say nothing, letting him tug me closer to rub his short stubble over my neck and collarbones. My legs start shaking again as he bends low to brush his stubbly chin over my right nipple, following it with a lick, and moves on to my left. I gasp, and he chuckles before coming up to kiss me, rougher this time, more intense, and I lose myself in it.

Daddy holds me up as we make out, and I'm grateful because my knees wobble. The taste of his mouth is all I want, and I feed on his saliva and live for the twists and touches of his tongue. When he breaks free, he's panting, and I'm shaking like a leaf. Daddy smooths the backs of his fingers over my cheeks and then smooths my hair down.

"Now," he says, and his voice is gritty. I can feel his cock pushing against mine through our jeans where he's clutched me tight during our kiss. "I'm going to have to watch out for that."

"For what, Daddy?"

"For how slutty-good your mouth is, baby. It makes me lose my mind."

I think I should feel insulted by "slutty," but I don't. The harsh words were said with such gentleness and lust that they feel like praise.

Daddy rubs his fingers over my lips, and I taste the salt of his skin when I poke my tongue out to lick them. "That's right," he murmurs. "Daddy's boy has a slutty-good mouth. But it's only slutty for Daddy. Understood?"

"Yes, Daddy," I pant. My balls are tight and aching, and my cock is leaking so fiercely there's a wet spot on my underwear that's all slimy and hot. "Please, Daddy," I say, pressing my hips against his. "I need…"

I'm not sure how to ask for what I need.

"Daddy knows," he assures me. "Daddy has his boy."

He starts on my pants, and I almost come as he jerks them and my underwear down. "Daddy," I whine. "I don't know if I can wait."

He eyes my red, leaking cock, the swollen head, and my balls pulled up tight to the shaft, ready to shoot. Grinning, he kisses the side of my neck again, and runs his hands over my chest, feeling my body fur before tweaking my nipples with his fingers and thumbs. "Can you come from this, sweet boy?"

I shift forward, my cock seeking contact with his jeans-clad hip, and he releases one nipple to pull me close, one hand on my ass. "Don't move. Don't thrust," he orders. "Let it happen."

I don't know if I can, but I let him hold me while his other hand works at my nipples. His mouth explores my neck, and the spot behind my ear makes me gasp with delight and need. I struggle to control my own urge to hump, trying to be good, but soon I'm writhing as he tongues my ear. I groan when he takes my mouth again.

I hump his hip while he tweaks my nipple in the same rhythm. I can barely breathe with his mouth on mine, we're huffing like horses, and I'm just about to come when he shoves me away, a wicked smile on his face.

"Daddy!" I cry, throwing myself back into his arms. I thrust against his hardness, the roughness of the jeans hurting in a way that keeps me from coming. I want to cry. "Daddy," I whimper. "Daddy."

"That's right, boy," he whispers. "Daddy's here. Daddy's here."

I kiss his throat and let myself explore, trying to get his T-shirt off. I find my fingers are clumsier than they've ever been. His skin is sleek, and his smooth flesh isn't nearly as hairy as my own. When he pulls back enough to tug the T-shirt up from the back and toss it to the floor, I'm torn between pressing myself to him, so I can get his skin on mine, and staring at his muscles, the firmness of his build.

"Here," Daddy says, taking my hands and putting them around his waist, tugging me close again. Skin-on-skin, my cheek on his shoulder, his hands around my back, wandering down to cup my ass, it's the closest I've ever been to another man.

I turn my head and take a deep breath. Daddy smells like Ivory soap and sweat, and I want to cover myself in his clean scent. I want to be owned by him, inside and out.

"Daddy," I whisper. It's so good to say it. To feel it. To trust this man can hold me while I learn to be a big boy.

My knees are shaking, so I'm barely able to stand. Daddy catches my aching cock between his jean-clad thighs, which stills my attempts to hump again, the fabric too harsh for real pleasure, and yet I stay hard.

"Hold still," he whispers, tugging my right ass cheek aside, exposing my hole to the cool air of the bathroom. "Let me feel you."

I nearly pass out as his hand releases its hold on my cheek, and his fingers slide to dip into the crease, skimming over my hole. I shiver. No one's ever touched me there.

"Mm. That's a tight sweet hole, boy. Let Daddy show you how good it can be for you."

I've played with my own hole. I've finger-fucked it. But nothing has prepared me for the sensation of being clutched to Daddy's strong body, hearing him spit on his fingers, and feeling him rub that saliva against my anus. I breathe in gasps and sobs, already overwhelmed by this experience. I dissolve in his arms like melting snow.

"That's my boy," Daddy praises me. "No one's had your hole. Daddy will have it first."

"Yes, Daddy, you're the first."

"Mm, that's beautiful, sweet boy. It's so generous of you to let Daddy have this."

I tremble as he works the tip of his finger into me, and I realize I'm breached by another man for the first time in my life. My knees give out, and Daddy holds me up. I'm clinging to him, my dick trapped between his thighs, my hole opening to his fingers, and I groan.

"That's so good, sweet boy," he praises, and I want to cry with relief. I'm pleasing him. "Daddy wants to come in your ass. Will you let him?"

"Yes, please, Daddy. Please."

"I can't wait."

"Do it," I urge. "Daddy, I want it."

"Oh, Daddy will give it to you. But not now." He pulls his fingertips out of me, and I want to beg for them back. I would have, too, but he kisses me again, and I lose myself in his lips. He shifts his hips back, releasing my caught cock, and when I start squirming on his leg, trying to get off, he mouths at my neck and my ears, and doesn't stop me.

The feeling escalates. I'm going to come. I want to come.

But Daddy said not until he…

I groan.

"Daddy, I—"

"Go on, boy. Give Daddy your cum," he says in a ragged whisper. "Give it to me."

I cry out, wracked with spasms, as I paint his jeans and the tiles of the floor. The orgasm feels ripped from me, and I'm panting, trembling, and near tears when it's over.

"That was beautiful, baby," he whispers, kissing my earlobe, and then my mouth again. "Such a good orgasm you gave Daddy."

"You came?" I ask, disappointed to have missed it.

"No," he says, nuzzling my neck. I can almost believe he isn't doing this for the auction at all, that he's doing it all for me. I *want* to believe it. I almost do. "Your orgasm is a gift. Your cum is a gift. Watching you surrender to it is a gift. Getting to be the first to give you this…" He kisses my throat, and I tremble. He's found a spot that makes me squirm every time he tongues it, and he keeps going back to it again and again. "Every orgasm I get out of you tonight will be something you gift to me. Understand, boy?"

"I th-think so." I've never stuttered in my life, but I'm so overcome now, I can barely think or make coherent words.

"Good boy. Now," he says, leading me toward the bathtub. "The enema."

CHAPTER NINE

Erik

MATTHEW IS AS docile as the newborn kid out in the barn, maybe more so, as I place him in the tub. The tub is big enough to accommodate two grown men, so it's plenty big for Matthew to lie down, curl on his left side, and pillow his arm beneath his head. His breathing is unsteady, as he's still recovering from his orgasm and anxious for what's to come.

I've tested his hole with my fingers and know that he'll easily be able to take the nozzle of the enema. As he waits and watches, I prepare the nozzle with lube, and turn the water on, making sure the valve is set to closed. I wait a few beats, letting the tension grow in us both.

"Now," I say, breaking the silence, and speaking over his harsh breathing. "This is a real treat for me."

"It is?" he asks.

He's still shaking, and I've noticed he has been pretty much since he arrived. Nerves. Excitement. Desire. He's in physical overdrive, and I can imagine every sensation is heightened right now. The newness alone of being touched, of being in another man's arms, must be overwhelming, and the addition of the dynamic between us—the Daddy/boy play, the command in my tone, his easy submission—must be staggering to him.

"Yes, this is when I'll see my true boy."

"'True boy,'" he echoes, already dropping into subspace. I wonder if he even knows what that is or that he's in it. I'll have to do plenty of aftercare. I certainly won't be hustling him out of the door tomorrow morning, either. I'll need to make sure he's safe to drive after our night together.

I smooth my fingers through his hair before trailing down his back to cup his ass. I push one plump cheek aside before taking up the heavily lubed nozzle in my other hand. "No one is more real than when they're exposed in this way," I say.

He tenses slightly, and I rub his ass cheek until it loosens again.

"Now, believe me, sweet boy, this is a gift you're giving me. Understand?"

Matthew nods, and his breathing grows shallower as I slip the nozzle between his ass cheeks and smear some of the excess lube over his hole. Teasing him with the nozzle, making sure he's slick, I test his entrance. There's some tension, so I back off and gently fuck the tip in and out until he lets out a strangled sort of sigh. I push again, and he opens to the insertion with just a little pressure.

With the nozzle settled, I let go and just let him feel it in there. I stroke his arms, legs, hips, and into his hair, cooing to him. He's still breathing shallowly, and I check to see if he's gotten hard again after coming. He hasn't. I feel sure it won't be long.

It'll surprise him, I think, when he gets another erection after blowing such a big load. Guys his age don't expect that kind of easy recovery, but I know he's too aroused for any other option. He'll get hard out of sheer submission to me. I can feel it.

"Daddy?" he says, and he sounds so young—holy shit, so, *so* young, despite his salt-and-pepper hair, the slight fans of wrinkles by his eyes, and the sleek body fur on his front.

"Yes, boy?"

"I've never done this in front of anyone before."

I tell him, "That's what makes this special."

"But I haven't done *any* of this before," he reminds me. "It's all special, Daddy."

"Yes, but after you do this for me, you won't be ashamed of anything else we do all night. This is the thing that'll be the hardest for you to share. Afterward, you'll be my sweet boy completely. You'll give me everything, and you won't be ashamed."

He shivers, and I can tell he doesn't know if he believes me.

To be fair, I'm not sure what I'm saying is actually true, especially given Matthew's life and upbringing. And his age. There's more shame to break through with him than I normally encounter.

But he won't try to hide his face in orgasm after he's done *this* in front of me. He won't try to hold back out of modesty when I pleasure him or ask him to pleasure me. He'll remember that he's already given me the most shameful act of his body. The thing all humans like to keep secret and private.

That's why I always start with this. I learned this technique from my Dominatrix in college. She stripped me bare just this same way.

"I'm ready, Daddy," he says. I can't understand how he can still sound so innocent at his age.

My dick is aching. I rubbed one out earlier before he arrived, so I'd have more control, but I'm still shocked by my arousal. I always love the first time with a new boy. I love the introduction to kink. I love watching them struggle with the enema. I love everything about the first encounter.

But this is exceptional. There's a magnetism to Matthew I can't deny. I want to rub my hands over his furry front and tease his cock back to life. I yearn to stand and jerk myself off until he's coated with my cum as he takes his enema.

But I don't want to lose my load quite yet. I need to keep my stamina. The longer I wait, the better the orgasm will be, and I want him to see me lose it. He should see me shake and shudder and hear me cry his name. My release and pleasure, knowing he's the reason for it, will pump his ego in a way he desperately needs.

So, no quick orgasm.

No seeing him striped by my jizz.

Later, I'll show him how much he turns me on.

For now, he'll take the water I give him and hold it until I say, and then he'll show me his true face. His shame. And his surrender.

I'll show him that I can accept him—love him—through it.

CHAPTER TEN

Matthew

I T'S SURREAL.

I'm naked in Erik's bathtub, an enema nozzle in my ass, slowly taking in warm water, as he bends over me, watching, caressing my hair, and murmuring encouragement.

The difference in position between us is striking. Me: naked and vulnerable, taking what he's giving me, struggling to accept what's happening. Him: shirtless now, but wearing jeans and socks, confident, aroused but at ease with it, and commanding me with his firm, gentle hands.

How did I wake up in my bed this morning, same as ever, only to be here now? To be doing this weird, shameful, embarrassing thing with this sexy, strong, handsome, and still-half-dressed man?

"Take off your pants," I say, as if our power imbalance will be righted by him removing his jeans, as if I'm not voluntarily in this position, taking his care and commands by choice.

"Mm-mm, nope," he murmurs, trailing his fingers down my back, causing goosebumps to rise, and a shiver to take me. "I'll take them off when I'm ready. Right now, we're cleaning you up. Getting you prepared for what I have in these jeans."

I squeeze my eyes shut. Am I truly ready for that? Is he going to fuck me as soon as we're done?

I hope so.

I'm scared he will.

It feels like we're moving at a million miles per hour, hurtling through space and time, and yet we're cocooned right here, in this quiet, clean bathroom, where all I hear is the soft rushing of the water in the tube, his steady breaths, and the tiny sounds I can't help but make as my colon fills, and the sense of pressure inside becomes distracting.

"Getting full, boy?"

I nod.

"Almost there," he agrees. "Just a little more. You can hold a little more for Daddy, can't you?"

I nod, keeping my eyes shut, squeezing my anus around the nozzle. I feel full in a strange way I never have before. Liquid warmth rolls inside me.

"There," he says, turning the valve off so the water stops. "Daddy's going to remove the nozzle now. Try your best to hold the water in, all right?"

I nod again. Words have left me, or so I think, until he says, "What's the color right now, boy? You feeling all right? Are we at yellow, or are we still green? Red's okay too."

"Green," I whisper. I don't know what I'm doing, and I'm not sure this is what I wanted when I bought this night at the auction, but I'm in this far. I'm not backing out now. Besides, I have water up my ass; it must come out. There's nothing to be done about that.

"Good boy," he says, stroking my hair again. "That's Daddy's good boy. Taking this so well. So brave."

I whimper. No one's ever called me brave. I've always been too shrinking and withdrawn. That's part—though certainly not all—of what was missing when I'd mistakenly pursued music. The bravery to actually *pursue* it.

Like I'm pursuing this night with Erik.

With *Daddy*.

I love calling him that. It feels so right to me. I want to wallow in the sound of it, the feel of it on my lips.

"Daddy," I say quietly, touching my lower abdomen, feeling the slight pressure from the fluid inside. "I need to go."

"You can't hold it?"

I shake my head.

"You can," Daddy says. "Look at you, being so good for me. You've done well so far, and I know you can hold it for…" He glances at the chunky watch on his wrist and smiles. "Thirty-four more seconds."

I wonder if that's a number he's made up, or if there's a reason he's chosen it, but I don't ask. I figure I can do almost anything for thirty-four seconds, surely, so I breathe in and out, noting the cramps starting in my colon, the urge to push and expel the water.

"Twenty-eight, twenty-seven…"

He continues the count, and sweat slides down the sides of my face as the numbers seem to take forever, especially near the end.

"Five, four…"

I open my eyes. The starkness of the white tub, the way my skin contrasts with it, and all the brown hair on my forearms, legs, and belly looks rich in this light, thick and soft. I breathe in. I breathe out. I shiver.

"One." Daddy rises from where he's crouched by the tub and puts his hand out to me. "Hold your anus tight, boy. Keep all of it inside until you're on the toilet."

I'm hot all over. I'm sure my cheeks have flushed red, as well as my chest, but I'm so embarrassed by what I know must come next, *and* so eager to get it over with that I would have hustled to the toilet if Daddy hadn't slipped his arm around my waist, and walked me carefully to the clean, white throne.

"Easy now," he says. "Keep it in until Daddy says you can go."

I search his face as anxiety spirals inside me. "I can't."

"You can. Try." He kisses my cheek and helps me sit on the

toilet. He squats in front of me, his expression keen, and his eyes on mine. "This is the hardest part."

I squeeze my eyes closed, trying to hold the liquid inside me, feeling the almost irresistible urge to push it out. But I fight it off. My heart pounds, my legs shake, and my teeth grind. I keep release at bay.

"So beautiful," he murmurs, carding his fingers through the damp hair at my temples. "Working so hard for Daddy right now. I love that. Thank you."

I groan, but keep the liquid locked in tight.

"Open your eyes," he says, and it sounds so gentle that I can't believe something that tender is directed at me. "Look at Daddy."

I take a steadying breath, slow in through my nose, and then release it even more slowly from my mouth. When I feel sure that by unscrewing my eyes, I won't unscrew my anus, too, I obey.

He's so handsome. The brown of his eyes is muted now, soft with a calm, sweet regard. His mouth is tipped into a gentle smile, and his jaw is relaxed, his brows unfurrowed.

He takes hold of my hands, strokes the backs of them with his thumbs. "I want you to look right at me, Matthew, right in my eyes…and let go."

I swallow hard, a shock of appalled nerves shooting through me. I can't resist him, though. I don't even try. I stare into his eyes, feel the stroke of his thumbs on my knuckles, and give in.

Sucking in a quivery breath, I blush hard as it all pours out of me.

He nods reassuringly and hums, "That's my good boy. Let it all out. So brave. You're so brave, Matthew."

I whimper, hot all over and embarrassed to my core, but he leans over and plants a kiss on my lips. Not a sexy one. Not a quick peck either. But a long, comforting press with a wet *pop* at the end.

"Now, wipe yourself."

He watches as I do, and it's dreamlike and weird. I see that he's not aroused by this. His jeans aren't distended in front the way they were when we'd been making out, not even the way they had been when he was putting the nozzle in my ass and filling me with the water. No, he doesn't seem turned on by what we've just done, just *pleased*. Calm and relaxed.

While I'm a shaking, shuddering mess. Wow.

"Now I've seen you at your most vulnerable, boy."

I swallow again, jittering as I sit on the toilet, not sure what happens now.

"*And* you let me watch."

I gaze at him, trying to understand what he's telling me, but I'm out of my depth for sure now. I'd told him I wanted him to control everything I did this weekend, and if this is part of it…

I don't hate it.

I feel exposed, and it's fucking weird, but his expression, his tone, makes it all seem like I've done what he wanted me to do, and that's *rewarding*.

"Let's get you cleaned up."

He leans over me, flushes the toilet, and then pulls me off the seat, closing the lid after. He puts his arm around my waist again and helps me to the shower area, checking that the temperature is set to something good, and guides me under the rainfall shower-head.

He steps right in with me, even though his jeans get soaked. As the water sluices over my shoulders and down my back, he wraps his arms around me, pulling me against his wet jeans and his naked upper body. He rubs his hand over my chest hair, and traces my body fur to my soft cock.

"Mm, such a pretty dick you have, boy."

I gaze at it as he runs a finger along the side, and my cock thickens under his soft strokes, growing by the second.

"Look at how you respond to me. Daddy knows what his boy needs."

Daddy reaches for a bottle of body wash, uncaps it, and puts it near my nose. "Does my boy like this scent?"

I take a whiff—something strawberry-ish and otherwise nondescript. I nod.

"Good." He pours some into his hand and starts to wash me. I wince as he cleans my ass, but he just makes another soothing sound and continues, like this is his job and he likes doing it.

"All this hair on you, boy. It's a beautiful thing," he says, lathering up my chest and stomach and then my pubes. My cock is at full salute now, and he washes all around it, soaping up my balls and perineum, but avoiding my shaft entirely.

"You were so good just now, with the enema. I want you to know that," he says, kissing my neck after the water has washed away the suds. "I'm so proud of you. Are you proud of yourself?"

"I don't know, Daddy."

"No? Tell me how it made you feel."

"Embarrassed."

"Mm-hmm." He washes my asshole again, but this time, he starts truly playing with it, fingering the rim, tapping at the entrance, but not actually pushing inside. "And?"

"And shy."

"Yes."

I swallow and add something disconcertingly true. "And relieved."

"Mm-hmm, how were you relieved?" He slides his hand from my ass, rinses it off in the water, and gets more of the soap.

I answer him as I watch him suds his hands again. "Physically. The pressure and cramps stopped."

"Is that all?"

"I was relieved that…" A wash of shame hits me, and I duck my head.

"Now, Matthew, show Daddy your face," he says, taking hold of my hard dick and pumping it with his sudsy palm.

I force myself to look at him, afraid he might stop touching me if I don't.

"Tell me, what were you relieved about?"

"Relieved that I didn't have a choice."

"In what way?"

"I could have said the safe word, and it would have stopped, and I would have—" I gasp as he twists his palm over the head of my cock. Gulping, I grab him around the waist so we're both supporting each other as he strokes me.

The water pours around us. His jeans are soaked and feel rough where I'm touching him. His hand, though, is perfection— heaven—and I want him to keep jerking me.

"You would have?" he urges me to continue.

"I would have used the bathroom alone."

"But you didn't want that?"

"I wanted to do this with you," I say. "To do what Daddy asks of me. To...to *show* you."

"And what'd I see?"

"Me. Doing...that."

"How do you feel about me watching?"

I pant lightly, the pleasure of his strokes on my cock catching up with me. "I...feel...seen."

"Yes, and what a beautiful sight you were."

Much to my disappointment, he releases my dick, and turns me to face into the shower stream, rinsing the suds from my front side. He walks behind me, wrapping his arms around me, and slides his palms over my front. His hard cock rubs against my ass, still encased in his soaked jeans. He's definitely into my body hair, and I don't mind. So long as he wants to touch me. I'm hopeful he isn't doing all this just because I bought him.

"I'm going to tell you something, Matthew."

"Yes, Daddy?"

"I've never had a boy *not* try to talk me out of the enema during our first experience."

I don't like the reminder that he's had other boys, but I feel like prancing and preening that I'm the only one who's never fought him.

His voice is quiet in my ear as he goes on. "The others have always been a bit of a brat about it, even though none of them opted to use their safe word."

"A 'brat?'"

"Arguing, trying to disobey, trying to stall. Crying. Begging me to turn my back. But you just did what I asked of you, *when* I asked it, and without making a fuss. It was beautiful, boy. The sweetest surrender. All that gorgeous trust. Sublime."

"I had to go." I explain, which is true.

He chuckles. "So did they. Believe me. But you…you gave me such a beautiful gift with that moment of submission, Matthew. Just like when you came for me earlier. You love being at Daddy's command, don't you?"

I nod, feeling dizzy with the truth of it.

"You're full of presents for Daddy, Matthew. I can't wait to unwrap them all."

I let him lead me out of the shower, rub me down with a thick towel, and then—after admiring me from head to toe, like he truly does see me as his very own Christmas gift—he hands me the boxer briefs he wants me to wear. He watches as I put them on.

When I see the trick to them, I gasp, and he laughs.

"Open in the back for easy access." He slips a hand over my hip, around to my ass, and pushes his fingers inside the neatly sewn opening there. "A roommate of mine makes these and some other, fancier lingerie for men. But I think simple black boxer briefs with that charmingly placed hole are the sexiest. I don't need lace and garters. I just want *access*."

I shiver as he slides his fingers into my crack and over my hole. Just a brush to tantalize me before he pulls away. "Let's go, boy. There's a lot to do and too little time to do it."

I let him take my hand and lead me from the room, though my heart skips a sad beat at that reminder of the shortness of our time.

CHAPTER ELEVEN
Erik

MATTHEW IS A dream submissive; there's no doubt about that. I can't imagine what a capital-letter Sadist might do to him—what Matthew might *let* him do.

I'm grateful to whatever God there might be that Matthew found me and didn't bid on the well-known sadist Greg Houser's offering five posters down from mine.

As I lead Matthew out of the bathroom, holding his hand, I guide him toward the bed intending to relieve him of various aspects of his inexperience. The remnants of his cologne, the one I'd admired the first time we met, trail after him, laced with the lingering scent of the soap I'd lathered him up with.

Tenderness blooms, and I want to rub my nose all over him, breathe him in. After I've taught him a few things about sex, I plan to take him downstairs and get a warm fire started, cuddle him on the sofa, and teach him about affection.

I'd intended to bake Christmas cookies with him this weekend, but my mother made a batch before she left—decorated them too—so there's no need for that. I have presents, but those are for tomorrow morning before he goes. And aside from sex, there isn't much else he's listed as being important to him—except for the cuddling, feeling cared for, and loved.

I'm going to make sure there's plenty of that before I have to send him on his way tomorrow.

But first things first.

Matthew is hard as a rock again and desperate to come, though he won't admit it or ask for more. He's dropped into subspace like a rock in a pond. I've never seen an inexperienced sub go so willingly into that mental bliss, but he's there. Lost in that floaty place where time and space stop existing, where it's just you and your Dom, or your Daddy, as the case may be, and you're living for the moment with him.

"That's good," I tell him as we come to a stop in front of the bed. "Take the underwear off and put them on the night table."

He frowns. "I just put them on."

I smile. There's the man I met the other night, the observant one, the one who surprises me. Apparently, even in subspace, he's sharp.

"Daddy wanted to make sure they fit properly. They do. Take them off."

He blinks at the underwear before shoving them off his hips, down his long, lightly muscled and hairy thighs, and kicks them over his feet. Picking them up from the floor, he folds them into a square, placing them on the bedside table neatly, just as I've asked.

"Now, come here." I take him to the wide sofa and sit him on the edge of it. I run my fingers through his hair again—it's soft, and I love how the silver glistens between the brown strands. "Wait here. Daddy's going to be right back."

Matthew watches me go but doesn't move. I head back into the bathroom and open the walk-in closet. Stepping inside, I tug my wet jeans off with some effort, and remove my socks before looking at my set of toys. Most of what I want to do with Matthew will be as natural as possible, without implements, but there are times when...

I pluck the items I might want, and grab a new bottle of lube, too.

His eyes widen when he sees me naked, and he gulps as he scans me from head to toe, his gaze lingering on my hard cock as I walk. It juts out in front of me, bouncing with each step, and I smirk as he blinks rapidly at the size of it. I'm thick, so my dick can be intimidating for some when they first see it, but I'm always careful with the people I fuck. Matthew is going to be well-prepared to take me when the time comes.

"Like what you see?"

He nods, and I smile again. Matthew's so quiet, and I desperately want to see if he gets loud when I start touching him. I think, given the sounds he made when we were making out and when he came earlier, he's going to be a very rewarding instrument to play.

"I might use these a little later," I tell him, showing him the blindfold, and the scarf I could use to bind his hands or feet, if the mood hits me, and if it seems right for him, too. I put them aside, showing him the bottle of lube. "This is also for later. But I'll be using it sooner than I'll be using those."

He shivers and nods.

"What do you say?"

"Thank you, Daddy."

I stroke his hair again. He's so good. So very good. I'd expected a "Yes, Daddy," or an "I understand, Daddy," but "Thank you?" Matthew is a natural. An absolutely delicious dream.

"Matthew?"

"Yes?"

"Daddy is so happy you're here with him tonight."

"You are?"

"Yes, I am."

He blushes, and his lashes touch his cheekbones. "Thank you, Daddy. I knew you could help me. When I saw the photos... I knew."

"Let me help you now."

"All right," he agrees with such guileless need my insides turn to mush. If I'm not cautious, I might mess up and have real feelings for this guy, because he's just so damn pliant and eager.

I love that in a boy.

I take my cock in hand. "Daddy's dick needs attention."

"What do I do?"

"Open up. Let Daddy show you."

Matthew dutifully opens his mouth, and his eyes don't leave my face as I approach. I place the head of my cock between his lips, rubbing it over his hot tongue before combing my fingers through his hair gently, murmuring, "Suck."

His eyes stay on mine, desperate, wanting, as he closes his lips around me. He keeps his teeth carefully back from my flesh. He's terrible at this, but his clear-eyed need is refreshing and sweet, so I hum encouragement as he sucks what he can of my dick, bobbing up and down and tonguing the slit.

I'm not going to come from this, no way, but it's good to let him feel me out. I let him work for some time, giving him guidance now and again about what I like "—hold my balls, that's it, pull off and lick the shaft, so good—" and when his lips are swollen and red, even redder than that night downtown when we were out in the cold, and he couldn't keep his teeth from his bottom lip, I finally pull out.

"Good job, Matthew. Now open again and let Daddy help you take him a little better."

That's when I take hold of his head and press my thumbs lightly into his jaw until he opens. Using my hips, I guide myself into his open mouth, pushing the head of my dick against the inside of his cheeks, feeling the slickness of them. I tell him to stick his tongue out as far as he can.

When he does, I press the hinge of his jaw again until he's wide open. I take my time sinking in until I hit the back of his throat. His eyes soften, and I realize how much better he is at this part. His gag reflex isn't strong at all. I push into his throat.

Matthew's face is flushed bright red, and his eyes go glassy with lust. I smile, holding myself there until he begins to struggle to pull breath around me. I draw back. Saliva strings from his lips to my cock. His chest is heaving, his eyes are full of reflexive tears, and his lips are still that bright red I can't resist.

"Matthew, that was so good, letting Daddy into your throat like that." I sink to my knees in front of him and take his chin. I kiss him, and his lips are hot on mine. When I pull away, I gaze into his eyes and praise him. "I'm so proud of you, and you're learning so well. Let Daddy reward you for your work."

"But you didn't come," he rasps.

"Because I come when I decide the time is right," I say, thumbing that sweet dimple. "The time's not quite right." He frowns, dissatisfied, and I laugh. "Is my boy upset he didn't get to drink my cum?"

He nods.

"You like cum?"

"Love it."

"You'll like it even more in your ass. And Daddy only has so many loads in him, sweet boy. I'm gonna make them last."

"Fuck."

I laugh. "Oh, sweet Matthew. Look at me."

He meets my gaze again, all hazel wildness, and I kiss his lips before I say, "This is your reward for letting Daddy watch."

I bend and engulf his cock.

"Daddy!" he cries, his hands coming to my head and gripping hard. I don't complain, letting him squeeze and try to grasp my short hair. I deepthroat him relentlessly. I'm good at this, and he's so inexperienced, and this is such a fresh sensation to him that he doesn't last long.

"Daddy, please," he whimpers. "Daddy, Daddy!" And then he surprises me, yelling, "Daddy, *help*!"

I grip his hips, taking his cock as deep as possible, and swallowing around him.

"Help me, Daddy," he cries. His cum shoots into my throat as he seizes up, shouting with pleasure.

When he's shaking and spent, I let his cock slip from my mouth, and sit back on my heels. I wipe my lips with the back of my hand. Matthew stares at me, his pupils blown wide, and his pulse thrumming in his throat.

"Matthew," I say, and my voice is a little wrecked from the deepthroating.

"Yes, Daddy?"

"Did you come in Daddy's throat without warning him?"

He blinks rapidly and looks down, pink staining his cheeks. "I'm sorry, Daddy."

"Are you?"

He nods.

"How do you feel right now?"

"Ashamed."

"Why?"

"I came in your throat." Matthew groans and covers his face, flopping back onto the wide sofa. "I should have told you, but…I couldn't."

I climb up next to him, stroking his arm. "You cried out for help."

His eyes dart to the side. "When I was young…" he stops and gulps a breath.

I wait, but when he doesn't continue, I prompt him. "Go on."

Matthew sighs.

"I've seen you at your most vulnerable, Matthew. Nothing you say can be more embarrassing than that, can it?"

"I don't know. Maybe." He takes a shivering, panting breath, curling onto his side. I stroke his shoulder, as he buries his face against my naked hip. I let him hide as he tells me his truth. "I used to pray for God to help me to stop feeling this way."

"To stop feeling gay?"

"Yeah. Once, when I was really scared because I couldn't stop wanting men, I went to my dad, and I asked him… I *begged* him. I said, 'Daddy, help me. Please help me.' But I couldn't explain what I meant. I couldn't admit it or tell him what I was. I just wanted him to take it away."

"What did he say?"

"Nothing. He hugged me. That's all."

I ponder this. "And just now when I was sucking you? You wanted it to stop, to be taken away? You can say red, or stop, or—"

"No!" Matthew says, pulling his face from my hip and looking at me with a frantic gleam in his eyes. "I didn't want you to stop. I didn't. I'd have died if you stopped."

I comb my fingers through his hair. "Then what was going on?"

"I felt…shame. About how much I want this, and how good it is. I didn't want to feel ashamed, but I was, Daddy. I'm so sorry."

I slide my fingers over his cheek to where the dimple shows when he smiles. It's not there now. "And you wanted my help to not feel ashamed? You want Daddy's help?"

"Yes," he whispers.

"I'll help you, Matthew. And I'll make you come even if you *are* ashamed. You'll never be denied with me."

"Please, Daddy," he begs, his eyes filling with tears. "Please."

"Please, what? Is there anything you need specifically right now?"

"Please love me."

I kiss the side of his face and draw him up into my arms. "I do, Matthew. Tonight, I do."

Deep down, I think I can love him for longer than tonight. If only I weren't recovering from a breakup, and if he didn't live so far away—but that's a flimsy excuse, isn't it? I can love him longer.

If I allow myself.

CHAPTER TWELVE

Matthew

I SLEEP LIKE a child, hard and deep.

When I wake, I'm so relaxed I think I'm in my comfortable bed at home, until I recognize Daddy's big, strong arms around me.

At first, I freeze, afraid to move for fear of waking the shame that has lived inside me for as long as I've been aware of the filthy, urgent sexual things I want, and for fear of what might come next between me and Daddy as well.

My mind spins through every moment since I stepped out of my car and into this new space and time with Erik. Everything about it feels surreal but it's also the most fiercely authentic experience of my life.

The sandwich I ate when I first arrived seems ages ago and like a dream. The horses and goats, even the dogs, feel like figments of my imagination, and yet I felt them all with my own hands. And the review of our contract for our time together…

My cock stirs at the memory of how intense Daddy had seemed as he'd gone over every item, confirmed it, and solicited my verbal consent yet again. And then how he'd shone with power as he'd led me by the hand up the stairs to his bathroom…

Holy fuck. What had happened next! I'd let Erik take charge of me. I'd allowed him to control even my bowels. I'd done it willingly, and I'd *liked* it.

My cheeks go hot, my dick grows even thicker, and my balls tingle as I recall the terror and excitement of allowing myself to be

Erik's boy.

"Hungry?" The breath of the word washes over my ear. I shiver in his arms. "Thirsty?"

I don't want to move or open my eyes, but Daddy knows I'm awake, and so I stir, turning to him. I press my face to his strong chest. He strokes my hair as I huddle against him, breathing in his scent. His cock lengthens and smears pre-cum between us. He doesn't push or comment, though.

I turn my head, pressing my cheek to his pec, and I open my eyes. It's peaceful here on the giant sofa, covered with a light blanket, and drifting in the pale light from the window. I sigh as Daddy kisses the top of my head.

"What color are we, boy?" Daddy asks, his voice a rumble in my ear. "Red, yellow, green?"

"Yellow," I admit. I want to say green. I'm horny still, and want to come again, but I'm overwhelmed. I don't know what happens next. I know all that we've agreed to do together, but not knowing the specific "how" of each activity is its own kind of anxiety. While I'm still processing what we've just done, the idea of something more is too much to take.

"Good boy," he whispers. "Thank you for being honest when you need to go slow." He holds me tighter, and I melt against him. It feels so good to be in his arms, to have his strength around me.

I haven't felt *this* safe since I was a child in my father's arms, since before I felt my first hint of sexual desire, since before I knew my father would never accept me or approve of what I fantasized about.

Tension grows and then breaks. A small sob breaks free.

"That's it," Daddy says, rubbing my back and kissing my head again. "Feel that feeling. Just let it come."

I hold on to him, and tears prick my eyes as he murmurs encouragement. The world tilts and rights itself, over and over, like

I'm on an amusement-park ride.

"My father would be ashamed of me."

Daddy says nothing at all for a long moment. "Maybe so, but *I'm* proud of you, Matthew. You're a beautiful man, and a wonderful boy. Your heart is pure, and—listen to me, this is important—your needs are valid."

"I need too much," I say; his heartbeat is steady and certain beneath my ear.

"Tell Daddy what you need."

I hesitate, because *a lot* is coursing through me—emotions, thoughts, fantasies, memories—and I'm not sure what will come out if I open my mouth.

Daddy strokes my back again. "What do you need, Matthew?"

"So much," I gasp.

"Get it out. Just say the words."

"I need to be held down and fucked," I say, my voice breaking. "I need to be chased, and caught, and choked."

"Go on, boy."

"I need to be forced to come."

"All right."

"I need...I need..." I bite my lip, and tears slip over my lashes and down my cheeks. Fuck, I'm a mess. He doesn't need this shit. I should go. I should stop ruining his day with my—

"Tell Daddy what you need," he says again, firmly. "Tell me everything."

"I need to be loved!" I cry.

A floodgate opens, as hiccupping sobs take over. Daddy holds me through it, rocking me, telling me again, "Your needs are valid, Matthew. *You're* valid. You deserve to be loved."

He doesn't say I deserve to be chased and choked, or held down and fucked, but when I finally stop making a fool of myself, he helps me sit, hands me a tissue from the box near the sofa, and watches as I wipe my eyes before he says, "I'll hold a boy's throat, but I don't choke my boys. There *are* other Daddies who do that."

I shake my head. "I don't know, I don't know…"

"You don't know what?"

"I don't know if I *want* that? I just sometimes *need* it."

He touches my cheek in that way he likes, and as he fingers the place where my dimple shows, he tilts my head up and asks, "What's the difference to you in those words? 'Want' and 'need?"

"I…want to love myself," I say.

He nods.

I can't look at him as I go on. "But I need to give up control because I can't do this—"

"Do what exactly? Specify, please."

"I can't even think about having sex without feeling ashamed. I don't want to feel that way anymore. I'm trying not to, but it keeps happening anyway. But, in my fantasies, if someone *makes* me? If I'm forced? It's not my fault…"

"Is that why you let men use your mouth?"

I nod. "That way, it's not my fault. If they use me, and I don't come? If I hate it and myself afterward, I'm still innocent."

"Oh, Matthew," Daddy says, tugging me into a hug. "Sweet boy, you are always innocent. Always."

"Am I?"

"Yes."

"But—"

"Matthew, when I fuck you, it's going to be because you ask me to and when you come, it's going to be because you wanted me to bring you to orgasm."

"But Daddy?"

"Yes?"

"When I…when I begged for help earlier?"

He nods.

It's so humiliating to say. I see his eyes soften, encouraging me with just a look, and I force myself to admit, "It made it feel so good? It made it better?"

"Mm, I see." He gazes into my eyes. "We're in a little bit of a conundrum then."

"Why?" My throat tightens. This is it. This is when he tells me that what I want isn't right, and the shame will own me, and I'll shrink enough to crawl under this sofa and die. To make it worse, my stomach picks this moment to rumble.

"This is a conversation to have over food," Daddy says, standing and putting his hand out to me. "Let's go downstairs and refuel."

I want to protest. I want him to tell me that I'm too much for him to handle and for him to send me home. More than that, I want him to hold me close and tell me that I'm lovable. I want him to flip me over, spread my cheeks, and fuck my hole mercilessly. I want all these things at once, but I definitely *don't* want to go downstairs.

His hand is still there in front of me, his naked body so strong and handsome, the light from the windows outlining every muscle, sinew, and scar. I swallow hard, take a breath, and fall back to the role I've agreed to play tonight.

"Yes, Daddy," I say, and let him pull me to my feet.

He picks up the assless boxer briefs I discarded earlier and hands them to me. I put them on, and he takes a moment to admire how I look. I feel silly and embarrassed by all we've said and done so far, but there's no disguising the heat in his eyes. He wants me again. I haven't disgusted him with this show of perversion and weakness at least.

Erik crosses to open a drawer in the chest near the bed and pulls out sweatpants. He tugs them on. Reaching out his hand to me again, he praises me when I take it. "Good boy." Sliding his arm around my shoulders, he guides me toward the stairs, and I'm aware of all the places our skin touches as we move.

"My mom made Christmas cookies," he says as we start down the risers. "Iced and everything. We'll have a few of those to get your blood sugar up before we talk."

I don't want to talk now. I want to eat cookies, open the stocking I've been promised, crawl on my knees to wherever Daddy is sitting, and suck his dick until I taste his pre-cum, and then…

"Matthew," Daddy says. "Stop thinking so loudly. It's Daddy's job to take care of you. I know what you need."

"Do you?" I ask as we hit the bottom riser, and step together onto the main floor of the lodge.

"You just told me." He tugs me around, so my back is to the counter dividing the kitchen from the dining room space. I'm facing him as he steps close, pushing me so the edge digs into my hip. He holds me with enough strength I'd have to struggle hard to escape him.

Erik's lips are delicious and slow, and I throw my arms around his neck as he kisses me. My knees go weak, and I'm dizzy with lust as I start to hump his leg while he lets the kiss draw out. When he breaks away, mouth red and his breath coming in pants, he slides a hand up over my chest to take hold of my throat.

He doesn't choke me, but he holds me there, gazing into my eyes. My hips keep flexing against his thigh, and if he grips even a little tighter, I think I'll come. But his hand remains a little too loose for that.

"Daddy," I whimper. "Please."

"What do you want?"

"Choke me."

He leans his head close and rubs our noses together slowly. "Tell me what you really want, sweet boy."

"Make me."

"Make you what?"

"Make me come!" I groan as the shame flows over me. It's sinful wanting this. My father would hate me, my mother would be ashamed, and my community would…

"Feel that?" he asks.

"What?" I feel nothing but arousal and the tormenting shame that's followed me my whole life.

"If I make you come now," he says calmly, as if he knows for sure he can, and quite easily, too. "If you come just like this, feeling these emotions, it will be explosive, sweet boy. Because the thing is, shame can make it hotter. Filthier. Shame can make you shoot so hard you see stars."

I pant and seek his mouth, but he holds me away, that little bit of extra grip on my throat making my balls tighten. I'm just about to come when he says, "Don't do it. Don't come yet, boy."

I groan and grit my teeth. "I need to, Daddy."

"You're doing great. Just hold on. Let Daddy tell you something important first."

I shake as pleasure arcs through me, and orgasm seems nearly inevitable as I hump his leg, but I focus my attention on where the counter is digging into me, the unpleasant irritation of it, and I close my eyes on Daddy's intense gaze.

"Tell me, Daddy. Please."

"Stop humping me," he says. His tone feels like affection, but also like an order.

I take a shuddering breath and still my hips.

"Daddy doesn't want you soiling these yet," he says, sliding his other hand around my hip over the waistband of my boxer briefs. He opens the fly and works my cock free. Each rough touch is almost enough to tip me over, so I bite into my lower lip to hold back.

"Now," he says. "Tell me about your father, boy. What was he like?"

I shake my head. I don't want to think of him. "Please, Daddy."

"Because it's not sexy?"

I nod.

"Too bad. What would your dad think of you right now, hungry and hard, and trying to rub off on me? What would he say?"

I suck in a ragged breath. "I don't know."

"What would he say?" Daddy demands.

"That I'm a sinner, that he's ashamed of me, that I'm no son of his."

"Imagine he's here now. He sees you."

I can imagine it all too easily, and my stomach turns over. I whimper.

"Good," he whispers. "Now, tell me again, boy. What do you want me to do to you?"

"I want you to..." I can still imagine my father's disgust. "I want you to fuck me."

"Mm. And?"

"I need to come. Make me come, Daddy. *Make me come.*"

"Not yet," he says, kissing my cheek. I want to scream, but I can't even pull in a solid breath between all my panting and near-sobbing. "How does it feel to beg for Daddy's dick? To want his cum in your ass?"

"Like I need it to live."

"You need Daddy's cum more than you want your father's love, don't you?"

The words hang in the air, and I can feel the potential behind them, something hard and forbidding. "Yes," I admit.

"That's my boy," he says, fiercely, and strokes his hand over my dick.

Crying out, I shoot, coming with a rough, hot force that's heavy with shame and embarrassment and a sick sense of loss, but also carrying a shimmery top note made from a defiant, beautiful spark of truth. I spurt onto the wooden floor, the heat of my seed hitting our bare feet and dotting Daddy's sweatpants.

I'm still shaking as Daddy releases my neck and pushes on my shoulders until I'm down on my knees. My eyes roll up as he pushes his cock into my open mouth, and I tip my head back, letting him slip into my throat like the men who used me. He slides in and out slowly, his fingers tracing my eyebrows and cheekbones before slipping to grip my hair.

"Christ, boy. Gonna shoot in your throat." He lets loose a light growl. "So you can deepthroat but you can't suck yet. I'll teach you how. Don't worry. Holy shit, this is good. Look how deep you take me. Almost to my balls." He says all this in an awed tone, and once he's on the edge—I can tell by the shaking in his thighs, and the way his knees buckle—he takes hold of my face, and demands, "Watch Daddy come. Watch what you do to me."

And I do.

I stare as his chest flushes, and his pupils blow wide, and his face twists into a grimace. All the while, he stares down at me, his intensity pouring into me like light, and when he grunts, I feel the first jerk of his cock on my tongue.

I can't taste his cum as much as I'd like, with him thrust so deeply into my throat, but I swallow as best I can around him, taking his seed in. He curses before pulling free, cum and spit stringing from his cock to my mouth, and he wipes them away with his hand.

I stay on my knees, gazing at him as he stares down at me, strokes his thumbs over my eyebrows, and says, "Now cookies and cuddles, and *then* we'll talk about what just happened and why that was so damn good for you."

"Was it good for you, too, Daddy?" I ask, and my voice sounds rough, battered from the throat-fucking.

"Beyond good. Never fucked a throat so willing." He looks conflicted about that, but he leans low and kisses my forehead. "Get up. Put your cock away. Daddy's going to feed his sweet boy."

CHAPTER THIRTEEN

Erik

WE BOTH WASH our hands, and I take Matthew back to the sofa. "Get settled here," I command as I tuck some blankets around him. "Rest."

He stays upright, but barely. His gaze follows me to the fireplace, where I grab some logs from the stack by the hearth. Within a few minutes, I have a nice fire going for him. Matthew's drooping a little, despite the nap upstairs.

I'm not surprised after the emotional, messy connection we just made. That kind of intensity can take it out of a boy—and a Daddy, too, to be honest. But I don't have time to snuggle with him and drowse. Not quite yet. I need to take care of his other bodily needs.

Like water and food.

After washing the log residue and sap from my fingers, I go to the built-in pantry near the back of the room and retrieve the lap tray. I've prepared plenty of food for him in advance, so I have a Pyrex container of mixed fruit (cantaloupe, orange slices, and grapes) ready to go. I also have a hearty tofu stew in the instapot, so I ladle out bowlfuls for each of us.

Placing them on the lap tray, I glance over at him, and notice the way his gaze lingers on the Christmas tree before drifting to the red and white stockings on the mantel. When his eyes widen, I smile. He's noticed the little extra step I took.

I had Charles embroider his name across the top of one stocking, and mine across the top of the other: Matthew and Daddy. He takes a shuddery little breath, and I know it's pleased him.

I add the dessert—four of my mother's iced Christmas sugar cookies—and carry the tray to him. He sits up from his exhausted slump, and I place the tray over his legs, drop down beside him, and take up the spoon. I lift a bit of the soup to his mouth and murmur encouragement as he opens to let me feed him.

"Good boy." I wipe a stray drop from his lip with my thumb, licking it clean. Matthew obediently accepts a few more bites from me before I hand the spoon to him and pick up my own. "Go on, feed yourself," I say, as if he needs that permission.

Matthew blinks, drowsy and drugged by orgasm, the warm fire, and the shock of what he's shown me so far. It's been a long time since I've seen a man as easily tossed into subspace—if ever.

As I eat, I ask, "How do you feel?"

"Good," he says, simply.

"Dreamy? Loose? Like you're floating?"

He nods, focusing his big eyes my way before turning back to his soup and taking another bite.

I open the lid of the Pyrex container and indicate the fruit. "Eat some of that, too."

"Yes, Daddy." He chooses cantaloupe first, and chews it with his eyes closed, as if he's enjoying the taste and the wet slide in his throat.

"This is subspace."

He looks at me, brows furrowed.

"This feeling you have. You're not fully in it now, but you're still drifting there. You could go deeper, or you could pop up out of it and back to your usual state of mind."

His brows draw down even more.

"Do you like this?"

He nods.

"You're my boy in this space, aren't you, Matthew?"

"Daddy's boy," he whispers, placing a grape into his mouth.

"Yes." I stroke his head and return to eating. The grayness of the day lends an ethereal, otherworldly vibe to the light shining through the wide window by the downstairs sofa. It's foggy, and a light snow had begun while we played upstairs.

After a few more bites, I say, "Let's come out of that space a little. Daddy needs to talk to you."

Matthew shakes his head, frowning, and I'm surprised to see him resist me, but I'm pleased, too. He's not a doormat, even if he's the most submissive boy I've ever had—hardly even a hint of the brat in him.

"Yes, Matthew. Daddy needs his boy to listen with a clear head."

"All right," he agrees, still sounding distant and dreamy.

"Let's start by centering you here. Tell me five things you can see."

"The fire, my stocking, your stocking, the tree, the foggy mountains out the window."

"Tell me four things you can touch."

Matthew touches each thing as he says the words. "The blanket, the tray, the fruit, and you." His hand rests on my chest.

"That's good. Now, three things you can hear."

"The crackle of the fire, your breathing, and the heating unit kicking on and off."

"Two things you can smell."

"The soup. The pine scent of the Christmas tree."

"One thing you can taste."

"The tang of the grape I ate."

"You're here with me?"

Matthew meets my gaze, and his eyes are clearer than before. There's still a shine that tells me he's aroused and exhausted, but he's no longer floating away in his head. "Yes, Daddy."

"Good. Now eat and listen to me."

He nods, and I take another bite, pondering how to broach this without scaring him too much. "Matthew, shame isn't something you can necessarily excise from your life. Feeling it to some degree, especially when it's been indoctrinated from as young an age as yours was, can be inescapable."

He doesn't respond but continues to eat, alternating between soup and fruit.

"Loving yourself, learning to demand good things for your life doesn't mean you'll never feel ashamed of what you want, who you are, and what you crave. The key is to use that shame for the best outcome. When playing with shame, as we did earlier with the enema, and again by bringing your father's memory to mind while you begged for my cock—" He shifts, and his cheeks grow red in that way that's gorgeous in its intensity. "Playing with shame in those ways can be freeing, thrilling, and, as you saw for yourself, deeply arousing. You shot like a boy of fifteen today, didn't you? When's the last time you came this hard?"

"A long time, Daddy," he admits.

"How do you feel about what we did?"

"Embarrassed."

"What embarrasses you most?"

"That I imagined him here, seeing me, loathing me..." He puts down his spoon and takes a jerky breath. "That I *did* want your cum more than his approval. That's not just embarrassing; it's messed up. But the way I came? The way all that made me just—" He groans and shifts. "Fuck."

"Getting hard thinking about it?"

"Yes, Daddy." The shame is in his voice again.

"Daddy loves that."

Matthew meets my eyes. "I don't know if I'm a good person,"

he confesses. "Why did I come so hard, Daddy? Help me, please."

"Shh," I tell him, rubbing the back of his neck, and kissing his cheek. "That's my good, sweet boy. Just breathe a minute. Feel those feelings."

Once I'm sure he's not going to tip over into a panic, I go on, "You came so hard because coming for me, eating my cum, is a giant 'fuck you' to the way you were raised. Just like doing something 'bad' or 'wrong' can feel exciting because it's forbidden, the pleasure was amped up because you were being brave enough to confront those feelings head on. Pushing through them to ecstasy. Do you understand?"

Matthew ponders and nods. "It's still humiliating."

"That's fine. Daddy doesn't need you to feel any particular way about what we do, so long as you don't feel worse than you did before we touched."

"I don't. I feel…embarrassed, but relieved. Better."

"Good. Because I can hold your shame, boy. I can hold it, and mold it, and turn it into orgasms for you. Understand? That's in my power. It's in your power, too. Don't turn your back on the shame. Dive into it. Fuck it if you can. Ride it."

"Ride it," he whispers.

"Yes," I urge. "It'll be the most empowering thing you can do, to learn to manipulate the shame for your own pleasure. Then it will lose its power outside of scenarios set up and controlled by you and your Daddy, or your lover. Understand?"

"I think so."

"It's a lot to take in. Do you want to continue to play with shame tonight?"

He hesitates. "If Daddy wants to."

"But what do you want, boy? Tell me."

"I want you to fuck me," he says. "And I want to come for you. However Daddy makes that happen, I'm sure I'll be happy with it."

I kiss his forehead, and we start eating again. I fret slightly at his pliability. He's so sweet, so quick to agree. Another man, another Daddy or Dom might abuse this in him. I have one night to teach him about sex, kink, and shame, and how to negotiate his boundaries in a safe way. It's too much. I can't do it all tonight.

My stomach twists. I *can't* do more, though. Matthew doesn't tick any of my boxes.

He lives too far away.

He's middle-aged.

He's…

He's never said he wants more than this. I need to honor his wishes and not put pressure on him just because this feels right to me.

Still, I feel in my bones I can help him beyond this experience. There are so many things I can guide him through and pleasures I can help him embrace. Holy shit. Am I really contemplating the complexities of a long-distance Daddy/boy mentorship with an older man?

I think I am.

Damn.

CHAPTER FOURTEEN
Matthew

AFTER THE LATE snack Daddy prepared, there's more cuddling and watching the fire. It's unbelievable to me that this is real. I'm really wrapped up in another man's arms after all these years of yearning. My heart aches, and more than once, tears prick my eyes. I have to squeeze them shut to keep the tears from falling.

I know Daddy won't care if I cry again. He's already seen me sob like a baby and sit on the toilet, so leaking a few tears has nothing on the embarrassment of all that. And yet these tears are private. They're mine, and I'm not ready to share them.

Which may seem strange since I'm sharing so much else with Daddy, and most of it for the first time, but these tears are different. They're not new. They're very old. And I don't want him to soothe me or try to ease the reasons for them. All of it will have to be grieved in its own time. My therapist says so, and I know it must be true.

This evening, I'm in a man's arms, and I'm ashamed, but I'm happy. Most of all, I'm relieved.

While the snow piles up outside the window, lending a blue glow to the light from the early-rising moon, Daddy strokes me all over. It's hypnotizing and erotic, and I'm hard again before it seems humanly possible. Three orgasms in under twenty-four hours are already more than I've achieved in years.

Though I haven't had a reason to try for a record, like I did when I was in high school, and my parents were away for a weekend. I scored fifteen in less than a day back then, aided by the half-naked male models in underwear ads in the various catalogs my mother received.

I didn't see my first gay porn until my late twenties, when I bought a computer and kept it in my bedroom. I had a few marathon masturbation sessions after that, but in recent years, I've been too snowed under by responsibility and grief to want to wank for days.

I don't want to wank now, either. I want to *be* wanked, and kissed, and cuddled, to be sucked and fucked. I want to struggle against Daddy while he takes me to that glorious state of orgasm. I need to claw at the sheets and bite the pillow. I need to scream.

I wonder if he'll let me. I wonder if that's okay.

I suppose I'm going to find out.

But first, Daddy wants me to relax with him, to get used to being held by another man. As he strokes me, we listen to the soft, jazzy Christmas album he's put on the turntable after washing up our dishes. I soak it all in, melting into him, sweaty from the fire and the blanket, but unwilling to move a muscle unless it's to be fucked.

"This is what two men can be together. This and nothing more if that's what you want," Daddy says. "If it makes you feel loved."

"Oh, I want more," I say, and he chuckles.

"Most men do."

"But some men are happy with just this?"

"Yes."

"Any of your boys?"

"No, all of my boys have been sex fiends," he says with another rumble of quiet laughter. "Like you."

"Am I a sex fiend, Daddy?"

"For a virgin? Yes. Definitely so."

I smile, sitting up to straddle him. He cups my ass to still me, pressing me even more firmly against him. I'm hard, and my cock digs into his groin. He's *not* hard, but, as he holds me steady, I feel his dick begin to wake, fill, and throb next to mine.

"Let's start slow," he says.

I chuckle. "Daddy, we're way past slow."

He grips my ass tighter and kisses my chin. "We're hampered by just having one night," he explains. "Or I'd have taken more time with you."

If only we could have more than one night. Perhaps…

No. I have to stay in the now. This one night is what I bought.

Somehow, I know he wouldn't have gone much slower than this, no matter the circumstances or his intentions. He seems to get as swept away in the moment as I do, and the part of me that's never had a man's true interest feels like I could live off his avid regard alone. I could eat it like bread and butter, and it would feed my body and soul.

"Daddy?" I venture, feeling timid even after all we've done.

"Yes, boy?"

"Will you lick my hole?"

"How do you ask? I want to hear it nicely."

"Daddy, will you please lick my hole?"

"Ah, boy, you sound so sweet." Daddy slides his fingers into the opening at the back of my underwear and trails them into my crack. I shiver as he traces my hole with the pad of his middle finger. "Such a sweet, tight little hole, and it's all for Daddy, isn't it?"

"Yes, Daddy. All for you."

He growls lightly, and I grin. It's unreal to have this kind of effect on a man. I never imagined that I could.

"Fuck—" He rolls us over, so I'm underneath and he's on top. Sitting back on his haunches between my spread legs, he smiles at me. "First, let Daddy see it."

I nod and wait, but when Erik lifts his brows, I realize what he wants. I go hot all over, embarrassment rising despite everything, but I pull my legs back at the knees, canting my hips up, and feeling the open back of the underwear stretch wide.

The air in the room is warm from the fire, and a trickle of sweat slips down my crack. Erik presses my ass cheeks apart and regards my asshole. It's an evaluating look and an appreciative one. When he shifts his gaze to meet mine, he's got wide pupils and glassy eyes. He wants me.

Even now, I can't believe it. This sexy, younger Daddy wants me. Boring, accountant me. How is that possible?

And yet it is. It's undeniable. And not just because I see the evidence of his erection in his sweatpants. It's in his eyes, on his face, and even in how his fingers touch me: firm, sure, and yet so hungry somehow.

How can fingers be hungry? I don't know, but eyes can be too, and right now, Daddy's eyes are eating me up.

My breath catches as Daddy pulls my underwear off, tossing it over his shoulder. His focus never leaves me, gaze trailing over my skin in hot, almost palpable strokes. With another of those light growls, he tugs my chest hair, and skims his hands over my stomach, brushing against my hard cock.

"Such a fucking gorgeous boy," he whispers. "If you only knew what you do to me."

"What?" I ask, breathlessly. "What do I do to you, Daddy?"

"You make me want to forget you're a virgin. All this manliness, all this fucking gorgeous lithe muscle, and sinew." He touches me as he talks, trailing his fingers over my arms, shoulders, and down my pecs. "All this fucking hair," he whispers, sliding his hands over it again. "Delicious. Like a dessert. And I never knew…" He clears his throat, and his brows furrow. "Never even thought…"

"What didn't you think, Daddy?" I can't believe I'm talking right now, asking questions instead of insisting on him licking my hole as I'd asked. But I need to know what he's so surprised by, because I think it's something inside *him* and not about me at all. I've shown him so much of my vulnerability, and now, I want something in exchange.

"I didn't know how intoxicating it could be. All this innocence and trust in this manly package." Daddy's hands wander over me again, never touching my cock, though it flexes up from my stomach, trying to get attention. "The power of it, the sexual intensity…"

I moan as he cups his hands beneath my knees and shoves them back farther, exposing my asshole to his gaze.

"Look at that," he whispers. "Some people like to call their asshole a bussy—a boy-pussy. You like that?"

"If Daddy does," I say, shaking.

"Mm. What about calling it a boy-cunt. You like that?"

"I like it all. I'm so horny, Daddy. Call it whatever you want. Please. Just lick it."

Daddy takes his time, though. "How do you feel about hole? It's not as crude, but it's not prudish either." He continues to examine me as I try to catch my breath; excitement sings in me.

"Bussy's good, Daddy," I say, hoping that if I give him an answer, he'll stop teasing me. "I like bussy."

Daddy smiles. "Thank you for telling Daddy what you like." He kisses the side of my knee, and then spreads my ass cheeks farther apart. "Mm. Now that's a pretty bussy. Never been touched. Never been fucked."

I squirm, desperation building in my core, wanting to be either or both of those things, and the sooner the better.

"All for Daddy." It's a command.

"Yes!"

"Tell me."

"My bussy's all for Daddy."

"Mm, you're delicious. And *fuck*."

He doesn't say more, falling on my ass with a hungry, urgent kiss that jolts a sharp cry from me. I dig my hands into his short hair, trying to clutch and hold on, as I garble pleas for him to never stop, desperate to let him know how good he's making me feel with his lips, his tongue, his teeth.

I've never felt anything like this—*wet, soft, hot* all over my asshole, and as he works his tongue into me, I squirm again with pleasure so intense I can hardly breathe. My cock throbs, and pre-cum slips down the crown to pool on my shuddering stomach. My legs jitter, and I realize I'm hyperventilating as spots begin to swim in front of my eyes.

"Daddy," I grit out. "Daddy, yellow. Yellow." It's hard to say because I don't want him to stop, and yet I don't want to pass out, either.

At once, Daddy stops licking my hole and sits back on his heels. Concern creases his forehead as he grips my hips solidly. "Breathe in on the count of four with me," he says. "One, two, three, four. Hold it. Now out." We breathe together, gazes locked, for four rounds like this. When he senses I'm all right again, he says, "Talk to Daddy. What happened? It's all right. I just need to know."

"It was too good. I've never felt—" I swallow hard. "It was almost like being tickled, which I hate. But not. I want more of it, please, Daddy, but maybe with some breaks. Not so much all at once."

He massages my hips and down my thighs. "Not so relentless?" he offers, nailing it.

"Yes, Daddy. Your boy couldn't breathe." I feel so small saying that, but not in a bad way, in the way where I know this muscled, handsome Daddy is going to take care of me. "It was too good. Can you help me?"

"Daddy will always help you. Let's try this first. C'mere," he mutters, gathering me up in his arms, and changing our positions so I'm on top of him again. "I want to kiss you."

I blink. "After…?" His tongue has just been in a very private place.

"Oh, baby, hell yes."

"Okay." The thrill of doing something so taboo drives me to line my mouth up with his and let him take control again.

Time melts away in the heat of the fire, his kiss, and the sensations of his fingers sliding up and down my crack and teasing my damp hole. His stubble scrapes my chin, and I get lost in the feel of his lips, his tongue touching mine, and the hot, wet delight of making out with a man, of being kissed, and of kissing.

I'm still not good at it, but I'm learning, and when I do something with my tongue that makes Daddy gasp, there's a jolt of pleasure in my core, almost as good as an orgasm—satisfaction of a different kind.

After what feels like an eternity lost in the most thorough and heated kiss I've ever imagined, Daddy breaks away, and shifts me off to the side, so he can retrieve a bottle of lube from the drawer in the coffee table next to the sofa. "Does my boy want Daddy to finger his hot bussy?"

I roll onto my side to face him, pushing my hard dick against his hip, and nod.

"Tell Daddy what you want."

"Daddy, please finger my bussy," I beg. "Please."

"You're so pretty when you beg," he says, rubbing our noses together before kissing my mouth again. "So pretty all the time."

I shiver. I've never been called pretty. I've never even been called handsome, being far too little of everything traditionally desirable in a man. I could get used to this feeling of being seen and loved, of being appreciated, and found sexy. I could get used to it far too fast, and that's scary. And exciting.

I whisper, "Even when I was… on the toilet?"

Daddy sucks in a small gasp, his pupils blowing wider, and he leans in to bite gently at my lower lip. After kissing it to take away the sting, he says, "Even then, Matthew. My boy was gorgeous showing Daddy his true self. Thank you."

"You're so handsome, Daddy," I say, rubbing his chest and shoulders. "Your body, your face… This is like a dream come true."

"I'm glad, sweet boy. Let Daddy take you deeper now. Spread your legs for me."

We shift, and I lie back on the sofa, letting my legs fall open, and Daddy goes up on one elbow above me. He flicks the lube bottle open with his teeth, and I help him to slick his fingers.

As he stares into my eyes, he begins a wonderful, slow assault on my asshole. He starts by massaging the rim until I'm squirming, panting, and close to begging. Only then does he press in one finger and start to slowly fuck my hole.

"Daddy," I whimper. The kick of having another man inside me, even if it's just a finger, overwhelms me. "Help me, Daddy," I say, and his lips curve up at the edges.

"Feeling ashamed, sweet boy? Got a man's thick finger inside you?"

That kernel of shame bursts open, blooming in me painfully. I nod. "Help me, Daddy."

"Don't worry. Daddy's going to make you come again. But not for a long while. So relax. Feel everything."

I groan as he presses deeper, reaching my prostate. The sensation is almost enough to block out the pulsating shame.

"Like that?"

I whimper and nod, breaking out into a fine sweat as he does it again.

"Where are we, boy? Green, yellow, red."

"Green. Don't stop."

"Daddy's got you."

I turn to him, and we start kissing again. Daddy works his finger in and out, kissing my lips with passion.

Once I'm humping up to rub his belly and whining desperately into his mouth, he adds a second finger. The stretch feels right and good, and I groan in deep, satisfied pleasure.

"Daddy's boy is so responsive," he breathes against my lips. "Does it feel good, Matthew?"

"Yes."

"And where's that shame now?"

"Still here, Daddy," I say, pulling him closer with my arms around his neck. "Still right here."

"Is it making your dick hard?" he asks.

"Yes."

"Good boy. Feel that?" He presses against my prostate again. I don't know how I can possibly avoid feeling it. It's so intense and consuming. I groan and shiver, my hips jerking helplessly and my cock pulsing pre-cum again. "That's what you get when you confront that shame. Pleasure. And this too—" he kisses my lips. "Affection. Along with this—" he licks into my mouth, kissing me with that hunger I've been drowning in all day.

"And all of these," he says, his voice all grit and honey, as he pushes in a third finger. It's a lot, and I pant harder, straining to relax my asshole enough to let him push all three in at once. "So tight, sweet boy. You're going to feel so good wrapped around my cock."

I whimper again, and he sinks in deeper, fucking me for long minutes with all three fingers. When we go back to kissing, I'm lost in a sweaty, lust-filled wonderland I've never imagined possible. We kiss for what feels like hours, with me riding his fingers. He reapplies lube several times as it grows tacky, but I accept him back gratefully each time.

As the minutes flow by, his fingers begin to move in and out of me easily, sometimes with two digits, sometimes three, and sometimes just one, always keeping me guessing and desperate, always moaning and on edge, wanting more, or less, or harder. But I'm unable to control my responses—my grunts against his lips, or my cries when he hits my prostate.

As he works the pads of his fingers over that delirium-inducing place inside me, driving me into a state of sweaty, hot lust, he keeps kissing me. I love being invaded on both ends by him, by his tongue and his fingers, and I suck at his mouth, trying to capture his fingers by squeezing my bussy around them.

After a long, glorious time, Daddy grips my hair with his free hand and pulls my mouth away from his with a sharp tug.

"Enough."

I'm dazed, confused, and still riding his fingers.

"Calm yourself," he whispers, kissing my chin and the tip of my nose. "Calm."

I pant and squirm on his fingers. "I need to come, Daddy."

"I know, but I think it's time we took this upstairs."

My stomach trembles, and butterflies dance in my gut. "Why?"

"I'm going to fuck you, sweet boy."

CHAPTER FIFTEEN
Erik

GETTING MATTHEW UP the stairs is easier said than done. His legs are trembling like they're made of Jell-O, so I have him lean on me, and together we make our way up the risers to the top floor.

The mood in the room is different from downstairs, which is warm and golden from the fire. Up here, it's chilly and blue, with reflected light from the moon bouncing off all the snow piling up outside. There's a thick pad of fluff out there on the deck now, and despite the almost-full moon, I can't see the mountains for the low-hanging clouds, the darkness of the fallen night, and the swirls of flakes dancing in the air.

The bed is blue, too. Blue sheets, blue pillows. Calm and serene.

Once I have Matthew in the middle of it, it's calm no more. He's shaking with lust. He reaches for me as soon as he's settled, and I cover him with my body. I love the way his chest hair and stomach fur feel against my skin. He's the hairiest otter of a man, and I find that it's sexier than I knew.

His little whimpers of need encourage me to rub my chin over his jawline, feeling the roughness of his incoming stubble, listening to the susurration of our facial hair coming together.

The room is peaceful but a little cool, and I pull myself away from Matthew's warm body and hungry arms to position and turn on a space heater. "There," I say, coming back to the bed where he waits restlessly. "Daddy doesn't want his sweet boy to be cold, now, does he? There," I soothe him. "Let Daddy take care of you."

I cover him again, and he draws his legs up, cradling my hips, and wraps his arms around my neck. "Daddy," he pleads in that way that makes my balls ache. "I need it. Please. Don't make me wait anymore. I've been a good boy. I've been so good."

"You have," I agree, nuzzling his throat but not kissing it. "You've been Daddy's best boy."

"Please," he urges. "I need it."

"But what does my boy need?" I smile as his breath hitches.

"I need Daddy's cock. I need Daddy to fuck me."

"Mm," I agree, kissing the side of his sweaty throat and licking up to his ear, sucking the lobe, and tonguing the shell. He squeaks, and the sound shoots right to my groin, making my already hard cock even harder. He jitters in my arms, groaning as I continue to lick and tongue-fuck his ear.

"Daddyyyyy," he whines. "Daddy, please."

"Let Daddy see the other side," I whisper, taking hold of his jaw and turning his head. I press his hard dick with my own, sliding our hips together and using my bigger size and weight to hold him down, preventing him from getting any friction on his cock. "There you go," I whisper. "Let me see this ear, too."

He tries to grind up on me as I kiss, lick, and tongue his other ear. He grips my back hard with both hands, begging me to fuck him with every breath. I love it. He's adorable this way and sexy as hell.

His eager need, his virginal innocence, his responsiveness, and his desperation are one hell of an intoxicant. I want to drag this out until he can't stand it a moment more, until he's crying along with his pleas.

But I've already pushed the envelope multiple times with Matthew. I should take it all down a notch. He's inexperienced, and putting him through the wringer has been intense and fun. But he's going to have a confusing time going forward, when most sex is get in, get your nut, and get out. But hopefully, that won't be the future for Matthew. Maybe he'll leave this experience with the insight and desire to find a Daddy who can—

I suck in a breath, struck by the twist in my gut. I know what that is, what it means. It's not appropriate. It's ridiculous and wrong.

But I don't want another Daddy handling this beautiful man, touching his soft skin, tongue-fucking his ear or his ass, eating up his whimpers and moans. I can't stand the thought of another man seeing his face as he comes, or playing with his shame, or teaching him how to use it for his own pleasure. I want—

Something I can't have.

Not with Matthew.

"Daddy," he begs. "Please stop teasing me. *Please*."

There's a thread of such need in his voice that I can't help but give in. I kiss his forehead, his nose, and the dimple in his cheek. "That's my sweet boy," I encourage him. "Begging so prettily for my cock."

"I want it," he groans. "Waited my whole life for your cock, Daddy. Please."

The truth of that hits me hard. Matthew's older than me, and he's never been touched like I've touched him, and he's never been kissed like I've kissed him—*where* I've kissed him—and he's never been fucked.

I'm going to change that. Right now.

"Yes, boy. It's time. Stay right there."

I heave myself off him, kissing his neck, chest, and stomach as I do. I wonder how crazy I can drive him with some attention to his nipples, but first I'm going to get inside his hot, lithe body.

As I reach for the lube on the bedside table, I realize my hands are shaking. It's been a long time since I've been so spun up for a boy, or any man. I tremble despite having already shot once.

Matthew has some kind of hold over me, and I shouldn't be indulging it. I should be running scared, back out to the barn and the horses and the goats. Back to my work downtown and to younger men who have never made me shake like this...

"There now," I soothe him. As I get back between his legs, I spread the lube over my hard, hot dick, stroking a few times for the pleasure of it. When I'm ready, I ease his legs apart. "Lift them for me, hands behind your knees, just like that...yes, good boy. Good boy."

I can see his beautiful bussy again, dark hair swirling around its pinkness, and I lick my lips. I want to eat it again, get my tongue up there, but he'd called yellow earlier when I did that, and I don't want to slow down right now.

I want to slide into him nice and gentle until I'm balls-deep, and he's stretched out tight around my thickness. I'm dying to see his face when I draw out and thrust back in for the first time. I ache to capture that. Own it.

So I do.

I lube his hole, hushing him again when he hisses at the chill. Lining my dick up, I shift my weight so I can help him hold a knee back, opening him just that much more. I drag my eyes away from the sight of my cock about to breach him up to his face.

I study him for a long moment, hovering on the edge of giving him what he wants. He's a study in beauty. His hazel eyes blown wide with lust, his cheeks flushed with need, and his lips bright red from our kisses and his teeth, which even now are digging into his bottom lip as he tries to be patient, waiting for the big push in—

And there it is.

He squeezes his eyes tight shut as I work my thick cockhead past his sphincter. His breath comes in shallow huffs, and his stomach rises and falls with each one. Matthew's nipples are hard and pink, and I make plans to assault them once I'm buried to the hilt.

For now, I just rock my hips, going deeper and deeper, little by little, watching the beautiful struggle play over his face between pleasure and pain, between ecstasy and fear. He's a delight. A beautiful, pliant, sexy, delicious delight. I want to lick him everywhere, eat his cum, and feast on his saliva. I want to grow sharper canines, turn into a vampire, and live off his blood. He'd let me. Matthew will let me do anything.

And with that thought, I push hard and fast, bottoming out in him with a groan that seems to come from my balls. I'm all the way inside, and he's hot as blood, tight as a glove, and throbbing with wonderful life.

I breathe in and out through my nose, trying to take a moment to gather myself before I give in to my animal needs and pound him into this mattress. He makes me feel mad with lust. It's scary how much I want to take all of him. I've never wanted that with a boy before. What they gave was always enough. This, though, this is so close to something vital and pure, something I've dreamed of but never imagined could exist—

"Daddy," he says, rough and desperate. I watch his Adam's apple bob as he swallows, and I remember the way his throat had opened to me. So expert in that one thing, so eager to be used like that in the past, and so good at bringing me off with that skill now.

I want to fuck his throat again at the exact same time as I fuck his ass. It's so unfair that I can't.

"Yes, boy?" I ask.

"I feel—" His eyes fill with tears, and when they spill over, I lean over and lick them from his cheeks, the salt like life on my tongue.

"What does Daddy's sweet boy feel?" I ask, shifting my weight onto my knees, and taking hold of his legs behind the calves. I lift them to my shoulders, getting ready to fuck him for real.

"Full," he whispers. "Full and afraid."

"Mm, what color are we, boy?"

"Green, Daddy."

"Are you sure? We can be yellow." Christ, I don't want to be yellow! "Or even red. It's okay. Be honest with Daddy."

"Green," he whispers. "Please fuck your sweet boy."

I grit my teeth, holding back the urge to outright pound him after that beautiful plea. I take a slow, calming breath, and I move. His head tosses back, putting his throat on display, and he arches up, his nipples peaked and rosy.

I fuck in and out of him several times, slow and even, breathing to match my thrusts. I watch as he absorbs the sensation, and I'm pleased when his cock—which had softened when I entered him—grows to full rigidity again, the head purple and slick with pre-cum.

"You look so hot taking my dick, boy. So sexy."

"Yes, Daddy."

I smile, his breathless agreement adorable. "Your bussy is so tight around Daddy's dick."

"Yes, Daddy."

"Is this good, boy? Is this what you've wanted your whole life?"

His asshole tightens around me. He groans, his legs trembling in my hands, and he whispers, "Yes, Daddy. This is what I want. Fuck me, Daddy. Fuck your boy's sweet bussy. Fill me with cum, Daddy, give me your cum."

"Shh," I urge. I don't want to ruin all this by giving him what he wants right now. "Shh, boy. Take Daddy's cock. Feel it."

He groans and tosses his head on the pillow. He looks amazing twisting on my dick, and I watch him like he's a miracle unfolding before my eyes. His tension as he absorbs my quickening thrusts, his writhing as I nail his prostate, and his flushed, sweaty responsiveness all drive me harder and faster.

I release his legs and collapse on him, digging in deep with my cock and capturing his hands next to his head on the pillow. Held in place, he opens his eyes and gazes up at me. The trust I see is mind-blowing and still far too unearned. I honor it by thrusting into him at a steady, even rate, watching as he struggles with how good it feels, how right.

"This is what you're made for, Matthew," I tell him. "To take Daddy's cock just like this."

"Yes, Daddy," he says, a sob in his throat. "Yes."

"See how Daddy knows how to make his boy feel good?" I reach between us, sliding my fingers around his cock, holding it limply, not giving him friction enough to get off. "Is your cock hard for Daddy?"

"Yes."

"Are you hard because you love having a big, thick dick in your asshole, Matthew?"

"Yes, Daddy."

"Tell me."

His voice breaks as he says, "I love your big, thick dick in my ass, Daddy."

"Mm-hmm. All good boys do."

"Please," he whispers. "Come inside me."

"Oh, I will. Be patient, sweet boy. Daddy knows what you need."

"I don't...I can't..."

"Shh, shh now. Daddy has it under control. Just take my cock, Matthew. Just feel how good it is in you. Made for this, baby. You're made to be fucked."

"Daddyyy," he whimpers, his cock flexing as a spurt of pre-cum slicks the skin between us.

"Don't come yet, boy," I whisper. "You'll thank Daddy if you wait. I promise."

"Please."

"Mm-mm, no. Wait." I smooth his hair back off his forehead, kiss his lips and his throat, and then move to his collarbones. "Such a good boy," I praise as he manfully resists coming. "Daddy's best boy."

I turn to his nipples and realize I've made a mistake in not playing with them more before. He turns into a jittery, sobbing, moaning mess. His knees knock my sides, his asshole convulses around my cock. His grip on the back of my neck tells me that despite his tears and pleas, he likes this.

"Oh God!" he shouts. "Help me, Daddy! Help me!"

I don't stop fucking him, keeping my thrusts steady and even. I suspect what's about to happen, but it's far from certain. Not every man experiences prostate or anal orgasm. Only one of my boys did—Garrett—and a few guys I've fucked casually over the years have come apart like this on my dick. But I sense it like a tidal wave, pleasure gathering in Matthew's body, starting to crest—

"Daddy!" he shouts as he loses control.

I keep fucking him, knowing it will prolong the pleasure. His throat pounds with his pulse, and his legs and arms jerk as if he's having a seizure.

"Daddy!"

I'm relentless in nailing his prostate, making the episode drag on.

Once it's passed, I slow my thrusts, gripping his hips with both hands and moving away from his teeth-reddened nipples to capture his mouth. He's huffing like a horse after a long race, but I kiss him thoroughly, feeling the way even his jaw trembles after that climax.

"Enjoy that, boy?" I ask after he's calmed enough to open his tear-sticky eyes and gaze at me.

He glances away, shame sliding over his face. I think I know why, but he surprises me, saying, "I'm sorry, Daddy. I came when you told me not to."

"No, boy," I tell him, bringing his hand between us to touch his still-hard cock. "You didn't. See?"

He blinks, a stunned expression taking over from the shame. "What? How?"

"You're a lucky boy," I tell him, tweaking his nose and kissing his chin again. "Such a lucky boy. You just experienced the bottom's greatest bliss. You know the prostate feels good when stimulated, but it can also make you feel like *that*. An orgasm without shooting, like a full-body climax. It doesn't have a long refractory period. I can make it happen again. Do you want that?"

"Oh fuck," he groans, and his eyes roll up, his teeth chattering as an aftershock glances through him.

"Do you want that, sweet boy? Green? Yellow?"

"I want it, Daddy. Green."

"Mm. I'm so proud of you," I tell him. "You take Daddy's cock like a champ."

"Make your boy feel like that again, Daddy."

"You want that bliss?"

"Please, yes, please, Daddy."

"Hold on to Daddy tight," I tell him. "Daddy's going to ride you hard now."

CHAPTER SIXTEEN
Matthew

I GENUINELY DON'T know if I want to do this shocking "bottom bliss" thing again. After the third time, I'm fucked out, touched out, and yet when Daddy asks me if I want to go again, I beg for more.

The way I'm shaking is terrifying, and the pleasure is, too. I'm quite sure this isn't normal. *Nothing* I'm feeling tonight with Erik—with Daddy—is normal. I don't even want it to be. This is outside of my day-to-day life, a fantasy, a joy, a gift. And I want to ride his cock for all eternity if I can. Because nothing can ever compare to this.

"Sweet boy," Daddy says to me after I've sweated and cursed my way through another episode of pleasure. "Are you ready for Daddy's cum now?"

I almost burst into tears. I want his cum so badly. "Yes, give it to me. Fill me up. I want it."

"First, I have to make my boy come," Daddy says, taking hold of my cock, which is still hard and, despite having leaked an enormous slick mess onto my and Daddy's stomachs, still loaded.

I whimper, not sure I want that, but it's more important to do whatever Daddy wants of me than to have my own way. His cock is divine, a wondrous thing. It fills me and stretches me wide. I'm on fire for it and want to live with his dick buried inside me forever and ever. But it's just tonight, and I don't want it to be over.

"Daddy? Will you fuck me again later?" I ask, my voice quavering. I've cried while he's fucked me, I've screamed, and yet this plea is what embarrasses me.

"Do you want me to, Matthew?"

"I need it," I groan. "I need your dick, Daddy."

"That's because you're a boy, and boys always need Daddy's dick." He sighs. "So, so sweet. I just don't know what to do with you," he whispers. He kisses my mouth tenderly, making me lose my mind. "Let's make you come. We'll figure out what happens next after I've left my load in you."

"Fuck, Daddy," I grit out. "Stop teasing me and do it."

Daddy laughs, and with a quick rush of movement I didn't see coming, pulls out, sits back on his heels, shoves my thighs apart, and sucks my cock into his mouth. I shout and tug at his hair, wanting to come while he's in my ass.

"Please, fuck me!" I yell as he sucks and sucks. I'm going to explode in his mouth if he doesn't stop now. "I want—I want—" The orgasm is undeniable, but just before it starts, Daddy pulls off my cock, thrusts hard back into my ass, and jerks me through the first spurts.

I love how full I feel as I shoot with Daddy's dick deep in me. The cum goes everywhere—in my chest hair, all over the pillow— and my asshole squeezes his thickness with each pump. When I come back to earth, I'm sweaty and covered in cum, but Daddy's watching me with an expression of intense pride. A glow starts in my chest, and soon I'm smiling, as Daddy bends low and kisses me for what seems a very long time. I follow his mouth, trying to get more as he pulls away.

"Now it's time for Daddy to fill you up," he says, fondly stroking my face and touching my dimple. "Sweet boy, are you ready for Daddy's cum?"

"Yes, give it to me, Daddy. I want it. I want it so bad."

He grins, hitching my legs back. "This might be a little uncom fortable at first since you just came. Give Daddy a few seconds, all right? But if it's too much, just use your safe word. Daddy won't go harder than you can take."

"Yes, Daddy. Green, green, go."

He kisses me, and I dissolve under his heat and weight, his cock thrusting into me at a quick rate that takes my breath away. It's not the best feeling, not half as good as it was moments ago before I got off, but it's not unbearable. I stroke Daddy's back, kiss him with my newfound skills, poor though they are, and whimper as he strives for his climax.

"This is it, boy," he grunts, lifting onto his elbows and watching my expressions. "Such a gorgeous face you've got. Such sweet eyes. Those *lips*. Fuck...here it is. Here it is, sweet *fucking* boy. Fuck, *fuck*!" He shudders on top of me, convulsing as his cock throbs. It thuds against my tight rim, and perhaps I imagine it, but I swear I can feel his jizz filling me.

We kiss some more, as Daddy keeps himself deep inside me. When he begins to soften, he slips out, along with some of that hard-won load. "Daddy's got it," he assures me before I can even express my dismay at losing his cum. "Hold on, let me get it..." He uses his fingers to push the stray cum back inside me, urging me to cant my hips up so it doesn't slide back out again. "Good boy, just like that. Hold Daddy's semen inside."

I'm weak with delight and satisfaction. This is what I've wanted, what I've needed, and it was every bit as good as—no, infinitely better than—I'd even imagined. Daddy has taught me so much about my body and pleasure, and this fuck has been the perfect cherry on top.

I know we have the rest of the night, but a small amount of dread mars this moment: what if he doesn't fuck me again before I go? What if this is all I ever have of him? What if he feels like his duty is discharged, and now we can cuddle, open presents in the morning, and—

"Boy," he says, snapping me out of my mental spiral. "Do you know what's happening right now?"

"No, Daddy?"

"My semen is in your colon, and do you know what happens to it there?"

I shake my head, though I suspect it'll dribble out.

"Your body absorbs some of it. Absorbs the hormones and nutrients it can glean, takes them into your bloodstream, and feeds them to your cells. Even more so when you swallow my cum."

"Daddy…"

"Is that as hot to you as it is to me?" Daddy asks. "You'll have part of me in you for years to come. So long as there are cells in your body that have fed from the semen you've swallowed or I've shot into you? I'll be part of you. Understand? This—" He motions between us. "Isn't just tonight. I'm in you, boy. I'm in your memory, your blood and body. Don't forget that."

Daddy lies next to me, exhausted, but he pulls me close, and we cuddle. I think about it, what he's said about his semen, part of him being inside me, becoming part of me, and I love that. I want more of him.

And, I realize, I want to reciprocate. I want to put myself in his ass, his throat, and his bloodstream and cells. I want to be part of him for years.

"Daddy?" I whisper before he can fall asleep.

"Yes, boy?" He drags his eyes open, and I can tell he's about to get up, maybe get me some water, or worry about food, so I put my arms around him to keep him in place.

"Daddy, I want to fuck you, too."

He smiles, kisses my mouth, and nods. "After we get some rest. Maybe tomorrow morning."

"You'll let me?"

"Of course, boy. Daddy's ass is yours if you want it."

"Okay," I agree and close my eyes. I'm exhausted, filthy, covered in drying sweat and cum, and yet I can't make myself even begin to get out of this bed to clean up. I think Erik feels the same.

He nuzzles my hair, sighs his pleasure, and pride fills me again. I've made my handsome young Daddy so tired. I've given him good orgasms and worn him out. Me, Matthew Angel. Me, the virgin.

The *former* virgin.

And later tonight or tomorrow, he's going to let me fuck him. I'll be part of him for years to come—in his memory, his blood, his body. Even though after tonight we won't see each other or do this again? Daddy will never forget.

I'll be his boy this way forever.

CHAPTER SEVENTEEN
Erik

MATTHEW IS ASLEEP with drool slipping from the side of his mouth, the darkness of his stubble coming in like a shadow. He's adorable.

And I'm in trouble.

I stand by the window, gazing out at the newly cloudless sky. At some point, the storm has blown through, and all that's left is piles of white snow. It looks like more than enough for a white Christmas, and I wonder if that will delight Matthew. He'd seemed thrilled by the tree and stockings. Does he decorate his home for the holidays? Does he celebrate with friends? Or does he spend Christmases alone with no fanfare?

I have the sinking suspicion it's the latter. The thought of sending him packing on Christmas Eve to a cold, empty house creates a hollow ache in my chest. With my mom away, I'd have been fine to spend the holiday with my animals catching up on some downtime.

Now, I imagine watching Matthew drive away, his red taillights disappearing around the bend. I imagine spending Christmas alone like I'd planned, and instead of peace, quiet, and rejuvenation, that hollow ache grows deeper.

The moon is low in the sky, and its light bounces blue and serene around the mountains and into my bedroom. It's in that pale light that I watch him sleep.

I know this feeling.

I've had it before. The first times with all three of my prior boys were special in their own ways, but none could hold a candle to the intensity of what Matthew and I have shared in the last few hours.

The funny feeling in my stomach? The fond warmth in my heart? The urgent protectiveness and desire to keep him safe and mine? These are all familiar from my past experiences with the boys I made a full-time Daddy commitment to.

But Matthew didn't sign up for that. He wanted one night with me. That's what he bid on, so that's what he's getting.

And even if he does want more, I don't do long distance. It never works. Not that I've tried it, but I'm a man who needs his boy close—to kneel at his feet, to suck his cock, to touch, and love, and protect.

I can't protect Matthew if he's in Nashville and I'm here. I can't make sure he's fed, warm, safe, and getting suitably fucked. It would drive me crazy to try to be his Daddy from a distance.

I know some people are exclusively virtual with their submissives or boys, but that's never appealed to me. When Duncan asked me to do a video call with him after he left for grad school, I did it once because I cared about him and knew he needed the support, but there was nothing erotic or satisfying for me in seeing Duncan jerking off through a screen.

Just pixels. No flesh, no cum, no spit. I love all that. I love the warmth of a boy's body against mine—and it's a surprise to find out a boy with so much fur is nice to cuddle, especially in the winter. For as long as my Daddy/boy relationships last, I like to share my meals, my life, my time. I don't want what Matthew can offer me, and yet...

I gaze at him, watching the blankets I've piled on him rise and fall with his breathing.

Have I ever had a boy so pliant and good? Have I ever fucked a man who falls so fast into subspace? No to both. And have I ever seen into a boy's shame so fast, known what he needs, and dug it out like a precious jewel to present to him mid-fuck, making him come like a volcano? Of course not.

This is something special between us. I've known it from the start, from the first day when I found him so unaccountably arousing and chalked it up to just being horny after a dry spell.

My spell isn't dry anymore. I came my brains out twice in a few hours, but I'm ready to go again.

He'd allow it too. If I wake him, if I tell him, "I want back inside you," he'll agree. He'll open his arms and legs and bring me in. I'll fuck him full of cum again, and he'll take it happily.

Jesus Christ. Now I'm hard.

It's stupid. This won't work. It can't happen.

I turn my attention back to the snowy landscape outside. It's piled up on the deck and drive. I know that beneath the snow is slick, black ice from the fog laying down moisture before the storm arrived. I consider the roads back to the interstate. The pass over the mountains. I sigh.

You know what else can't happen? He can't go home tomorrow.

I reach for my phone on the bedside table and wake it up for the first time since he arrived. There are multiple texts—a few from my mother and a couple from clients wanting to know if we're still going to train after Christmas and what if the snow doesn't melt? One from Nick, and a text from Charles that appears to be about a heating problem with the house in town. Great. Just great.

But that's not why I picked it up. I open the weather app. No more snow ahead, but the temperatures are supposed to remain in the low teens. No hope for melting this snow away. Which means that Matthew and I are trapped up here until a plow comes through, which, since it's the weekend and almost Christmas, probably won't be for a few days.

I should be upset. This wasn't the agreement.

But I'm not upset. My heart flutters, my dick fills with blood, and I smile.

I glance back at Matthew, who hasn't stirred—he must be exhausted. Three loads at his age! Christ, it's hard to believe. I hope he's not going to be too disappointed by being trapped here with me.

Maybe I'm wrong, and he has holiday plans in Nashville that he'll be sorry to miss. Even if he does, which I doubt, I'll make it worth his while to stay. He might not be able to spend the next three days having sex, but I know other ways to impress him.

It looks like the one-night December Daddy Experience Matthew bid on has turned into a multi-day Snowed-In Christmas Experience. I feel nothing but excitement about that. *Joy.* I hope when he wakes up, he's excited, too. There's just something about the way his eyes glow when he's happy…

Oh, Christ. I'm in so much trouble.

PART THREE

The Snowed-In Christmas Experience

CHAPTER EIGHTEEN
Matthew

MORNING LIGHT BLARES in my face, forcing me to wake up. I don't want to. I've been half-awake, drowsing in and out of sleep, for the past hour, enjoying the sound of Erik's snores, and the firm, warm feel of his form next to mine.

As soon as I admit I'm awake, and as soon as he's up too, it's the beginning of the end. I'm due to return home sometime today. *Home.* The word has never felt so empty and meaningless.

There'll be no colorful glittering tree or twinkling lights or sugary Christmas cookies with jolly snowmen piped in frosting. No Erik holding me close and fucking me hard and giving me more than I could have ever hoped for.

And while Daddy's going to let me open my presents and fuck him this morning before I go, I also know that it won't be enough. I'll do anything he asks of me if he just allows me to stay. But he won't be offering that. I need to let it go.

Each second feels so precious. I don't want to lose this, lose him, but this is all I've got.

"The sunrise is worth seeing." Erik's voice is rough from either sleep or from the jagged cries he'd released as he'd fucked me.

I pry my eyes open, and sure enough the sky outside is streaked with the most stunning shades of orange, pink, and coral. The fog around the mountains gives it an almost pearlescent glow. "Wow," I breathe.

"Mm." I suppose that's agreement.

Erik rolls to clutch me in the little spoon position, one arm slipping beneath me and around my waist to take hold of my cock, the other hand sliding up my chest, and—

"Oh God," I whimper, as his hand comes to my throat and wraps around it lightly. "*Daddy.*"

"Relax. Daddy just wants to remind you whose boy you are."

I'm hard now. But I don't move or say another word, just let him hold me this way as the sun rises—pink, coral, blue, white, orange. Colors peaking and collapsing, until I'm certain I'm blind from them all, but it turns out I've closed my eyes.

My cock aches in his grip, and my breath comes in soft, quick pants.

"Are you hard for Daddy?" Erik asks, squeezing my dick.

I don't speak, just breathe a little faster when he begins to stroke me.

"Last night, you let me fuck your bussy, boy, and you came on my cock."

Heat rises in my cheeks. Why am I embarrassed now when I wasn't then? "Yes, Daddy."

"How do you feel about that?"

"Like I want you to do it again. Now. Please, Daddy." I can feel my throat moving against his hand as I talk, feel the vibration of my voice.

"You beg so prettily." He releases my throat and my dick. "But we have things to do this morning."

I roll onto my back, blinking at him in confusion. "Daddy?"

"There was a snowstorm. Bigger than they predicted." He gestures toward the window, his military-short hair still managing to have a bit of bed head to it, with short tufts sticking out in awkward directions. He's sweet. Cute. It's hard to believe that just seconds ago, he had his hands on my throat and my dick, commanding me with ease.

Erik adds, "What do you want to do today? You're not going anywhere until it melts, so we can do whatever you'd like after breakfast once I shovel the walk to the barn and check on Molly."

"Whatever I'd like," I repeat, sitting up to peer out the window. *Wait. I'm staying here?*

Sure enough, the predicted inch of snow is more like a foot and a half. We get more snow in Nashville than in some parts of the South, but I'm still not prepared to drive on winding mountain roads with snow and ice. I'm trapped here.

Trapped in a winter wonderland with the hottest man on the planet. My heart flutters, and I can't conceal a giddy grin. Christmas is just a day on the calendar. Two, if you count Christmas Eve. It shouldn't mean anything to open my presents on actual Christmas morning. I'm a grown man.

Yet being with Erik on Christmas for real does mean something. Far more than it should, but that's a problem for the future. I clear my throat, trying to contain my excitement before asking, "You don't have any plans with friends and family? I don't want to intrude."

"I don't." He frowns. "Do you?"

I shake my head. "After my parents died…" I shrug. "Christmas hasn't been the same. For better or worse."

Erik gives me a piercing look, nodding slowly. "The Christmas aspect of this experience was an important factor in your decision to bid."

It's not a question. I nod.

"Then this will be a special Christmas for us both."

Erik may have only said that to be kind, but my heart soars regardless. "Thank you."

"It's Christmas Eve, and you've been such a good boy. What would you like to do? Sledding? Snowman-building?"

"Daddy," I say, turning to where Erik is getting out of bed, naked as sin and just as gorgeous. "Last night, you said I could fuck you."

He grins. "Oh, I'll keep that promise. Wouldn't back out on it for the world. But we've got all day and all night. I don't think you can keep up the pace we started yesterday, refractory periods being what they are. I think it's best if you don't come this morning. Or maybe even this afternoon."

I let out an undignified squawk.

Daddy laughs. "Oh, so you have big feelings about that, I see."

"Daddy, please—"

"No. I'm in charge. Remember our contract."

I want to cry, which is stupid because I'm a middle-aged man who shot his load three glorious times just yesterday after a lifetime's dry spell, so waiting a few hours shouldn't be a problem. But my eyes prick with tears.

Erik's expression grows serious, and he sits next to me on the bed. "What are you feeling? Tell me what's going on."

"I don't know, Daddy. I feel scared?"

"Scared of what?"

I swallow hard. "Scared that you won't let me fuck you, and I'll have to go home, and—" A tear falls, and it's embarrassing as hell, so I cover my face, feeling the heat of humiliation flowing over my skin. Despite knowing I can't drive on icy roads, the fear that I'll somehow have to spend Christmas alone in Nashville, after all, devastates me.

"Ah." He pulls me into a hug, and tucks my head against his chest, kissing my hair. "When you were growing up, did your daddy promise you things and fail to deliver?"

A myriad of memories flash through my mind.

"Yes, Daddy."

"Tell me about what he promised."

I tell him about the times my dad said he'd teach me something, like how to throw a ball well, or to fix my own car, but he never took the time. How he'd promised he'd consider buying me a guitar for Christmas when I was twelve, but there'd just been the usual socks and practical shirts and corduroys under the tree. Because Christmas was supposed to be about Jesus, not gifts.

Or how often my father had told me he'd come to one of my events to watch me in the school contemporary band, or my recitals, or the Christmas pageant, but then he'd never show up, claiming he had to work.

"Claiming?" Daddy asks.

"Yeah. Sometimes it may have been true, but most of the time?" I shrug, and the tears that had started earlier slip down my cheeks in hot streams. I don't try to stop them. Daddy says he wants me to feel my feelings. I let them rage, and the tears fall.

"I think—" I stop myself because this is my secret. I've never even said this out loud to myself.

"Go on."

I take a shuddering breath. "I think he avoided spending time with me because if he did, then he'd know. He'd see the truth, and he didn't want to see the truth of me."

"But didn't you say you lived with them until they died?"

"Yes, Daddy."

"All those years, you didn't spend time with your father?"

"You can live with a person, love them even, and never really get to know them. He didn't want to know me. Because he'd have to admit I'm gay, and he'd know that I..." I hiccup a breath and bury my face in Erik's chest. "That I want a man's dick in my ass, Daddy."

"I know you do," he coos, so soothing and warm. "I know you want that, baby, and Daddy's okay with that. Daddy knows."

I cry as Erik rocks me in his arms, rubbing my back, and hushing me for long minutes, until I stop.

It's embarrassing as hell once I have. There's no getting out of the awareness that I, a grown man, am letting a younger man hold me and treat me like a kid, letting him calm me like a child who's skinned his knee. Shame soars on in, and Daddy knows it.

"Feel that shame, Matthew?"

I nod.

"Would you like Daddy to spank it away?"

I hitch a breath, swallow hard, and another tear squeezes out. "Yes, Daddy."

"Get on your stomach across my lap, boy." He says it so easily, as if he's not offering something that I need like a heartbeat. "This will clear your head," he says as I get in position, ass up, his hand resting on it. I bury my face in a pillow I've pulled over to hide my shame. "This will get all the ghosts out."

I shudder as he rubs his hand over my ass.

"Ever been spanked before?" he asks.

I nod.

"By your father?"

I nod again.

"Did he use his hand?"

"Yes."

"A belt?"

"Sometimes."

"Anything else?"

"A switch from outside. A wooden spoon."

"Did he only spank your butt?"

"Yes, Daddy."

"Anyone else ever spank you?"

"My minister," I say with a hoarse throat. "He caught me look-ing at the other boys in the shower at Bible Camp."

"With his hand?"

"A strap."

"Did you cry?"

"Howled, Daddy. I screamed and *howled*."

"Mm." He sounds so noncommittal. I don't know for sure what he's thinking, but I guess I don't need to know. He asks, "What are your safe words?"

"Yellow and red, Daddy."

"Use them, Matthew. Promise me you'll use them."

"I promise."

"Do you still feel that shame? The hot, dark, bloody shame that filled you when that awful minister caught you looking? Do you feel that, Matthew?"

"Yes."

"Were you afraid he'd tell your dad?"

"I think he did."

"What did your father say?"

"He ignored me for a week."

"And how did that make you feel?"

"Even more ashamed."

"Think about that, sweet boy. Feel it." He rubs my ass again, squeezing my cheeks. "Think about how much you need a dick in your ass to be happy. Now that you've had it, you know, don't you? You've never been truly happy a day in your life until yesterday."

"Daddy…"

He spreads my ass cheeks apart and slides his fingers into the crack, touching my hole, and I bite my cheek, so close to begging him to finger-fuck me. "Imagine telling your father the truth, Matthew."

"He'd have hated me."

"He might have."

"He'd have told me I'm going to hell."

"Are you? Going to hell, Matthew?"

"I don't know, Daddy."

"Mm." Another swipe over my hole with his big, dry fingers. "Shame is a powerful thing. Let's shake it free. Hold on to those memories. Now be ready to let go." He grips one of my hips, holding me steady, and lifts his other hand. "We begin."

The crack of pain is both intense and silly. I want to laugh, but I can't because another one lands almost right on the back of the first, and I gasp. Daddy rubs the pain away before smacking my ass again. He sets up a smooth rhythm, alternating cheeks. As the pain begins to grow, the stinging, aching burn crowds out all other feelings in my heart and forces them from my throat in shouts.

As the pain expands, I can't shift away from it without disobeying Daddy and rolling out of his grip. Truly, the pain isn't that bad. Not half as bad as when my father used his belt or the minister used that strap, and yet it's consuming enough that I'm absorbed by it, cocooned in it. Safe.

Which strikes me as hilarious given that Daddy is currently slapping me again and again, my ass stinging, and the ache mounting. I shouldn't feel safe at all. This is violence. This is pain. This is...

Perfect.

I submit to Erik's hand, collapsing against his legs, and my shouts turn to sobs as I let the shame go, letting Daddy's hand and the sting of his spanking fill the space it leaves behind.

"There you go," he says to me. "Such a good boy. Knowing just what to do. Almost done here. Your ass is rosy. You've got such a pretty butt." He smacks me again. "Tell Daddy how you feel."

"Empty. Full." I gasp as he spanks me again. "Both, Daddy. It's both."

"Mm. Empty of what? Full of what?"

"Empty of...the past. Full of this. This *feeling*. This big feeling."

"Where's that shame, sweet boy?"

"I don't know, Daddy. It's gone. I don't feel it. I just..." Another smack lands. "I just feel you."

"Good boy, such a sweet boy." He smooths his hand over my butt. "Look at you. Christ, the things you do to me."

I can feel what I do to him. He's hard, and I'm greedy for what he can offer. I want to suck him, take him in my ass, anything. But when Erik tells me to rise, he doesn't give me either of those things. Instead, he pulls me into a kiss, and we hold each other, tongues and lips touching, much more tenderly than most of our kisses yesterday.

When he moves away, I'm hard. He is too, but all he says is, "Let me get some lotion for your ass. It won't bruise. I didn't hit hard enough for that. But it'll be a little tender, and I plan to take you horseback riding later. You're going to feel it."

The time he takes to rub in the lotion is excruciatingly long when there seems to be no promise of orgasm in sight. Eventually, he holds me again, kissing the top of my head and running his hands over the fur on my body he seems to like so much.

"It's time for breakfast," he says at last.

I see his cock has gone down, and while mine is still hard and raring to go, he's ready to move on.

"Daddy," I try. "Your boy's horny."

"My boy's going to have to wait. Daddy already got sidetracked from his morning plans. Breakfast, then shoveling, then the barn."

"But what about the presents?"

"Not yet. Santa doesn't come until tonight. We can enjoy this playtime a little longer."

A river of joy flows through me. Daddy is enjoying this, enjoying *me*.

The thought fills me with a sunbeam of pride that washes away the shadows of lingering shame.

CHAPTER NINETEEN
Erik

As I shovel the wet snow off the steps and sprinkle salt so the ice will melt, I'm thinking about Matthew. I can't help *but* think of him, and what we've done together. It gets me all twisted up inside—in a good way that steals my breath—and even when I scold myself, tell myself to focus on the here and now, on the steps in front of me and nothing else, I can't do it.

My mind turns again and again to Matthew's lithe body squirming under me as I smacked his ass, to his cries of pain and ecstasy, and to the pleasure I took in taking him to those places.

Christ. I've been pushing the boundaries with him in ways that I'd normally work up to for months with a boy, and I've just had one day with Matthew. It's irresponsible. Who knows what genie I'm letting out of the bottle with all this shame play and psychological mind-fucking?

And yet the thought of stopping now, of trying to reverse course, seems cruel. He's in this with me, and he has at least one more day here, maybe two, given the wet, icy thickness of this snow. Not to mention the fact I don't want to spend Christmas Day without him now. And if we can break down these walls, tear open his issues, and fuck them away...

But that's not how this works. Kink play isn't some magical fix for whatever hurts a person carries. It can help or soothe if applied well, or it can aggravate if applied poorly.

Which am I doing now?

It's hard to say. When I'm in the moment with Matthew, I have such clarity. I can see the path to guide him on like the hand of God himself has shown me the direction and urged me to take Matthew's hand and lead him. So I have been. It's the most natural feeling in the world. The easiest choice to make—not because it's simple, but because it's right.

Or so it seems at the time when the passion is high, and his eyes are on mine, so innocent and yet not young at all…

I want him in ways I've never wanted a boy before. I want him because not only do I think I can guide him to be a better man, but when I'm with him—when I'm his Daddy—I'm the man *I* want to be. The scenes unfold in my mind with pristine clarity, purity of intent, and roaring arousal. His issues blend into my innate knowledge like the sunrise bleeds into the sky outside my window each morning: bright, beautiful, clear, and hopeful.

I think of Brandon and his silly morning-after smile after he'd been fucked within an inch of his life, his teasing giggle, and his wet eyes when he'd told me about Ferko and confessed his future plans no longer included me.

It still stings. I still miss him.

But when I think of what it was like to be Brandon's Daddy? It was nothing like this.

Digging out even the simplest of Brandon's issues had taken months of soft-domming him, and he'd enjoyed being a brat more than he'd enjoyed being a boy. He'd never been particularly needy, either. Not like Duncan, who'd required so much care and handling—he'd been more like Matthew—except he'd been so young, just out of his teens. There hadn't been much depth there. It'd been me giving, him taking, and I'd thought that was the way I preferred it.

But with Matthew, when I give, it doesn't feel like he's taking. It feels like he's giving too.

I don't want to talk to Nick about this. Not even a little. He'll have far too much to say and not about the real issues, just about how he was right, and it's a good thing I participated in the auction. And, yeah, it was, but given how knotted up I feel, it's not as simple as all that.

I clomp back up the stairs when I'm finished with the work and pause on the deck. Through the window, I see Matthew on the sofa, bundled up in the blankets I laid over him, head back, mouth open, asleep again. His scruff is starting to grow in, and I'll have to get him to shave it before we have more sex, or I'll suffer beard burn on my chin and maybe other places.

I'd shaved while he ate the breakfast I made for him—oatmeal with plenty of butter, berries, chia seeds, and some protein powder to make it stick. But afterward, he'd looked so sleepy and sweet, still exhausted after his big day, that I'd taken pity on him. Losing most of his virginity had really taken it out of him.

So I'd tucked him in on the sofa, made a fresh fire, and turned on soft, jazzy Christmas music, to help him rest while I did the outdoor work.

He hadn't protested, simply saying, "Thank you, Daddy," with that sweet, sexy voice that makes my balls twinge with lust every damn time.

He'd fallen asleep in minutes.

A cardinal flits past, bright red against the white snow, breaking my reverie.

Glancing at my watch, I realize I need to check on Molly and her kid. I don't want Matthew to wake and be confused about where I am, so I text him. His phone is by his hand and hopefully he'll sleep through whatever alert comes through. He needs the rest.

Heading to barn for horse and goat maintenance. Stay here and wait for me.

I send it, watching him through the window. He doesn't wake.

Relieved, I make my way toward the barn. The snow is crusty on top, and my boots make a satisfying crunching noise with each step. The sky is blue as a robin's egg above, and the mountains are awash with light and glittering snow. The view from Tully's Lookout will be beautiful, no doubt. I already planned to take Matthew on a ride today, but now I know which trail I'll use.

As I work, I realize I'm humming "Winter Wonderland."

Caring for the horses and goats takes time and effort since each animal needs extra love and attention during a snowstorm when they aren't as free to roam. I spend time with them and find that as I do, I'm able to stop obsessing about Matthew.

But the effect is temporary. As soon as I've finished checking on my final charges, Molly and little Miss Merry Joy-Joy, my mind returns to the worries at hand.

Aside from Nick, I do know some folks at the local kink club, but none of them are confidants of mine. It would feel odd to contact one of them and confess that I'm in the middle of a big, gorgeous mistake with a boy, and I don't want to stop making it. But I don't know if it's ethical to charge on ahead just because it feels natural, right, and good.

I glance at my phone, checking the last string of texts I'd exchanged with my out-of-town, kinky friend RJ Blitz. The last chat had been months ago, but RJ had stated: *If you need anything at all, or just want to talk about this stuff again, hit me up. I'm here for you.*

That'd been back when I was dealing with Brandon leaving me. RJ'd been supportive and kind, and, best of all, not in Asheville, so I didn't have to worry about running into him out and about or gossiping to other local kinksters.

With a sigh, I text him now, even though it's still early in the morning. RJ travels a lot, and there's no telling where in the world he might be—literally. The chances of him being on Eastern time like me are quite slim.

Straightaway, my text shows as read, and without delay, reply bubbles appear.

While I wait to see if he can chat, preferably by FaceTime, I think about how I met RJ and his husband, Aaron, a few years ago. A record company had hired me to train the members of a female-led country band, as well as their mixed-gender entourage, in self-defense.

RJ had been the band's traveling lead guitarist at the time—for all I know, he still is—and Aaron, a former teacher, had worked for the group tutoring their kids on the road. Both RJ and Aaron had taken my self-defense classes, and I'd liked them from the start. Since I had to travel with the group for a couple of months, similar to when I worked on film sets around the world, I got to know them both pretty well.

During casual conversations over drinks at a hotel bar, or eating takeout dinners on the bus, I'd learned Aaron, a handsome guy who was older than RJ, had been RJ's English teacher back in high school. While RJ had always crushed on Aaron, Aaron had been oblivious to RJ altogether, much less his charms, until *long* after he'd graduated.

After a few beers on a Friday night halfway through the tour, RJ'd inadvertently revealed they were in a soft D/s relationship. A few days after that, I got brave and confessed I was kinky too.

As the tour had gone on, the three of us often discussed the merits of Daddy play vs. other D/s play, and pain play vs. shame play vs. humiliation play and where they all overlap. All kinds of kinks had been analyzed between us before the job came to an end.

RJ and Aaron had met Brandon out on the tour, too, when he'd come to visit me for a few days. And they'd hung out with him a few times afterward when we'd gone out as couples for nice meals. So, when Brandon left me, I'd reached out to RJ to share my shock and grief.

RJ understood how I felt. He told me that even though I'd never imagined the relationship with Brandon lasting forever, we'd had something beautiful—he'd seen it for himself. That insight, plus the fact he didn't live here locally, made it easy to share my feelings with him.

After Brandon, RJ had been able to help me in ways Nick and the local kink club couldn't. Maybe he can help me now.

I hold my breath as the bubbles disappear and then appear again.

Fuck autocorrect. Bus is bumpy. Can I call?

Please do, I reply.

An incoming FaceTime pops up. RJ looks good. He's grown his hair out some, and it brushes his cheekbones in a very rock-n-roll way. He looks healthy, with rosy cheeks and shining eyes.

He also appears to be crammed into one of those tour bus bunks I remember too well. It's not a very comfortable area, but it gets the job done. Aaron isn't there with him, so I ask about him first.

"He's chatting with Larissa about her daughter's grades. It could be a while."

"Ah, yes, I imagine Larissa is a real mama bear about things." So he's still touring with the same group. Larissa is the lead singer and a lovely woman, but also the very epitome of a Type A personality.

"Yup," RJ says. "She's gonna need some hand-holding to accept that her baby girl is on the dim side, and we *all* need to lower our expectations of her future collegiate prospects."

"Ah, sounds fun."

"Like stubbing your toe. Twenty times. Poor Aaron."

I laugh, but it's distant. My mind is whirling, trying to figure out how to ask RJ what I want to ask him, how to explain who Matthew is and what's different about him, and I'm already trying to guess what RJ's response will be.

He senses my distraction and cuts to the chase. "What's up? You okay?"

"I'm all right. I'm just…" I hiss through my teeth. "It's about a boy."

"Ain't it always," RJ says with a laugh. "Brandon again?"

"No, no, he's gone for good."

"I'm sorry about that, man."

"Me, too," I say because it's habit, and I realize that for the first time since Brandon left, maybe I'm not so sorry after all. "It's a new boy. He's a man, really."

RJ's eyebrows lift. "Aren't all your boys men? I sure hope so."

I roll my eyes. "They've all been legal, if that's what you're asking, but they've always been young. This boy, he's older than me."

"Awesome," RJ waggles his brows now. "Kinky fun. Older men know all the tricks."

"That's the thing," I say, pausing, trying to figure out how much I can share without violating Matthew's privacy. Not that RJ will ever meet him. That's part of the problem. We were supposed to have one night together, and that's all, but I'm already raising the kink to higher and higher levels with him. *Fuck.*

"What's the thing?" RJ prompts.

"He's a virgin. Or he was. Practically. He'd performed some oral that was more about being used than anything else. Nothing sensual. Nothing real between men. You get what I'm saying?"

"Yeah, I get it. And let me guess—he's fresh out of the closet, right?"

I nod and rub a hand over my eyes.

"Got yourself an ugly duckling situation? He's following you around now, wanting more, but he's not—"

"No!" I huff, irrationally irritated on Matthew's behalf. "Nothing like that."

RJ laughs. "I'll shut up and let you tell me then. What's going on?"

"He's gorgeous and sexy, and I want him like I've rarely wanted a man before."

"So far, so good."

"But he's not from here. I don't do long distance. He just wanted one night."

"Okay, back up. Where's he from, why don't you do long distance, and why just one night?"

"Yeah, okay, let me just…" I rub my forehead and sigh. "Let me start at the beginning."

RJ listens as I describe Nick's plan for me to "get back on the kink horse" with the charity auction. I even confess to him about setting the opening bid incredibly high so no one would bid on me. He whistles under his breath when I tell him about seeing Matthew across the coffee shop before I knew he was the auction winner, and how I'd wanted to fuck him in the bathroom.

He gets serious, though, when I confess to him about the intensity of the last day and night, how I hadn't ever expected to be so into a guy like Matthew, or so aroused by *his* arousal.

"When Matthew arrived here at my cabin, things went into overdrive so fast I should have whiplash. But I don't," I say. "I feel like when I'm with him, I know who I am, who I'm meant to be, and what I'll grow to be, and it's fucking beautiful."

"Sounds like a winning combination to me. What's the problem?"

"I don't do long distance."

"Why? Where does he live?"

"Nashville."

He blows a raspberry. "'Long distance?' You make it sound like he's from Australia. You can see a guy who lives in Nashville. There are even direct flights, and they're pretty cheap if I recall correctly."

I grunt. It's true, but… "I need a boy who sleeps by my side every night. I don't want a relationship that's weekends only."

"All right, then move to Nashville."

"My business is here."

"Move him to Asheville."

"I barely know him!"

RJ laughs again. "Oh boy."

"What?"

"You're scared."

"Bullshit." I huff again, but I'm lying.

"Go on," RJ says. "Get out all the reasons why this won't work. Let's hear them."

"He just wanted one night."

"Did you ask if he'd be open to more?"

"It snowed. We're stuck here for Christmas. So, he's got 'more' whether he wants it or not."

RJ cackles, and I start to second-guess my choice in texting him at all. "Did he seem upset at the prospect of being stuck with you? Was he averse to more time spent coming his brains out and falling apart on your dick?"

"So crass," I say, though in my head, I'm no better.

"Did he?"

"No. He seemed…" I'm annoyed, because RJ is calling me on my shit, and it sucks. He's no better than Nick after all, though less self-congratulating.

"How did he seem?" RJ presses.

"Happy?"

"Sounds about right."

I sigh. "The thing is, I'm not sure I'm doing this right, and by 'right,' I mean ethically."

"Oh?" RJ frowned. "Why are you worried about that?"

"He's so inexperienced, and I mean that in every way that matters in kink, and yet when we start a scene…" I clear my throat, embarrassed. "I just start to *fly*, and I don't want to land. He doesn't seem to want to land either. I check his safe words often, and he's honest with me when it's yellow or even red. But if he's green, I end up just going with it, and it's so fucking *good*. For both of us. Yet in the light of day, I worry, what if I've taken him too high? What if when this is over, he falls?"

"Isn't that what you do? Teach people to fall?"

"Yeah, but this is different. What if I hurt him?"

"Ahh."

I wait for him to give me some words of advice, something smart or even stupid, something that will clarify what I should do by either being correct or so wrong the right thing comes to mind. RJ says nothing.

"So what do I do?"

"Well, bud, I think you've just got two options here."

"What's that?" The hope in my voice is embarrassing.

"You're going to have to get real fucking honest with yourself and admit that you want more with this guy at whatever price, or you're gonna have to admit that you're too fucking scared to dive into the realest thing you've ever known."

I suck in a breath like I've been punched. In a way, I have. I'd wanted the truth when I'd texted RJ, but it turns out I don't want it like *this*. "It's not the 'realest thing I've ever known.' I was with Brandon for years, for fuck's sake."

"Mm-hmm, and Brandon made you feel like this guy does? Ever? Even in the beginning?"

I remain silent.

"So it *is* the realest thing, and you're afraid. I get it. It's a big deal."

"I'm not afraid," I insist.

"You're scared you'll get hurt. That you'll fall, and you won't be able to hop back up like one of your trained stuntpeople. That it'll be Brandon all over again, but worse."

"You're wrong. I know what I want and what I don't want. That's all. And I don't want a long-distance thing."

"Right," RJ says and shrugs. "Whatever you say."

"He deserves a Daddy who'll be with him day in and day out. It's not just about me," I say, like he's accusing me of being selfish.

"Probably."

"I care about what he wants and deserves. It's my duty as his Daddy to prioritize him above all else."

"Uh-huh."

"So this is about *him* and what *he* needs, not just what I want."

"And he needs a second-rate Daddy who can't see him the way you do, just because that guy's in the same town? And you need a shiny new boy with no wrinkles on his face who can giggle insipidly at everything you say and suck your cock for a few months or years before he takes off and leaves you alone?"

"Fuck you."

"You wanted my opinion."

"I didn't ask to be insulted."

"It's not an insult to have someone point out that you're afraid to be fully loved, or to remind you of that conversation we had in Albuquerque when the bus broke down. You remember it?"

"I remember."

"Brandon wasn't with us, and you were drunk on that blackberry wine Aaron bought from the shitty liquor store, the only place in walking distance, and you said—"

"I know what I said," I snap.

"And *you* said, 'I can't ever have what you and Aaron have.' I asked you why and—"

"I know what the fuck I said!"

"You told me, 'Boys always go because, in the end, I'm not worth staying for.'"

"I was drunk. That's got nothing to do with this situation."

"What happens if someone stays, Erik? What happens if you do find something like what I have with Aaron? What if this boy sees you—*really fucking sees you*—and stays anyway? What then?"

"He won't stay."

"This guy? Or any boy?"

"I don't know," I admit.

"Figure that out before you lose something precious over a few shitty excuses." RJ's head swivels to the side. "Oh, hey, babe. Just talking to Erik about kink stuff."

Aaron's face appears at an awkward angle on the right half of the screen. He's as handsome as ever, with dimples that rival Matthew's. "Hi!" He grins and waves.

I smile and wave back, though a little half-heartedly.

RJ goes on, "I was just telling him he should be brave and take on this new boy he's been seeing."

"I haven't been 'seeing' him," I say. "I was won in an auction, and he's got my cock in his pocket for a couple of nights. That's all."

RJ rolls his eyes. "That's all, he says. That's *all.*"

"You wouldn't call RJ if that was all," Aaron says, with a know-ing smile. "Take his advice. He's good at cutting through BS and getting to the heart of things."

I sigh. It's true. That's part of why I reached out to him, but I don't think I can take his advice. It's too real. The thought of *trying* with Matthew makes me feel...

Fuck.

RJ's right. I'm terrified. But if I put that aside, and imagine a future of fucking Matthew, of having days, weeks, months, and *years* of time to see what else is deep inside his closet of shame, to excavate it, to air it out and let it run free? I just want to laugh, and spin, and scream at the sky.

I'm in so much trouble. So incredibly fucked.

"I *would* take his advice," I agree. "If I weren't a coward."

RJ cocks his fingers like a gun and shoots at the screen. "Bam. He sees the truth of it."

I don't know about that, but I see there's no way to pull back from what I've started with Matthew. I don't know how to go forward with it either, but at least RJ hasn't fed me full of bullshit and called it truth.

I chat with Aaron for a few more minutes about light things—we're both teachers in a way, and we like to compare notes on the best way to reach our students. After that, we all wish each other a merry Christmas before ending the call.

I sit on the stool by Molly and Miss Merry Joy-Joy's enclosure, watching them together. Molly rests while the kid frolics and falls. Gets up again. Falls. Gets up.

That's what I teach, isn't it?

So why *am* I so afraid of this fall? This thing with Matthew is a Christmas gift of the kinkiest sort. But it's also beautiful. Unexpected. Intense. It makes my balls ache and my heart sing.

RJ's right. I don't want it to end.

But, fuck, what if he stays, and I let him in? Let him see the real me, and it turns out I'm not the man he thinks I am, or I'm not the Daddy he needs? What if I let myself believe in having more than just a few years with a boy? Let myself see this as something with potential? *Forever* potential?

What if, after a while, he gets sick of this kink, or outgrows me, and then he's gone too? Like Brandon, like Duncan and Garrett, but this time I can't tell myself it's part of the process. This time it'll be an older man leaving me, and maybe that hits far too close to home.

My mind skitters away from memories of my father.

Maybe I've got just as much baggage as Matthew does. Hell,

I've been carrying Santa's giant toy bag full of issues.

Fuck this. RJ can go suck Aaron's dick and spank his ass. I might preach falling and getting back up again, but *this* kind of vulnerability and risk? It's just too much. I've never given that much power to anyone, and I'm not going to start now.

This weekend with Matthew is only this intense because it's a time-out-of-time, a bubble of pure sexual energy and connection, and I've been missing that for far too long. I've forgotten how good it can be. Any other boy could probably give me just as much of a buzz after such a long dry spell. I'm projecting far too much onto this situation. I should give Matthew the best Daddy Experience I can and stop worrying about it.

RJ's wrong. This thing is beautiful *because* it's fleeting. It's not meant to be more. I don't know what I was thinking of calling him for advice. I'm older than he is—hell, I'm older than Aaron, too, and I've got a ton more experience with kink.

So, yeah. I'm going to take Matthew flying as high as he can go and bring him safely down. Once he's back on the ground, I'll give him a peck on the cheek, a pat on the ass, and send him off into the world to find a permanent Daddy. Someone who lives near him and can take him on for good and for real.

Even if that thought makes me feel vaguely sick, it's still the right thing to do. My hesitation is probably just because my open, trusting Matthew in the wrong man's hands? That could do so much damage.

However, the right man could change Matthew's life for the better.

I'm not the right man.

But I can help Matthew find him. I've got kink connections. I can put Nick on a mission to find a quality Daddy in the Nashville area. We can set Matthew up with him after this is all over. I'll feel better about everything if the Daddy who takes him on has at least been vetted by someone with his best interests at heart.

Sure, he's got that friend Doug who drew up the very solid contracts for our time together, but that guy used him in the past. As far as I'm concerned, he can't be trusted.

A Daddy vetted by me is exactly what Matthew needs. I'm sure he'll agree to that if I mention it to him. He agrees to most everything.

The roiling that sets up in my stomach is stupid. I'll ignore it. Just like I'm going to ignore RJ. I'm in control. I've got this. It's Christmas, and we're going to celebrate our bonus time together, and that's that.

Even if I fall a little during my time with Matthew? It won't be too far. I can still get back up.

CHAPTER TWENTY

Matthew

I WAKE AGAIN to the blare of midmorning sunlight on my face. In a daze, I peel my eyes open and take in the fireplace, the Christmas tree, and the snow glistening outside. A smile grows.

I'm here in Erik's lodge—or cabin as he calls it—and this is real. I've done it. I've finally had sex with a man—a caring, intense, passionate man—and it'd been everything I'd dreamed of and more. The languid feeling in my muscles? That's all real too. The satisfaction in my bones? Real.

Oh Lord, everything about the last twenty-four hours has been mind-blowing. I feel like a newborn colt, slick and fresh, all wobbly legs and knobby knees. Or maybe I'm like the baby goat out in Erik's barn—fuzzy, frisky, and giddy, like I can climb mountains, or trot around everywhere in a paroxysm of joy.

When I flex my ass muscles, squeezing the cheeks together, I grin at the tenderness of my hole—or "bussy," as Daddy calls it. I do it again. It's like a shot of ecstasy straight to my heart, which is galloping like a horse.

I clench the blanket over me in both fists, pull the material up to my mouth, and let out a small shout. It's as if I'll burst if I don't let the feelings free. I have a few more shouts where that first one came from, so I let them out, too.

Holy shit. I'm so happy. I didn't even know it was possible to be this happy. Every part of me feels awake and alive. My blood is fizzing, my heart is clamoring, my brain is spinning, and my cells are zinging. My nipples are hard. My cock is at a half chub. Another small scream comes up, and I smother it with the blanket, too.

Some inane part of me wants to capture this feeling, and the only way I can think to do that is to take a selfie documenting this moment in my life when I'm perfectly happy. I'm not sure I've ever felt the sensation before.

I wake my phone, and a dozen or more text messages come through. I ignore them long enough to take the shot and smile at the image of myself: eyes gleaming, bed head messy, and a red mark on my stubbled chin—beard burn. From kissing Erik. I bite into my lower lip and think about how good his cock tasted, how much I want to suck him off again, but this time his jizz will fill my mouth, and I'll—

My phone buzzes in my hand. Another text message comes through. From Doug.

Opening our message thread, I see that he's sent a number over the last twenty hours. Nine to be exact, and they're all different versions of the same thing:

Where the fuck are you?

Why haven't you replied?

Has he killed you?

Don't you know you can't just go to some strange guy's house without giving a friend your location? If you're murdered, I'm not responsible. Got it?

I scroll through them all and smile at the odd, warm feeling in my chest. I didn't know Doug cared this much about what happens to me. He sounds genuinely scared. I'm sorry for that, but it's kind of nice to know he still has strong feelings for me. Maybe we're really friends again, after all, and I didn't ruin everything by begging Forest to fuck my mouth. Maybe I've earned back an invitation to Christmas next year.

I type in a response.

I'm fine. Thanks for checking on me.

Location?

I send through the address.

Proof of life?

I send the selfie I just took.

You look happy.

I am.

When will you be home? I want to see you when you get back to town.

Why?

Forest has a friend he thinks might be right for you, and since you've popped that cherry, I think you could be game.

My good mood flounders. *Who's the guy?*

It takes a while for Doug to reply. His bubbles keep on bubbling, though, so whatever he has to say, it's long. My stomach tightens, and I find myself standing to search out the big window, peering toward the barn, hoping Daddy comes to save me from this text exchange.

I hate thinking of my inevitable future where I'll end up saying yes to sex with a man who isn't Erik. And since Daddy won't keep me, I know I'll eventually say yes. Because after last night with Daddy? I can't go back to being celibate and alone. I just can't.

The phone pings.

Paul Adler. He's the attorney Forest's company works with when the shit hits the fan. High-powered. Wealthy. Turns out he's also looking for a short-term situation with a submissive man his own age. He's got good creds. I checked out the references. Past subs say he's fair and fun. No reports of problems.

I stare at those lines for longer than Doug seems to think is necessary because he sends through: *You don't have to decide right now. That's why I wanted to see you. Talk it through, and then maybe introduce you.*

My gaze returns to the stockings that are still filled since Erik says I need to wait for the real Christmas morning now. As curious as I am to open my presents, it'll be even more special to wait.

I know this can't be my home, but…

I want to spend Christmases here with stockings and lights and gifts and a fresh tree that fills the air with pine. I want Erik to be my man and this cabin to be our home. A place where we're honest together, and kinky together, and where I learn all about what's behind his calm exterior. A place where I help him care for the animals, and I take over his accounts for his business, and—

All that's silly and naïve. But I don't want to meet this Paul Adler. I don't want to see if he might be a good fit for my *"needs"* or anything else.

I want Daddy to come back from the barn, take me in his arms, kiss me, and make all this dissolve away into heat, passion, and sex. I want him to cuddle me on the sofa, feed me at his table, kiss me in the shower, and fuck me in his bed.

I rub my forehead. Christ, so much of that is all about sex. Is that all this is?

It doesn't matter when none of it's on offer anyway. Not after the snow melts and I have to leave. So, if I want to ever experience something like last night again, if I don't want to crawl back into my lonely life to die alone, I'll have to put myself out there, as I did with this December Daddy Experience. Look how well that's paying off.

Maybe Paul Adler will pay off too. And maybe he won't, but it can't hurt to check.

I'm not sure when I'll be back.

I thought you were due home today? Is this guy holding you hostage?

I'm snowed in. We have to wait for them to plow the roads before I can go.

Sounds like poor planning on his part, or did he want you trapped there with him for Christmas Day? Is he that lonely?

I wince, knowing I'm the one who's thrilled to not be alone at Christmas as usual. I tap out: *He knew it was supposed to snow, but it hit harder than they'd predicted.*

So all the serial killers say.

You checked his references yourself.

I did. And he's stand-up, according to everyone I spoke to. But if he tries anything weird, get out of there.

How? My car's under a pile of snow. But I'm not worried. He's been nothing but kind so far.

And intense, and gorgeous, and attentive, and gone to the barn for far too long.

I'm going to need proof of life every twenty-four hours you're away, or I'm calling the police.

Aye, aye. Didn't know you cared.

I care. Don't appreciate you asking my husband to fuck your face, but I care a lot about you.

I wince, shocked he actually brought my big mistake up. It's been the elephant in the room for so long. Fingers shaking, I type: *I'm really sorry about that. You know I am. How can I make it up to you?*

You can't.

This is a bridge he can't seem to get over, and the warm feeling I'd had toward him only moments ago goes cold.

Doug texts again: *I mean you shouldn't have to make it up. After what I did to you in college and how you forgave me for using you, I shouldn't have given you hell over one mistake. Forest is hot. I get why you'd want to suck him off.*

I ignore what he said about Forest and address the past again. *I wanted what happened between us back then.*

You deserved better than what I gave you. I shouldn't have treated you the way I did. I was rough with you, used you for relief, and didn't reciprocate.

I didn't want reciprocation. I wanted to feel bad.

The next message takes a long time to come through.

When you asked Forest to fuck your mouth, I wasn't jealous. But all that stuff? You and me back in the dorm? It came flooding back. It makes me sick with guilt whenever I'm reminded of it. Sometimes I think if I'd treated you better, you'd have found someone years ago and not let yourself feel so worthless.

I don't know what to say, so I stare at the words, trying to make sense of them.

So that's why I've been a dick to you, Matthew. I know that's selfish, but I really hate feeling guilty, so I've avoided you when I could. I'm sorry.

I gape at the text, agog at his confession. It hurts, but at least I understand now. *I forgive you*, I type in.

And then, as if he can't stand being serious and emotional another second, he asks, *If you're still with this Daddy, why are you texting me and not getting fucked?*

He's in the barn taking care of the animals.

Barn? Animals? Is this a scene from Deliverance?

He's got horses and goats and some dogs and cats.

And this is us, back to normal. It's weird how long I've wanted this, and now that it's here, and after his confession of selfishness, I just feel a strange calm. I do forgive him. Maybe I shouldn't, but I do.

They told me he was a business owner.

He is. That's a long story. I'll tell you all about it when I see you.

Why aren't you helping Daddy do his chores, boy?

Because Daddy told me to stay here and rest in front of the fire like a good, pampered boy.

Well, don't get used to that. Paul is probably more demanding. He'll want you to crawl under his desk and let him warm his cock in your hole while he does his paperwork, I bet.

My dick reacts to that image, but I don't conjure an image of this stranger Paul Adler. Instead, I imagine myself on my hands and knees on the floor of an office, crawling beneath a wooden desk, and putting my head on my folded hands, my ass up in the air, and Erik—Daddy—will pull his chair in behind me, cock out.

With some creative positioning, he'll thrust into me and just…*hold* it there, maybe sliding in and out incrementally, as he works at the desk above, scribbling away. I can picture it so well I can almost hear the scratching of his pencil moving over paper, the smooth roll of a pen when he signs his name, and when he's done with his work, he'll take hold of my hips to fuck me for real.

I'm hard now. Hard and aching. The front of the underwear Daddy's got me wearing is distended by my growing cock. I'm tempted to get on my knees, head to the floor, ass up, and wait for Daddy just like that.

What will he think if he walks in and sees me so ready and—

The ping of my phone brings me back to reality.

Paul is on board, btw. He'd like to meet you too.

I thought we were going to talk about it first?

We will. But getting on his schedule can be hard. He's penciled you in. You'll be able to meet him after Christmas, have a day or two to think it over, and iron out an agreement for six weeks of service by the New Year.

Six weeks of service? I just got fucked for the first time. Isn't this moving fast?

Matthew, I've known you a long time. You need a Daddy or a Dom. You'll see.

I can't disagree with Doug. Here I am right now, aching for the return of my Daddy, wanting him to save me from this conversation and the future.

Save me from ever meeting Paul or taking his dick.

CHAPTER TWENTY-ONE

Erik

WHEN I RETURN from the barn, I pause on the deck outside and look in the window again. Matthew's awake and frowning at his phone. As I open the door, he tosses the phone aside, relief washing over his face.

"What's up? Is there a problem?"

Matthew's expression clouds again as he glances toward the phone. "No, it's just…"

"Work stuff?" I suggest. It's a common excuse for avoiding an uncomfortable conversation.

He nods, the divots between his eyebrows deepening. "Something like that."

I take off my boots, putting them away neatly before hanging up my coat, unwinding my scarf and brushing off my hair. It's a little damp from the icy little pellets the sky is still spitting down now and again. "Something like that, but not that," I say, turning to the fire and carefully laying more wood on it. When I turn back to him, I cross my arms over my chest and say, "Tell Daddy what's bothering you."

"It's nothing, Daddy; I'm fine."

"Red," I say.

"What?" Matthew gasps and goes pale.

"Red. This ends until you talk to me. If it's work, fine, it's work, but I want to know that's really what it is. If it's not work, then we can't possibly go on with this until we've sorted the issue out. It wouldn't be safe. You wouldn't be in the right headspace, and I wouldn't be either."

Matthew licks his lips and darts a nervous glance at his phone. "My friend Doug was checking on me."

"Doug," I say, trying to keep my disdain out of my tone. "He's your safety-check friend."

"Yeah, I guess. I didn't ask him to be, though. He was worried about me because I hadn't replied to his texts, and I hadn't given him a location where I am with you."

"You're telling me no one knows where you are?"

"Doug does. Now."

"Matthew, you can't—"

"Doug already scolded me."

I blink, surprised by his pushback. He's been so perfectly compliant before. Then again, I've never truly scolded him, either. And I did call red. He's not in boy mode right now, so I shouldn't be trying to play Daddy, either.

I dial back my tone. "Good. I'm glad he did. Is that why you looked upset when I came in? Because your friend was giving you grief?"

"No, Daddy."

"It's Erik right now," I remind him gently.

"Can we go back to Daddy, please?" he asks, his lashes against his cheekbones, and his lips turned down sadly.

"Will you be honest with me?"

"Yes. I promise."

"And you won't hide from me?"

"I promise, Daddy."

"All right, boy. We're green."

Matthew's shoulders relax, and he chews his lower lip before peering up at me with that wide-eyed innocence that undoes me, especially set in that face with the salt-and-pepper stubble and the signs of aging by his eyes. "Doug wants me to meet a man when I get back."

My stomach flips, and I try to play it off by turning to grab a poker and jabbing at the fire until it lights just right. "Is that what made you frown?"

"Yes, Daddy."

"Tell me about him." I put the poker back.

"He's a Dom, or maybe a Daddy, and he's looking for a short-term submissive. Doug has vetted him already, and he thinks we'd be a good match. Doug says this man, Paul, is eager to meet me. Paul wants a boy his own age, so at least I won't be a surprise to him."

I try not to flinch at that.

Matthew keeps talking. "I don't know if I want to meet him."

I don't want Matthew to meet this man either, but isn't this just what I'd been hoping for in the barn? Someone else to take Matthew on?

"Do you want me to check into his credentials and references?" I ask. I assume the man has some decent ones if Matthew's "friend" Doug has recommended him. I know Doug checked up on me before my first meeting with Matthew last week.

"Would you want to?" Matthew asks, and I can't read his voice. There's something more there, but I'm not sure just what.

"I'd be honored to make sure you're in good hands when you leave me. In fact, I'd consider it a duty."

Matthew swallows and looks down. "Yes, Daddy."

"Get his information. I'll check into him."

"Of course. I'll get it from Doug right now."

And he does. He texts his friend, and when the reply comes through, he forwards it to me. My phone vibrates in my back pocket. I resist the urge to check the message now. As soon as I do, I'll start imagining it: my Matthew with another man, under him, taking his dick—

Fuck. I'm imagining it already.

Wait. *My* Matthew? I might be his first, but Matthew isn't mine, no matter what boorish urges have been awakened in me by his potent combination of age and innocence.

I shake myself and approach him with a smile. "Ready for the next thing, boy?"

"Yes, Daddy," he says, eagerly, and I just know he thinks it's more sex. Sorry to disappoint him, but...

"Let's get you dressed. We're going out to the barn for some light exercise and horseback riding, like I promised."

Matthew adjusts his crotch, and I consider taking a few minutes to blow him, but I want him aching for it later when I let him take my ass. "I appreciate my boy is eager for me. I love how responsive you are." I kiss the side of his neck, tweak his nipples, and suck on his earlobe. "Listen to you moan for Daddy."

"Yesss," Matthew hisses, rubbing his crotch on my thigh.

"But now's not the time for this, sweet boy. Daddy's gotta work out, and you need to get some exercise, too. Plus, this snow has left behind some beautiful views that are too amazing to waste."

GETTING MATTHEW BUNDLED up is pretty fun.

I let him put on the basics by himself: some of my silk long underwear—which are far too big on him—and his jeans. But when he starts to put on the MTSU sweatshirt he brought, I take it from his hands and lay it on the bed. His eyes linger there, like he's hoping this is some indication that I'm going to give up on our workout and instead just throw him on the mattress and strip him again.

It's tempting, but we both need to conserve our orgasms for the big event tonight.

I turn to my chest of drawers, removing two silk undershirts—one red and one green. "These will hold in your body heat."

He slips the red one on first, and I admire the color against his light skin and the dark base of his hair. Then he pulls on the green. He looks like an elf. A very sexy, sweet elf. I kiss his cheek, reaching into another drawer to take out a red sweater. "Now this."

"I have my own sweatshirt," he says, glancing over his shoulder at the bed. "Yours is a little big."

"Yes, but I want you to wear it." I lick my lips, wondering if he'll press the issue or ask why. I'm happy to tell him: I've got a mild kink for a smaller man in my clothes. I've always enjoyed dressing my slighter boys up in my shirts. There's just something sexy about the way they hang, how the arms come down too long, and the way the collar exposes their neck in a kissable way. Not that I'm leaving Matthew's neck exposed. The scarf will come later.

But Matthew doesn't ask. He just puts on the sweater and turns to me with those eyes basically begging me for approval.

"Good," I say, and fist my hand in the front of the loose sweater, tugging him close. He comes easily, shaking as I mouth his neck, his earlobe, and the spot behind his ear I've discovered makes him moan like a wild thing. When I've turned him on again, and he tries to hitch his hips against my thigh for friction, I let him. Kissing his mouth because I can't resist him, we fall into the moment. After a few minutes, he's panting, and I'm panting, and we're both aching and hard.

Dumb, but hot.

"Now," I say breathlessly. "Downstairs."

"Really?" he asks. "But…"

"But what? Daddy's boy needs to exercise."

"I do?"

I nuzzle him again. "It's good for you."

"Is my body not—"

I gently bite the side of his jaw. "Your body is gorgeous. Absolutely fucking beautiful. This isn't about that. It's about taking care of you. Daddy's responsible for you, and since our plans have been extended, I'm going to make sure your body is tended to in every way."

"I'm okay with the naked-in-bed way," he whispers and shoots me a sly grin.

My stomach flips over. I'm pleased to see this version of him again. I met him at the café, and he showed himself several times on that first day, but he's mostly been in pliant-boy mode since he arrived. I'm glad to see he's coming around to his typical self again. "You'll be naked in bed before long. Got it?"

"Yes, Daddy."

I kiss his mouth again, and when he tries to draw me in for a more heated exchange, I pull away. "Now, get your cute ass downstairs." I smack his butt as he walks by. "That's it. Go."

He glances over his shoulder, his cheeks flushed, and his neck red with the friction from my stubble.

Downstairs, I lead him to the coatrack. Wrapping a red-and-green checked scarf around his neck, I'm reminded of the one I never used last night in the bedroom. Maybe he'll be up for that kind of mild bondage play tonight after I've fulfilled my promise to let him try out my ass.

I must admit, I'm not desperate to be fucked. The truth is, I'm not particularly into bottoming. Not because I have any ridiculous ideas about it being a "passive" or "anti-masculine" position, though. I can top from the bottom just fine, thank you very much. It just never gets me off.

I enjoy the feeling of it, and sometimes I can get pretty hot while being fucked, but I've never tipped over into ecstasy while taking a dick. I find the sensation too distracting to get and stay hard. In the end, I typically end up fucking my boy's mouth or flipping him over, so I'm on top to finish.

But with Matthew, I'm into the idea, if only because he's never done it before. I like that I'll oversee how he experiences that distinct, perfect, physical pleasure for the first time. Having that control over him is definitely arousing. So is the thought of starring in all his future memories of every first he shares with me.

It probably doesn't say much good about my character that being the man he'll remember until the day he dies as his true first turns me on deeply.

I've never realized before now how much a similar feeling has led me to my boys. I love being the man they'll look back on as their guide into gay adult manhood. And now I love being the man who's going to initiate Matthew too.

"You like dressing me?" he asks, as I help him pull on his coat.

"Yup."

"A kink or something?"

"Little bit."

"Oh." He smiles, his eyes crinkling at the edges, and I want to kiss those fans. He has no idea how charming he can be.

"I don't consider myself a service sadist or Dom. I've always been more of a service Daddy." I turn to the door and open it, gesturing for him to go first. "Not all are."

"What do you mean?" he says as he crosses the deck to stand by the railing, peering out at the view. It's stunning today. Yesterday the clouds, the fog, and the snowstorm had obscured it, but today you can see the mountains against the pure blue sky.

"Service is when you do things for the other. I like to cook for my boys, dress them, bathe them sometimes, cuddle them. That sort of thing. Some Daddies like their boys to service them more than the other way around. They want their boys to wash *them*, cook *their* dinner, do *their* laundry—I admit, I'll have my boys do the laundry from time to time, but I'll always handle the dishes."

"Why's that?" He turns to me, and the way the light shines in his hazel eyes makes them look like sun on a mossy pond. I'm flustered by it.

Reaching out, I cup the back of his neck and pull him close, kissing the shell of his ear. "Because I like doing them."

Matthew chuckles and smiles at me when I pull back. Christ, he's beautiful. How is it possible he's made it to his age without once being seduced by a caring man? Who wouldn't want to take care of him?

"I like doing the laundry," he admits. "My favorite part is unloading the dryer. Getting the clothes out while they're still warm is comforting, and the fresh scent that fills the air? I love that."

"I love that you love it," I say, a rush of emotion making me feel like an awkward teenager. I compensate by taking charge. "Let's go."

He lets me guide him past the small deck with the hot tub and down to the path to the barn. I didn't show him all of it yesterday. Around the back, there's another door leading to the training area. That's where I take my clients if or when I bring them up here, and it's where I'll start training Matthew on how to get up after falling.

But first, we must cross the distance between the cabin and the barn. Birds call, the cold scent of snow fills our nostrils, and there's a creaking sound coming from the mountains. The trees around us are straining under branches full of snow. Matthew takes it all in quietly, and when Brodie and Scott come running toward him, he pets them and accepts licks on his hands, all without stopping his long trudge next to me in the snow.

"They're happy you're still here," I say. It's a lie. The dogs don't care one way or another about Matthew—not yet anyway—but *I'm* happy he's still here.

"Are they?" he asks, but he's looking at me. Busted. He knows.

I clear my throat. "Even if they aren't, I am."

He blushes, and I want to lick his red cheeks. "I'm happy to still be here."

"I feel like one day with you wouldn't have been enough. I wouldn't have been fair to you."

"Yeah? Why?"

"Because you deserve more than one night with anyone. You deserve to be cared for, and I think, even if we'd had the amazing night we did, and even if we'd woken to the planned stockings, Christmas breakfast, and presents, I think you'd have felt…" I don't know how to explain it.

"Used?" he asked.

"Maybe, but I was thinking more along the lines of you needing more aftercare."

"Aftercare. That's the cuddling and holding that comes after a kink scene, right?"

"Yes, but it's not just that. This? What we're doing right now? This is aftercare, too. I'm showing you that I've got space for you, whether it's naked or not, and whether an orgasm is promised or not."

"I want to give you orgasms," he says, and his grin is cheeky even if his blush comes rushing back. So ridiculous. I love it.

"I will happily accept them and even demand them, but I'm also happy to spend time with you when we're not fucking. That's key. You're more than just holes for pleasure."

He says nothing for several long moments, and the dogs come racing past us again. Scott has a stick, and he tosses it in the air to catch it, misses, and Brodie grabs it up.

"You're right," he says. "I wanted to feel cared for. That's part of what I've yearned for and missed out on. And this, being with you in a nonsexual way—being made to wait for sex, even—makes me feel cared for."

"Good. I'm glad to hear that."

"And I know it wasn't planned, but actually being here for Christmas is…" Matthew swallows hard. "Special."

My chest tightens. "It is."

"I do want to have more sex, though."

I laugh. "I promise."

He reaches for my hand, and I take it. I can't feel his skin through our gloves, but our connection is there all the same. It hums between us like a living thing. I try not to analyze it and just enjoy it. Because truth be told—I've never felt anything like it with another man.

CHAPTER TWENTY-TWO
Matthew

ERIK'S TRAINING ROOM is large. When he flicks the light on, illuminating the inside, I'm surprised by both the size and the professional vibe of it—though I suppose I shouldn't be, since training actors, dancers, acrobats, and even active stage musicians is his job.

I suppose, now that I think about it, the barn is much bigger than the area I saw for the goats and horses. I hadn't noticed it before because I wasn't analyzing the shape of the building, but now it seems obvious. If I had given it any thought, I'd have imagined this area was all filled with hay. But, no, Erik says that's all kept in the hayloft.

A black, orange, and white cat is asleep on a stack of thick mats by the inside of the door. I guess it snuck in from the barn some-how. I pause just next to it, taking in the chill of the room—minimal heating, it seems—and the vast number of items and equipment it holds.

The cat opens its eyes halfway to peer at Erik and me. It tracks Erik with its gaze as he tosses his puffer coat aside and crosses the room. He passes the barbells, and moves around to the square portion of the floor covered in soft mats where he stops near a selection of kettlebells in various sizes and weights.

"Take off your coat and come over here," he calls to me, and I run my fingers over the cat's soft back before obeying. "That's Dolly, by the way."

"She's cute." Soon I'm standing a few feet from him with my coat in hand, not sure what to do with it.

"Just toss it on top of mine."

I do, and the cat moves from her perch to settle on our coats, purring as she does.

"Damn cats," Erik says without any heat. "One of them has a sense of humor and likes to jump on you out of the blue. Watch out for that."

I turn around, but I don't see any other cats in the room.

Erik sets aside two metal baseball bats. "We try to have all the cats fixed regardless of sex, before we have way too many cats on our hands. But sometimes a stray cat shows up, already pregnant or in heat, and we end up having to find a home for six little ones."

There's a long mirror on the wall next to him, and I can see us both reflected in it. Erik is tall, muscled, and so handsome I wonder why he didn't try to go into acting himself, instead of just training actors to do what he does effortlessly. And then there's me. I admit I'm not unattractive. With this strange manic glow in my eyes, Erik's too-big clothes, and an exhausted languidness to my stance, I think I'm even a little sexy.

I tilt my head, considering us both.

Maybe it's wishful thinking, but we look good together. Big and tall next to shorter and lithe. Light brown and tan next to salt-and-pepper and pale. And his thirty-five years doesn't seem too young next to my forty-one. It's clear to me that anyone seeing us together would know that Erik's not only large but in charge. He moves and speaks with such easy confidence.

I, however? Even standing still and soft with this new rush of feelings, I hold myself in a way that can only be described as passive, submissive. I imagine this is what Erik must see when he looks at me.

I like it.

I like *myself* when I'm next to him. Even if I'm not "his boy" right now, and he's not "Daddy," I approve of this Matthew. He's not tied in knots, he's not ashamed of his life or desires, he's not trying to be someone he's not. He's just Matthew.

And Erik is just Erik.

I lick my lips. No, Erik is still Daddy, and when I'm with him, am I ever not his boy? I don't think so. Our roles are just so natural and clear. There's no fight in me when I'm beside him. I can just relax into this place of trust.

I don't know that I've ever felt this way in my life. Not in my home or school, definitely not in my workplace. I've always had to mask who I am. This is the first time I've ever just been raw and real and me.

It's like I became his boy the moment he saw me in the café and recognized me for who I was—the man who'd won him in the auction.

Now I can't stop being his boy. Not in his presence. Not even when he calls red.

"You warm enough?" he asks, pulling my attention back to the present. I realize I've wrapped my arms around myself as I've been thinking. "I can turn on the space heater."

I shake out my arms. "I'm good." Between the layers of silk undershirts and his sweater, I'm plenty warm.

"All right then." Erik tosses his sweater aside too, leaving just one silk undershirt over his toned flesh. I can see his muscles through it, and the darkness of his nipples. I realize I haven't kissed them or licked them yet.

There's so much I want to do. And so little time to do it. What if I'd had to leave this morning? What if I never get the chance to rectify this situation?

Erik tsks at me. "Pay attention, please. I understand you're still processing last night, but this is important. I don't want you to get hurt."

"Right. Sorry."

"You don't have to apologize; just watch me carefully. I'll explain what I'm doing as I go."

I nod, studying Erik's strong body as he hinges over, sticking his firm ass out—I remember gripping it last night as he plunged into me—and places his hands around the handle of the kettlebell.

"Keep your back straight," he says. "That's important. Don't bend it."

I chew on my bottom lip as he lifts his torso, so his back is perpendicular to the floor before swinging the kettlebell between his legs, letting it fly to the same level as his eyes as he stands and flexes his ass before hinging over to let it swing between his legs again. He does ten reps of that before letting the kettlebell rest on the floor.

"Now, let's talk through the key points."

He has me come stand beside him as he goes through the movements without the weight, and watches as I do the same thing. "Good, good," he says, directing me to the second kettlebell.

"Now, just lift it to start. I want to see whether this is the right weight for you."

I move the weight off the floor, but it's a bit too heavy, so I let it drop again. It clangs on the concrete. "Sorry."

"It's all good. Let me get a different one. Hold on."

We try out two more weights before he's satisfied that I'm not going to hurt myself doing the exercise. He stands next to me, watching carefully as I do a set of eight.

"Good."

I'm panting already, and a fine sweat has started, which is mildly embarrassing, but Erik doesn't say anything about it. Instead, he studies his watch, and after a set amount of time, he tells me, "Again."

Now I'm really huffing, and Erik watches me with an impassive expression.

"One more set, and then you can rest while I do mine."

I don't argue with him, and when he tells me to start, I do. The next set feels tougher, but it's soon over, and while I'm sweating—especially with the layers of undershirts and the sweater—I'm not entirely exhausted.

I am also more than happy to watch Erik. His body is beautiful, and after a few sets of ten, he strips off his undershirt and I'm blessed with the sight of his glistening chest and shoulders.

"Now, we'll do squats."

I strip off the too-big sweater and silk undershirts after the first set of squats. I notice his eyes lingering on my body, hungrier than I'd have expected, given how easily he'd turned down the prospect of an orgasm this morning.

After I finish with the squats with a light kettlebell, he comes around behind me, and I don't protest or move as he presses against my back and slides his hands over my upper body, scratching through my chest hair, and down to the fur beneath my belly button. I'm hard now, which will make doing any more squats inconvenient to say the least.

He kisses the back of my neck, my shoulder, coming around to kiss my chin, my jaw, and the front of my throat until he moves to suck on my nipples. My knees go weak, and I grip his head, using his strength to hold me up.

First my left, then my right, and back again; he teases me with his teeth and tongue. When he pulls away, his chin is red from the scratchiness of my chest hair, but my nipples are even redder from his work.

I pant, steadying myself on his biceps, which flex beneath my palms as he puts his hands on my waist, and holds me back, not allowing me to rub my erection on him.

"Now I'll show you the Turkish Get-Up," he says, all throaty and aroused. At least I'm not alone in my lust. He can't seem to keep his hands—or lips, rather—to himself to finish this workout. They roam over my collarbones and up to my mouth, where he gives me a thorough, wet kiss before pushing me physically away from him. "Watch carefully. If we're still snowed in tomorrow, I'll expect you to do this. But I'll let you get away without it today."

"Yes, Daddy." I sound drugged. I wish he'd stop whatever it is he's doing and just bend me over the—

"Matthew, are you paying attention?"

"No, Daddy," I admit.

He laughs, adjusts his own crotch, and says, "Watch me."

He's on the floor now with a kettlebell, and as I watch, he proceeds to do a complicated series of moves, all the while keeping the weight above his head. For the first time since I woke up, I hope the snow has melted by the morning. I don't think there's any way I can do what he's just done.

"That's the Turkish Get-Up."

"What's it for?"

He smiles. "It trains your muscles on how to get up." He does it again. And again. "The core strength needed for any feat that requires getting up from the ground can be developed with this move."

"I don't think my accounting job is going to call for that, Daddy."

He laughs and puts the weight down, coming over to me, running hands over my chest again like he's helpless to stop himself. "It probably won't. But core strength—" He touches my abs and slides his hands to my lower back. "Is key to aging well, and there's something to be said for the correlation between a strong core and inner strength."

"Is there? So all bodybuilders have inner strength too?" I raise a brow.

He chuckles again. "Look at my boy now. Showing Daddy his sarcasm skills."

"I just have my doubts, Daddy, that someone who's physically strong is also always emotionally strong."

"Fair enough. But I've seen it time and again with the people I train. As they learn to get up, literally, from the ground, as their core grows stronger and they can more fluidly rise to their feet with minimal or no use of their hands, I see an inner strength rise as well."

"Do I need more inner strength, Daddy?"

He grips my hips and gazes into my eyes. "All strength isn't good strength. I think you know that. You've been strong for a long time in ways that have hurt you. You held a lid down on your desires while your parents lived, and you're strong enough to go to a job every day that doesn't fulfill you because you need the money, because it's the responsible thing to do. You were strong enough to keep the truth from your parents because you didn't want to cause them pain—and that was just as strong a desire, wasn't it, as keeping them from turning on you?"

"Yes," I say, breathlessly. I haven't told Erik any of that, and yet he saw it. He knew I hadn't kept my secret out of fear alone, but out of love. And he knew how strong I'd had to be to hold that lid down for all those years.

"But that strength isn't the kind of inner strength I want to cultivate in you, boy."

He wants to cultivate things in me? We have one more night, two at most, can he plant seeds that will grow without the light of his regard shining on them?

"I want you to learn the inner strength that comes from doing things you think you can't—from being brave, like you were when you bid on me at the auction, or like when you came here or when you let me give you that enema. That's a different kind of strength from the kind that does what's respectable at your own expense. That's the kind of strength that lets you grow."

"And the Turkish Get-Up will make me grow?" I don't resist the urge to be cheeky. Daddy wants to see the real me.

He laughs again. "Tall as a house."

"I like being your boy, though, Daddy."

He nuzzles the side of my face, his sweat mixing with my own. "You can stay a boy as long as you want. It takes a ton of strength to be a dedicated boy."

I hold my tongue. I want to be *his* dedicated boy.

I long to be here in a month, a year, with Erik watching me as I do this damn Turkish Get-Up a dozen times in a row. I'd show him how strong I can be, and how much inner strength and bravery I can cultivate.

But I guess I'm not there, yet, because I don't have the guts to tell him.

Instead, I kiss him again, and he lets me. Minutes pass before he summons the will to push me away again.

"C'mon," he says, taking hold of my arm and leading me to the door, leaving our shirts behind us. "Let's cool off. We can't ride horses with hard dicks."

"YOUR ASS DOING all right?"

"Yes." I tighten my thighs around the big body moving beneath me.

"You're doing just great. A natural."

"Thank you."

I don't feel like a natural on the back of a big beast like Zebra Cake, who is every bit as sweet as Erik promised yesterday. I'm just not sure I'm cut out for horseback riding. The saddle isn't entirely comfortable, and while I haven't lied to Daddy whenever he asks about my ass, I'm not being entirely honest either.

Every jolt—and there are plenty of them as Zebra Cake makes his way up the rocky, mountain inclines on the trail through Erik's property—reminds me that not only did he spank me this morning, but I had his thick, wide cock up inside me last night. But I like being reminded of that, so while it does hurt, I'm not going to complain about it.

The memories of what he did to me are too good, too precious, and every ache brings them to mind with a crystal clarity that makes my heart race. If it weren't so cold, and my anxiety wasn't so high, what with the way Zebra Cake's feet are landing on what seems to me very treacherous stones, I might even chub up over it.

But as it is...

"Erik," I ask. "This is safe?"

"Of course," he calls back over his shoulder. "I'd never take you out on a hazardous trail or put you on an unsafe animal. Zebra Cake is a steady sweetheart. He won't let you fall."

"But what if he trips on one of these rocks?"

"He's sure-footed."

I don't reply, watching as Zebra Cake's feet land on another smooth, round stone, and his frail-looking ankles don't twist.

"Matthew, what color?"

"Are we in a scene?" I ask.

I hadn't realized we were in a scene right now. I thought this was just Matthew and Erik out for a ride in the glistening-white snowy day.

"Even if we aren't in a scene, you always have a right to call a halt to whatever we're doing. If this is red for you, say so, and we'll stop."

"Here?" I ask, blinking at the drop-off over the edge near the trail. "Like right here?"

"Yes. If you want that. If you need to stop so you feel safe."

"No. I'm fine. We can keep going."

"Or we can get up to the flatter part of the trail ahead, if you prefer, and call red on this."

"No," I say again, shaking my head. "I'm all right. I trust you." And I do. I trust Erik more than I've ever trusted anyone in my life, except maybe my mother, and even she had never been trustworthy enough for me to come out to her. I've shown Erik more of my true self in the last twenty-four hours than I've shown anyone in my entire life. I trust him that much. I trust him with the truth of me.

"All right, boy. Use your colors if you change your mind."

Noting his use of "boy," I answer in kind. "Yes, Daddy."

As we continue up the side of the mountain, I can't decide which is the better view: the wondrous landscape unfurling around me, all glittering white and magical, or Erik's wide shoulders, slim hips, and gorgeous ass undulating with each of Tyrone's steps. Erik's not wearing more than a sweater over silk undershirts, jeans and sturdy boots, and gloves.

"It's all in the underclothes," he'd assured me earlier when he was dressing us again after our workout. "Silk long underwear on top and bottom, thick socks, and a sweater is more than enough to keep us warm." He'd handed me each item as he'd named it and watched carefully as I'd put them on.

So far, he's right. I'm cold, but it's not unbearable, and I make a note to buy some long underwear for my next winter trip to an annual accounting convention up north. I always freeze at those.

After almost an hour of a slow, rolling walk around the mountainside, next to a frozen stream, and passing by striated rock faces, we arrive at a clearing. It's wide and covered in snow, and both the horses have to work to make their way through the dense, unblemished blanket. Once we reach the middle, Erik draws to a halt and nods at the horizon.

I tear my gaze away from admiring his ass and gasp at the gorgeous view. The mountains are like a layer cake of earth and sky, the white of the snow is almost blue, and the blue of the sky is so pure it takes my breath away. Evergreens add smears of green, and the fog, so common in this part of the Appalachian Mountains, lies over it in wisps and snatches like icing.

"Wow," I say, as Zebra Cake shuffles underneath me. "It's beautiful. Thank you for bringing me here."

"I wanted to share it with you," he tells me, turning to slide off Tyrone's back. "C'mon. Off you come now." He reaches for me, and I let him help me down like some damsel in distress, because I'm genuinely not sure I can get off Zebra Cake without falling. Erik says falling is good for a man, but I don't think I want to risk getting hurt all the way up this trail.

Erik seems to agree because he's careful with me. Even once I'm fully on my feet, he doesn't let me go. I'm about to tell him I'm fine, he can release me now, when he drags me close and kisses me.

The view is forgotten in the passion of Erik's mouth. It's a hot anchor in the cold air, and I chase his lips when he pulls back. It's a bad habit of mine to want more than Daddy is giving me in the moment, but he doesn't seem to mind, and he's never scolded me for trying to prolong our kisses.

Not that he's ever truly scolded me for anything yet. And given the shortness of our time together, it's unlikely that he'll be given the chance.

Because I plan to be so good for him. So perfect.

When I go, I want to leave behind a memory beyond his wildest dreams, so whenever he thinks of me, he thinks of what a good boy I was for him. I want him to think of me every Christmas. Far more often than that, to be honest, but I'll make this Christmas one to remember for sure.

"You're so tempting," he says by my ear, making me shiver with the heat and tickle of his breath. "If I were a little younger, and a little stupider, I'd shove you down in that snowbank and suck you off right here."

"You can," I tell him. "If you want to, Daddy."

"I know, boy. You'll let me do anything to you."

"I just want to be your good boy."

"You already are, Matthew. Holy shit, you are *such* a good boy." He nuzzles my neck. Tyrone stands next to us, huffing lightly in the coldness. "I didn't realize how hungry I've been for this. How much I've needed to connect like this with a boy. I'd hoped to find my love for this kind of play again, to find meaning in it, and *fuck me*, I've found all that and more. Thank you for showing it to me."

I smile at his echo of my own words regarding the view. "It's been my pleasure, Daddy."

He laughs. "It has been, hasn't it? You're so eager and such an avid student, a quick learner."

"I want to learn to fuck you, Daddy."

"Oh, I plan to teach you," he says, drawing me in close enough I can feel his hardness through our layers of long underwear and jeans. I'm not hard, but lust rises fast as he thrusts against me. "But that's for later, once we're in the warm, dry house. What can I teach you here, boy?"

"Anything. I'm ready to learn."

"On your knees."

I obey immediately despite the snow, and when he opens his pants, I realize he's using Zebra Cake's body to shield us from the cold wind. Erik leans back against his side, and he takes his weight easily. "Suck me," Erik says, indicating his cock, dark with blood and probably aching from the cold.

I open my mouth and suck on the head of his dick, taking hold of the base with my gloved hand.

"That's my good boy," Daddy says, dashing the knit beanie cap he's lent me into the snow, to slip his fingers through my hair. "Slower, move a little slower for me now."

I obey and bob my head, careful of my teeth. When I start to go even deeper, to take him into my throat, he clucks his tongue.

"No, sweet boy. Face-fucking is great, and deepthroating is fantastic, but you use it to shame yourself, and we're not playing with shame right now. We're playing with pleasure. *My* pleasure."

My knees grow wet from snow melting and seeping through the layers, but I work on his cock like my life depends on it: kissing, sucking, licking, and taking him halfway down before bobbing up again. I get a rhythm going, and I can tell it's good for him because he's panting and grunting. His thigh tenses beneath my palm, where I'm holding myself upright.

"Just like that," he whispers, carding through my hair more gently now. "Daddy's going to come." His voice sounds strained. "Swallow it for me, sweet boy. Swallow all of it."

It takes a few more minutes of my dedicated work before he grabs my head, holds me steady, and jets cum into my mouth. I swallow greedily, hoping that no drops leak out. It tastes bitter and strong, but I don't care. It's good because it's Daddy's. I'll drink gallons more of it if he has more to give.

"Fuck," he breathes. Slipping free of my lips, he tucks himself away, and joins me, kneeling in the snow. Zebra Cake stomps and huffs, but otherwise remains passively at our sides.

"Thank you, Daddy," I say as he rubs his gloved thumb over my lips, which feel rubbery from the exertion and cold. He presses his thumb inside, and I suck at the leather. The taste is familiar somehow. It brings back a flash of my childhood: my father's leather gloves on the steering wheel.

Erik pulls his thumb free. "That was special. You're special."

"You're special, too, Daddy."

"Yes," he agrees. "*This* is special." He sounds sad about that, though, resigned, and I don't know what to make of it. But then he smiles. "Does my boy need to come now?"

"No," I tell him honestly. "I'm not hard."

"Oh?"

I duck my head, worry creeping over me. "Is that okay, Daddy?"

"Boy, if you're not hard, that's just fine. So long as you're only doing the things you want to do, I'm happy." He pauses. "Did you want to suck Daddy and eat his cum?"

"Yes. So much."

"I'm satisfied." He fluidly rises to his feet and helps me stand. "There's a longer trail over to the other side of the mountain. Are you up for that, boy?"

"I just want to be with you, Daddy."

There's no more honest answer than that. If Erik wants, I'll camp out with him in a tent in the middle of this clearing. If it pleases him, I'll walk with him in the snow until we find a cave to fuck in. If he asks, I'll get naked on all fours and let him rim me here in the snow even if I get frostbite. Anything to make him happy. If I can service him and be served by him, I'll be happy.

This is better than I ever imagined.

I'm ready to give up everything to make each second with Erik last just a little bit longer. When this snow melts away, and this extended reprieve is over, I think my heart is going to break.

But Erik doesn't want a boy like me. This is special, like he said, a time-out-of-time sort of thing. He'll want a younger, sexier boy with that glow of youth, the shine of a life still unlived. He'll look back on this with me fondly, with yearning maybe, but if I ask for more, it'll pop the bubble, and I'll ruin it all.

Yet I'm on the verge of doing just that as he kneels again, clasps his fingers, turns his hands upside down, and indicates I should step into his palms. When I do, he boosts me onto Zebra Cake's back again. He clucks his tongue, and Tyrone comes plodding back over from where he'd wandered while I was sucking off his rider.

My mouth goes dry as Erik climbs onto Tyrone in one swift movement, like it's no big deal at all, and when he sidles his horse up to mine, he leans over to kiss me again. I feel like I'm in a movie. This can't be my life, and yet I want to keep it so badly it hurts.

Erik gives the command, and both horses clomp toward the trail he wants us to take next. Tears well in my eyes.

Fuck, he's amazing. I want to know more of him.

I want more of *all* of this.

But I can't have it. I need to be okay taking what I can get. One Christmas. That's all.

Daddy's hungry for a boy, isn't he? And I'm too much of a man.

CHAPTER TWENTY-THREE

Erik

Aꜰᴛᴇʀ ʀɪᴅɪɴɢ, I show Matthew how to care for the horses, and we check on the goats again, especially Molly and Miss Merry Joy-Joy. He's delighted by the goats' antics, and that makes me smile. I always find them charming, too.

It's good to see he takes joy in animals. When Tammy Back-Breaker, one of the fat barn cats, demonstrates how she got her name by leaping from the hayloft onto Matthew's shoulders, he screeches, but within moments he's laughing. He bends down to smooth his hands over her solid black back, while she weaves between his legs chirruping at him.

"She likes the element of surprise," I say, feeding handfuls of feed to Jerrykins the goat and his best friend Bobbins. "It's a good thing you're wearing so many layers, though, or her claws would have hurt like hell."

"I don't see any milking apparatus. You said you keep goats for their milk. Do you sell *any* of them for meat?" he asks. I can tell he's hoping we don't. Which is sweet. But he doesn't need to worry about that.

"No, we rent them out in the spring, summer, and fall for various maintenance purposes. Goats will eat a lot of invasive plant species folks don't want in their yards, in city parks, or on their farms—like kudzu, poison ivy, English ivy. Things like that."

"Huh, cool. I never knew."

"We've been lucky to be able to build a life we're passionate about, doing careers we love. Mom raised me to believe in making my life meaningful and helpful to others."

I wonder if Matthew will see how this relates to me being drawn to Daddy play, but he asks something else instead about a topic Brandon used to say was *also* very relevant to my kink interests.

"What about your father? You've never mentioned him."

"He wasn't around."

"Oh?"

Matthew doesn't press, but I can see the curiosity in his eyes. I don't owe him an explanation, but he deserves one. Relationships of all kinds should be reciprocal, and no one should ever have the upper hand, especially in vulnerability-dependent kink interactions.

Not all boys or subs want to know their Daddy's or Dom's weaknesses, and of my own boys, only Brandon ever tried to peel back my skin at all. Only *he* ever got a peek underneath. Which is probably why it hurt so much when he left. Not probably, definitely.

And yet Matthew's different, isn't he? He's here to learn, and what I teach him during this precious time together is what he's going to take home and think is right, what he'll accept going forward. Matthew isn't in this for kink alone. He's not looking for a way out, so much as a way in, and he's yearning for self-love. So what's it mean to him if the Daddy he's with doesn't trust him with his own darkness and past pain? If his Daddy doesn't let him in?

I don't want Matthew leaving me and thinking he's the only one required to share and strip down to truth and bone. That's not what he wants. Furthermore, it's not what he needs. He needs to develop self-love from someone else seeing and accepting every single part of him. Even more, Matthew needs that *same* person to hold him in a place of trust. Meaning whoever his Daddy or partner is, the man will need to be comfortable revealing his own fragility and truth, too.

I know it in an instant, like truth dropped into my heart from a higher source. Just like every interaction with Matthew, at least when we're together, I don't have to puzzle out what to do or what he needs, or even what *I* need. It all just comes naturally, like breathing.

I turn away from Tyrone and lean on the wall next to Dora's stall. I put my hands in my pockets, aware that I'm displaying a hint of insecurity and a small urge to hide. I push on with it. "My father left when I was six. He was in the horse business. That's how he and my mom met."

Matthew seems to sense what I'm saying is important to me. He steps closer, touches my arm, and gazes up with an open acceptance which I usually consider to be my domain. But he does it well, and as his hazel eyes soften, he feels truly older than me for the first time since we met.

I don't mind it.

"My dad traveled a lot, showing horses, selling them." I figure I'll just cut to the bone right away. Let Matthew and me both see whether I still bleed over it. It's been some time since I checked. "It turned out he had another family. We didn't know about them. They didn't know about us."

"Oh." Matthew's hand tightens on my forearm.

"Yup."

"And now?"

"Haven't seen him since I was ten. I used to spend summers with him and his other kids—the first wife divorced him after she found out about my mom and me, but he still got some rights to the children. Me, though… That was all voluntary. He had no legal right to see me after my mom took him through the courts."

"Ah." Matthew's soft sounds of listening encourage me to keep talking.

"I wanted to see him. He was my dad, and I loved him. I wanted to be with him. So he'd take me and my two half-brothers out on the road with him in the summers to help with the horses and to spend some time with us. But we started to realize he had a different woman in every town, and he'd say, 'Don't tell her about Miranda,' or 'Don't tell her about Lydia' or whoever the last lady was in the prior place."

My brows draw low, and my throat tightens. "But I liked Miranda and Lydia and Susan. I liked them all, and I had my mother's voice in my head telling me this wasn't right. That he wasn't a real man, not the kind of man I wanted to be. So I stopped spending summers with him and started helping my mom build the farm's business up instead."

"I'm sorry," Matthew says, his fingers holding on to my forearm as if he can press the pain back inside. I'm not even sure why this is so hard for me to say. It's not like how it was with Matthew's father. That man had never let Matthew be his honest self and opted to never really know his son. I *chose* to walk away. My dad wanted to know me. I just didn't want to know him after a while.

It still feels like he left me, and, fair or not, it hurts like he did too.

"Brandon used to say…" I see a small wince in Matthew's expression.

"Go on," he says, his words contradicting his physical reaction. "What did Brandon say?"

I decide to trust him. "Brandon said I have daddy issues, and that's why I became a Daddy—to parent myself by parenting other people."

"Do you think he's right?"

"Maybe."

"Do you think it's worth investigating?"

I smile at him. "Maybe."

"Erik," he says, and I don't correct him for using my name.

Right now, I'm the younger of us, and his guidance isn't something I should scorn or toss away. "Did Brandon ever see you? The *real* you?"

I tilt my head, considering him. I could lie right now, and he'd believe me, I know he would. "No."

"Why not?"

"I never trusted him enough to show him everything."

"Do you trust me?" he asks. In this moment, I'm not Daddy—I'm the real Erik, and he's seeing me.

I think of what RJ asked me on the phone. I lick my lips before I reply. "I guess I do, yes, because this is me. The real me."

"Have any of your boys ever…" he trails off. His eyes darken before he drops his lashes to his cheekbones.

"Ever what?"

"Seen you do an enema?" he asks quietly. "Like I did when I first got here? Have you ever shown one of your boys that?"

I shake my head. "No."

I've only ever shown that to Daniella, my Dominatrix from college, and just once. She's the one who taught me to start there, to get right to the heart of it in that way.

"Do you think you ever will?"

"Boys don't want to think of their Daddy like that," I hedge. It's bullshit. I've been in the kink community long enough to know there's a way to have a boy administer an enema to me, and for me to still hold a Daddy-space, to turn it into an act of service from my boy. The truth is, I just don't want to be that vulnerable with anyone. What if they let me down?

Like your dad did? I can imagine Brandon asking me, or even Matthew. Especially Matthew—if he had a little more time to get under my skin. It's a good thing he's leaving when the snow melts. He sees too much about me.

I don't hate it.

Matthew

AFTER A LONG shower, I dress in nothing but the clean underwear Erik has given me—this time with the entire back cut out—and come downstairs to ask if I can help with dinner. Erik waves me off. "It's nearly finished. Go wait at the table."

I do, taking the seat next to the head, allowing me to see into the kitchen. I watch as Erik puts together our plates. The scent of rosemary and sweet potatoes rises in the air.

It should feel silly, me wearing just these undies, while Erik is dressed in jeans and a light sweater—unfortunately not a Christmas sweater, but the navy blue suits him. But it doesn't feel silly. It feels sexy and different. New. Like everything else in the last few days. Exciting because it's so fresh. Precious because it's Erik who's there with me, Erik who's asked me to do this, be this, feel this.

I can't get over the way Erik finds me attractive; he can barely drag his gaze away from me as we eat. We don't talk, aside from niceties where I compliment his food, and he asks if I want more salt, but that's not uncomfortable either.

It all feels right after a long day. I'm warm despite being half-naked, thanks to Erik turning up the furnace and getting the fire roaring. I relax with him in the relative quiet, enjoying just the sound of forks on plates, and the light holiday jazz Erik's put on in the background. It brings back memories of playing in a jazz ensemble during my first and only semester at Belmont. At the Christmas concert, we'd presented soft, contemporary jazz versions of "It Came Upon a Midnight Clear" and "Soul Cake." I hadn't been very good, and the group would have kicked me out if I hadn't quit. Still, I have fond memories of that time.

After dinner, Erik leads me to the sofa and instructs me to get comfortable. I don't hesitate to obey. Watching him make a fire in the grate for a second night in a row, I'm surprised to see the stocking with my name on it, which had always been hanging from the mantel, is now on the coffee table in front of me. As tempted as I am to dig into it, I know I'm not allowed yet.

My thighs and buttocks are still aching from the horseback ride earlier, and I'm weary all the way to my bones. It's a nice exhaustion, though, born from exertion unlike any I've put out since I was a little kid. Sexual exertion, physical exertion working with the kettlebells and on the horse, and emotional exertion trying to keep my footing under the onslaught of so many feelings.

Because I'm drowning in them.

And what feelings they are! Nothing I've ever experienced before. So shiny and new. Effervescent *and* fluorescent. I feel like I'm glowing with surprisingly heavy, yet glossy emotions filling me up like bubbles.

But not soap bubbles, more like the tapioca pearls in the boba tea I get near my office in Nashville. The very idiocy of that analogy makes me smile to myself.

If I try to name these feelings, like those same slippery tapioca bubbles from my tea, they just slide away, skittishly avoiding any commitment to a specific sentiment. Almost like I'm hiding the name of the feelings from myself. I suspect I know why.

I can see myself at home in the kitchen, learning where Erik keeps the spices and the coffee filters and in which cabinet he keeps his strainer. I can see myself sauntering along the grassy path to the barn, the dogs racing alongside me, all of us so familiar with each other. I'll pick up a stick. I'll throw it for them. And off they'll run again.

I can see myself learning about the horses, how to help with them, how to care for their hooves and manes. I can learn about the goats, loading them into the trailer and driving them off the mountain, all the way to the suburbs of Asheville to munch on some wealthy hippie's yard.

I can watch as Erik trains people in the barn. I'll hold back, stay out of the way, be unobtrusive, and yet I'll be there to see both minor and major celebrities learn how to fall. And I can learn how to fall too. Erik will give me one-on-one lessons, until I'm so good at it that I help him sometimes, acting as a body for demonstrations with his clients.

I'll work on Erik's accounts for his business, taking them over from whoever handles them now, reviewing receipts and balancing books, bringing my education to him as a gift.

And I can see myself picking up the guitar again, just for my own pleasure, of course, strumming on the porch on a summer evening, as fireflies dance around the mountainside, without a worry in my head about it being good enough for anyone but me and Daddy. In my fantasy, Erik sits with a beer in his hand, his head tilted back, eyes on the stars, just listening. Never criticizing. Taking me and whatever music I offer for what I am and what it is.

I can see it all. I want to at least try for it.

The question is: Can Erik even want this? And if he can, would he want it with *me*? It's clear he wants to fuck me. I can see it clearly in his eyes, feel it in the way he touches me, and I tasted it in the cum he couldn't resist filling my mouth with earlier on our sexy horseback ride. But more than that? With *me*? I just don't know. I doubt it.

I don't have time to slide into despair over my yearning for something so far outside the bounds of what Erik has agreed to, because at just that moment he turns from the fire. I sit straighter as he joins me on the sofa.

"Is Daddy's boy ready to see what's in his stocking?"

I nod, swallowing hard, wishing he could read my mind and know what's going on there. Why can't he answer my questions without me having to risk asking them? "I didn't think I was allowed until Christmas morning?"

"Well, in my family, we have our own tradition of stockings on Christmas Eve, and gifts on Christmas Morning. Santa always comes a bit early when we deserve it."

I grin. "Even if we're naughty?"

He laughs and kisses me deeply, breaking away to say, "Especially then."

I feel like a kid pulling the stocking toward me, but soon lose myself in surprise as I tug out items. There's the handmade soap I'd ooh-ed and ahh-ed over the day we walked around town. There's a small box of candies from Chocolate Fetish with each of my favorite flavors. That he'd remembered all this makes my heart soar.

I remove a pair of socks knitted in rainbow yarn from the store on Wall Street, and laugh as Erik insists I put them on right away. The wool is soft and warm, and even though I'd resented the boring socks from my parents under the tree as a kid, these are wonderful.

I giggle at how I must appear, sitting on Erik's sofa in nothing but assless underwear and rainbow socks. His twinkling eyes are worth any amount of silliness. Socks have never made me so joyful.

There's a packet of patchouli incense, my favorite, and a number of crystals and stones—each with a small note about what they are supposed to do "energetically" for a person.

"I didn't think you'd be into this kind of thing," I murmur, stroking my fingers over the sea jasper shaped into a small heart. The note with it says it helps to provide a calm, uplifting energy during trying times, moving the holder into a more optimistic outlook on life.

"Oh, I'm friends with Ella—the witch who runs the crystal shop—and she's never steered me wrong on shiny rocks."

"You believe they work?"

"I think they're pretty, so it doesn't matter one way or another.

If they help, great. If they don't, that's okay, too."

I pick up the round red stone. The note says it's carnelian and it brings the holder bold energy, courage, and a lingering joy. There are four other crystals—yellow, pink, aqua, and purple in color—but I move on to the next thing in the stocking.

A buttery leather wallet.

Then a cat mug. The very same one I'd held for a few longing moments in one of the gift shops we'd gone to that day. It's full of Christmas candies.

"This is too much," I say. "There are still presents under the tree." I can't stop smiling.

Erik winks. "Take it up with Santa. But those have to wait until the morning. In the meantime, how do you feel about getting naughty?"

How do I feel? Like this is the greatest Christmas ever. I never want it to end.

CHAPTER TWENTY-FOUR

Erik

THE STEAM FROM the hot tub clouds my eyes as I watch Matthew ease his way in. I can tell his legs are aching, probably from the horseback riding, but maybe also from the positions I put him into last night.

His body is lean and quickly turns pink from the heat. I admire how sexy that is, along with his groan as he positions himself in front of one of the jets. "Ahh," he lets out, tipping his head back and gazing at the stars above us, visible above the steam. "This feels great."

I don't reply because the comment doesn't need an answer. The hot tub is one of my favorite aspects of life at the cabin, and I make use of it every time I stay up here. It sure beats the hell out of the rinky-dink shower I have in the house down in Asheville proper.

If Mom and I can get a better handle on our finances this year, maybe I can give up my aerialist clientele, shut down the training facility in town, give up the lease on the house, and move up here permanently. I'm sure there's a way to build the business to make it a profitable option.

I say all this to Matthew, as he bobs lightly across from me.

"What's the issue with your finances?" he asks, and then looks chagrined. "Sorry. I'm so accustomed to seeing other people's income numbers at work that the information just feels like a math problem to me and nothing more. I probably shouldn't have asked. Most people consider money to be personal."

As if taking your virginity wasn't personal? I almost ask.

Instead, I say, "It's fine. There's nothing shameful in our situation. It's not as if we are actually facing money problems. I do quite well, and so does Mom. She keeps the farm profitable, training special-needs kids with the horses and hiring out the goats. Still, my own private training brings in most of our income. Plenty of people are willing to travel here for my expertise, which is great—but generally, I charge less than I do if I go to them or if I have to travel."

"That makes sense."

"Everything changed during the COVID-19 pandemic," I explain. "Before, I did any training that didn't involve the horses in the center in Asheville. I have a nice facility there, with plenty of space for aerialist work."

"Aerialist work sounds so amazing."

"It can be, but I admit, after a fall a few years back where I busted my ankle badly, I don't always enjoy teaching it. But it pays well, and nationwide there are very few trainers who do it."

"Ah."

"Things were going great, but then the pandemic came along."

Matthew's brow creases with understanding. "Oh, yeah. That was a tough time for a lot of folks."

"Shows were shut down across the board—dancers, actors, martial-arts tournaments, TV show productions, movies—all canceled. Well, not all, but mostly. Which left me with just a few folks still needing my work. Because of the virus, I found it safer to move most of my practice up to the barn here. I could more easily control who my mom and I were exposed to that way. Of course, that also meant we needed a place for the clients to stay, since we couldn't send them back to Asheville every night without increasing the risk of exposure. With just the one bedroom in the main house, and my mom's room downstairs, we took the opportunity to add a guest residence behind the barn. Building it depleted our reserves more than I'd like."

"A guesthouse?"

"Ah, I didn't show it to you yet. It's just a small cabin set off behind the barn—one bedroom, a full kitchen, living room, and bath."

"In that case, I don't understand why you'd want to keep on renting a place in Asheville at all? How could anyone *not* leap at a chance to come train up here?" Matthew waves a hand around. "It's beautiful. Even in winter, the landscaping around the cabin is lovely. It feels so peaceful."

"That's Mom's doing, too," I say. "She loves to get out here and dig around in the dirt." I grin, thinking of her last spring, so proud of the way her wisteria was blooming. "I haven't let go of my house in Asheville for two reasons. One, it would leave the other renters high and dry, and two, I need to be in town to train aerialists. I don't have the facilities to do that kind of work up here. Not yet, anyway."

"Renters?"

I explain my setup in Asheville, and the guys living there.

"You have such an active social life," Matthew says, maneuvering his back to be more directly over a jet. The rising steam has his salt-and-pepper hair curling. "It must be nice."

"You're lonely in Nashville?" I already know the answer. To have stayed hidden in the closet until he was nearly forty, to bid on a Christmas fantasy with a stranger—he couldn't have been close friends with very many people.

"I don't know." Matthew sighs. "There aren't many people I want to be close with there. Sometimes I feel like I need a clean break."

Just thinking of Nashville has brought a disquiet to him. He looks as if he's dying to take flight, but he's chained in place.

"What's stopping you?"

"Nothing, I guess," he says, peering through the rising steam out into the night. "I mean that sincerely. There's nothing at all keeping me there now."

My heart aches for him. "Before, it was your parents?"

"Yeah. And then settling their estate. And afterward just…not knowing what else to do with myself. Maybe I'm lacking in imagination."

"Doubtful."

Matthew shrugs, the water rolling off his shoulders. He changes the topic. "It must be nice to travel like you have. Where all has your work taken you?"

By the time I get through listing the cities, states, and countries I've traveled to, Matthew's eyebrows are at his hairline, and his eyes gleam with a kind of envy I want to extinguish. I can take him with—

No.

I shouldn't even think about it. I can't take him with me the next time I leave the country. He's not here for that kind of future.

Unless, maybe, he is…

"Matthew," I start, but I don't know what to say or how to say it. For the first time in his presence, I'm tongue-tied and unclear. I don't know how to move forward.

"Yes, Daddy?"

I smile. Here we go. This is better. Just hearing that one word, I feel more clear-headed already. "Boy, do you like being here with me?"

"I love it, Daddy."

"And, if you could, would you stay longer?"

Matthew's lips roll in, as if he's holding in his innermost feelings. A beat and he asks, "How long?"

I'm a little dizzy as the words come out of my mouth. I try to make them sound light, as if I might be joking. But deep down inside, I think I might mean them.

"How about forever?"

Matthew

FOREVER?

Is he serious? He can't be, and yet, in my heart of hearts, I want him to be. Because even if it's too soon to say I've fallen in love with him, I've already fallen in love with this cabin, and these mountains, and the barn and the goats.

I've already built a life in my own head, a beautiful dream where I get to see what spring, summer, and fall look like on these hills. I get to learn how to ride a horse, and fall off one, and get right back up again. It's absurd how much I love this fantasy.

I hardly know the man in front of me, and yet if someone held me at gunpoint and said, "Decide now. Go back home to Nashville and your job, your history and life there, or stay here in Asheville in this cabin with Erik—with Daddy?"

I'd stay in a heartbeat.

I'm not sure if that says more about how dull my life is at home, and how worthless and lacking in value it feels, or if it says more about how wonderful it's been with Erik. After just a day in his presence, at his command, I see how vibrant even a second can be when it's filled with the right person, place, and pursuit.

I'd want to bring Simmony Sunshine with me, of course. He'd have an exalted life as a housecat here in the cabin, never becoming a barn resident like Erik's cats, but aside from His Royal Furriness, I'd leave everything behind if I could just stay.

"You can't be serious," I say, laughing because I think it might hurt less if he agrees it's a joke.

Erik touches my face, fingering the dimple, rubbing his thumb over my lower lip. His voice is rough. "I shouldn't be. But what if I am?"

My heart soars. "That's too much."

"It is." He nods. "It really is."

I see the unspoken "and yet I want it anyway" in his eyes. My heart feels like it's coming out of my chest. The steam chokes me, and I'm dizzy.

"I have work in a couple of days," I say as a deflection.

I want Erik to tell me to fuck work forever, and to stay and fuck *him* forever instead. I want him to grip me by the back of the neck and haul me in for a wet, hot kiss, that devolves into us getting wild together here in the hot tub. I want him to take me upstairs, tie me to his bed, and keep me there until the end of time…

Well, maybe not exactly *there*.

Because I want cuddles on the sofa, and horseback rides at sunset, and to find out just what his house situation in Asheville is like. I want to meet his mom.

I want a lot of things. I always have. My whole life, I've wanted and wanted and wanted. And I've never had any hope of getting any of it until now. Maybe I still don't have any hope. We're both old enough to know better than to race into this headlong.

Yet when he slides me into his lap, and takes the back of my neck and pulls me down for a kiss…

I don't care if I'm supposed to be *years* past all these fluttering, aching, wonderful feelings bursting through my every cell and consuming my higher thoughts. I don't care if Erik is thirty-five and smart enough to know that saying these things to me, to anyone, at this point in a relationship, with my level of inexperience, is irresponsible, and promising way more than he can deliver.

I don't care whether we're both being idiots.

I just want his lips on my neck, on my collarbones, and sucking on my earlobe. I want his hands skimming over me, taking hold of my cock.

"C'mon, boy," Daddy says, lifting me off his lap. "Let's go inside."

I don't hesitate, following him without question out of the tub and into a warm, fluffy towel. I giggle with him as we hop up the snow-covered stairs, back to the main floor lit only by the Christmas tree, and drip our way across to the stairway taking us to his bedroom.

I can't wait to see what's going to happen there. Whatever the future might bring, I know everything that happens tonight will be heaven-bursting-open, angels-singing, the-child-is-born *glorious*.

CHAPTER TWENTY-FIVE
Erik

I CAN'T BELIEVE I'm doing this. I've never done this before with any of my boys. I could tell myself I'm doing this now with Matthew because I want him to understand a good Daddy can top from the bottom, but the truth is I want to give him something I've never given another man or boy.

He's earned it. After all he's allowed me to have and to hold for him, I want to give him something special, too.

Even if it's something as scary as this.

"That's it," I say, encouraging him. "Turn the water on now."

"You're sure?"

I'm lying naked on my left side in the tub, a clean enema nozzle inserted into my ass, and my sweet submissive boy is asking me if I'm sure? "Turn it on."

He does. It's always a weird sensation, the rush of warm liquid and the pressure building over time.

"How long?" he asks.

"A little more," I tell him. "Stroke yourself."

"Yes, Daddy." His cock is flagging, but he strokes it to hardness again. "Now?"

"A little more," I whisper. Beads of sweat pop out on my forehead, my heart is beating harder, and my pulse is rushing in my ears. The urge to go is growing, and I breathe through it. "Now," I say. "Turn it off and ease it out."

Matthew does as he's told. His fingers tremble as he works the nozzle out of my asshole. "How can I help you, Daddy?"

"Give me a second," I say, the urge to expel the liquid strong. I wait for it to pass before I rise to my feet. I take his hand and step out of the tub. Despite the fullness in my gut, I feel strong as I lead him to the toilet. I point at the floor beside it. "Kneel."

He does, and I take my place on the toilet seat. I hold myself tight, keeping it in, and I try not to chuckle—that would be disastrous—as I see Matthew's red cheeks and his fanned lashes. He's embarrassed and can't meet my gaze.

I touch his hair, and he looks up. "Keep your eyes on me. I'm giving you something I've never given anyone before."

He nods, Adam's apple bobbing with the rough swallow.

Shame pulses through me as I flash back to when Daniella put me through this when I was nineteen. But I let it all roll away. This is my boy at my feet, gazing at me with the kind of pure innocence I've rarely seen in someone half his age, and waiting for me to show him my raw, true self.

"This is a gift," I say.

"Thank you, Daddy," he whispers.

Matthew doesn't blink, doesn't move or turn his face. He keeps his eyes on mine, steady and observing, his lips trembling, but no words coming out.

"Thank you," he whispers again when it's over.

"Now you've got a piece of me no other boy has," I say. "Respect that."

"I do."

I clean up and take us over to the shower. The water and soap washes away all but the memory, and we kiss until my cock grows hard and insistent. Matthew is clinging to me, wet and hungry, his own erection throbbing with need, and I whisper, "Now it's time. Come fuck your Daddy."

Matthew

I WASN'T WRONG.

This is bigger, better, more intense than I could have known. I kneel on the cold, hard tiles and hold his eyes as he empties himself. Not once does he look away. No blush of shame colors his cheeks. He never hides himself. He's brave in a way I aspire to be.

He is Daddy—not Erik—and he is strong enough to do this without flinching or fear.

My heart feels huge, like it's pushing against my ribs. If I just find the right words, I'll use them to worship his masculinity, his strength, and his steady certainty. I want to let him support me. His strength will keep me from ever falling.

Even if he says falling is a thing everyone needs to learn how to do.

And then it's over.

We finish up, move to the shower, and Daddy proceeds to tease me to insanity.

"This way," he says, as he finishes drying me off. "We aren't done yet."

The bed is still messy from this morning, and I'm surprised he hasn't made it. But when he pushes me down onto it, I don't care that the sheets retain the scent of our pleasure from the night before mixed in with that of his laundry detergent. This is us, together.

It's beautiful.

"Are you ready to fuck me, sweet boy?" Daddy asks, as he climbs over me, straddling my hips, and sitting on my thighs. My cock strains up from the mound of dark pubes surrounding it, and he strokes his fingers through the fur there, avoiding touching my shaft or balls.

"Yes, please, Daddy."

"First, you have to prep my ass. It's been some time since I had a cock in there. I'll need you to loosen me up."

I squirm under him. "Show me, Daddy?"

He grins and bends to kiss my lips and neck. "Hell yeah, sweet Matthew. I'm going to show you everything you need to know. Starting with how to eat my ass."

I groan.

"What color are we?" Daddy asks.

"Green."

"You want to put your mouth on my hole?"

Thinking of how the small, wrinkled entrance had felt against my fingertips when I'd helped him wash himself in the shower, I nod. "I do."

"You want to tongue-fuck me?"

"I want to every-fuck you," I whisper. "*Any*-fuck. Please, Daddy, let me."

He laughs. "Sweet boy, you're going to get what you want. Don't worry."

He kisses me, and the sweetness of our mouths connecting, the touch of tongues, and the sharing of breath makes my mind whirl. This man has taken me over, changed my life, shaken my soul. I want to bury myself inside him and never climb out.

Soon enough.

When he's got me so spun up I can hardly breathe, he rises over me, standing on the bed. The arched ceiling behind him shines blue in the moonlight from the windows, and I am panting as he moves so his feet are on either side of the pillow where my head rests.

"I'm going to squat," he tells me. "And you're going to eat me out."

"Okay," I agree, my voice a breathless thing.

"Color?"

"Green."

"If you need to end this, and you can't say red or yellow, tap my leg three times."

"Yes, Daddy."

He squats, and his ass, that muscular, gorgeous butt, is right in my face. I don't know what to do next, but he grips the back of my head and grits out, "Eat it. Go on, sweet boy. Make Daddy's asshole sing."

I spread his cheeks apart and bury my face in between, my lips finding the spot I'm looking for. I relish the sensation of his anus spasming in response to my touch, and when I lick him there, he hisses, tugging on my hair again.

"Go for it, sweet boy. Treat my asshole like you want to eat it up, swallow it whole, fuck it. Don't be timid now."

I grunt and obey. The scent of his groin, his balls resting on my forehead and blocking my eyes, all serve to make me feel like all that exists is this, here and now. I go wild on his ass, licking, kissing, even biting softly, and when Daddy lets go of my hair to grip the bedhead with both hands and his legs start to shake, I hope it's at least in part due to my efforts and not just because his muscles are getting tired.

When he rises off me, the cool air on my face is a disappointment. I want to pull him back down, but he flops onto the bed next to me, reaching to hold me close and kiss me. Sharing his taste with him, I moan into his mouth, and he teases my hole with his fingers before pulling away to whisper, "You've got me so hot, sweet boy. I want to eat your bussy next."

"All right," I agree, and he laughs.

"So compliant. So easy." He kisses my throat, my nipples, and my belly as he slides between my legs. He grabs me behind the knees, shoving back. I help him by taking hold of my calves.

"So goddamn pretty," he grits out, stroking his hard cock.

"Want to paint your fur with my jizz."

"Please, Daddy."

He laughs. "You'll say 'please' to anything, won't you?"

I nod.

He laughs. "Let's hear it then. Scream it for me, baby."

I scarcely have time to get my mouth open, eager to give him what he's asking for, before he's between my ass cheeks licking me open. I cry out, twisting, the sensation overwhelming just like the last time, and yet I hold back, refusing to call out the words that will make it slow or stop.

Flipping me onto my stomach, he eats my bussy until I'm clawing at the sheets, trying to get away from him and how damn good it feels. But Daddy holds my hips in his big strong hands, keeping me in place. I kick, I scream, and I plead just like he asked.

"Please! Daddy, please! I need you to fuck me, Daddy! Please!"

"Mm-mm." He rubs his stubbled chin on my ass cheek. The leftover soreness from the spanking makes it feel more intense. "That's not what we're doing, sweet boy. You're going to make Daddy feel good with your dick this time, remember?"

I pant and twitch. I don't know what I want anymore. I'm tempted to call yellow and renegotiate, beg him to fuck me instead. But I do want to sink into his hot, hard body. I want to feel his ass convulse on my dick. I want to praise him for taking my cock into his tight bussy, just like he's praised me.

"Daddy…"

"Let me just eat you a little bit longer, sweet boy, and then I'm going to teach you to finger me."

I don't know if I can take it, but I nod, whining into the pillow as he goes back to making my asshole the center of our world. When he pulls away, I'm a slobbering, teary-eyed mess, but that doesn't stop him from lubing up three of my fingers and telling me to finger-fuck him.

"Just one at first, but then however many you like. My hole knows how to take it."

"Can I call it your 'bussy,' Daddy?" He's positioned us on our sides, face-to-face. His right leg is bent, with his knee resting on my hip. My left hand is slick with lube.

"Bussy is for a boy's hole. Or at least, that's how it is in this bed and when you're with me. Other men might have different rules." He tenses, and I feel those words have taken him out of the scene, out of the room.

I pull him back in. "What if I *want* to call it a bussy, Daddy?"

His eyes take on a new light. "Bratty is a new look on you." He touches my hair. "It's a good one. But if you call my asshole a bussy, I'll have to punish you."

I'm shaking as he guides my fingers. "How will you punish me?"

"I'll tie you up and rim you, but I won't let you come."

"You'd do that?" I gasp. It sounds intoxicating.

He laughs. "You like the idea. Of course you do." Daddy touches my wrist, positioning my hand. "Now focus. One, and then a few more—ah!"

I look into Daddy's eyes as I push my middle finger into his hot, gripping heat. "Oh," I let out, shocked by the visceral satisfaction of being inside another man—inside Erik, my Daddy. Even with just a finger, I'm shot through with power and passion. This is *right*. I've needed this for so long.

"Now play with my rim," he murmurs, shifting his knee higher up my hip, opening up to me more. His cock is half-hard. I reach with my other hand to hold it. "That's good," he encourages. "I usually lose my erection during anything ass-related, but I'm still turned on. Don't worry. It still feels nice."

But he doesn't go soft in my hand. He grows hard, and I stroke him as I push another finger inside before using three at once.

"Ah!" Daddy jolts. "That's my good, sweet boy. Now get Daddy's prostate. Find it."

I work my fingers deeper, twisting, trying to get the angle, and when Daddy jerks, his cock jumping in my loose fist, I know I've found it. I work the pads of my fingers against the spot, rubbing the nub.

"Fuck, sweet boy," he grunts. "This is so..." Sweat slips down his face, and he gazes at me with hot, wild eyes. "You're so beautiful." He says it with an awe that touches my soul, and I whisper my own truth back.

"I want to be your best boy, Daddy."

I mean this in so many ways. I want to be the best I can be for him, and I want him to think of me as his best boy of all the boys. I know it's unlikely. I have no skills, no youthful resilience or bubble butt or charm or shiny teeth and eyes, but I have devotion. I could give him devotion. Forever, as he'd said. If he'd let me.

"Baby, right there," he whispers, his hips twitching as I finger-fuck him and tag his prostate with each push in. "You've got this. You've got this so good."

I let him babble as I kiss his forehead and lick the sweat from his brow. I jerk his cock as I tongue his ear and kiss his hungry, demanding mouth. He's sweating with need and still babbling praise when he reaches down to stop my hand from moving.

"Enough."

I halt.

"Out."

I slide my fingers free.

He's shaking as he reaches for the lube again. He passes over a tissue from the bedside table container and opens the lube once I've wiped my fingers free of stickiness.

"That's good." Straddling my hips, he tangles his fingers into my chest hair, pulling slightly. "Daddy's going to take your cock now, and you're going to make Daddy feel like a king, got it?"

"Yes." My pulse thrums. The room darkens, clouds passing over the waxing moon outside.

"Yes, what?"

"Yes, Daddy."

He runs his hands over me again, and positions himself. "What color are we?"

"Green."

"Do you want to come in Daddy's ass?"

"Yes, please, Daddy."

"Good boy."

I'm not prepared for how fast it happens.

"Fuck, Daddy!" I cry as my cock is fitted into the tightest, hottest, sweetest, and sexiest place it's ever been. I convulse in sheer delight, ripples of pleasure coasting over my skin, rising in goosebumps and lifting my nipples to agonizing hardness.

"Baby, you're doing so good," Daddy croons as he lowers himself. When I'm fully sheathed, he grinds down on my hips, pubic hair to ass cheek. "Look at you," he murmurs, rubbing his hands over my body fur and tweaking my nipples. "So happy to be inside your Daddy, aren't you?"

"Yes," I hiss. "Daddy, I'm so happy."

"Is this what you want, boy?"

I take hold of one of his hands and lift it to my throat. His eyes darken, but he holds my neck so my Adam's apple bobs against the palm of his hand.

"Mm, boy, you need to be owned, don't you?"

I nod, and his hand tightens on me, so I feel like I'm being held down. He's got me under his command, even though it's my cock in his ass.

"That's good," he whispers, gazing into my eyes with a weighted, knowing gaze. "Lie back and let Daddy ride you."

The sweet slide and tight friction are mind-blowingly good. Groaning in bliss as he lifts and falls on my cock, I try to thrust up, to get some control of my own.

Daddy releases my neck and lightly slaps my cheek—not even hard enough to sting—scolding, "Your pleasure is Daddy's property now. Hold still. Feel this. Do nothing but *feel*, boy."

I let him have me. There's no doubt in my mind I'd have come if we hadn't tested the boundaries of my refractory period so much already over the last day. I'm grateful it's lasted, though. I'm beneath a gorgeous man, his stomach, chest, and leg muscles flexing, sweat making him smell delicious, and his ass gripping my cock as he rides it hard.

When he releases my neck, I reach up to put my hands around his throat. So thick, so strong. I don't press, but I hold him there, and he gazes at me as he takes my cock again and again, whispering things that make my toes curl and my balls ache. All of it filthy. All of it what I need to hear.

"My dirty sweet boy," he says, taking hold of his own cock—still hard—and stroking it. "Feel Daddy's pulse under your palms? That's my life, boy. It's strong, and powerful, and it can sustain us both."

"Daddy," I grit out, my balls twinging with need, but orgasm lingering too far away. "Daddy, take care of me, please."

He knocks my hands from his throat and takes hold of my neck again, this time with both of his hands. He presses harder than before and stops riding my cock.

"I feel your life, too," he says.

I groan, feeling his heartbeat thudding around my dick, the heat of him pulsing around me.

"Your life feels beautiful. You're stronger than you know," he mutters. "You're like catnip or angel dust. You make me high. You make me feel too much."

"Let me on top?" I ask. "Please, Daddy?"

He nods and pulls off me. The cool air of the room is a shock to my tender cock, already so accustomed to the heat of Daddy's body. On his back, Daddy is so gorgeous I want to cry. He reapplies lube, lifts his legs, and lets me get between them. As I inch forward, he reaches to guide my cock into him.

I stare into his eyes as I push in past the tight ring of his ass. He doesn't break eye contact, letting me see his face react to the sensations, letting me watch his eyes soften as I push inside, allowing me access to his inner world.

I remember how we'd stared at each other earlier after the enema, and this is no less intense. Daddy is giving me these pieces of himself, and I'm going to hoard them away inside.

These are things that will always be mine, even if this cabin and life are not. I wish they could be.

"Good boy," Daddy says, as I lodge myself deep. "Feel that?"

I nod.

"Tell me what you feel."

"Your heartbeat on my cock. Your life. Your strength. You're so strong, Daddy. You can handle anything."

He smiles. "Oh, sweet boy, come here." He pulls me to his chest, kissing the top of my head as I cling to his strong torso and hunch in and out of his hot ass. He rubs up and down my back, whispering to me as I fuck him. "Daddy's sweet boy is doing such a good job making me feel good. You're so good at this, sweet boy. So good for Daddy."

The fuck becomes something different than when he was riding me. It's languid, slow, and I'm cuddled close as I press into him again and again, letting myself wallow in the support of his strong body, the softness of his comfort, and the sweet heat of his ass.

"Matthew, Daddy's so proud of you," he whispers. "You're my sweet boy. My good sweet boy."

The scent of his sweat and the tenderness of our joining lasts until I reach a point of no return. The soft, beautiful fuck goes up in sparks of pleasure exploding from me in pulses of cum. I cling to him, kissing his pecs, shaking from the jolts of pleasure.

"That's my good boy," Daddy whispers, his voice strong and sure. "My *best* boy."

I jerk and unload in him again, biting his nipple. I moan, the words settling in my heart. Best boy. *Best.*

It's over. We lie together, my cock slipping from him, while his still presses hard against my stomach, both of us breathing and feeling too much.

CHAPTER TWENTY-SIX

Erik

LAST NIGHT IS still swimming in my brain as I sip coffee and stare out at the melting snow. The latest news from TDOT's posts on Twitter declares the highway through the mountains open, as are most of the main roads, but the mountain roads are still waiting for salt trucks. I have an excuse to keep Matthew with me for one day more. One of those Christmas miracles folks like to believe in.

I want him to stay. I might even need him to, after what we did last night.

I don't think I'll ever forget the expression on his face last night as he'd climbed on top and then bottomed out, the surrender to pleasure and his tender affection for me glowing in his eyes. He's a loving man. A deeply needy man, too.

I don't know how he's stayed so innocent at heart when he's lived with homophobia and had to hide himself growing up. I can't imagine what that's like. He deserves a respite from all types of pain.

I left him in bed, letting him sleep off the intensity of the last couple of days. He deserves to sleep in this morning, even if my inner clock will never allow me that luxury—even on Christmas morning.

Not to mention the animals in the barn—they need minding come rain, shine, or days of exhausting rounds of sex. So I'd hauled myself out of bed as quietly as possible, trudged to the barn with a twinge in my ass I haven't felt in a long time, and did my duty by the horses, goats, dogs, and cats.

The whole time I'd worked, my mind had kept replaying the night before. The way he'd knelt by the toilet, the earnest expression he'd held as he'd watched me empty myself of the enema, and how he'd held that moment, witnessed it, without judgment, without letting shame win. I'd shown him something only Daniela had ever seen before. No one else. No other boy.

Sipping my coffee now, I can't keep my mind from coming back to it again.

What had I been thinking? I'd wanted to give him a piece of me, something unique, but why? I'd taken myself to a place I'd never intended to go this weekend. It's too much. I'm too far into this.

But I don't want him to leave. I'm grateful to have another day with him. I'd keep him here a week if I could, make him share New Year's Eve with me, introduce him to my mom.

Speaking of, I missed a call from her this morning while I was working. I pull on my heaviest coat and a beanie and head outside to the porch swing, taking a heavy blanket out with me. Once I'm settled, I put the FaceTime call through and grin when her face fills the screen on my phone.

"Hey, baby!" A wide smile creases her weathered face, and her blue eyes twinkle with happiness. "Merry Christmas! How's it going with Molly?"

"She and the kid are doing just fine."

"Good! That's good news! Got a name for the little one?"

"Miss Merry Joy-Joy."

Mom's eyes blink rapidly. "That's unusual."

"Yeah, a friend chose it." I can see the questions coming and decide to head them off at the pass. "How's Aunt Meryl and the crew there?"

"Well, you know how it is, always some kind of drama. Right

now, your cousin Leo and his husband—you remember Dr. Anderson?—are here with their little girl, and she's quite the odd little thing."

"I remember from their wedding. Do they still call her Lucky?"

"Sure do."

"Good name for a horse or a dog, but I don't know about it for a child." We'd had this same conversation about the little girl's name after the wedding, too. Mom and I do that a lot—rehash the same things a few years apart. It's comforting. "Leo's health all right?"

"You know how it is. He'll always have problems. But with a devoted doctor for a husband, he's been doing well for himself. They're a handsome couple." She pauses. "So your, ahem, *date*? How did it go? I'm guessing well since he named Molly's kid."

"Subtle, Mom."

"Wasn't trying to be. I just want you to be happy."

"I am happy." It's a reflexive answer. We both know it's not true, or at least, it hasn't been since Brandon left.

"I'm sure you're plenty happy right now after getting some hot ass. Very little makes a man happier. But I'm talking long-term happiness. It's what matters the most. Was this date someone who might make you that kind of happy, Erik?"

My face is red from the cold, but it's also flushed with something else. Rubbing my eyes, I realize it's embarrassment over how poorly I've conducted myself during all this, how I've fallen under Matthew's spell.

I've given over parts of myself to him—intimate, personal parts of myself. I've let him give me so much too. My heart feels on the line here, and that was never what this time with Matthew was supposed to be about.

How reckless have I been? Christ.

"Oh? It went badly?" she asks, her brow crinkling with worry.

"You look miserable."

"No, no. It went well. It's still going well."

"Oh?" Mom's eyes take on a gleam again, and this time it's complete delight. "He stayed for Christmas? What's his name?"

"Matthew."

"And one night has turned into *two* with Mat*thew*?" She chuckles at the rhyme.

I roll my eyes. "And given the state of the roads, it might turn into three."

Mom senses something in my tone, and the delight leaves her eyes, replaced with concern. "Oh, and how do you feel about that?"

My cheeks get hot again. "I'm fine with it."

"'Fine with it.'" She rolls her eyes and brushes her blonde hair back from her eyes, revealing her plucked eyebrows. "Where is he now?"

"Sleeping?"

"At this hour?"

I laugh. "He's not accustomed to farm life, Mom. He's accustomed to sleeping in on the weekends."

"Well, you must like him more than 'fine' if you're letting him do it anyway," she says. "Other boys of yours have been out in the barn mucking out stalls or lifting kettlebells, getting started with 'training' from day one."

I don't point out to her that doing something *different* with Matthew might be an indication I don't have any interest in keeping him around to train up the right way. But she's right, of course. I'm so soft for Matthew in a way I never was for Brandon, Duncan, or Garrett, and definitely not with any of my other temporary playmates.

When I'd woken up this morning, turned onto my side, and saw his face in the glow of the dawn light? I'd melted. His dark lashes lying on his cheekbones, his brow smooth in relaxation, and the little fans of wrinkles by his eyes? All so kissable.

As I'd watched him breathe in and out, the sweet scent of his skin drifting to me, I'd thought of the story about the long-ago Chinese prince who'd cut the long sleeve off his robe because his lover had fallen asleep on top of it. He'd destroyed his own royal and priceless clothing rather than wake the man. And at that moment, I'd known—if I'd needed to cut my way out of the bed in order to not disturb Matthew? I would have.

"He's different," I admit to Mom.

"They're all different," she says.

"True. But he's…older than me." I think it's the best way to get across to her how very different Matthew is from my former boys.

Her brows leap out of view beneath her bangs, and her mouth opens and closes a few times before she says, "How *much* older?"

"Just a few years. He's forty-one."

"Ah." She blinks. "I see. So… In this scenario…" Mom bites her lip like she's trying to think of the perfect phrasing. "Are you the boy then?"

"No." I laugh. "He's still the boy."

"Oh?"

"Age doesn't matter. It's the role." It wasn't long ago at all I'd been troubled by the age thing. Now it doesn't concern me at all. I had been prejudiced about it, but Matthew has shown me the light.

"Right, right. I get it. I think." Mom tilts her head, a thoughtful expression falling over her fine features. "I suppose this could be good."

I laugh again. Mom—always the optimist—thinks this could be good. No surprise there.

She grins. "Tell me about him. What's he like?"

"He's handsome," I say, kicking my feet against the porch floor to get the swing going. "And naïve in a charming way. More naïve than Brandon or Garrett, maybe just as naïve as Duncan?"

"At his age?"

"I know. It's amazing he's maintained this level of innocence. It's unique." And beautiful. But I don't share that. "He was sheltered in a lot of ways. Raised by religious parents."

"Ohhh," she says, nodding her head. "I see."

"He lived with them for his whole life, so he's never had a chance to—" I wave my hand around. "And now they're gone, passed away, and he wants to discover himself in all the ways he never could before."

"You're helping him do that? How beautiful, Erik. What a special start to a relationship."

I huff out a laugh. She has no idea. None at all. It's been beautiful and altogether too much, too fast. It's been irresponsible and wild and exactly what I needed but shouldn't have ever had. Worse, it's doomed to failure. "He lives in Nashville."

"Well, he doesn't have to stay there, does he? It won't kill him to move here, would it?"

"Mom…"

"Well?"

"It's not like that. Matthew's just here because he won my Daddy/boy experience in the Christmas charity auction. He's not going to stay. He's got a whole life of his own. He was never meant to stay."

But I know he wants to stay. I saw it in his eyes last night when I asked him to stay forever, and I saw it on his face when he pushed into me. I felt it in the way he clung to me as he fucked me gently, and as he huffed and shuddered in orgasm in my arms.

He doesn't want to go home any more than I want him to go. And my mother, angel though she is, won't try to talk me out of these irrational feelings. She's an eternal optimist and always thinks every guy I so much as flirt with is "The One."

But what if, for the first time ever, I want a guy to be "The

One" too?

No. Stop. This will never work for so many reasons.

"Does he not feel the same way about you?"

"He's just a one-night stand who got snowed into a three-night stand, Mom."

"No, I know you, Erik. You've got the starry-eyed look you always get when you first fall in love. I'm well familiar with it. You got it when you fell for Jason Doloman in high school, and then for Ellie McGuire in college, and of course Duncan and Garrett. Admittedly, it took a little longer with Brandon because he was quite the brat, but I knew when you fell for him. It was during the trip to Canada for the film shoot with that actor ex of Leo's—Curtis Banks—"

"What a dick."

"—it was the first time Brandon traveled with you. I don't know what changed during that trip, but when you came home, you had stars and moons in your eyes, and you were a complete goner for him. Until he left."

I sigh. She's right. I *had* fallen in love with Brandon during the Canadian shoot, even if I hadn't been willing to admit it to myself then, or for way too long afterward. "Don't put it like that."

"How do you put it?"

"Brandon didn't leave. He grew up. Moved on."

"Right. Well, whatever euphemism you need to use to feel better about what happened. The fact is he left you, and it broke your heart. Is that what's holding you back from embracing this new love, baby? Because, if it is, I understand. It's easy to want to wall up your heart. But don't steal joy from yourself. Life's too short."

"What if he doesn't bring me joy in the end? What if he has some horrible habit? Or some baked-in ways of thinking and being which aren't compatible with mine? What if he's a Republican?"

"I've never known you to ask questions like that about one of your boys in the past. You always dove in headfirst into each attraction. You never tested the depth. What happened to 'the details don't matter, Mom?' What happened to 'it'll all work out as it should.'"

"It's different with Matthew."

"Why?"

"Because I always knew the others would leave! I *wanted* them to leave!"

There. I said it. It's out on the table, and I can tell by Mom's expression she knows as well as I do what I've admitted. Matthew thinks I'm so strong. The truth is I'm a coward. A fearful coward who can only live "big" by staying "small" with my heart.

"No, I remember how it was with Brandon. You wanted him to stay…"

"In the end, maybe. But when it started…" I shake my head. "I never expected him to stay with me. I knew he'd take off when the time came, right from the start. It's why I let him into my life at all. If I'd known I'd fall in love with him? If I'd known how much it would hurt to lose him? So much more than it hurt when Duncan and Garrett left. Christ, Mom, I wouldn't have let him in my life. I'd have walked away the very first day."

"Brandon was your first heartbreak."

I rub my chest. It hurts just remembering. An echo of the pain that's finally fading. "I don't want to go through that again. It's not worth it."

"Baby, the chance for a happy ending is worth it. This Matthew could be your happy ending."

I sigh. I won't ever say this to my mom, but she didn't get a happy ending, so why should I expect to? It wasn't Brandon who stole my faith in men, but Dad. He betrayed us. Since that day, I've never, not for a moment, believed men were a safe place for my heart. It's why I've always had *boys*, why I've always been Daddy to them.

Men? I've never trusted them to stay or believed I could depend on them for my own happiness. A quick fuck? Sure. Anything else? Never.

That's why *I'm* the man I always wanted my father and the men around me to be—responsible, loving, soft, caring, dominant, commanding, and *there for my boys*. The play during sex? It's just one way of expressing the kind of man I want to be. The kind of man I never expect anyone to ever be for me.

The whole point of "getting back on the horse" with this auction was to see if I could enjoy being a short-term Daddy. If I can still play this life-affirming role without turning my life—or someone else's life—upside down. But looking back to our first date, for lack of a better term for it, I haven't harbored short-term Daddy sorts of thoughts about Matthew. From the beginning, I was having spontaneous fantasies of what it might be like to keep him in my life long enough to teach him about NASCAR, poetry, and so much more.

A little voice offers, *Hell, he's trapped here, you could start to-day...*

I want to slap my own face. Instead, I scrub through my hair and groan.

"What are you thinking about? You've got your forehead all screwed up." If she were home, Mom would press her fingertips between my eyebrows to smooth my frown away. Her voice softens. "I'm sure it's scary, but don't let fear and what happened with Brandon steal everything from you. He's not worth it."

"Brandon just followed what was natural and right. He grew, changed, and left. I'm proud of him for recognizing it was time even when I didn't."

"Oh, you accuse *me* of being a romantic, but here you are, dusting shit with gold."

I snort. "How's that?"

"That boy got horny for what another man was tossing, and he left you so he could run off and catch it. That's all that happened. He didn't 'grow up' any more than any man grows up. He did what he's always done—what men always do—he followed his dick. He left you high and dry for a nice set of orgasms on a fresh dick, that's it."

"Mom," I choke out. She's always frank, but this is beyond the pale even for her.

"It's the truth. I've let you tell yourself this nonsense about how you did your job as his 'Daddy,' and he 'grew up,' and all that BS because I thought it made it easier for you to let him go." Mom shakes her head. "But now you're sitting there looking like an angel fell from the sky and into your bed, but you're telling me this Matthew can't be your man because he might *stay*? Am I getting this right?"

I laugh.

"What?"

"His name is actually Angel. Matthew Angel."

"There you go! It's a sign."

I roll my eyes. "I don't know what's worse. If he stays or if he goes… What do I even do if he stays, Mom? How does it work? I've never seen a relationship like that in the wild."

"Because your dad left us."

"Yes, and most of my friends' dads, too. And all my boys. They leave. It's what men do. You just said so yourself. If Matthew *stays*…" I shake my head. "I don't know how to even imagine it."

But that's a lie. I can picture it perfectly.

Matthew in his underwear sitting on our sofa, nipples pebbled from a chill, lower lip red from chewing it, and his eyes alight for me.

Matthew sitting at the kitchen counter, dressed in a button-up shirt, typing on a computer, sipping coffee, and looking thoughtful.

Matthew strumming a guitar by a bonfire next to the barn. I haven't seen him play yet, but it's there in my mind's eye all the same.

Matthew on the back of Zebra Cake, trailing behind me through the mountain passes, and stopping to roll around with me in a grassy clearing.

I can picture him in the training room, sweating as he pushes himself harder, his lithe muscles growing stronger with each passing day.

I can imagine him in my bed, naked, quaking with pleasure and need, eyes going hot and wild just before he comes. I can see his quiet, pleased smile as I kiss his face afterward and tell him how good he is, how much I love fucking him, how he's my boy, my angel…

"What nonsense is this?" Mom prods. "There's no recipe for making a relationship work. You just make a life together however it fits, with whoever you love. That's all. It's not rocket science. You don't have to solve equations or anything. You just start taking the other person into your life, you make them important, let them grow roots in your soil—" She lifts a brow. "Notice I said grow roots, not wings. You've always talked about your boys growing wings. Not this time."

"You haven't even met him. You know nothing about him."

"He's forty-one. His name is Matthew. He makes your eyes shine like a sun is rising behind your irises. I know enough."

"That's nothing, Mom."

"It's more than I knew about Brandon, but what did I say about him when you brought him home the first time?"

I sigh and scrub a hand over my hair again. "'This one will break your heart if you let him.'"

"But I *also* said it will be worth it."

"It wasn't."

"Oh, baby, loving is always better than not loving. Having is better than not having. And losing is better than never having had at all. Those clichés exist for a reason, Erik."

"Maybe so, but you're wrong about this thing with Matthew."

There's movement through the window, and I watch as Matthew moves into the kitchen wearing just his underwear. "I can't have him."

She blows a raspberry, and I roll my eyes at her.

"Gotta go," I tell her with a half-smile. "Sleeping Beauty has awakened."

"Don't ruin this for yourself," she says, waving goodbye and blowing me a kiss. "Let him know you want more. See what happens. And, hey, have a merry Christmas."

I blow a kiss back and end the call. The fact is, I've already told Matthew I want more, and he said it was too much, and he's *right*. But I also know if I ask him to stay tomorrow night, and the next night, and the next? He'll find ways to say yes.

I am sure of it, down to my bones. And in the cold light of day, it scares the shit out of me.

Matthew turns to the window, stretching, displaying his fine body. He seems boyish despite being so manly with all that sexy fur. His tummy is flat, and his hips are slender. I lick my lips as I watch him.

I think it's time to have him kneel for me again.

I want to see his sleek body on his knees for me, ripe mouth taking me in…

Even if this is all against my better judgment, even if I'm taking things too far already, he's here for at least one more night. I'm not going to let my emotional upheaval ruin it for us. And I am going to take as much as I can before he leaves.

He must leave.

Because I can't afford to see what happens if Matthew stays. I won't be able to keep him happy. I don't even know what that looks like outside of a Daddy/boy relationship, and I can't afford to find out. Not after all these years of trying to be the best man I can be. I can't handle having it confirmed I'm not worth sticking around for, and every man I love leaves, just like my dad.

Matthew thinks I'm strong, but I'm a coward.

For all my preaching about the importance of being able to recover from a fall? It turns out I'm lacking the core strength to accomplish the feat myself.

CHAPTER TWENTY-SEVEN

Matthew

ERIK ENTERS FROM the porch, carrying a blanket and sporting rosy cheeks from the cold. I shiver as the chill from the door opening and closing wafts across the room, and I wrap my arms around myself.

When I woke alone in bed, I figured he had gone out to take care of the horses and other animals, but I was surprised he'd let me sleep. There's no particular reason why. I just imagine that in his role of Daddy he'd normally have roused his boy, even after a long night of fucking, and put him to work in the barn, too.

But me, for whatever reason, he's left me to my dreams.

I don't know what to make of it, or if it's even true, whether he's given me special treatment or not. Maybe this is all in my head. I push all thoughts of it aside when he smiles at me. He's so damn handsome, and I'm already so owned by him. I want to kneel at his booted feet.

"Merry Christmas. Sleep well?" he asks, tossing the blanket and his phone aside, onto the soft chair next to the door.

"Merry Christmas to you, too. And yes. Thank you, Daddy."

"Of course, boy." He stoops to take off his boots before putting his beanie back on the coatrack and adding his big puffer coat as well. "Let's get some breakfast in you."

The way he says it, though, I have a feeling he's not talking about eggs and bacon. My stomach is empty, and I could use some food, but the thought of sucking Daddy's cum down first makes me weak. I go to my knees right where I am, at the threshold between the living room and the kitchen.

"Fuck, boy," Daddy says, unbuckling his belt, and shoving his jeans and underwear down so his cock rises out of his light brown pubic hair. My mouth fills with saliva, and I save it to slick his dick with. I reach out for it as he strides toward me, but he knocks my hands away. He takes a handful of my hair, gripping it hard but not painfully, and tilts my head back, so I'm gazing up at him.

He runs his thumb along my jaw. "You shaved."

"Yes, Daddy."

"Good boy."

Pinching my chin between his thumb and fingers, he opens my mouth. My heart pounds, and my cock presses against the front of my underwear. "You've got gorgeous eyes, boy," Daddy says gruffly. "Such pretty lashes. Fuck." The last word is ripped from his mouth like he's almost angry. "You're just so fucking hot. Christ."

I stick my tongue out, wanting his cock, begging for it with my face, and he moans before giving me what I need. His flesh tastes musky from the work in the barn, and I open wide for his thickness, feeling the sides of my lips stretch. Daddy scoots closer, making my head tip back; I focus on not gagging as his cock hits the back of my throat.

"Breathe in through your nose for me," he murmurs, his hand in my hair turning gentle. "Good boy. Now stick your tongue out as far as you can, cradle the underside of my dick. Yes, just like that. Fuck." Beneath my palms, his thighs shake, and I grip tighter, holding on. "One more breath, boy. In and out. Good. And now open your throat for me."

It's easy. All those years of letting men use my mouth have blessed me with this one skill, which, right now, seems to please Daddy. Saliva wells around my lips and slides down into his pubic hair, wetting his balls as they press to my chin. Daddy holds me there, his thick cock in my throat, his hand in my hair, and his intense, emotion-filled eyes on mine.

I can't read his feelings, but mine are clear. I'm happy. Deeply, truly happy. Tears slide from beneath my lashes, and Daddy shifts his hold on my head to brush them away with his thumbs.

"Such a good sweet boy," he murmurs. "Taking Daddy's cock like an absolute angel. God, I love it." He runs the pads of his thumbs over my eyebrows, smoothing them just as I start to feel the urgent need to draw fresh breath. "Go on," he encourages me. "Suck in a breath around my dick. You can do it."

I try, but he's thick, and I'm afraid I'll gag. Daddy just holds steady and when I gasp a gross-sounding wet breath, he smiles at me. "That's my angel. That's so good. Mm, your throat is perfect." I gasp again. "Fuck, Matthew. You're perfect. So damn perfect."

Sucking in a desperate breath as he pulls himself out, I pant at his feet, saliva all over my chin and cheeks, and my throat feeling raw. As soon as I've caught my breath, I open my mouth, begging with my eyes.

"Oh, sweet boy, you want more of Daddy's cock? Hungry this morning?"

I don't answer because he feeds his dick into my throat the way I want, but I hope he sees it in my eyes: *so hungry, Daddy. So hungry for you.*

The world seems to shimmer around the edges, and I'm hazy, both light and heavy, like I'm flying and also pinned here in place by Daddy's thick cock. I cling to his thighs, feeling the denim on my palms. I rub up and down, using the friction to center myself. I'm here on the floor of Daddy's kitchen, letting him press into my throat and choke me with his dick.

I love it. I love it so much.

"That's beautiful." Daddy says, touching the tight edges of my mouth where I'm open so wide for him. "*You're* beautiful. Made to kneel for Daddy. Made to worship me with your body, aren't you, Matthew? Daddy's little angel."

I can't answer him, so I close my eyes and open them again, hoping my emotions shine out from my soul. I want to kneel for him and only him. I want him to think my efforts here are worth the time and energy required to keep me as his boy. I don't care anymore if he deserves someone younger and better. I want this man. I want his dick and his home, his life and his love.

I want to be his boy forever and for real.

"Now, suck me until I come," he tells me, pulling his cock back out of my throat, and moving my hands from his thighs to grip the base of his dick. "Use your hands. Get me off."

I croak, "Yes, Daddy."

I'm still not very skilled at this, but I'm enthusiastic, and I can see by the gleam in his eyes he likes that as much as he likes what I'm doing to his cock—which is everything I can think of which might feel good. Licking, sucking, jerking, bobbing my head up and down his shaft and fondling his balls, I'm doing all of it.

I hit a rhythm he seems to especially like. His knees weaken, and he grips the counter to hold himself up.

"That's my boy. You're getting me there. Just. Like. Fuck!" Daddy grips my hair, his face screwing up tight, and I eagerly lap at his slit until jizz spurts out, hitting my lips, my teeth, and the back of my throat. "That," he whimpers, as he shakes through his orgasm. "Just like that, boy."

Daddy's fingers card through my hair as I lick him clean. I sit back on my heels to wipe the excess from my chin, and lick that off, too. It tastes sour and bitter, like baking soda and lime. I love that it's his cum, and I made him lose his load. I love that I get the privilege of eating it for breakfast.

Not another boy.

Me. Matthew Angel.

"Thank you, Daddy," I whisper. "Thank you for this delicious breakfast."

He laughs, his eyes crinkling at the edges, showing the effects of sun exposure on his face. He's so handsome. My stomach swoops and dives, and a grin breaks over my face, unbidden. I've made him happy. I've made him come and laugh. What more could a boy want?

"Thank you for eating it," he whispers. "I made it just for you."

I kiss the head of his cock and help him tuck it away and zip back up. Once Daddy's dressed, he pulls me to standing, running his hands all over me, touching me everywhere but where I need it most—my aching dick.

"You're too old, Matthew," he murmurs, and I stiffen, but he goes on. "Too old to come so often in just a few days, so you're going to have to wait."

"Daddy?" I ask, confused, but I don't mention that I'm supposed to leave today if the roads are clear. I don't want to go. If he wants me to linger here with him, if he wants me to stay…

"The roads up to the house still aren't safe," he explains. "You have another night with me." Daddy kisses my lips, my nose, and then my collarbones. Despite his orgasm, he sounds out of his mind with lust when he murmurs, "Merry Christmas to you, sweet boy. Time to open more presents."

"You've already given me too much," I insist, but my heart still swells, and I eye the colorfully-wrapped boxes under the tree. I don't think there'll be any practical corduroy trousers in there.

"This is how a Daddy should treat his boy."

"Unless the Daddy wants the boy to treat him," I remind him.

"Is that how you'd prefer it?"

"No," I whisper as he leads me to the sofa. "This is perfect."

The presents are wrapped so well I wonder if he's done them himself or had them done professionally in a store. Regardless, when he puts the boxes in my lap one by one, he encourages me to rip the paper—which was forbidden in my house growing up. My mother always reused it to line shelves or wrap other gifts.

It's fun to toss it around, to let the ripping sound tear through the room, and he and I both laugh when I accidentally rip the box on one trying to get the wrapping free of the stubborn tape.

"This is ridiculous," I say, giggling, as I lift the absurd and wonderful Christmas sweater. It's a Fair Isle style with a black base, and red, white, and green alternating colors, with three rows of goats wearing scarves, and across the front, the face of a giant baby goat who looks a lot like Miss Merry Joy-Joy.

"Put it on," he encourages.

It's soft beneath my fingertips, the finest wool imaginable, and so I slip it over my head, enjoying the soft, warm embrace on my skin. "Do I look silly? In nothing but this sweater and these underpants?"

"Nah, it's hot."

Erik reaches behind the sofa and pulls out another box. "This one's for me." It's a similar sweater with a red background color, and an adult black-and-white goat face. He discards his T-shirt and pulls the sweater on.

My throat grows tight. Hadn't I pictured just this?

"Go on. Open another," Erik urges.

I gaze around at my haul when it's over. Two beautiful green shirts, and a blue sweater he's picked out just for me. A handmade jar of "junk rub"—a deodorant for my nether regions in a scent he's chosen. A book of poetry by another one of his favorites, and a small, empty picture frame.

"What's this about?" I ask, indicating it.

"Just a minute, and you'll see." He indicated the final box. "Open that one, too."

I tear into it, and inside is a Polaroid camera, already loaded with film.

"Here," Erik says, taking it from me. "Let's get a few pictures of us."

My chest tightens. I'm not sure I want photos. If I can't keep having this, then I'm not sure I want to remember it in vivid color later. But I let him position us on the sofa and take pictures. The camera spits them out, and as they develop one by one, laid out on the coffee table, I'm overwhelmed by the pureness of them.

It's me and Erik in Christmas sweaters, like I'd imagined back at the auction, both of us glowing from the inside, even brighter than the tree lighting us up.

"What do you think?" Erik says, lifting one of the photos and holding it up to the frame. "This one's good."

I nod, throat tight, a popping sensation in my chest, like I'm breaking open.

I take the frame from his hands once he's secured the photo of us inside.

There we are: brown eyes beside hazel, dark hair next to lighter brown, and my smile as wide as his. What is this? What have we made together? All I know is—

This is too beautiful.

Erik

TEASING MATTHEW IS a delight.

Even if I have doubts about how deeply I'm getting involved in kink with him, I still can't stop myself from going harder than I'd intended. We're so far off the terms of our contract now—though still consensual—I can't believe my own urges.

At least all the ramped-up adrenaline from doing these scenes allows me to put aside all the feelings and fears which came up during my conversation with my mom. I can focus on him, on the present, and what we have right now.

After negotiating the details, Matthew lets me tie him naked to a dining room chair with scarves and brutalize him with kisses to his most ticklish areas, licks to his cock and balls, and tons of nipple play. I've never seen a man so responsive to touches to his nipples. I crouch in front of him, just running my fingers around his areolas and watching him squirm.

When I add my lips, tongue, and teeth, he nearly comes off the chair—or he would if he wasn't tied down.

"Beautiful," I praise him. He deserves so much praise. He has no idea how good he's been these last few days. Having never done any of this before, he's clueless. Right or not, it makes my heart pound to know I'm the first man to see him like this. The *only* man.

Matthew tilts his head back, perspiration pooling at the base of his throat, and his breath coming in short, sharp pants. He goes very still. "Daddy," he whimpers, and I laugh as his cock flexes and his balls wrench up, trying to come around the supersoft rope I've used to tie his orgasm off. I run my fingers over it, testing it's not too tight, and confirming there's no chafing.

Satisfied, I whisper, "Your orgasm belongs to Daddy, boy. Doesn't it?"

"Yes, Daddy," he groans. "Please."

"No."

Matthew trembles, but when I go back to playing with his nipples, he keens, his cock leaking copious amounts of pre-cum. He's so damn hard now and his guileless face gives away how deliriously pleasured he feels. Grinning and struck with a good idea, I duck my head and suck his cock while still pinching his nipples, gratified by his hopeful cries. So eager to come. When I feel he's reached a point of arousal where even the soft rope isn't going to hold off his orgasm, I pull away.

"No, Daddy!" he cries. "Please! Fuck, Daddy, I'll be good for you. I promise. Just, please, let your boy come, Daddy. Let your boy come…" He's close to sobbing now, and I let the grin slide from my face, I let the grin slide from my face, growing serious as I comfort him with kisses to his lips, chin, earlobes, and neck.

"That's my sweet boy," I murmur. "Doing such a good job for Daddy. Aren't you, baby?"

"Am I?" he pants, voice breaking, and tears slipping down his cheeks again. This time they're not from choking on my cock, but from his wild need to come.

"Do you have a word for me, Matthew? We can end this."

He takes a shuddering breath before shaking his head. "No, Daddy. No word for you."

"So I can do this, then?" I lick one of his nipples. His breath hitches. "And this?" I kiss my way to his furry stomach, licking the soft hair down to his mound of pubes. "And this?" I suck one straining ball, tight from being tied apart from the other.

"Daddy," he groans, twisting his hands against the scarves binding him to the chair. "I can't. Please. I can't, Daddy."

"Then use that word, Matthew."

He shakes his head, and I laugh, kissing along his inner thighs, back over his balls, and taking the head of his cock into my mouth again.

"Shit!" he cries, convulsing, pulling at the scarves but not breaking free. "Daddy! I need…I want…Help me, Daddy! *Help me!*"

I slurp and suck, patiently making him come unglued. He's shaking, crying, and shouting for release, but I don't give it to him. I can be a real bastard of a Daddy when I've decided to tease my boy, but there's another reason for this madness. I want him to come while I'm fucking him, and I'm just not ready for that yet. So he has to wait.

I kiss his cock and blow on it. "Matthew, you've been a wonderful boy for me today. I've put you through so much. It's time you got a reward, don't you think?"

His head comes up from where it's been resting chin-on-chest. His eyes gleam with hope. "Yes, Daddy, please."

"All right," I say, untying his balls, and touching them carefully. He hisses at the stinging release of his tenderest parts. "You're going to love this reward."

"I will, Daddy," he agrees. "I promise I will."

"I *know* you will."

I untie his feet and hands, rubbing them before I help him stand. He's unsteady on his feet and shaking like a leaf as I lead him to the sofa. He's been brought to a fever pitch of arousal, and he's so beautifully ready for release. I kiss him hard once I've got him on the sofa.

Matthew goes mindless, trying to rut against my stomach as I straddle his legs, but I keep just out of reach. His kiss is messy, desperate, and out of control, and when I pull back, he gazes up at me with lost, wild eyes that are barely coherent. He's deep in subspace, far, far away, and yet he's never been more present than he is with me right this second.

"That's my good boy," I praise again, standing, and taking his chin between my fingers.

Matthew's panting and red all over with arousal. "Daddy?"

"Get comfortable." I turn to the coffee table, the place where I'd left his underwear earlier. "Lift your feet. That's it." I see the clouds of understanding drawing across his face as I pull the underwear up his legs, over his thighs, and cover his straining, hungry cock. "Good boy." I stand again. "Now, stay right here. Don't touch yourself."

"Daddy," he growls, and it's the closest to angry I've ever heard Matthew come, I think. The realization shoots me through with hot, sweet lust. I've pierced his armor. I've cut through to his id. He's here with me now, and he's about to demand what he wants. I wait for it and then—yes! "Daddy, make me come."

"There it is," I say, clapping like he's executed a lovely performance. "Very good. Now, use your safe word and this can be over, or—" I know what he's going to choose. "Or sit back and take what Daddy gives you."

He moans, licks his lips, tries to focus his eyes, and fails. "Daddy...Daddy, please."

"Wait here, Matthew. Don't touch yourself."

"Or what?"

"Or Daddy will punish you."

He swallows hard. "How?"

"You'll have to make yourself come for the rest of our time together," I say. "No coming in Daddy's mouth, or from his hand, or in his ass."

Matthew's lips wobble, like he's going to cry for real, the ugly kind of crying, but then he nods. "Yes, Daddy. I'll wait here. I won't touch myself. I'm a good boy."

I comb my fingers through his hair, tilting his head back so he meets my gaze. "You are," I say. "The best boy." I've never felt so in control, so powerful with a boy before. So right.

Fuck. I have to get a grip, I tell myself as I stride across the room to the Christmas tree. Beneath it is one last present hidden way in the back, tucked behind the limbs so well he hadn't noticed it earlier. It's a big, long box labeled *To Matthew, From Daddy*. I drag it over to him.

"This is my final gift for you, boy."

"Final?" he says, blinking and confused.

"Open it." I don't dare address his unspoken questions: what does "final" mean? Is this really over after tonight? "Go on. See if you like it."

"I love it, Daddy," he whispers before he's even started to peel the paper away. He strokes the box, and then, with trembling fingers, tries to pick open the taped edges.

"Rip it, baby."

He tries, but his hands are shaking too much, and he's so weak with lust that he's practically melted onto the sofa, so I open it for him. Matthew's hands follow my own, tearing the paper with me, until he's faced with the box itself.

"Now, if you hate it, I'll replace it with one you like better."

Matthew lifts the lid, his breath stops, and his eyes fill with tears. "Daddy…"

"Is it good, boy?"

Matthew lifts the guitar case from the box, unbuckling the clips, and exposing the guitar itself. The wood of the classical guitar gleams in the light, and the nylon strings make discordant, echoing sounds as he places it face up on his lap. "Daddy, it's beautiful."

It sure the fuck is. I'd noticed him eyeing it during our time in Asheville at the Woodrow Instrument Company, and I almost didn't buy it for him. In fact, when I went back to the shops to buy his presents, I'd just planned to get things which I could easily fit into his stocking and into a few shirt boxes. But I'd kept thinking of the guitar and went back for it two days later.

"You can play, right?"

"Yes," Matthew whispers. "Or I could. It's been a long time."

"Do you have a guitar?"

He shakes his head. "Dad sold mine. When I quit at Belmont. Gave them away to a family down the street with three teens learning to play. He'd never wanted me to have them in the first place, said I wasn't a musician in my soul, and maybe I wasn't. But it'd felt so important back then that I try, at least. So, I'd saved up enough money from my summer jobs and bought a classical and an acoustic. They were mine, and… He sold them."

Matthew's voice is clearer now. He's leaving the deepest sub-space, but there's no doubt he's still drifting there. He's got the floaty vibe, the faraway feel like he's living inside a dream. That's what this feels like for me, too.

"Play," I say. "Daddy wants to hear your music, boy."

"I'm so rusty, and I never was very good," he murmurs, plucking the strings. "It's in tune, though."

"I had it tuned, and I've been real careful with it ever since."

"Mm." Matthew positions the guitar, closes his eyes, and begins to strum some chords. It's nothing impressive, but the steady rhythm and the sweetness of the sound rise around us. I smile at the picture he makes—sitting in the underwear I've given him, playing this music, still so dizzy from our play. I love this. He's beautiful. I want to keep this moment forever.

I can.

In my heart.

That's what memories are for.

"My fingers hurt now, Daddy," Matthew says after fifteen minutes of playing chords and strumming. He holds the guitar out to me with shiny, hazel eyes. "Can I stop now, please?"

"Of course," I say, taking the guitar and placing it aside, leaning it against the wall behind the chair next to the sofa. "Now," I say, coming back to the sofa. "Daddy wants to hold you."

Matthew nods and waits as I strip myself down to just my underwear, too. "So sexy, Daddy," he says, as I step in front of him, my hard cock jutting from the top of my boxer briefs. I put his hands on me, and he rubs them over my abs, my thighs, and around to cup my ass. Leaning forward, he nuzzles my balls, smelling me, breathing me in like he wants to drown in my odor.

I clutch his face to my crotch roughly before letting go. "Let Daddy hold you now."

"Yes," he agrees, lifting his arms. "Hold me."

I scoop him up and carry him toward the stairs. He's not light, but carrying him is no problem after all the work I've done with kettlebells, and other weight training over the course of my life.

Matthew scents my throat, kisses my earlobe, and whispers, "I still want to come, Daddy."

"I know you do, angel. But Daddy decides when."

He shivers and I hitch up him a little higher, getting a better grip before I start up the stairs. I'm strong, but this is a challenge, and by the time I'm at the top, I'm breathing hard and sweating. He holds my neck and doesn't let go.

I take him to bed.

Matthew stretches out on the clean sheets I put on after playing earlier. He's so lithe and gorgeously furry, I can't resist sliding my hands over him again, cock twitching at the way his body hair feels on my palms. So sexy, so manly, and yet he's such a natural submissive. My boy.

I climb in next to him and pull him into my arms, resting his head on my chest, and I kiss the top of his head. Holding, breathing in his scent, I memorize the feel of him against me.

Making memories for later.

CHAPTER TWENTY-EIGHT

Erik

"THIS IS YOUR mom?" Matthew asks, pausing with a mug of hot cocoa by the collection of photos on my dresser.

"Yup."

"She's young."

"She had me at seventeen." I smile at the photo of the two of us with our long-gone horse Smoky during the filming of an old Western show which had been one of my first training gigs. "We were more like friends sometimes than parent and child. I didn't mind. Still don't." Though I don't want to think of the things she'd said to me earlier on the phone. Not now when I've made peace with this ending.

Sort-of made peace. Mostly. Almost?

"Oh?" Matthew's lips tilt sideways in a sad expression. I wouldn't call it a smile, but it isn't a smirk either. "It's strange, I lived with my folks my entire life, but they were never my friends. They were always just...my parents, you know? I never felt like I was fully grown up when I was with them." He looks down at himself, wearing just the clean underwear I put on him earlier. "I guess I'm still not. Here I am as your boy."

"Hey," I say, beckoning to him. "Come here."

Matthew pads over to me, a vague expression of shame on his face.

"There's nothing childlike about being my boy. It takes great strength of mind and character to surrender to me as you have."

I'm trying to convince myself as much as I'm trying to convince Matthew. I know he has to leave and go out into the world. I know other men will use him and take advantage of him, but I want to believe he'll be strong enough to cope with it. The depth of his submission is evidence of his strength.

But Matthew senses the bullshit. "No," he says, gazing at me with sad eyes. "I'm very much a child in some ways. I might be in my forties now, but there are parts of me—big parts—that are still in need of parenting." He swallows. "Daddy, will you…can you…" He clears his throat. "When you said last night I should stay forever, was that just lust talking? I mean, what if I could…" He takes a shaky breath and rushes on. "I guess I want to know: do you want me for more than just this?" He motions between us. "More than this time I've won from you?"

My heart pounds, and blood rushes in my ears. My mouth goes dry. I don't know what to say, so I say nothing. Understanding dawns on Matthew, and his gaze goes shy and ashamed before he nods once, looks away, and says, "I understand. You don't have to say anything. I can see it on your face."

"Matthew…"

He puts his hands up. "No, please don't. It'll just ruin the time we have left. I shouldn't have asked. Forget I did."

Like a coward, I stand, pull him into a hug, and take the out he's given me.

Which makes me an asshole, too.

LATER IN THE barn, Matthew is petting Dipsy and watching me do my sets. He isn't working out because I think he needs to rest. It's been an intense few days physically, emotionally, and mentally. I've already crossed so many lines with him, made this time together so much more than I ever intended, and way more than he can expect from future men. I'm ashamed of myself for not having the guts to talk with him earlier, get it all out on the table. So I'm trying to at least take a more hands-off approach for the rest of the night.

"So you teach your clients martial arts, too, right?" Matthew asks, running his fingers over Dipsy's head, making him purr.

"I do."

"Can you teach me? Just a little, before I go tomorrow." He smiles wryly. "I could use some help in the self-defense department. What if the next man I meet isn't as good to me as you've been?"

My stomach knots up, and I almost drop my kettlebell on my toe. The thing is—it could happen. It most likely *will* happen, and the thought of Matthew out there with some other guy using him with less grace and love than I have? It sickens me.

And not just the thought of him being pressured into doing something he doesn't want, or even forced, but the thought of any other man getting to see his face in orgasm, or watch him writhe with bliss, or sweat for joy, or witness that rapturous expression when he's just been entered…

"Fuck," I whisper, wiping a hand over my sweaty face, but I put a smile back on before I turn to Matthew and beckon him over. "C'mere. I can teach you a few things."

I take him to the mat. It's soft and makes for a good place to fall.

The basics are simple enough, and soon I have him bouncing between his left foot and his right, hands up, hitting the air.

"Nice form." He's a quick learner when it comes to physical things. "Did you play sports as a kid?" I ask, demonstrating the moves for him again.

He repeats them easily. "Baseball and basketball. My mom didn't want me in football."

"You move well."

He smirks. "I know."

Ah, my boy's getting cocky now. He's adorable when he's feeling good about himself. "All right, let's take this to the next step."

We move through several basic setups for punches, which I emphasize he should only do if he has no other option. "Running is always your first choice. It's *always* the best choice."

Panting, he bounces back and forth, sparring a little with me, tapping my hands. "Teach me something useful then. I already know how to run."

I smile. "All right. Let's talk about breaking holds."

He's less of a natural at this, but he catches on quick enough. Grabbing him from behind, I demonstrate how to break a hold from on top. He performs it multiple times. So I seize him from the front and demonstrate another technique.

He struggles a bit, but eventually he manages to break my hold. When I go to show him the neck choke break, he nods that he understands. But when I grab him again, he just stands there, hands raised to grip my forearms, and his breath coming in rough pants.

"Go on," I encourage him.

He doesn't.

I release him, spinning him around, and I see what's going on. He's turned on. His borrowed track pants are distended in front, and his cheeks are flushed with both exertion and arousal. His eyes have gone dark.

"What's this?" I ask, taking his chin and lifting it. "Do you enjoy being rough with Daddy?"

"A little," he whispers, gaze darting to the floor. "You could..." He blushes darker.

"I could what, boy?"

Matthew's eyes lift to meet mine, those dark lashes outlining the hazel so prettily. "You could chase me? Grab me? I'd fight you, but..." His throat clicks as he swallows hard. "But I'll let you win."

Well, shit, if the kinky little fuck wants to get super dirty with this? We can play. We sure as fuck can.

"Verbal protests?"

"Yeah. I'll ask you to stop, but I won't mean it."

"Safe words are red and yellow."

"Yes, Daddy."

"Ready?"

He tenses.

"Now."

Matthew rushes to the door of the training room, wrenches it open, and races outside. I give him a little bit of a lead, though he's quick enough I'll have to work to catch him, and then I go after him.

It's wild running through the fields of melting snow, panting, swerving to avoid puddles, and racing over uneven ground which leaps up to trip me. I train my clients out here sometimes. Especially those who have shoots that require outdoor dramatic running or battle scenes, but never have I chased a lover over snowy mud and grass, knowing that when I catch him, he's going to fight me.

But he's going to let me win.

I'm more practiced at running over bumpy ground than Matthew, so I catch up fast enough, but I toy with him, letting him dart to the left and burst ahead, only for me to catch up to him once again. Grabbing him from behind, I swing him up off his feet, and tumble him to the muddy grass.

Matthew pounds against me, but I haven't taught him how to escape when someone's got you down yet, and he fights uselessly, pushing, shoving, even trying to kick me off, but I pin him with little effort. He's red all over again, and panting hard, his eyes bright as he whispers, "Don't, Daddy. Don't."

Not red. Not yellow, but "don't."

"Got a color, boy?"

He shakes his head. "Don't, Daddy," he says again, this time almost slyly.

I flip him over. "Here. I'll show you how much you love Daddy's dick in your ass."

I don't have lube, and this is madness, but I start saving the spit in my mouth to slick the way. It's going to hurt, but I sense in Matthew's quickened breath, in his fingers clenching in the snow-laced grass, that he's gagging for this. He has his safe words if he wants them.

"Daddy," he whimpers. "But Daddy…it's wrong. It's bad. It's a sin."

If things were different, I'd play with his baked-in shame until he only associates it with coming for me, coming for his Daddy.

"Stay there," I order, releasing my hold on his wrists, and pulling down his track pants to expose his sweet ass. It's perfect, and in the sun it glows as white as the melting snow across the field, dusted with dark hair instead of grass.

"Fucking love your ass," I mutter.

"Daddy, it's wrong," Matthew whispers, but he lifts his ass up in a plea for me to do something, anything with it. "Stop."

"Got a color?"

"No."

"Shh," I soothe him. "Let Daddy show you how good it feels, sweet boy."

I push his ass cheeks apart and reveal the treasure of treasures—his sweet, tight hole, which has brought me so much pleasure the last few days. And it's brought him pleasure too. If I do this now, he's going to be sore when I fuck him again tonight, and there's no doubt in my mind I'll have to have his ass one more time before he leaves. But Matthew wants to play this game, he wants to play with his shame, and I'm not afraid to take him there.

We can do this.

I go to work on his asshole, licking and spitting, getting it wet, and all the while he keens and begs me to stop. "It's wrong, Daddy. It's bad. Stop, stop, please, Daddy, *don't*."

My own pulse beats wildly, and for a moment, I get lost in the role. I'm the Daddy who's doing something wrong, who's taking his sinful lust out on his innocent boy, and my dick grows stiffer with the dirtiness of it all.

When I have Matthew wet enough to risk trying to sink in, I rub a wad of spit on my cockhead, line up, and shush him as I push. Slow, slow, *slow*.

"Daddyyyy," he whines, straining back. He goes up on his elbows, nearly slamming his head into my jaw.

"Shhh," I hush. I slide my hands around his throat and rest my elbows on his shoulder blades. I increase my hold on his neck until I can feel his pulse pounding hard against my fingers. Not enough to choke him, but enough to make him feel my control as I concentrate on moving into him.

Little by little.

In and out.

Slow and sure.

Stretching him open, raw and rough, as he whimpers and begs beneath me. When I'm balls-deep, I pause and kiss his hair. He squirms beneath me. So I squeeze his throat a touch more before relaxing my hold again, just so he's aware I still have him.

"Feel that, boy?"

"Yes, Daddy."

"That's Daddy's cock, right where it belongs. Deep inside his sweet boy."

He sobs in the sexy way he has when we're playing with his shame. "Daddyyyy."

I don't think any other man will ever see him like this, or if they do, they won't know how to handle it. That terrifies me for him. It terrifies me for *me*, too. How is it possible I'm so sure when we're playing with fire like this?

"Feels good, doesn't it?"

Matthew shakes his head. "It's bad. It's a sin."

"Sin feels good," I whisper in his ear and rock my hips, nailing his prostate at this angle. He jolts beneath me. "Feel that sin, boy? It's gonna make you come."

He groans, and his fingers spasm against the muddy ground. The cold air burns in my lungs, but my cock is hot in his ass, and my body on his is keeping him warm. Kissing his temple, I find it's sweaty, and his throat is hot beneath my palms. But it's his gorgeous internal heat driving me onward. I feel like I could fuck him here on this snow-wet earth forever.

"Daddy, help me," he whispers, and I bite the shell of his ear. He gurgles and shudders beneath me, moving one hand down, working it under his hips, tipping us slightly.

Releasing his throat, I roll us both over, him lying flat on top of my belly, still pinned on my cock, and both of us are now staring up at the bluest of blue skies. Matthew's hand moves, jerking himself off, seeking his release, and I whisper filthy things in his ear, making it better for him, poking at his deepest hurts.

"Are you gonna come on Daddy's cock? Gonna come for your Daddy like a dirty little sinner?"

"Daddy." He pants, his hand moving faster.

"See? Daddy knew you'd like it. All your begging 'don't, Daddy.' All your pleading for me to stop. But you *wanted* me to put it in you, didn't you? You wanted Daddy's dick splitting your ass."

Matthew groans, and his head collapses back, narrowly missing my face. He strains, jerking himself faster, and I just hold his hips steady, keeping my cock as far inside as possible.

Christ, how are we fucking again? It's so damn good between us, that's how. Every time with Matthew is like a fire out of control.

I think we're going to do one thing, and then we just…do something like this. And I can't regret it. It's always perfect.

"Daddy, I'm…gonna…" His voice is so strained, so beautiful and sexy. I want to swallow the way it sounds and make it part of myself. I want to keep it forever. "Gonna…come, Daddy."

"Show Daddy how much you like his cock," I whisper. "Come for me. Show me, sweet boy."

"Oh fuck," he grinds out.

I feel it—the wonderful clenching and fluttering of his anus around me as he comes hard. I shove him roughly onto his stomach again and thrust into him sharp and hard; he gasps in broken little sounds. My climax rises as I hold the back of his head so that he's face-down in the dirt, and whisper in his ear, "Take Daddy's load. Open up and *take it*."

He shudders under me, a second orgasm ripping through him, and I breathe hard in his ear, making him squirm, as I struggle to get there.

Almost. Almost.

And…

"Yes! Yes, baby, *fuck*." I kiss the shell of his ear as I kick the wet grass, my orgasm rioting through me. "What a good boy," I croon as I crash, still shaking with bliss. "What a filthy, sinful boy. Daddy loves you. Daddy loves you so much."

Matthew slips his hands out from beneath himself, and reaches back to clasp my head, keeping my mouth next to his ear. I breathe there, shuddering through a few aftershocks. I whisper, "Goddammit, Matthew. You make me wild."

I struggle to dislodge myself from his hole, and then use my own jizz as a kind of balm on its reddened rim. Matthew lies motionless on the muddy earth for a few minutes, and then he flips over. His front is covered with mud, much like my back, and his eyes are wet, his cheeks red, and he has a vulnerable look in his eye.

"What is it, boy?"

He licks his lips, seems about to say something important, but finally offers, "It's cold, Daddy."

Normally, I'd insist on knowing what it was he hadn't told me; it's my duty as a Daddy to make sure all hesitations and concerns are addressed. But I suspect what it's about, and cowardice stops me from demanding the truth. I help him up, get his track pants up, and put my arm around him as we walk, filthy with mud, toward the house.

"C'mon," I murmur. "Let's get a shower. Afterward, more hot chocolate. Then we rest."

It's only later, once we're both clean again, and bundled up with the promised hot chocolate on my sofa, watching *Die Hard,* that I let myself remember what I'd said, what I knew Matthew hadn't wanted to address out there on the ground.

I'd said I loved him. While my dick was still throbbing in his hole, I'd told him not once, but twice that I love him.

Fuck.

Fucking, fuck fuck.

I kiss his hair, and Matthew snuggles tight against me.

Some Daddy I am. What a mess this is turning out to be.

A gorgeous, delirious, addictive mess.

CHAPTER TWENTY-NINE

Matthew

I DON'T WANT this Christmas to ever end. Not because it's perfect—I think there could be better, more beautiful Christmases than this one even, given the right circumstances—but because I don't want my time with Erik to be over.

Dinner is from my recipe, even though we make it together. Working as a perfect team, we chop the vegetables, make the dumplings, and monitor the stove before plating the results to perfection. Daddy is happy with it all, moaning around his first bite of chicken and dumplings.

"Who taught you to cook like this?"

"My mama," I say, slipping into a Southern-boy drawl easy as pie. It's not a traditional turkey dinner, but this food is a good fit for Christmas—rich and carb-heavy. I'm still just wearing my undies and a Christmas apron.

"She did a favor to the world."

I blush. "I'm glad you think so."

"So what was it like? Growing up in your house?"

"I've already told you some of it."

"Tell me more."

I don't know if this is an Erik and Matthew talk right now, or a Daddy and boy thing, but it doesn't matter. I want to tell him everything anyway. If I had the time, I'd spill it all. "I know you must think it was horrible for me, growing up in a house with parents who thought being gay was a sin."

Erik doesn't deny it, looking at me over his next bite of food and waiting for me to go on.

"But we had a lot of good times. Mom and I weren't close, not like it seems you are with your mom, but she spent time teaching me to cook, clean, and take care of myself. She liked to dance, and she and I took a ballroom dance class together when I was in high school."

"Oh? You still good at it?"

"I doubt it. I remember a few steps. You dance?"

Erik shrugs. "A little. Nothing fancy. Go on."

"Anyway, she was sweet, you know? And she loved me. I was the child she'd longed for. But once she had me, I think I was a disappointment. Not the *worst* disappointment, but not what she'd hoped for either. She'd have liked to be a grandmother, would have liked to see me married and all that. But whatever the case, I have a lot of fond memories of her. She made my lunch for school every day. She took me to baseball practice, and later to guitar lessons. She liked to watch soap operas with me, and she'd record *Days of Our Lives* while I was at school to save until the weekend so we could catch up together."

"Do you still watch soaps?"

I laugh. "From time to time. When I'm missing Mom or something, I'll tune in. Soaps move simultaneously fast and slow, you know. So you can check out for a year, and when you come back, not enough has changed that you're confused. You can always jump back in."

"I watched *The Young and the Restless* with my granny when I visited her on summer vacations."

"Then you get it."

Erik nods. "Tell me about your dad."

"Oh. Well, Dad and I..." I poke at the next dumpling, spearing it with my fork. "We didn't fight or anything. We did a lot together, in fact. He taught me about car and house maintenance, and he was the one who made sure we were on our way to church by nine-fifteen every Sunday morning. He taught Bible study, and he believed in it all very deeply. He tried to instill that same belief in me."

"Did it take?"

"In some ways."

"You go to church?"

I shake my head but then take back the denial. "Well, sometimes. I grew up in the church. My family's friends and community are all there. Sometimes I do go back just to remember why I left. And because I miss them, you know? I mean, I miss my parents and the life we had. Not because it was all sunshine and roses, but because it was my normal, comfortable existence." I flash him a wry smile. "I'm tired of being comfortable."

"So I gather," he says, raising a brow. "You pushed the edges of comfort for both of us earlier today, didn't you?"

I blush, thinking about the way I'd egged him on in our kinky play out in the field. For me, that's all twisted up with the way my dad spoke to me about Christ. "I did."

"No need to be embarrassed. Like I said before, shame play can be a part of kink."

I smile to acknowledge his statements, but my mind is still on my father. "Dad—my dad, I mean—he didn't lecture me about God so much as steep everything about our lives in the church. I stopped saying prayers before eating a few months after they died, and it'd seemed like a big rebellion. You can imagine how having this time with you has been a colossal fuck-you to everything I was raised to believe in? So thank you. I needed it."

"There's a shadow side to all of us, and kink can be a good way to acknowledge it and give it what it wants. For you, you have a cape of shame hanging over you, and until you can find a way to take it off, twirling around in it can be a way to cope."

"I did love my parents. I do."

"I'm glad it wasn't worse than it was."

"There was no physical abuse, and the emotional and mental abuse was…" I consider how to best put it. "It was low key, unintentional, and almost impossible to call abuse."

"I'm guessing, due to your submissive nature, you didn't do anything to provoke them either. You went with the flow, and they never noticed how, for you, there was internal friction in that life."

I sigh. "They genuinely believed they had a good life, and because they believed it I guess they did. They also thought if everyone just lived like them, those people would be happy, too. They were a compatible match. They loved each other. I was loved—" I huff a laugh. "I was *loved,* but not known. And that's the difference, isn't it? Some people say it's not possible, but I'm living proof you can love someone without knowing them. That's what my parents did."

"Did they love *you*, though? Or did they love an illusion? They loved something, but whether it was you?" Erik shrugs. "That's a question for someone smarter than me."

"They loved parts of me."

"True."

"And I loved parts of them. Who really sees *everything* about another person? You've seen me at my most vulnerable. You've see me come, and sleep, but all those years I lived with my parents are part of me, too, and you can never *know* all that. No one can. Maybe if I'd had a sibling, we might have shared some memories of my parents and agreed those memories represented who they were, but even with siblings, the story isn't always consistent. Sometimes siblings might as well have different parents because they're treated so differently as kids."

I frown, realizing I sound defensive. "Sorry, I don't mean to be..." I gesture to encompass however it is I am. "My parents are still a touchy subject for me. It's hard because they're gone, and I want to honor the good parts of them because there were plenty, but it's also true being their son fucked me up."

"Understood," Erik says, his eyes full of care for me. "I'm pretty sure that's true for most folks. I'm not perfect."

I start to argue. Erik has been so much more than I ever imagined when I put my bid on him at the auction. So much more. For me, he's been perfect.

But then I remember his declaration of love while we were fucking in the field, and the way he'd avoided addressing it afterward. I also think about how over-the-top some of the scenes we've done have been, given how short a time we've had together, and I know…

He's not perfect.

But the way he's flawed appeals to me. I'd like the opportunity to peel back more layers and find the part of Erik which makes me mad and annoys me. There's got to be a part of him underneath this perfect-seeming exterior that will surface to poke me hard enough to prove his humanity. His failure to address his verbal slip-up earlier is close, though. It does rub me the wrong way.

Taking a deep breath, I decide to call him on it. "Daddy?"

Blinking, Erik takes a moment to reply, and it's clear now our prior conversation has been as Matthew and Erik. When he answers, his voice has that surety it sometimes loses when he's not in his role. "Yes, boy?"

"Earlier, when we were fucking outside…" I can tell by the way his face goes neutral he knows what I'm about to bring up. "You said—" my face grows hot, but I go on. "You said I'm a filthy, sinful boy—"

"It was role play. I don't think you're sinful. I'd never think what we do with each other is a sin. I don't even believe in sin."

"I know, Daddy. That wasn't what I wanted to ask you about."

Daddy clears his throat, and I can see him decide to man up before I can ask the rest.

"I said, 'I love you.'" Daddy smiles with tenderness. "I meant it at the exact time I said the words. I was in you, feeling so good and strong, and there was affection in my heart for you." He touches his chest. "It's possible, as you said, to love a man without knowing him. But that doesn't mean I'm *in* love with you. There's a difference there, isn't there? I can love you abstractly, but I can't be in love with you without knowing you better than I do."

"I want you to know me, Daddy."

"Matthew..."

I put my fork down, my heart going wild. "Is there a reason we can't have more time than this?" My voice sounds raspy, and my throat has gone tight. "Is there a reason this has to be over?"

Daddy—no, he's Erik now, there's something that shifts in his shoulders, in his face when he's dropping the role—sighs heavily. "Matthew, there are so many reasons."

"Will you tell me what they are?" Tears sting my eyes, but I blink and hold them back.

"You live in Nashville."

"There's the internet. Phones. Texts!" I'm growing upset. "Planes! I have a car! You do too!"

"I don't do long distance," he says. "It's a deal-breaker for me."

My throat grows even tighter.

"There's also the fact that you're so inexperienced—"

"I'm not good enough at this? You need someone better at sex?"

Erik blinks. "No, that's not it at all. You're beautiful in bed. It's been an honor and a pleasure to share this time with you. It's for *your* sake I bring it up. You should explore more. Have more men. Experience different types of sex. Have *fun*. Live the life you should have been living all these years."

"What if I don't want to?" Indignant hurt rises.

"Then you don't have to."

"But what if I want to be with you instead of having 'fun' with 'more men?'"

"Matthew, you can't give up your life, change everything, and dive into something with me just because of this time we had together. This has been intense for you—and for me—and I understand not wanting to let it go. We've been in an intimate, passionate bubble which exists outside of our regular life. That can seem like the most wonderful, beautiful experience that should never end. But it *will* end. It *does* end. It has to."

"What about your other boys?" I get out around the lump threatening to choke me. "You let them be with you for years sometimes."

"Yes, but those relationships ended too."

Is that what he's afraid of, and why he won't admit this thing between us is extraordinary? "What if this one doesn't?"

"You can't want a commitment with me, Matthew. You don't know what you might be missing out on."

"My parents were high school sweethearts. They never even dated anyone else. They were happy. They didn't have to experiment, or fuck other people, or 'have fun' the way you're recommending, and they loved each other until the very end."

"It can happen. But it's rare."

"So you're saying if I leave here, sleep with other men, have other Daddies—" Erik can't disguise his wince "—and experiment with other kinds of sex, only *then* will I be able to know what I want? I can't know what I want right *now*? As a grown man?"

"Matthew…" he says it so kindly a tear spills from my eye. Erik shifts forward to wipe it away with his thumb. "Boy, don't cry now. There's a big world out there waiting for you. Daddy loves you enough to send you out into it. You'll thank me for this later."

Standing, I drop my napkin by my plate and turn away. "I won't."

It sounds as juvenile as the times when my own father insisted I'd eventually thank him for some harsh lesson he'd taught me, but I feel as adamant now as I did back then. Only this time, I have the vantage point of being an adult, and I *know* this is bullshit. I'm just too hurt right now to be able to figure out why.

I take myself upstairs, and Erik doesn't follow me. In the privacy of his bathroom, I lock the door and gaze at the tub where he'd performed the enema on me just two days before, and marvel at how that single act had torn down so many of my walls. He'd known it would. He'd done it on purpose.

And yet his walls haven't even been shaken after he let me do it to him, have they? They remain fully intact.

How is that fair?

Sitting cross-legged on the bathmat by the tub, with my back to the porcelain rim, I cover my face and try to breathe. The long-distance excuse is absurd. It's not like Nashville is in another country.

He thinks I'm infatuated because he's my first fuck. Maybe I am. But don't all relationships start with a crush or an infatuation? He thinks I need more experience before I can know what I want. Maybe I do.

I have a Dom, Paul Adler, lined up to meet after all, and it would be interesting to see how being with him is a different experience. But if Erik says I can stay and we can try? I'll cancel that meeting without a second thought.

I growl and scrub my hot face with my palms.

Hadn't I been wanting to see a part of Erik that would annoy me?

Looks like I found it.

CHAPTER THIRTY

Erik

I WAIT FOR Matthew to come back downstairs, and when he finally does, I sit him on the sofa, take his hands in mine, and say, "Matthew, all men fall for their first fuck."

"It's not—"

"Let Daddy finish talking," I say. "I'm flattered you want more with me. This time with you has been beyond special. I'll never forget a moment of it. I'm grateful for what you've shown me, and for what I've learned from you."

He tries to speak again, but I put my fingers over his lips.

"What *I've* learned is I'm not ready to commit my heart to someone again. I was hurt when Brandon left me, and I'm not brave enough to risk that pain again. You're amazing. I've loved getting to know you, getting to hold you, and being allowed to give you all this pleasure, joy, and play. Introducing you to kink has been a blessing in my life, one I can't begin to measure the value of... But extending anything longer than this? I'm not ready for that. Do you understand?" I lift my fingers from his mouth.

"It's not me, it's you? Because you fell in love with your last boy?"

I sigh, sidestepping his comment about Brandon. "Well, it's a little you. I do believe you deserve to have a diverse set of experiences before you decide what you want to commit to. Right now, this seems exciting, and all you could ever want, but that's because it's the first thing you've had. You're in a fishbowl with me right now, but there's an ocean outside of here."

"Really? Now it's 'there are plenty of fish in the sea?'"

The disappointment and disdain in his voice catch me off guard. I sit with it for a moment, trying to decide what I want to say. But he speaks again before I have a chance.

"Erik—Daddy—Erik—whatever, whoever I'm talking with, both Daddy and Erik, I need you to understand this right now." Matthew takes hold of my hands and looks me deep in the eyes. "I'm a grown man. I might not have had my dick in many guys or gotten fucked ten ways to Sunday by half a dozen men, but I know what I want. And what *I* want is to pursue a relationship with you. I'm quite clear on that, both in my heart and in my head. I understand you don't like the idea of long distance, I don't love it either, but if you wanted this with me, I think you'd try to make it work. I get that you think I need more experience, but I don't give a shit about that, and so neither should you. Unless what you really mean is I can't satisfy you, and then that matters a great deal—"

"No, it's not—"

"Shh." He actually shushes me, and I stop talking. I blink at him as he gazes into my soul and goes on. "I also understand your last boy broke your heart, and it hurt more than you imagined. I think it must have surprised you a great deal since you've protected yourself from feeling brokenhearted by dating men you know are going to leave because they've got somewhere to go, a different life trajectory, and it doesn't include you. So, to have fallen for him, to have loved him with your whole heart just to have it smashed—"

"It wasn't my *whole* heart." Christ, I sound ten years old right now. Where's my Daddy persona now?

"Even half of a heart getting smashed up hurts like hell. I might not know about romantic love, but my parents are gone, and it broke my heart. I understand what that's like." Matthew lifts one of my hands and kisses my knuckles. "So you're right. If this isn't about me not being able to satisfy you—"

"It isn't."

"So this *is* you and not me. That's rough because you're not something I can fix or change. Only you can do that. So this means I have to leave here tomorrow and get on with my life. That's okay. I get it. I don't love it, but I get it. You're not ready for someone like me. You need training wheels a bit longer before you're ready to ride the bike."

"Matthew..."

His audacity should gall me, but instead, I'm pierced by the sharpness of his truth. He's nailed me to this wood, and now I'm squirming on it. Leave it to a religiously-raised shame-slut to know just how to crucify me.

"So I'll go home tomorrow, and I'll move on with my life. I have an appointment with that Dom I mentioned, and I'll keep it. I'll see if *he's* what I want, and if he is, we'll see where it goes. I'll be okay, Daddy. Don't worry about this boy. But if you're ever ready to take off the training wheels, and get on a real bike? Call me. You know where I am."

Matthew stands, takes my hand, and leads me toward the stairs.

"We have the rest of tonight, and I don't want to waste any more of it like this. Let's go, Daddy. Your boy wants to play. Christmas will be over soon."

I follow him, my heart pounding and my knees feeling weak. I'm out of my depth. He's just called me Daddy, but I've rarely felt so young. From the start, I've thought of Matthew as naïve, as weak and vulnerable. But he's shown me the truth.

He's strong and brave and wiser than me by far.

Yet when he climbs on the bed, turns his gaze on me, and reaches out, saying, "I need you, Daddy. Take care of your boy," I'm the man in charge again. I'm his charity-auction Daddy.

Even if I've technically delivered on what he bought, in my heart, I still owe him tonight.

PART FOUR

The After Experience

CHAPTER THIRTY-ONE

Matthew

PAUL ADLER IS gorgeous.

He's got slicked-back black hair, blue eyes, a jawline that could cut paper, and a tall, lean build speaking of wiry strength.

I'm sitting across from him in his loft apartment in downtown Nashville with a spectacular view of the skyline, sipping a bourbon, and looking over the agreement we made earlier in the week. My stomach is in knots. I want to believe it's anticipation, but as I ponder the various scenes I've agreed to, I can't help but wish I was going to be doing them with Erik instead.

But that's not a possibility.

Since I left his cabin, I haven't heard a word from him, and I've had too much sense and pride to reach out. If he isn't that into me, he isn't, and I need to face facts and move on. And if he *is* that into me, but too afraid to admit it? Then that's a whole other load of problems I don't need in my life.

I want to love myself, embrace my sexual needs and my queerness. I need a man, a Dom, a Daddy who can handle me, who wants to make a *commitment* to handle me.

Paul Adler isn't that man.

But he wants to sign a six-week contract, which is more than Erik offered. After it's over, Paul has said he'll help me find someone else.

Just like Erik, it seems Paul has an aversion to long associations at this point in his life, but enjoys having a boy or sub at his beck and call for the weeks when he's not swamped with work. He's a Very Important Man, from what I understand, and has the fate of many country music stars' contracts, as well as other rich folks' lives, in his hands by virtue of being their lawyer.

When he takes a break, he takes a long one, and then he goes back to his highly stressful, but lucrative, career. As he told me when we first met up, "Normally, I take six weeks off around the holidays, but this year I couldn't get the time for various reasons. Which means I'm late to my vacation and have some real steam I'd like to blow off. Typically, I hire a companion for this time, and it's not always sexual. It's not even always Dom/sub. I'm a busy man. I don't have 'friends.' Sometimes I need companionship more than I need orgasms or kink. But this year…"

His smile grows somewhat sadistic. "I've had a few hard months. I want *all* the orgasms and kink. Are you sure you're up for this? Doug has filled me in on your situation, and I understand you're new. I get the responsibility of handling you, and I'm not afraid to do it. Do you trust me to?"

I had at the time, and I do now, too. The pen is right next to the paper. I can sign it, and the first scene can begin tonight.

Part of me wants to do it. I'm horny, and I yearn for the pleasures I've just learned and experienced with Erik.

But another part of me is desperate to get back to my Daddy. The man I've not stopped wanting for even a moment since I pulled out of his driveway.

"It's all right if it turns out you're not ready for this," Paul says, crossing his legs. He stretches his arm out along the back of the sofa opposite me. We're separated from each other by a long wooden coffee table that's artisanal and must have cost somewhere over ten thousand dollars. I admire the way he leans sexily against the cushions. He's a dream to look at. A few weeks ago, imagining him taking control of me would have had me panting and in a puddle on the floor.

It still could if I let it.

"I just have a few more questions," I hedge, struggling to come up with a genuine one. Finally, I ask, "Do you know Erik Garner? He's a Daddy in the kink scene in Asheville."

Paul's left eyebrow goes up, but he shakes his head. "No, but I assume he's the man you've been with before. The only man, yes?"

"Right. It's just…I keep thinking about him. Is that normal?"

"Normal?" Paul ponders his glass of bourbon. "I'd say it's pretty common to think quite a bit about your first fuck if it wasn't a bad one. Or maybe even if it *was* a bad one."

"Who was yours?" I'm stalling now, and we both know it.

Paul licks his lips and rubs a hand over his dark stubble before saying, "We can play the getting-to-know-each-other game; I'm happy to do that. But if you want to leave, all you have to do is walk out the door."

I bring my clenched hands to my forehead. Bowing my head, I close my eyes and breathe. "I'm not sure what I want."

"You seemed very certain during our last meeting, when we drew up this agreement."

I nod, but don't lift my head, keeping my hands against my forehead, and breathing in and out with my eyes closed. "I know."

"What's changed?"

"I was angrier then," I whisper. "I wanted to prove to myself and to him that I could move on. That I wasn't the weak, naïve man he thought I was, and I'm prepared to take the steps I need to in my life to get what I need. Steps he's not brave enough to take."

"And now?"

I laugh under my breath and lift my head. "Now I just really miss him."

Paul swirls the liquor in his glass, pondering me. "You had him in your life for how long? Three days?"

"Four." If I count the day we met to make our contract, and I do.

"And he's been out of your life now for how many days?"

"It was over on the twenty-sixth, and today's the thirtieth, so…"

"Five days."

"Yes."

"I'd say you've got at least a few more weeks of thinking of him before you start to move on."

"Sir?" That's what he's told me to call him.

"Yes?"

"I don't want to move on."

He smiles, cocking his head. "Of course you don't."

"And you want me here with you anyway?"

"This isn't a forever thing, Matthew. You can want this Erik whether you're here with me or whether you're out there alone. I'll be all right either way. It's your choice."

"If I choose to be with you, we'll do what's in this agreement?"

He nods. "And you'll get paid the stipend I pay to all my subs when it's over."

It's a large sum. It means I can leave the accounting job. It means I can consider some kind of new life without dipping too far into the funds my parents left for me.

"And if I leave right now, just walk out, then I…" I bite into my lip. "I go back to a life with no sex, and—"

"Whoa, whoa," he says, lifting his hands. "You're an incredibly sexy man. You can have sex whenever you want. There are apps, clubs, bars, and even a BDSM club you can try. There are more ways to skin that cat than signing our agreement."

"I like you, though. You're the kind of man I'm looking for."

"I am, yes."

I groan and chew on my bottom lip.

Paul stands, crosses to me, and lifts me to standing. He's shorter than I am, which is strange, and yet when our eyes meet, I do feel he's in charge, and I could obey him. He runs his hands into my hair at the side of my face and smiles up at me. "You don't have to know tonight. I won't rush you."

"But your vacation… If I say no, you'll need another boy."

"I can get another boy. I wanted you, but I'm not hurting for offers right now. The stipend makes me a pretty exciting catch." He laughs, slides his hands to my shoulders, and squeezes. "Go home. Think it over. Let me know tomorrow morning."

"I wanted to come for you tonight," I confess, blushing.

"Me too. You'd look so good on your knees for me." He shrugs. "But c'est la vie." Paul guides me toward his loft door. "I'll be waiting to hear from you. Don't take too long, but Matthew? Do be sure next time."

He kisses my cheek and sends me on my way.

As I pull out of the parking garage beneath his building, I'm sweaty and confused. I wanted to be used tonight, to be fucked, and made to come, and I'm curious about how Paul is in bed, how he'd touch me, and what pleasure he'd wring out of me. Would it be different from what Erik gave me?

But curiosity is simply that.

What I truly want?

Is Erik.

CHAPTER THIRTY-TWO

Erik

THE BLUE RIDGE Kink Club isn't where I want to be, and yet here I am.

Nick coerced me to come down with promises of conversation and whiskey, but I find that here, in the moment, I don't want either. The place is packed with wall-to-wall kinksters ready and willing to play. Some are even pretty hot, like the boy who pranced past me wearing bunny ears and a fuzzy tail stuck just above his bubble butt.

But none of them are going home with me tonight.

"Talk," Nick says, spinning on his swivel stool before propping an elbow on the bar and setting his chin on his fist.

I roll my eyes. There isn't much to say I haven't already said. "I'm not ready. That's all there is to it."

"So the Auction Boy was a bust?"

I sigh. Nick always wants to boil things down to something simple, and this just isn't. "He was great."

"But you don't do long distance, yadda yadda, all the rest of your excuses, right?"

"They aren't excuses."

"Well, I guess he was no honeypot."

I make a face. "What?"

"Honeypot. You know." Nick rolls his eyes at me. "You don't know? Okay, so have you ever been at an orgy, and there are like three fine asses lined up across the back of a sofa just ready for you to fuck?"

"This sounds very specific. Are you sure this isn't a story from your own life?"

"It is a story from my life, and it's how I know honeypots are real."

I wave my whiskey glass his way, urging him to get this ridiculous story over with. I've just had a sip of it. Alcohol always seems more appealing in theory than in reality. At least for me.

"So, three asses, all lined up. You fuck one, and it's nice, but there're two more, so you pull out and fuck the next one and the next one. It's hot. They're all hot. But for some reason, one boy's ass just feels so good. The best ass of the set. And you keep wanting it, even though some other boy's moaning like a bitch in heat, squirming on your dick, and begging you to go harder. So that's a honeypot."

"A bitch in heat is a honeypot?"

"No, the inexplicably good ass is the honeypot. Jesus, pay attention. A honeypot is precious and rare. If he'd been a honeypot, you'd have never let him go. So maybe he wasn't the one." He waved around the room. "There are plenty more to pick from for a play date."

"I don't want a play date." I want Matthew, who's no honeypot. He's more than that. He's an angel. Not just because it's his actual name.

"Are you actually calling it quits on kink?"

"I don't know what I'm doing, Nick," I sigh. "I've got no patience for this tonight."

"Well, what *do* you have patience for?"

I shake my head and look at my watch before casting my gaze over the room again. There's no one I want to talk to here, and definitely no one I want to fuck. "I guess not much. I think I'm going to head home."

"This'll be the last time I see you here," he says with his frank astuteness.

"I think it might be."

"Thirty-five is awfully young to hang up the Daddy hat for good."

"It is, but I just don't have the appetite for it anymore, I guess."

I do, though. For one beautiful weekend—the best Christmas since I was a kid who believed in Santa—I had plenty of appetite, and it'd been beyond delicious. I don't think I can ever achieve that kind of perfect play with anyone ever again. Matthew was my last boy.

"A broken heart can ruin a lot of good things, but it heals. Eventually. Maybe I rushed you into this too fast."

"Maybe you did, but I can't say I regret it." I'd never regret Matthew, but at the same time, damn, do I wish I'd never gotten a taste of him. It's not the same thing as regret, but it's too fucking close. "Tonight, none of this appeals to me. I just want to go home."

"Go on," Nick says, patting my shoulder. "If I see you around these parts, then I'll see you. If I don't, well, we can meet up for coffee or some shit."

"Or you could come up to the cabin, ride some horses, get in some training with me."

"I'll pass. Horses are too big for any man to mess with. My mama taught me that."

"Horses require respect, it's true, but they're wonderful animals."

"So you say."

I clasp his hand. "Thanks for trying, Nick. Getting me out in the scene again was a good idea. I learned a lot. Including that I'm just not in the right headspace for kink right now."

"It's better to know than not," he agrees. "Later, Erik."

"Later." As I walk away, a redheaded twink in nothing but a blue thong and high heels saunters up to Nick, saying something to make Nick guffaw and slap his ass. The kid leans on Nick, and as I round the bar for the exit, I feel sure Nick's found his plaything for the night.

The ride back to the house is short and quick. All the various roommates are out doing their thing—whatever particular thing that might be—except for Charles, who is sewing away in his room with the door and windows open and a fan circulating.

"Trying to heat all of Asheville?" I ask.

He doesn't stop working as he calls out, "Heater's stuck on high. Blowing full force."

"Great," I mutter. "How long has that been going on?"

"Off and on over the last few days. The others took off to find somewhere else to sleep for the night. I'm heading over to my uncle's place soon. I just need to finish…" He grins, a slash of pretty white teeth across the bottom of his boyishly handsome face. "There. Done." Charles stands and shakes out a lacy, frilly thing I suppose is another sample of his "lingerie for men," but I'm not sure how the pieces go on and where.

"Pretty," I say, because it's easier than asking questions.

"An upcoming best-selling piece," he proclaims.

"No doubt. When are you going to make enough money to get a real studio?"

"You want me out?" Charles asks with a twist of his eyebrows.

"Of course not, but surely you have bigger plans than this place."

"I do." He smiles cheekily. "I'm going to buy a whole house and hire assistants. In time, I won't just be a lone lingerie designer. I'll be a fashion icon."

"I approve of that plan."

Heading back out into the hallway to fiddle with the thermostat, it's only a few seconds before I give up and retreat to my own bedroom. It's a sauna in there, and I sit on the bed for a long moment, staring at the ceiling. I don't know what else to do right now, so I open my windows too. In the dead of winter.

What a mess.

Curling up on my bed, I take out my phone and do what I do far too often. I read over the last texts I exchanged with Brandon.

I wish you all the best, but please don't text again.

I chew my bottom lip as I re-read his reply: *I'm sorry this is so painful for you. You were the man I needed for a long time, and I'll never forget you. Ferko sends his regards.*

I close my eyes and picture Brandon's face. His blue eyes twinkling as he laughs. His red lips around my dick. His lithe body shuddering beneath me as I fuck him. The jiggle in his ass when he walks. I love all that. Or I did. I think I probably still do.

But I don't want him back anymore.

Even if he walks through the door right now, drops to his knees, and begs to be my boy again, I'll send him on his way because I meant what I said to Matthew: none of my boys are meant to last.

I choose them that way.

I close my eyes, and my mind betrays me by showing Matthew waiting for me at the cabin. I think of him moving his things in, of him taking up a permanent place in my life. Beneath the terror those images evoke, I feel warm and right inside.

But when I think of growing old with him, of him staying with me, being my boy even when he's sixty and I'm fifty-four. Or hell, even older! How does that work? What does that *look like*?

My mom is alone; she's never found true love, and it's always been just the two of us. How do you build a future with a lover? Maybe I should call my cousin Leo and ask him how he and his doctor decided to get married, how they knew it would last, and how he knew they could make a family and a future together.

Or maybe I should ask RJ and Aaron.

But instead, I pull up the text stream I shared with Matthew.

The last message is from when he let me know he'd arrived home safely in Nashville after our time together. Since that afternoon, there's been nothing. Which is right, and what I asked of him, and yet it's not what I wanted. For the last five days, every time my phone pings I've hoped it would be him.

I read over our texts from the night following our very first meeting. Then I double down on this mistake by opening the photo he'd sent me: post-orgasm, cum all over, and that wild, beautiful expression on his face. I let this guy—this gorgeous, submissive, sweet guy—walk away because I'm a coward. He took such a risk with me, trusted me with everything important—body, mind, and soul—and I let him down.

I've let myself down.

I put the phone aside, staring out the open window and feeling the cold air coast over my face. Heat pours from the vents in the room. Hot and cold blowing on me at once. Is this some kind of metaphor for my life? I feel like it might be.

"Hey," Charles says from my open doorway. "I'm leaving. You going to be all right here?"

"Sure am."

"Really? You're okay?"

"Yup."

"Did Brandon call or something?" he asks, stepping into the room carefully.

"No."

He stands half in the room for just a moment, considering. "Ah. You haven't been this down in a while. I thought maybe—but never mind. I'll just go now. Goodnight."

"Night," I say, but I sit and watch Charles saunter down the hall, his ass waving back and forth in that pretty way he has.

Maybe I *should* reach out to Brandon. Maybe that's what's wrong with me. If I had more resolution with him, more closure—

I grab my phone and swipe it open. I'm confronted again by Matthew's sex-drenched body and his beautiful eyes.

I don't text Brandon.

Instead, I thumb in a message to Matthew, read it half a dozen times, and delete it. I wait a few seconds, considering, before I thumb it in again.

I want to ask if he's all right, if he has regrets about me, about us, if he wants to meet up again, if we could maybe consider having something casual until I'm more certain of myself…

But instead I send: *Can I call you? It's important.*

My stomach knots up, and I break out into a sweat. What am I doing? I'm not sure.

But it feels like bravery.

CHAPTER THIRTY-THREE

Matthew

*C*AN I CALL *you? It's important.*

I breathe in and out. I'm at the elevator in the parking lot under Paul's building. I slept on it, and I've come here after going home to change after work. I've been too nervous to eat dinner, because I've decided I'm ready to sign the agreement and let Paul take me through a basic scene as his sub.

This, with Paul, is what I want.

Or it was.

Until this text came through.

Because I *want* Erik. It's only if I can't have him that I want to continue my journey of self-discovery, and Paul seems a fair and good man, a trustworthy person to carry on with. I want to be with trustworthy people.

But more than anything, I want to be with Erik again.

I find myself back in my car, shivering in the dank chill of the concrete lot. I stare some more at Erik's text. I can't get my hopes up. This is probably just about some small issue he needs to resolve. Maybe I left something in his cabin, and he needs my mailing address. Maybe there's been a problem with the check clearing for the charity.

Maybe…oh, God, what if he wants me to act as a reference for him for another boy? To verify he's trustworthy and safe.

I feel sick.

I squeeze my eyes tight, take a deep breath, and reply with: *Sure.*

When?

Now?

Yes

The call comes through immediately—a voice call—and I answer. Thank goodness there's a signal down here.

"Hi, what do you need?" I breathe out in a rushed gust, as if by asking it this way, I can stop him from hurting me or denying me again. He doesn't *want me*. He's made that very clear.

There's a long silence at the other end of the line before Erik says something that takes my breath away.

"You. I need you."

My heart pounds, and my pulse throbs. Paul Adler and his four-million-dollar loft and his steady smile disappear from my mind. I'm here with Erik on the line, and he needs me.

"How?" I ask. Maybe he needs my accounting skills? My address? Maybe he needs me to return the guitar?

"Lots of ways, but mainly I need you to forgive me."

"For what?"

"For being a coward. I never should have told you I didn't want to try a relationship with you. The truth is I *do* want to try with you, but I don't know *how*. I've never done that kind of commitment before. I've never even *seen* it done. My mom and I? Well, my dad left us, as I told you. And most of my friends' parents divorced. I've only let myself be with boys of a certain kind. Boys who are just passing through."

"Yeah?" I'm dizzy. I grip the steering wheel even though I'm parked. This is happening. He's telling me he wants me.

"And the thing is, you came to me because you wanted to learn to love yourself by embracing all the things you've held at arm's length your whole life, and I thought I could show you that. But how can I? When I hold at arm's length the people and things that will make *me* grow the most?"

"I make you grow?"

"Shit, I should have said all this in person. I should have gotten in my car and driven right to your house."

"Do you even have my address?"

"Somewhere in our legal documents for the auction. I could have found it, driven to you, and begged forgiveness on my knees for acting like I knew so much, when you were right. You were absolutely fucking right. I *was* running away from us, from how good we are, in all ways, because I'm scared. I'm fucking terrified. And you're the brave one, the adult, the one who was going to take a leap of faith for us, and after all you've been through—"

I jump to defend him from himself. "You've been through a lot, too. You have good reasons to not trust that someone will stay. You've got reasons to fear you're going to get hurt."

"I want to make our lives better, Matthew. Both our lives. I think what we shared last week was special. Irreplaceable. No one else has ever come close to making me feel as alive, whole, and right."

"You mean it? You're not just lonely or horny or—"

"I mean it. I can get ass whenever I want. But I don't want just any ass. I want yours. Do you understand?"

Do I? There's just one thing I can say. "Yes, Daddy."

His breath hitches. "Oh, God. Say that again."

"Yes, Daddy. I understand."

"When can you come home to me?"

My mind spins. "I have a few things I need to take care of."

"Your job, yes, and your cat. Maybe we can figure out—"

"The most pressing thing is backing out on the Dom I was about to meet with again," I say. "I'm in the parking lot under his building."

Erik makes a garbled growling sound. "*Again?*" He clears his throat. "It's fine. That's fine." He doesn't sound like he means it.

Which shouldn't thrill me, but it does. He adds, "I'm glad you're exploring. If you want to play with him, I'll understand and—"

"I want *you*, Erik." I gaze around the space at the incredibly expensive cars parked nearby. They probably each cost more than I make in a year at my job. Which I very much want to quit. "I don't want him."

"Did he touch you? It was this *Paul Adler* person?" He says the name like it's leaving a bad taste in his mouth. He's jealous.

I can't stop a grin. "A little?" We'd shaken hands, and he'd kissed my cheek.

"Did you come for him?"

"I don't see why it's your business, but no. We haven't signed the contract yet."

"Why not?" Erik sounds skeptical.

"I wasn't sure about it. But I'm here now because I'd decided to go ahead with what we planned. He was a perfect gentleman in the meantime." And then, because I like the raspy, angry edge to his voice right now, I say, "His hands are nice. He's been gentle so far, but he had some plans for later, which included pain play."

"You *agreed* to that?"

"I don't think I'd hate pain play," I admit. "But I'd rather you chase me across a field and roll around in shame with me instead."

His answering needy gasp makes me dizzy with joy.

Erik

THIS IS HAPPENING. Matthew's letting me back in. I'm dazed by my luck. "When can I see you?"

"Soon," he answers. "I have some problems to solve here at home, and I need to tell Paul I won't be signing the contract."

I want to get hold of that contract and rip it into tiny shreds.

"But on Friday, I think I can make the drive."

"Fly. I'll pick you up at the airport. I'll pay for the flight."

"That's silly and expensive."

I need to make this *right* with him, and I don't think I can wait until Friday. "I'll come to you."

"You don't have to."

"Actually, I do. You've been too lenient with me, Matthew. I might play the role of Daddy, but I'm still learning too. You should ask more of me. That's something we need to figure out together." He's quiet for a beat, and my stomach flips anxiously. "Do you understand what I'm saying? I should give you more than I have. I should have given all my boys more than I have."

"Like what?" he chokes out.

"I should have given you a real chance at my heart, at being part of my life. You deserved it; they all did. Maybe Brandon would have stayed if I'd ever given him the impression that I expected him to."

"Maybe he would have."

"*You* would have."

Matthew laughs, and it sounds like it hurts his throat. "Yes. I would have."

"I don't want Brandon," I tell him. "I want you. But is it too late? Have you moved on?"

"No."

"But you were about to sign a contract with another man…" I can't believe I'm being needy now, but some part of me wants Matthew to spell it out explicitly. I want to know for sure he doesn't prefer the idea of another man instead of me. How ridiculous, how anti-kink, how not the way of the game…

And yet this isn't a game. This isn't kink. This is my heart on the line.

"Don't be silly, Daddy. I'm your boy. How can I move on from that?"

My eyes fill with tears, and my throat tightens. "You could. You're strong enough to do anything you want, Matthew. But I'm happy you haven't. I want you to be my boy. I want to see if it can work between us for a long time."

"I want that, too."

"Is it all right with you if I come see you—" I glance at the clock. I need to figure out how to turn the heater off in the house, and it's already getting late in the day. Driving to Nashville tonight means a late arrival, but I don't want to wait. "Tonight?"

"You don't have clients, Daddy?"

"No, boy."

"You don't mind driving?"

"It'd be my honor to come to you."

Matthew hesitates, and I wonder if I've put too much on him. It's short notice for a visitor. He's not even at his home. He's outside a Dom's apartment. He's in his car. I'm an asshole, but—

"All right, Daddy. I'll text you my address."

I heave a sigh of relief.

CHAPTER THIRTY-FOUR

Matthew

I HANG UP the phone, feeling jittery and unhinged. Is it really possible that an hour ago I'd resigned myself to being with Paul for the next six weeks, and now I'm going to have to renege on it all, rush home, clean the bathroom, vacuum the floors, and sit in anticipation until Daddy arrives at my *home*. The place I grew up. The house still crusted over with my parents' life and energy.

I feel like I might hyperventilate, but I can't just text Paul that I'm backing out. That's not fair to him. I'm still at his loft, after all. So, I get out of the car, take the elevator up, and knock.

Paul's brows go up when he opens the door, and I wonder what he sees in my face. Obviously not what he was expecting. He gestures for me to come in. I shake my head.

"I'm sorry, sir, but I won't be signing."

He presses his lips together, his expression shading toward disappointment, but when he squeezes my shoulder, it's full of kindness. "Thank you. I understand."

"But I haven't explained."

He smiles gently. "I don't think you have to. Unless there's something you need me to know, or something I did which you think I need to be aware of? Because I get the sense this isn't about me."

"It's not, sir."

"Are you okay? Do you need to talk about it?"

"No."

Paul squeezes my shoulder again and releases me. "I wish you all the best. Maybe I'll see you out and about in the scene. Thank you for everything."

I want to make it better, soothe any hurt to his ego, but he doesn't seem affected in that way. He's disappointed but nothing more. I suppose it's good and right, but I do wish a man I'd almost pledged myself to for six weeks would have had more of a reaction. I suppose this means it's good it shook out this way. I'd have been setting myself up for regret if he's this emotionally unavailable.

"Thank you, too, sir."

Paul doesn't shut the door until he's seen me get back on the elevator, and I breathe a sigh of relief as the gap closes on his blue gaze. I lean back, letting the elevator take me back to the parking garage and my car. Guilt tells me I should be thinking of Paul, of the lurch I've left him in for his much-needed vacation, but I'm not. I'm thinking of one thing only.

Getting home and preparing for Daddy's arrival.

As I pull out of the parking garage and into the dark winter night, I calculate the time. If Daddy is leaving soon, I can count on him being here by two a.m. It's always slower going over those mountain roads in the dark.

I'll want food ready for him in case he's hungry. I'll want the house to be clean. I'll have to replace Simmony Sunshine's litter first thing. I'll need my *body* to be clean, and—

My mind spins with all I want to do before he arrives.

I wonder what he'll think of how I'm living.

I wonder how it might change how he feels about me and how seeing him in my home might make me feel about myself.

I'll know soon enough.

CHAPTER THIRTY-FIVE

Erik

IT'S LATE, AND I'm tired. The chipper voice of my navigation app advises me my destination is ahead on the left.

As I climb out of the car, I notice Matthew's house is a two-story Craftsman-style, and it matches the rest of the neighborhood. Probably built in the nineteen-sixties or earlier, it seems no major overhauls have been undertaken over the years.

The moon in the sky above is white and round, nearly full, and I think of how one of the actresses I worked with once told me that in astrology, full moons represent reaping a harvest sown. Consequences and outcomes.

The land here is flat, and the wind rushes over it with a broad ease it lacks in the mountains. There, either the wind is funneled and focused, or soft and meandering. This is vast, open, cold, and fast.

I steady my nerves.

The lights are on in Matthew's house. I can see into the living room and note the furniture is reminiscent of my Aunt Meryl's back in Blountville: a plaid sofa with matching drapes in the window, and heavy wood furniture of various types.

While some other houses in the neighborhood are still decked out in bright holiday decorations, Matthew's isn't. It should be. He deserves every fairy light and bauble and glittering garland.

I'll make sure he has them in the future.

I see a light come on in an upstairs window and flick off again.

Taking a deep breath, I step toward the front door, ready to confront my full-moon consequences. But as I do, it swings open, and Matthew's familiar silhouette is there to greet me.

He says nothing, just leans against the door jamb, waiting for me. I start up the walk, and then up the three stairs into the light of the front porch. He looks good. Healthy. It's not like five days apart should have driven him into a pining-induced illness, but I'm glad to see he hasn't lost weight, and his eyes are shining.

"Hi, Daddy," he greets after a long, heavy silence I'm not sure how to interpret. "Come on in."

I follow him inside, and when he shuts the door behind me, I turn around and back him up to it. Placing my arms on either side of him, caging him up against the door, I examine the mystery of his expression. His chin is tilted up, his eyes are wide and eager—though a little nervous now—and his breath comes in excited huffs.

"Boy." I take his chin and lift it higher, bending to press a kiss to the dimple I've missed, the corner of his lips, his nose, and his forehead. "I've missed you."

"Have you, Daddy?"

"Tempted to fuck you right now against this door."

"Go ahead, Daddy." Matthew laughs and leans back wantonly. "I'll let you."

I nuzzle his neck, getting a good lungful of his scent before rubbing my lips on his. "Fucking hell, I've missed you."

"I've missed you, too."

My mind wars between backing off and talking things through like a reasonable person, having some tea and cookies, or whatever the fuck Matthew has planned—because there's no way he's been sitting here for the last five hours calmly waiting for me. He's prepared *something*—probably himself, and food, and this house, and God knows what else.

But I don't want to wait. I want to remind myself and him that he's *my* boy, I'm his Daddy, and he's not some other man's to touch and hold—or to appreciate in the way I initially hadn't had the balls for.

"Get on your knees." I push him down, pleased when he drops at once. I keep my hands braced on the door behind him. "Get my jeans open."

His hands shake as he works my fly open. Once it is, he looks to me for instructions, and I want to weep at his perfect, submissive, adoring gaze. I don't deserve this. But no man does. Matthew's a gift—a generous, beautiful gift.

"You know what to do next," I whisper. "Show me what you remember of what I taught you."

He works my cock free of my underwear and jeans, and I shove them around my hips to make it easier for him. Matthew takes hold of my cock, his hand wrapping around the base, and his dark lashes fanning on his cheekbones as he closes his eyes and takes a moment to enjoy the feel of me in his hand.

His lashes flutter until he's gazing up at me. "Like this, Daddy?" He opens his mouth, puts his tongue out, and licks the head of my cock.

"That's good, sweet boy. That's what Daddy needs. Show me how you can suck me."

He does just that, and fuck, I don't know if he's been practicing on a banana, or if he's just a fucking savant, because he's going to suck my brains right out of my cock if I don't slow this down. But I don't.

I just let him go to town on me as I stare down at him, letting him witness my pleasure when he sits back to take a gasping breath and gazes up to gauge his effect on me. Smiling, he gets back to work. I tangle my fingers in his hair, muttering praise and pleasure, and coming closer and closer to orgasm.

"That's right," I say as he opens his throat wide and swallows me deep. "That's my deepthroating little cocksucker." It doesn't make a ton of sense, but I'm shaking now with pent-up need. My palms are sweaty when I place them on the door again, and they slip and squeak. "Such a good boy. So good to Daddy."

Matthew's eyes are hot and desperate as he works me over, and when I get close to climax, I grip his hair, hold his head still, and whisper, "Let Daddy do it, baby. Let Daddy have your mouth."

I fuck slowly into his throat and back out again. Matthew's eyes roll back, and gasping, gagging noises erupt along with wet, sticky saliva as I thrust in. I know he's been throat-fucked by other men, but this is me owning him right now, taking my pleasure right in the doorway of his childhood home, with the remnants of his parents—who would have rejected him for this—all around.

"Daddy owns you, sweet boy," I whisper. "No one else. Nothing else matters but this. Remember that."

He moans, and I plunge into his vibrating heat. His throat grips as he swallows. "That's so good. You're made for this. Made to be my boy."

"Daddy," he whispers when I pull out and he catches his breath, eyes wet as he sits back and stares up at me, red-mouthed and swollen-lipped. "Shoot in my mouth, Daddy. Let me have your cum. Let me eat it."

"Oh, you'll have it." I grip his hair again, and using my other hand to press on the hinge of his jaw, I open his mouth. He doesn't need this kind of force, but he submits to it easily, and I push inside again until I'm balls-deep—his eyes tearing up, his lips tight around the base of me, and his throat gagging at my intrusion.

I hold tight, wait until his eyes start to grow frightened before pulling out to let him breathe. I repeat it. Once, twice, three times. I thread my grip into his hair and whisper, "Daddy loves you, boy."

He groans, and I tilt my head back, gasping, as pleasure grips me by the balls and pumps out in sharp, harsh bursts which take my breath away. Matthew gags but recovers, sucking down my cum greedily before pulling off to lick the excess from my balls and his own hands. He sits back on his heels and licks at his palms like a kitten.

"That yummy, boy?" I ask, gruffly, still panting, and leaning heavily against the front door to his home. "That what you needed?"

"Yes, Daddy. Thank you," he breathes.

I haul him up. Tasting my cum in his mouth with our first kiss since we parted is rewarding in a barbaric, caveman way. I feel like I can own him, claim him, and mark him as mine. I love knowing he's absorbing my proteins, my DNA, incorporating it into his own body and cells. I'm making Matthew my boy inside and out.

"Love that, Daddy," he whimpers when I finally release his mouth. He's limp, though I can feel his iron-hard cock digging into my thigh. "Love when you come for me."

"You deserve it," I tell him. "You're so hot, so good. You deserve Daddy's cum."

"Thank you."

"*Meow.*"

I glance down, and an orange-and-white cat, similar in appearance to Daisy, slips around our ankles, purring. We burst out laughing.

"This is Simonny Sunshine," Matthew says, indicating the affectionate creature. "He's friendly."

"I see," I say, tugging my jeans up and tucking my cock away. "He's pretty. Like you."

Matthew scratches lightly at the fuzz of hair exposed at his collar. His lips shine from the spit of our kiss, and his eyes are hazy. "Are you hungry?" he asks, lifting from the subspace he drops into so quickly for me.

"I don't know. What do you have?"

He takes my hand and leads me from the entryway, through the living room, and into the kitchen, both of us jittery and still shaking with lust, happiness, and the shivers which come with staying up late into the night. There he seats me at a table that seems right out of the nineteen-sixties, as does the linoleum, and the cupboards.

"I didn't know what to make for you," Matthew says, putting a plate in front of me. "So I made this."

It's the chicken and dumplings recipe we made together on Christmas Day. I'm hungrier than I realized now that it's before me, the steam from it rising deliciously. I lift the fork and begin to eat. I notice he doesn't, though. "Have you eaten tonight?"

"Yes. Earlier, when I made this."

"Have more."

He shakes his head, and his hot blush rises up his neck and into his cheeks. "I've cleaned myself inside for you. I want to stay ready, Daddy."

I'm vaguely disappointed he did an enema without me, and I won't be able to strip him down and lay him bare like that again, but I suppose it's not a right I've earned back. Not that I ever *earned* the right to start with, but now I'm determined to earn it every time going forward.

We drop the issue. I feel the weight of his gaze as I eat, but it's not heavy. It's like gauze brushing over me lightly, and when I look up, he smiles, his hope and heart in his eyes. How did I send this man away? Why did I think I shouldn't pursue something real with him? Something lasting?

I glance around the kitchen, the evidence of his family and the years of his life before me, and I wonder what it all means to him. I want to ask him, but I also want to give him what he wants. I can see in his eyes he's hoping I'll make him come soon, and I don't think he'll be able to concentrate on anything else until I do.

Or maybe all the serious stuff—like what do you want from life, and what do you want to do with all this stuff your folks have left you with, literal and metaphorical—needs to wait until the light of morning anyway.

Tonight, it's just too late to go into any of that.

"Daddy's sorry," I say. "Do you forgive me?"

Matthew shrugs. "Of course."

And maybe it can really be as simple as that.

CHAPTER THIRTY-SIX

Matthew

AFTER ERIK'S DONE with dinner, I lead him upstairs, past the photos of my family on the wall, past the door leading to my room, and down the hall to a part of the house I don't enter very often. I open the door.

My parents' wide bed is there untouched, though earlier tonight I changed the sheets for the first time since their death. I left on the bedside lamps, which bathe the room with a warm, shy light.

Erik makes a sound under his breath, but I don't dare pause to let him think about where he is, or what we're doing in here, because I can't explain this. It's too intense and too much, but I also know I *have* to do this, and I have to do it now.

Maybe when it's over, I'll be able to say why.

Erik doesn't ask. He runs his gaze over the room, the photos on the dresser, the wallpaper, the big bay windows which look out onto our backyard, and he says nothing at all. Instead, he turns to me and starts to strip me of my clothes.

The knot in my stomach unwinds, the heat ignites over my skin, and when I'm naked, heaving breaths in and out in wound-up arousal, I allow myself to say, "This is my parents' room."

"I know."

"This is their bed."

"Yes."

"I need you to do this here, Daddy."

"It's okay, boy." Erik crowds up against me, walking me backward toward the mattress, and pushing me down onto it. He kneels at the side of the bed, dragging me by the hips until my ass is half hanging off the edge of it. "I think I understand what you need."

The room spins a little as I let him press my legs back and open. Taking hold of my hard cock, I stroke it as he bends and breathes over my asshole. The atmosphere between us is solemn, even as he begins to kiss me there.

The room is so quiet except for our sounds—panting, wet licking, and our groans. The night is heavy outside, and the room is weighted with the past. I fight to keep my eyes open, to take in the familiar room, the memories assaulting me from every corner—the scent of my mother's perfume slipping in from their en suite bathroom, the glint of my father's belts on the wall where they still hang, the memory of him using one on me when I'd accidentally broken a neighbor's window.

Now I'm in their room with Daddy, with my legs up and spread, his face between my ass cheeks, and I'm letting him do something to me they would hate, something my father would use one of those belts on me if he knew about and which I fear, in my heart-of-hearts, is a sin.

And, *fuck,* it feels so good.

I groan, breaking into a sweat, as I grip Erik's head, his short hair rough on my palms, and beg him not to stop. "Please, Daddy, make your sweet boy come. Please."

Daddy doesn't stop licking and tongue-fucking my bussy, groaning with pleasure as he does. I moan and tremble, wanting the heat of him on top of me, feeling cold and exposed in the darkness of the room.

"Daddy, Daddy," I whimper. "Help me. Please, Daddy, help."

It's a cry that meant something deeply personal to me in the cabin, but now, here, in this house, in this room, surrounded by these memories, it means so much more. A deep ache starts in my belly, my heart, and my lungs. A rough sob.

It works its way out of me, and when it breaks free, I press my fist into my mouth to hold back more. Daddy doesn't stop his work on my asshole, and my legs shake, my heels beating a jittery tattoo on his back and shoulders as he works.

Tears leak down my face as I pinch my own nipples and tug my own cock, owning this—owning my sexuality, my pleasure, and my desire—owning that a gorgeous man is eating my ass.

I cry out, "Look at me, Daddy! *Look* at me!" But I don't mean Erik, and he seems to know, diving into my hole harder and with greater gusto. "See me! I'm gay, and I love this so much."

I sob again, but it feels better, less ripped from my soul and more relief. I stroke myself faster, reaching for the edge of bliss, and when I feel the urge to come, I ask, "Can I come, Daddy? Please?"

Erik replies by knocking my hand off my cock, forestalling my orgasm, but not stopping his oral assault on my bussy. I curl my hands into the coverlet my mother's aunt gave her for a wedding gift, and I arch as Daddy begins to finger me, too. Pleasure jolts with each brush over my prostate, and I cry out my need and perverse joy as my cock leaks pre-cum on my stomach, enough that it slips down the sides of my torso and smears the coverlet.

"Get on your knees at the edge of the bed, boy," Daddy says, and I'm shaking so hard with arousal, lack of sleep, and heady emotions that I have a hard time obeying. Once I do, though, I'm shocked to see my new position affords me a view of the big portrait of my parents on the opposite wall.

It's been there for as long as I can recall, but now that I'm naked, dripping pre-cum onto their bed, and about to take Daddy's cock into my ass, I realize what I've set up, the confrontation I've needed since the day they died.

"Sit back," Daddy says, standing behind me and wrapping his arm around my chest, pulling me so I'm seated on my heels. "Kiss me."

I turn my head, and though the angle is awkward, Daddy leans in to devour my mouth. His tongue and mine collide with purpose and lust. I melt into him, my lips tingling and overstimulated, my breath full of his scent and our saliva mingling on my chin. Erik huffs against my lips, "Let's do this, sweet boy. Let's show them who you are."

I nod, tears pricking my eyes again, as I position myself on my elbows and knees, ass up.

The *snick* of the lube bottle opening tells me he's found where I placed it on the nightstand earlier. The slick is cool over my hole, shocking and promising. I stare up at the portrait, at the lines by my father's mouth, the sternness of his eyes, and my mother's placid, innocent expression.

Maybe our first time together again, after thinking we could never have more than one weekend, should have been about *us*. Maybe it should have been about connecting as a couple who are agreeing to take on a future of some kind together, to try for one at least, but I know deep in my heart I can't do that until I've put my past to rest. As twisted as this may seem, doing this with Daddy is part of moving on with Erik.

As the blunt heat of Erik's cock pushes at my tight hole, I whimper, "Help me, Daddy. Help me."

"Shh, I'll help you, sweet boy. Daddy's going to fuck this shame out of you." He rubs the head of his cock over my hole and commands, "Show them your face. Let them see who their son is."

I curl my toes and groan as he pushes in. It's an intense stretch, and I bear down to make it easier for both of us. Grunting when his cock strokes my prostate, tears prick my eyes again as his pubic hair grinds against my ass cheeks, followed by the soft kiss of his balls on the back of my own.

"There," Daddy says, taking hold of my shoulders and shoving until his cock is fully seated. "This is who you are. Tell them what you need them to know, angel."

"I love getting fucked, Daddy. I love it so much." I don't know if I'm addressing my father or my Daddy who's slowly thrusting into me now, grinding against my ass with every push in. "I love to eat cum and suck dick. I love it, Daddy."

"Good boy. That's my good, sweet boy," Erik praises, stroking down my back to grip my hips. "Open that bussy up. Daddy's going to fuck you hard. Show them how you love it."

"Yes, please! Oh, *fuck*!" I cry as he begins to ride me so hard my vision wavers. I can barely focus on my parents' picture. My hole spasms, my muscles tighten, and my cells come alive with pleasure and erotic energy. I'm alive, this is true and honest. I'm getting fucked and I'm so *fucking* happy. "Daddy, make me come! Make your boy come! Please!"

But Daddy doesn't. He rides me until I'm panting, sweating, crying out, and my cock has drooled a mess on my mother's coverlet. I feel the creeping, shattering perfection of orgasm coming for me even though I haven't touched myself since Daddy batted my hand away. It's going to grab me. It's going to get me.

I shudder and grip the coverlet, focusing on my parents through the sweat dripping into my eyes. "See me," I grit out. "See. Me."

The crest of pleasure breaks, and I cry out, my hole spasming on Daddy's cock and my cum jetting onto the bed in thick white spurts. I whimper, my nipples peaking, and I'm swept with chills and sweet convulsions. It feels right, like I'm sweating out my shame, my self-hatred, and so much fear.

"That's my good boy," Daddy says, stroking my back. "Coming on Daddy's cock like an angel. Such a sweet, sweet boy."

I squirm and convulse again. The erotic moment pairs with my father's stern gaze peering at me from the portrait. My own need to be loved and praised overwhelms it all. "Daddy, love me," I whisper. "Love me, please."

"I love you, angel. I love you so much."

I collapse, burying my face in the coverlet, and as Daddy plunges deep into my ass and unloads with a grunting cry, I start to sob. But it's not with pain or shame. It's with relief.

"Thank you, Daddy," I whimper. "Thank you."

CHAPTER THIRTY-SEVEN

Matthew

"FEEL BETTER?" ERIK asks, pouring more hot tea into my mug. He sits next to me at the small kitchen table.

I'm wearing sweats and an old, soft T-shirt under a sweater my mother knitted for me when I was sixteen. It's comfortable and baggy, with a stretched-out neck and overly long arms. Mom wasn't much of a knitter.

Erik's back in his jeans and the shirt he arrived in, and I wish he looked more comfortable. I consider offering him something from my wardrobe, but it wouldn't fit him, and my dad's old clothes are far from what a man like Erik would find relaxing. I remind myself Erik probably has some of his stuff out in his car if he wants to go get it.

I can't seem to answer Erik's question, so I sip the tea in silence. I feel both better and a hell of a lot worse. I'm not sure what to make of this mishmash of emotion, but Erik stays right by me, touching me, and keeping my mug constantly filled with hot tea—which I'd asked him to make, though I don't even like it. My mom always made me tea when I wasn't feeling well.

Why don't I feel well?

Immediately after the sex, I'd felt so good, like I'd unburdened myself of a lifetime's worth of self-hate and anger at my parents, but it didn't last the length of the shower. Shame and humiliation had crashed in on me, making it hard to breathe or even stand as Erik had washed me from head to toe, and everywhere between, paying close attention to the state of my asshole after the furious pounding he'd given me.

I squeeze my anus and feel the sticky residue of the cream he'd spread on me afterward, something he'd found in my parents' bathroom drawers. I hadn't even asked what it was or suggested it might have been in there quite a long time at this point. I'd just let him take care of me.

"I don't know what it is about you, angel," Erik says, and this time, for some reason, the word holds a whole new meaning. I raise my gaze to his, wondering if he means it the way I'm hearing it. "But when I fuck you, things just seem to go sideways, don't they?"

"Do they?"

"I always tell myself I'm not going to let the kink go too deep or too fast, but the next thing I know, we're playing in your shame like pigs in mud, rolling in it until we're covered, and while I think it's a good thing—bringing all that crap out into the light—it can lead to sub drop sometimes too. Any kind of play can, but especially emotionally intense things like we did earlier. Do you know what that is?"

"Sub drop?"

"Yes."

I shrug. I think I remember hearing something about it some-where, but right now, it feels like my heart, mind, and soul are moving through the mud Erik just mentioned. I couldn't put two and two together to save my life right now.

"Sub drop is an emotional and physical low after an intense kink scene. It can be helped by things like aftercare like cuddling—"

"Hot tea," I quip tiredly.

"Yes, and sugary snacks, or fuzzy socks. Everyone's different." Erik rubs my back again. "Sometimes people want to talk."

"About what?"

"In our case, you might want to talk about what we did up there or about us, but sometimes people want to talk about unrelated things, something distracting." He pauses, and glances at the clock above the stove. "But right now, you should sleep."

I shake my head. "I don't want to sleep. I want to stay awake with you."

Erik seems about to argue with me, but he peers around the kitchen and through the door leading out to the living room. "Is there a place we can cuddle? Maybe watch some TV?"

"Yeah," I say, standing and taking him by the hand. "This way."

I've never imagined having a man here, in my folks' living room on the sofa with me, and I definitely never imagined if I did, I'd be lying with my head in his lap as he plays with my hair with one hand and uses the remote to scroll through Netflix options with the other.

Everything about tonight feels so surreal. It's hard to believe that earlier I was outside Paul's loft imagining a very different future than I'm letting myself toy with right now. It's even harder to believe Erik drove all those hours just to see me. He must have really wanted to be close to me tonight.

My stomach twists in on itself. And what did I do? I made it all about me, about what *I* needed and wanted to do, and now I'm a mess because of it. Erik must be so disappointed.

"I'm sorry, Daddy," I murmur.

"For what, angel?"

Again, angel instead of boy. My heart wants it to mean something, to mean he's shifting toward something more romantic with me, less kink-role based, and more personal.

"For making you do that with me."

"You didn't make me do anything. I have safe words, too, and if I hadn't been on board or okay with what we were doing, I'd have used them." Erik sighs. "Maybe I should have, if only because it all happened so fast. We should have talked the scene out, planned it…"

Erik tangles his fingers in my hair, putting the remote on the side table by the sofa, apparently giving up on finding a show. "I keep letting things go too far with you, trusting we can handle it all together, because it feels so right in the moment. I need to work on that."

"Please don't," I say, taking hold of his hand and squeezing before bringing it up to clutch to my chest. "I love how you are with me, how one moment flows to the next." I kiss his knuckles and press his hand to my chest again. "I didn't *want* to talk about it before we did it. I was afraid I'd chicken out. But I needed to confront all that. I needed to make them see me. But they can't, and they won't, because they're dead. This was the closest I could get."

"I understand."

"But I shouldn't have used you to accomplish it."

"You absolutely should have. Who else were you going to use? And if you needed it now, tonight, so you can move into whatever future you and I try to build together, so be it. Even if you needed it just so you can go *alone* into a future without me, then so be that, too, because you deserve to be free of these things, angel."

"You keep calling me 'angel.'"

"Is that all right?"

"I like it. Growing up, teammates sometimes called me Angel, but when you say it, it feels like you're calling me an angel. It's special."

"You *are* an angel, *my* angel. From now on, 'boy' is just for kink and play. 'Angel' is for all the time, any time."

I roll onto my back, so I can see his face. Well, more like the underside of his chin and up his nose, but it's at least a view of him when I ask, "What do you want us to be?"

"Lovers. Boyfriends," he replies. "That seems like the best place to start."

"I want to be your boyfriend."

"And who knows what happens after that? I sure as hell don't. This will be new territory for me. You'll have to be patient with me if I get scared sometimes, but I promise I'm going to get up every time I fall," he says.

"And I promise I'll help you up."

Erik smiles, brushing his fingers over my forehead. "I called my mom from the road to let her know I was coming tonight, and she's already set on you moving to Asheville and living with me." He laughs. "She plans to move out to the house behind the barn to give us space and privacy. I know that's a lot. I'm not pressuring you. She's just excited I've found someone I want to do this with. Try, I mean. Really try."

"I'm excited, too," I whisper. The night has been long, and the quiet of the house is deep. Even Simmony Sunshine is sound asleep on top of the Wi-Fi box. "Will she be happy in the house behind the barn?"

"Of course. I think she wants more privacy herself, anyway. And that will leave the lower floor available for any longer-term training clients until we can build a second tiny house." Erik goes on. "Oh, and my mom wants to meet you? But maybe it's too soon for that."

"I don't know," I say with a little half-shrug. "You've seen me in a lot of vulnerable positions; it seems fair that I meet your mom and see you in one for a change."

"You've seen me do the enema. That was vulnerable for me."

"Was it really?"

"Of course." He blushes. "I've only ever shown one other person that."

I touch his scruffy cheek, loving the scrape of his whiskers on my fingertips. "Thank you, then. You were so stoic. It seemed easy for you."

"I'm good at faking it," he says. "Being a Daddy, in the past, has been a lot of faking being strong and in control, but for some reason, with you, it feels real. Right."

"I want to see all the versions of the real you. Including who you are with your mom. I'm curious about her, too. You seem so close."

"She's a good woman. You'll like her."

"I think I will."

"When I left home earlier tonight, I told myself I want to start slow with you, but I don't know if we can," Erik admits. "You and me? We just jump right into things, and I think it's unlikely we can slow our roll for whatever it is we're going to be together."

"Well, it's probably like riding a horse, right? If we go too fast, we might fall off, but we can always get back on again."

"Unless we break our backs in the fall," he says.

"Or our hearts," I whisper, touching his chest. "I promise I'll do my best to protect yours, Erik. I understand you're scared to have it broken again, and obviously, I can't swear it won't happen, but I'll do my utmost to make sure you're never blindsided by it like you were with Brandon."

"Thank you. And I promise the same to you."

"We'll talk about things, like we are tonight, and we'll make sure the other person always knows what we want, and where we're going. We'll be a team."

"A team." He laughs. "You know, I've never been on one of those. In all my work, in everything I do, it's about individuals."

"Luckily for you, my dad made me play Little League," I laugh.

"You'll have to teach me this time."

The mention of my father sobers me again. I'd been feeling lighter, lifting on the wings of hope and excitement offered by this exchange of promises and opening up of feelings. But now, in a flash, I'm right back down in it again.

"He was a good man," I whisper, squeezing Erik's hand to my chest. "I loved him, and I know he loved me—what he knew of me, what he *wanted* to know of me—and that should be enough."

"It's enough."

"No," I disagree. "It can't ever be. I want it to be, but it's just not. Earlier, when we were…when I was…" I clear my throat, tears clogging it.

"Take your time."

I breathe in and out through my nose, slowly, like I'm catching my breath between thrusts of his big cock into my throat. When I'm not on the verge of breaking down again, I say, "When you were fucking me, and I was staring at their picture, I just wanted so much for them to be alive, for them to step out of it, to hold me while you—" I break off. That sounds perverse. "It's not as if I'd wanted them involved in our sex, but I needed and wanted them to truly embrace me, even the worst part of me."

"Is that the worst part of you?" Erik challenges. "Think about it. Is it?"

"No," I agree, my breath hitching. "It's one of the best parts. It's a beautiful part of me. This affection and feeling between us, what we'd like to grow, what we can do with each other to express it… All that reflects the best part of who I am. It's who I most deeply am at my core. I'm not an accountant, or a guitarist—though I do like to play. I'm not their son, or a good Christian boy, or a churchgoer. I'm not the clothes I wear or the things I eat…"

"You're Matthew."

"I'm who I am when I'm naked and getting fucked by my Daddy—by you."

"That's an important part of who you are," Erik agrees. "My angel, my boy."

"Yes, and earlier? I needed them to love that part of me, too. It's the best part of me, Erik, not the worst part. The *best* part."

"There are so many good parts of you, Matthew. You're kind, generous, smart, funny, and responsible. You're a good son, and you stood by them loyally until the end, and all of that is part of you. But what you had to hide might feel like the most primary part of your identity right now and for some time to come. That's natural. But there's more to you than being my boy, too. However, you *are* my boy. My hairy fuck-toy. My sweet bussy."

"Oh God," I whisper. "That's so dirty."

"Do you like it?" he says with a tired smirk. "You like thinking I own your body? And that tight bussy?"

"Yes, Daddy."

"Because I don't want anyone else touching it without my permission, do you understand? Not Paul fucking Adler, not anyone."

"No one." I can feel my cock growing hard again, and I hope the night, even though it's so very late, isn't over for pleasure. "Daddy?"

"Yes, sweet boy?"

"Make love to me?"

"I can do that," Erik says, helping me stand from the sofa. "Where do you want me to do it?"

"Here," I say, pointing at the sofa. "And there." I point at the kitchen table visible through the doorway. "And in my bedroom. And then back in their bed."

"I don't know if we can come that many times tonight," Erik says, nuzzling my ear. "But I can fuck you in all those places over time, no doubt about it. Where do you want me to make you come first?"

"In my room," I say. "I've masturbated in there for so long, dreaming of getting fucked in that bed. It's about time I did."

"You're such a filthy little angel."

I laugh. "Matthew Angel. That's me."

He kisses my nose. "It is."

Or is it Matthew Devil? I don't know. And I don't care, as I lead Daddy by the hand, past the boxes of Christmas tree decorations I'd pulled out of the attic. Erik sees them and stops.

"You did decorate for Christmas?"

I flush. "No. But when I got back from your place, I brought them down to look at. It seemed too silly to put a tree up after Christmas Day. Where would I find one even? But I unwrapped them. Enjoyed them. I'm definitely putting one up next year." I pause. "Wherever I might be for Christmas."

Erik nods and squeezes my hand. "Yes, you will."

Upstairs, I tell him, "This is my bedroom," opening the door to the room I've remade several times over in my life. "I've slept in it since the night they brought me home after the adoption."

Peering around at the queen-sized bed, the mood-lighting I set up earlier, and the carefully selected framed art on my walls, Erik asks, "Jerked off a lot in here, have you?"

"Yes, Daddy."

"Want to show Daddy how you do it?"

I chew my bottom lip for a moment, gazing at him from beneath my lashes, knowing it makes him hard when I play innocent. "Yes, if Daddy fingers his boy while he does…"

"With pleasure."

The world is splintered open now. My December Daddy experience is over, but my whole life is just starting. The one I'll live as Matthew—Erik's angel.

Daddy's sweet boy.

EPILOGUE
Erik

F ATE IS SUCH an odd thing, as Matthew likes to tell me, because if I hadn't let Nick talk me into putting my stupid trifold poster up at the charity kink auction a year ago, I wouldn't be sitting here tonight blissed-out on a Christmas Kentucky Buck cocktail while I watch my mom and my boyfriend put up the Christmas tree on the day after Thanksgiving.

It's been a busy year. Between moving Mom into the house behind the barn, my business picking up in the post-pandemic rush to get production schedules spinning again, and Matthew quitting his job to settle here with me not even three months after we'd agreed to be serious with each other, things have been hectic.

Especially since we chose to sell Matthew's parents' home after liquidating the furnishings and interior of it, and I let go of the lease on the Asheville house once it was clear Charles wanted to take it on. I also closed the facilities in town and stopped taking on aerialist clients. With all that, we haven't had a moment to breathe. And every moment we *are* breathing, we're fucking and playing, and peeling each other down to our most vulnerable, naked parts.

I love it. Matthew loves it, too. He's told me many times.

We couldn't possibly be a better match. We're both addicted to going deep and hard, and we do it so naturally together. Every kink session is like an excavation of our souls, which leaves us adoring each other more.

And what's more, I love him as I've never loved a man before.

I'm so grateful I got the chance to know him like I do. I sing the praises of fate, or God, or goddamn Nick for bringing us together last year.

The Christmas playlist is one Mom's put together, so it's a mishmash of festive classics, holiday country songs, and seasonal jazz. Totally strange, but absolutely Mom's taste and what I grew up listening to. Over dinner, she had Matthew add some of his childhood favorites to the playlist, too, including Christmas songs by contemporary Christian singers like Amy Grant and Sandi Patty.

I love hearing Matthew sing.

He's singing right now as he hangs ornaments from his childhood, some faded and fragile, but all still beautiful. It makes my insides buzz with joy to hear his warm tenor. I know he's comfortable and happy if he's singing, and that's all I want in this world.

His voice isn't great, but it's not bad either. I can see, though, why he wasn't destined to succeed in studying music. Matthew says he didn't have the talent *or* the guts, but we've proven time and again that Matthew has a lot of guts. He's brave and strong, and willing to confront the shadow parts of himself most people run from their whole lives. Hell, I almost ran from mine.

If I had, I'd be alone now, and maybe for the rest of my life.

I owe Nick a lot, and he never fails to remind me these days. I wish he could find someone to love as well, but he's certain he'll die alone. He shares my former affinity for the young ones, and all the boys he takes under his wing fly the coop within a few months. He just can't seem to make it last with any of them. I hope something changes for him soon.

I used to think all boys leave. But Matthew has shown me otherwise.

As for Matthew's friends, Doug and Forest, they've come to visit a few times, and I've nearly, almost entirely forgiven Doug for using Matthew the way he did in college. But I'll always hold a grudge.

As for the man I almost lost Matthew to, Paul Adler, rumor has it he's looking for a Christmas companion again this year. I hope he finds one. Every good Dom and Daddy deserves a match at the holidays, and I appreciate he was kind to Matthew during the time when I'd let him down.

Full after another wonderful holiday meal, I hike my socked feet up on the coffee table as I pet Simmony Sunshine and scroll social media on my phone. I'm admiring my cousin Leo's cute photos with his husband and their daughter when a text comes through. The preview flashing across the screen makes me almost choke on my Kentucky Buck. My thumb hovers over the message. I burn to open it, but is that urge a betrayal of Matthew?

I sip my drink, putting my phone aside to watch Matthew shimmy around the tree. He's laughing with my mom and stopping from time to time to take a swallow of his own champagne cocktail before going back to throwing tinsel on the limbs and hanging ornaments at Mom's direction.

"Here now," Mom says, pointing. "Fill that hole."

I bite my lower lip to keep from making a quip about how Matthew is very good at filling holes, but he prefers to have his filled, thank you very much. The holiday playlist starts at the beginning again, and I relax back into the sofa as sleigh bells and country strumming fill the air.

Matthew swings around to pick up his guitar, plops onto the pillow Mom had been sitting on by the tree, and begins to pluck out a simple counter-melody that flows nicely with the recorded music.

As he begins directing Mom about the holes to be filled, I pick up my phone again. It's okay to be curious. It's normal.

I open the text.

Hey Daddy, it's your favorite boy wishing you Merry Christmas from Budapest. Things here are good, though I'm single as a Pringle these days. I miss you, Daddy. Do you miss me, too? I'll be home in February. Let's meet up.

There's a picture attached. It's a selfie, showing Brandon alone, a cheeky grin splitting his face, and a red beanie on his head. He's glowing with youth and energy, and I can almost hear his laugh in my ear. He's beautiful. I loved fucking him.

But I don't love *him* anymore.

I flick a glance up at Matthew, who's still playing his guitar, and I type a reply into my phone.

Hey, Brandon. Glad to see you looking so healthy and happy. I'll be traveling for work in February. New production in Canada. My boyfriend's coming with me. His name's Matthew. I'm happy with him. Stay well.

I include a photo Mom took of me and Matthew earlier, standing in front of one of the many outdoor Christmas trees she's decorated all the way down the driveway. In the picture, Matthew's laughing and holding a baby goat he'd just named Holly's Holiday Harmony—or Holly-Holiday for short—and I'm gazing at him like my heart is fit to burst.

I press send.

It shows as read at once. I don't know what time it is in Budapest, but it's not early. I wait to see if he'll respond, and just when I've decided he won't, a thumbs-up reaction appears. That's it. Nothing more.

I'm forever through with Brandon. I wish him the best, but I have my man, my boy, and my angel now.

"Matthew," I say, and he looks up with those wide and somehow still so innocent eyes. "C'mere."

He puts the guitar aside and crawls across to me. If Mom wasn't here, I'd have a very specific reaction to that, but as it is, I manage to keep my libido in check.

I tug Matthew up onto the sofa and snuggle him close. "Thank you," I whisper in his ear.

"For what?"

For being forty-two, I almost say.

For being so handsome, and brave, and vulnerable.

For telling me I needed you.

For being right.

For letting me see your shame and fuck it away, or roll around in it with you, depending on the day. For loving me, for letting me love you.

"For winning me in that auction."

He beams. "Best money I ever spent."

THE END

Letter from Leta

Dear Reader,

Thank you so much for reading *My December Daddy*!

In November of 2021, these characters showed up in my mind unexpectedly. I must admit, I tried to reject them. They weren't part of my writing plan for the year, but they wouldn't go away. They made all kinds of sweet promises—"We'll be soft, fluffy, adorable, *easy*. We promise." Insert a Jim Halpert stare into the camera. Right? The audacity of those lies! Haha.

I suppose it's arguable that Matthew and Erik are adorable, but for all the rest? Soft, fluffy, *easy*? Laughable.

Perhaps it sounds a bit woo-woo to say that characters "show up" in my mind or that they lie to me, but that's the way I experience it, and I can't talk about it any other way.

While this book turned out to be nothing like I'd expected, I'm glad I let these men persuade me to write their story. Parts of this book upset me, some of it even frightened me, but the story represents Erik and Matthew's raw truth. I hope you feel that too.

If you enjoyed meeting RJ and Aaron from Mr. Naughty List, click through to grab it up. It's a wonderful read, and I know you'll enjoy witnessing RJ and Aaron's love blossom.

Be sure to follow me on BookBub or Amazon to be notified of new releases. The best way to keep up with what's happening book-wise is to subscribe to my newsletter for snippets of the day-to-day writing life, important announcements, sales, and more. Also to see some sources of my inspiration, you can follow me on Instagram.

If you enjoyed the book, please take a moment to leave a review.

Reviews not only assist readers in determining if a book is for them, but they also help a book to show up in site searches.

For the audiobook connoisseurs out there, *My December Daddy's* audiobook is available now, narrated by the amazing John Solo. Buy it now on Audible.

Thank you so much for being a reader!
Leta

TRAINING SEASON
by Leta Blake

Can a cowboy's firm hand help discipline this feisty figure skater—on and off the ice?

Matty Marcus fears he doesn't have what it takes to achieve his Olympic dream. His self-esteem is at an all-time low after figure skating coaches and skating judges have told him he's not skinny enough, good enough, or masculine enough to win.

Matty wishes he could afford the kind of coach he needs, a top-notch one who specializes in keeping their skaters focused. But those coaches are ridiculously expensive, and Matty is financially strapped.

Until a lucrative house-sitting gig brings him to rural Montana. And to Rob.

No one has ever looked at Matty the way rural cowboy Rob Lovely looks at him. No one has ever touched him, loved him, and healed him from the inside out. No one has ever made him feel so valuable and adored. Worthy. Strong.

No one has ever taught Matty how to fly. Or how to lose.

Rob might be a cowboy and a single dad who knows nothing about figure skating, but after only a few months, he's trained a new kind of bravery into Matty's soul.

But to achieve his Olympic dream, Matty will have to face the ultimate test. Has he truly learned what it means to win—on and off the ice—during his training season?

Training Season is a MM romance with a feisty, flamboyant figure skater and an easy-going dominant cowboy, opposites attract, hurt-comfort, single dad, winter holiday highlights, love beyond reason, multiple steamy scenes, and a well-earned happy ending. *This book contains some BDSM elements.*

Gay Romance Newsletter

Leta's newsletter will keep you up to date on her latest releases, sales and deals, future writing plans, and more from the world of M/M romance. Join Leta's mailing list today.

Leta Blake on Patreon

Become part of Leta Blake's Patreon community to support her indie publishing expenses and to access exclusive content, deleted scenes, extras, and interviews.

Other Books by Leta Blake

Contemporary

Will & Patrick Wake Up Married
Will & Patrick's Endless Honeymoon
Cowboy Seeks Husband
The Difference Between
Bring on Forever
Stay Lucky

Sports

The River Leith

The Training Season Series
Training Season
Training Complex

Musicians

Smoky Mountain Dreams
Vespertine

New Adult

Punching the V-Card

'90s Coming of Age Series
Pictures of You
You Are Not Me

Winter Holidays

North's Pole

The Mr. Christmas Series
Mr. Frosty Pants
Mr. Naughty List
Mr. Jingle Bells

A Boy for All Seasons
My December Daddy

Fantasy

Any Given Lifetime

Re-imagined Fairy Tales

Flight
Levity

Paranormal & Shifters

Angel Undone
Omega Mine

Horror

Raise Up Heart

Omegaverse

Heat of Love Series
Slow Heat
Alpha Heat
Slow Birth
Bitter Heat

For Sale Series
Heat for Sale
Bully for Sale

Audiobooks

Leta Blake at Audible

Discover more about the author online

Leta Blake
letablake.com

About the Author

Author of the bestselling book *Smoky Mountain Dreams* and fan favorites like *Training Season*, *Will & Patrick Wake Up Married*, and *Slow Heat*, Leta Blake has been captivating M/M Romance readers for over a decade. Whether writing contemporary romance or fantasy, she puts her psychology background to use creating complex characters and love stories that feel real. At home in the Southern U.S., Leta works hard at achieving balance between her writing and her family life.